The Making of the Lamb

The Making of the Lamb

A Novel By

Robert Harley Bear

Eirth Publications, L.L.C.
Rockville, Maryland

Copyright © 2014 by Robert Harley Bear
All rights reserved

No part of this book may be reproduced to transmitted in any form or by any means, electronic or mechanical, inluding photocopying, recording, or by an information storage and retrieval system—with the exception of a reviewer who may quote brief passages in a review—without the written permission from the publisher. For information, contact Eirth Publishing, L.L.C. through www.makingofthelamb.com.

Published in the United States by
Eirth Publications, L.L.C.
Rockville, Maryland

www.makingofthelamb.com

Trade Paperback ISBN 978-0-9893138-0-3
Hardcover ISBN 978-0-9893138-1-0

Cover Design: Peri Poloni-Gabriel, Knockout Design
www.knockoutbooks.com

Printed and bound in the United States of America
April, 2014

To all the donors who have registered to give life-saving bone marrow at Be the Match Foundation, marrow.org. Without this incredible act of generosity by an anonymous donor a few years ago, this book would never have been completed.

About the Author

Since 2004, Robert Harley Bear has studied late Iron Age archeology, writings about druids from Irish legends to the annals of Julius Caesar, biblical history, Roman history and stories and legends of the missing years of Jesus Christ.

Robert Harley Bear is an attorney and an information technology consultant. In 2005, he was baptized at St. Paul's Parish, K Street, in Washington, DC, where he remains an active parishioner to this day. He taught the high school confirmation class for several years.

Jerusalem

And did those feet in ancient time,
Walk upon England's mountains green?
And was the holy Lamb of God,
On England's pleasant pastures seen?

And did the Countenance Divine
Shine forth upon our clouded hills?
And was Jerusalem builded here,
Among these dark Satanic Mills?

Bring me my Bow of burning gold;
Bring me my Arrows of desire;
Bring me my Spear; O clouds unfold!
Bring me my Chariot of fire!

I will not cease from Mental Fight,
Nor shall my Sword sleep in my hand;
Till we have built Jerusalem,
In England's green and pleasant Land.

Words by William Blake, 1808.
Set to music by Sir Hubert Parry, 1916.

Contents

Prologue 1

Part I - The Journey to Britain 15
Prelude 16
Chapter 1 - What to Do About Jesus? 20
Chapter 2 - A Gift of Tongues 39
Chapter 3 - A Problem with Prophecy 61
Chapter 4 - A Perilous Passage 77

Part II - Growing in Wisdom and the Favor of God and Man 101
Interlude 102
Chapter 5 - The Tin Finder 110
Chapter 6 - Days of Awe 131
Chapter 7 - Rumps 153
Chapter 8 - Ynys Witrin 178
Chapter 9 - The Secret of the Lord 198

Part III - A Mission from God 225
Interlude 226
Chapter 10 - Of Lepers and the Law 230
Chapter 11 - A Chariot and Some Prodigals 253
Chapter 12 - Bangor 279
Chapter 13 - The Chosen 296

Part IV - A Painful Destiny 313
Interlude 314
Chapter 14 - The Path to Calvary 318
Chapter 15 - The Unblemished 331
Chapter 16 - Dark Satanic Mills 354
Chapter 17 - Arrows of Desire 377
Chapter 18 - Stonehenge 389

Epilogue 407
Author's Afterword 427
Glossary of Place Names 435

Illustrations

Jesus is Found at the Temple, James J. J. Tissot (Watermark) i
Legend (All Maps) 14
Lower Galilee (Map) 14
Mare Internum (Map) 14
Roman Gaul and Celtic Britain (Map) 15
Southwest Belerium (Map) 100
Ynys Witrin (Map) 101
Southwest Britain (Map) 225
What Our Savior Saw from the Cross, James J. J. Tissot 313
Tunic Cross Icon, Robert Harley Bear 407

Prologue

Oh, Vanity! Why do you stir this humble scrivener to pose these imaginings as answers to such mysteries of faith? Can pen and ink depict the beauty of those prehistoric Isles of Wonder or the cosmic forces of the Tor? Can they render the nuanced utterances, in language now lost, of the *Tuatha Dé Danann* or the Fisher King? Can they recapture the druids' arts or the boisterous gatherings in prehistoric Celtic halls?

Most challenging of all: can they hope to paint a living picture of the adolescent Jesus, as he walked the green hills of Britain, grew to manhood, experienced his own humanity, and came to terms with the fate that awaited him?

It begins with a legend committed to writing during the Dark Ages. In about A.D. 600, Pope Gregory dispatched Augustine of Canterbury to preach the gospel to the Germanic tribes that had invaded Britain. But there, among the native Celtic people, Augustine encountered an existing branch of Christianity that had been isolated from Western Europe since the collapse of Roman rule two centuries before. Augustine wrote to Gregory what the bishops of that Celtic church had told him:

> ...In the western confines of Britain, there is a certain royal isle of large extent, abounding in all the beauties of nature and necessities of life. In it, the first neophytes of Catholic law found a church constructed by no human art, but by the hands of Christ himself.

The legend holds that Jesus was brought to Britain by Mary's uncle, a trader in tin and known in Scripture as Saint Joseph of Arimathea, the wealthy man who buried Jesus in his own tomb.

The Knights of the Round Table searched for the Holy Grail throughout Britain. Some might call them mad. Why should the cup from which Jesus drank at the Last Supper be there, of all places? But the Arimathean is linked to that quest, too; legend credits him with bringing Christianity to Britain shortly after Christ's passion, perhaps bringing the cup with him and hiding it there to be sought.

The legend was still alive in William Blake's time, for him to put to verse:

> And did those feet in ancient time,
> Walk upon England's mountains green?
> And was the holy Lamb of God,
> On England's pleasant pastures seen?

To this day, you find the legend throughout southwest Britain. It is depicted on the banner of Pilton Parish, set forth on the website of the St Just in Roseland Church (sic), and mentioned in the history posted inside the Church of Saint Lawrence in Priddy. The town seal of East Looe depicts Jesus and the Arimathean arriving on a boat in the course of one of their trading missions for British tin. According to the legend, what grew to be one of the largest monasteries of Britain was founded by Saint Joseph in present day Glastonbury on the spot where Jesus built that first church. Although the monastery was dissolved by Henry VIII, its ruins still dominate the center of the town.

And yet, this legend might bear witness to a truth far more ancient still. The bishops assembled at Nicea in A.D. 325 decreed that there was no time when the Son was not. They pronounced his substance to be the very same as the Father's. They affirmed, quite rightly, that he was begotten of the Father before all worlds and not made. For Jesus was there as the divine Word even as the Father began the work of Creation by separating the light from the darkness. He was with God. He was God, and all things were made through him. In him was life, which was the light of men, and the light shined. So it was written.

However, so too was it written that when the time was ripe, he put aside his divine dignity and became flesh to live among us. He did not come with manifest power and glory or even as a great person, but rather as a helpless baby with a fully human nature born to a poor household in a ravaged land.

His earthly parents nurtured him as his humanity required. As a boy of twelve, though knowledgeable beyond his years and fully aware of his divine Father, his wisdom and favor with God and man were not then complete; rather, it was written that he went on to grow in that wisdom and favor. His human nature would have become more reconciled to his divine nature that also abided fully within himself. Maybe it was then that he accepted his destiny to suffer on the cross as the final and perfect sacrifice for all.

Perhaps, in that way, it can be said that the Lamb might have been made.

Allow me now, mere scrivener that I am, your patience to pray. As this prologue turns to the culmination of the incarnation, I put aside my feigned omniscience and give voice to the thoughts, words, and deeds of the players who play their parts, each blinded by their own vanities, desires, and limitations of mortal frame, save for one now grown back into true omniscience.

The Garden of Gethsemane outside Jerusalem, A.D. 33, during the reign of Tiberius, second emperor of Rome

Jesus

Their darkest hour is now at hand. Even the most steadfast will find their faith sorely tried until the morning of the third day.

They had come to Jerusalem in triumph less than a week before, greeted by the waving of the palms. His disciples and followers had seen Jesus work many miracles, even raise the dead, but no matter how he tried to tell them that his time for leaving would soon be at hand, they only comprehended the good news they wanted to hear. The power of his teachings and miracles made them expect nothing but more great wonders.

Oh, Father, any ordinary man, knowing what I know, would just keep walking. The temple guards will not be here for an hour. The Mount of Olives is such a small rise, and I have ample time to escape to the other side. I could have such a wonderful day tomorrow with Mary, Martha, and Lazarus in Bethany.

But I am not an ordinary man. I am your Son! Father in Heaven, I made the choice to accept this path so many years ago, and ever since, with every step, I have lived, I do live, and I will live in tomorrow's pain.

Jesus stopped with his disciples at the garden. He bade them stay, and he walked forward with Peter, James, and John. He told these three, "My soul is heavy with sorrow. Please keep watch."

He went forward another few yards and threw himself on the ground.

Abba, Father, all things are possible to you; take away this cup from me. But, let it not be my will, but your will to be done.

Jesus got up and went back, and he found Peter, James and John asleep.

See, Father. See how all now take a hand in my death. Not just the Romans or the Jews or even Judas now betray me. Even my closest disciples cannot stay awake for one mere hour. They will blame themselves for the weakness of their flesh, but is it not you and I who tire them?

They are now truly baptized in my death, and that is good. All can be baptized, and all are forgiven.

Twice more he prayed. Twice more he went back to those sleeping disciples.

The die is cast, as it was cast through all eternity. You command, Father, and I choose to obey. That is all that it comes down to. Not the Jews, not the Romans, not Judas, and not the disciples—just you and me.

I cannot bear the pain of this hour. Spare both of us. Let this be over quickly for the pain of this garden is worse than what is coming on the cross.

Joseph

Joseph felt relieved as he made his way north from the city on his way home to Arimathea. He was pleased that he would be with his mother on his birthday, but he had been unwilling to leave until they told him Jesus was on his way to Gethsemane. It would be so much safer for Jesus and his followers in Gethsemane than in the walled-in Upper City, where they could have been trapped.

Cursing the dilapidated state of the road, he kept his horse to a walking pace. A courier dressed in the garb of the Roman Legion galloped past, riding fast away from the city—an ill omen, to Joseph's way of thinking. Romans in a hurry spelled trouble, particularly at such an early hour, and at Passover as well. Could there be some disturbance back in the city?

Later, about mid-morning, he had to draw his horse off to the roadside for a party of legionnaires marching the other way. The legions always had priority, requiring all other travelers to make way. These troops speeding toward the city added to his suspicion of some disturbance.

As he resumed his journey, Joseph heard a shout from some distance behind. Another rider, this one in rags, approached at breakneck speed over that broken road. A vagabond? No, it was Thomas, one of the Twelve, coming after him.

Thomas pulled his horse up short. "Jesus has been arrested!"

"Tell me about it, and quickly."

"We were in the Garden of Gethsemane with Jesus." Thomas, an unskilled rider, turned his mount awkwardly and pulled alongside Joseph. "Most of us were asleep. Suddenly great shouting awakened us. Judas led in a group of temple guards, and they arrested Jesus and hauled him off."

"Judas? But he is one of the Twelve!"

"I saw it with my own eyes."

"Was Jesus hurt?"

"The guards treated him roughly, but I didn't see any sign that he was wounded."

"What are they doing with him now?"

"Peter sent me off to follow you two hours past midnight. They were preparing to try Jesus for blasphemy right then."

"They cannot try him in the middle of the night! All the members of the Sanhedrin must be present for such a trial, and we would need time to get there."

"That's what Peter said, and some of the Sanhedrin said it, too. But Caiaphas said the danger posed by Jesus was too great. He said if they waited, his followers might gather in force and cause a riot, and that would bring down the wrath of the Romans."

Joseph cursed Caiaphas under his breath, kicked his horse into a gallop, and raced toward Jerusalem, leaving Thomas far behind.

❧ ✤ ☙

Weary from his frantic ride, Joseph approached Jerusalem in the early afternoon. From the outskirts of the city, he could see the Hill of the Skull, the site the Romans used for executions. On the summit of the hill, visible for miles around, three men already hung from crosses. At this distance they were only tiny figures, too small to identify with his eyes, but the shouts of passers-by left him in no doubt: Jesus was among the condemned.

Joseph took a footpath, outside the city walls, the fastest route to the site. The steep climb to the hilltop left him winded and trembling, leaning heavily on his walking stick. What a windswept, forlorn, lonely place.

At the top, the sight of his beloved nephew in such agony knocked his remaining breath away.

Jesus's blood flowed in thick streams, all down his nearly naked body—from the horrible wounds of his scourging, from the nails hammered through his wrists and ankles, and from the ring of thorns that rode like a mockery of a crown around his head.

The nail through Jesus's ankles must be the worst. With every strangled breath, he had no choice but to bear down on that nail. What pain it must cause him!

A crowd had gathered to witness the proceedings. Some cried out for Jesus's death. The sooner the better, they seemed to think, eager for this troublemaker to leave Jerusalem in peace.

Roman soldiers were there, too. They were battle-hardened men, accustomed to scenes of horrible carnage. The crucifixion was nothing they hadn't seen a hundred times before, and they showed signs of boredom.

Searching through the crowd, Joseph located his niece, Mary, standing with Mary the Magdalene, Martha, and the young disciple John.

"Oh, Joseph, God be praised for bringing you here," exclaimed Mary. Tears spilled down her face. "Once again, you arrive at the hour of our greatest need."

Joseph's quivering legs gave out, and he fell to his knees. "I would happily give my life to relieve Jesus from his pain, but all we can do is watch as his life slips away." Tears streamed from his eyes. *Oh, Jesus—is this really the Father's will?*

Mary knelt next to her uncle and said, quietly but urgently, "There is one thing yet to be done for Jesus—and for me as well. Only you can do it, Uncle. When the time comes, we must obtain his body and give it a proper burial. The Romans will not hear me, because I am only a woman. As next of kin, you must ask for the body."

Joseph, exhausted from the long horseback ride and the climb up the hill, simply nodded.

John, Martha, and Mary the Magdalene talked as if they still expected Jesus to free himself. Joseph and Mary exchanged knowing looks. They knew that Jesus could do that if he so chose, but that he would not.

In a pain-wracked voice, Jesus cried out, "My God, my God, why have you forsaken me?"

Joseph shivered with a chill not due to the sweat cooling on his back. *Why are you so far from helping me, from the words of my groaning?* The twenty-second Psalm.

Jesus opened his swollen eyes and looked down at his mother. "Ma'am, here is your son." His eyes turned to John. "Here is your mother."

John nodded, and placed a hand on Mary's shoulder.

Jesus moaned, "I thirst."

A Roman soldier lifted a sponge with hyssop to his lips.

The long hours of the afternoon passed slowly.

At one point, Jesus forgave his tormentors.

At another moment, he turned his head toward the dying thief on the cross beside him, and he promised the man he would join him in Paradise.

Finally, with storm clouds gathering, Jesus commended his spirit into the hands of the Father. He spoke no more.

Soon the sun would set and Sabbath begin. Joseph watched one of the priests speak to the Romans. He knew what was coming. He had seen this before. To end things quickly, the Romans would break the legs of the victims, denying them the means to support their weight and draw breath. Sure enough, soldiers swung their heavy spears and crushed the bones of the other two victims. But the one who approached Jesus exclaimed that he was already dead.

The soldiers debated what to do. Then one of them stepped forward. He looked about the same age as Jesus, and he seemed oddly familiar, but Joseph could not place his face. The soldier placed the iron tip of his spear against Jesus's side. "Where is your almighty God now, Jesus?" he snarled, and then he plunged the spear in.

Joseph's breath stuck in his throat. *The Roman soldier. He's Longinus.*

Blood and water flowed from the wound and spattered upon Longinus. As the other soldiers mocked Jesus, Longinus suddenly wailed, "We have killed a god!"

Mary screamed in anguish, such a heart-wrenching cry.

What power that precious blood and water possessed! Joseph hobbled forward as quickly as his old, weary legs would carry him. He had with him two fine cruets he had intended as gifts for his mother; he used them to collect what he could of the spilling blood and water. How Joseph wished for a funnel. So much of it spilled into the ground and was lost.

Pilate

In his palace, Pontius Pilate was in a foul mood. Not because he had condemned a man to death. He was used to that. Not even because he knew the man whom he had condemned was innocent. Pilate liked to think of himself as a man who was firm but fair. He took no joy in shedding innocent blood. Sometimes it was necessary, but that was not the cause of his trouble, either.

Caiaphas had played him for a fool, and Pilate knew it. Pilate had condemned Jesus simply to placate the mob that Caiaphas had manipulated.

Eventually, Pilate would have to show Caiaphas who ruled this province. To spite Caiaphas, he had written a plaque identifying Jesus as "King of the Jews," over the objections of the temple priests. People might take that as a mockery of Jesus rather than as Pilate intended, but no matter.

Adding to his troubles, his wife Claudia had locked herself in her room and was not speaking to him. Why did she not understand? This Jesus was nothing, just another charlatan prophet. Would she have him risk everything for the sake of one crazy man? Did she not know that if a riot had broken out and word got back to Tiberius, Pilate would be blamed?

Caiaphas is sure to come barging in soon. Why is Jupiter trying me so much today?

Pilate scowled at an approaching attendant.

The attendant bowed. "Begging your pardon, Prefect. The *noblis decurio* Joseph, a merchant from Arimathea, is here to see you."

Pilate smiled. "Very well." He ceased his restless pacing and moved to his seat. Of all the Jews in this accursed place, Joseph was the only one Pilate trusted. He gave sound advice. Most importantly, he understood Pilate's perspective. The other Jews did nothing but complain. Yes, Pilate would happily grant Joseph an audience.

But when the attendant brought Joseph into the private audience chamber, Pilate was struck by Joseph's haggard appearance. The smile that typically brightened his face was missing. "You look terrible, my friend."

"I come on a matter of great urgency." Joseph paused, seemingly at a loss for words. This was unusual. In a halting voice, he continued. "I'm here to claim the body of my great-nephew, who was crucified today."

So, that was it. Pilate hadn't known that Joseph's family had a black sheep. One of the robbers executed along with that crazy prophet. Pilate nodded. A simple matter. "I'm sorry I had to order his execution, but I must enforce the laws. I did not know he was related to you. Maybe it's better that I didn't know; it would only have delayed things and put your family through more pain."

Joseph stood there, weeping.

Pilate rose from his chair and laid a gentle hand on Joseph's shoulder. "We executed two robbers today. Which one is it? I will release his body at once and ensure no word of this gets out. There is no need to bring shame on your family."

"It was Jesus. He is my niece's son."

Astonished, Pilate drew back.

Joseph was a member of the Sanhedrin. It was inconceivable that his own family would have a blasphemer within its midst.

Pilate cared nothing about the distinctions between the various Jewish sects, so long as they heeded the authority of Rome. "Jesus is a different matter. If he had stuck to teaching. . . ." Pilate sighed. "But that business at the temple the other day. Overturning tables, and. . . . Joseph, he ran the businessmen out with a whip! I couldn't overlook such rebelliousness, especially during Passover."

Joseph nodded.

"And his followers. . . ." Pilate stopped for a moment. "If he is buried anywhere but in the pit of criminals, his grave site might become a shrine."

"Jesus was innocent of any crime. You know this. So, if it becomes a shrine there is no harm in it."

Pilate's job was to keep the peace and see to the collection of taxes; these Jewish sects could sort out for themselves what shrines were built. And Joseph was right, of course, about Jesus's innocence. It would only insult Joseph's intelligence to defend the charges against his kinsman. "I had no choice, Joseph. Caiaphas and the mob were threatening a riot—"

"It isn't for me to lay blame. Jesus's death and sacrifice were the will of God. You were only his instrument."

"Caiaphas said that Jesus claimed to be the son of your god. You have a strange religion, my friend, if you worship a god who would sacrifice his own son."

"Jesus's sacrifice offers salvation and redemption to the entire world."

"I guess I must have burned that bridge. I doubt that your god will save me after I condemned his son."

"The mercy of God has no limit." Joseph pointed his crooked old finger at Pilate. "Just claim Jesus as your savior. God will forgive even the death of his only son. But without Jesus there is no hope of salvation." His hand dropped.

Pilate paced the floor, considering the matter. "Jesus was a fool, Joseph, and so are you. I have seen how he brings hatred to the eyes of your countrymen. Eventually, they will turn on you as well. I fear you must leave this province. I cannot protect you, and I will not have your blood on my hands."

"What about the body?" Joseph asked. "Under our law, it must be buried before sundown."

"Take it. I will send soldiers to protect you and to make sure he is dead. But remember my words. You must leave this province."

Joseph nodded, said his good-bye, and left.

Pilate smiled, smoothed his toga, and stood straight. His decision to release the body to Joseph could appear as a simple matter of discharging the law, but Jesus was supposedly a dangerous heretic with followers. Pilate could have delayed matters and manipulated things so Jesus's body would be thrown anonymously into a common pit for criminals, as Caiaphas would have wished. *Better yet, Caiaphas will surely know that. Best of all, Caiaphas will come to know that I know. Let the place become a shrine. It will serve Caiaphas right. He will think twice before threatening me with a mob again.*

Joseph

One by one, once they realized that the vengeance of Caiaphas and the mob had been spent, most of the Twelve had returned from hiding and gathered at Joseph's house. Judas was dead, and Thomas was still missing.

THE MAKING OF THE LAMB

Peter was the most distraught, still berating himself for denying Jesus three times—just as Jesus had foretold.

Joseph lowered his creaking bones onto a cushion as he once again relived the evening of Jesus's death in his mind.

Upon returning to the Hill of the Skull, he had found Mary cradling the body of Jesus against her bosom. The soldiers on the execution detail were happy to let Joseph deal with the body, in accordance with Pilate's command. Fortunately, Joseph's friend Nicodemus, a secret follower of Jesus, was skilled in the art of burial. Together with Mary and some of the other women, they had carried Jesus's body to the tomb Joseph had set aside for himself. Working quickly, they had prepared Jesus for burial, barely finishing the job as the sun set, signaling the commencement of the Sabbath and the cessation of all work. A group of Roman soldiers had arrived to guard the tomb; they rolled a boulder over the entrance. The resounding thud as it dropped into place still weighed on Joseph's heart.

They were all now sitting so quietly. That was a good thing, as Joseph had no desire to talk to anyone. Eager for a distraction, he fiddled with his thorn-wood walking stick. The smooth, spherical handle comfortably fit his palm. A small bronze ferrule protected the bottom. Vine-like swirls in the wood grain evoked the Celtic patterns in the wares he had encountered during his career as a traveling merchant. Joseph liked how the stick bent when he put his weight on it; that flex had always energized his gait. *It feels alive, as if it might take root and grow if I plant it in the ground—but not in these parched Judean hills.*

Joseph had been unable to sleep. He ate and drank little.

Finally, on this morning of the third day, he ordered a servant to bring him a cup of wine. He heard a few whisperings among the others as he lifted his cup. *Why should an old man not be allowed the relief of a cup of wine?* Then they all went silent.

He did not care. He was thirsty. He was in a world of his own as he sipped the sweet wine from that old wooden cup. It was the first simple pleasure he had allowed himself.

He began to shake. Throbbing pain wrenched his body. *Is this death? Oh, rapture! Sweet death will bring me with Jesus once again.* But the pain quickly ceased.

Everyone in the room stared at him.

"The spasms are ended. What are you all babbling for?"

James, hands trembling, tipped the fruit from a polished platter and handed it to Joseph. Puzzled, Joseph peered at his own reflection. *What? I have become younger!* His hair was dark brown again, his skin smooth. The ravages of several decades—erased.

John pointed to the cup. "Jesus said that anyone who drank from his cup would live forever."

Andrew and Matthew grabbed for the cup, fighting over it.

The tumult shocked Joseph from his reverie. "You fools!" He leaped to his feet, his bones and muscles no longer protesting. He snatched the cup back and hurled it to the floor. "Why do you wish to abide in this world of sorrows longer than necessary? Don't you wish to be with the Lord as soon as you can?"

Peter bent down and picked up the cup. He handed it to Joseph, saying, "The Lord appointed this cup to you, Joseph. Keep it secret, for there is too much power in it. Keep it safe."

Suddenly, the door of the upper chamber burst open. Mary of Magdalene stood in the doorway, gasping for breath. All attention in the room turned to her. "He's alive!"

∽ ✤ ∾

Over the next forty days, the risen Jesus remained with his disciples, preparing them for their task of spreading the Word to distant lands.

One morning, on a hillside near Emmaus, Jesus appeared to Joseph alone. "Uncle, soon I will give my followers their commission. But for you, I have a more specific mission."

Joseph nodded.

Even before Jesus spoke, he had known he must return to the island of Britain to fulfill a promise on Jesus's behalf.

It was a promise Jesus had made many years before.

Lower Galilee

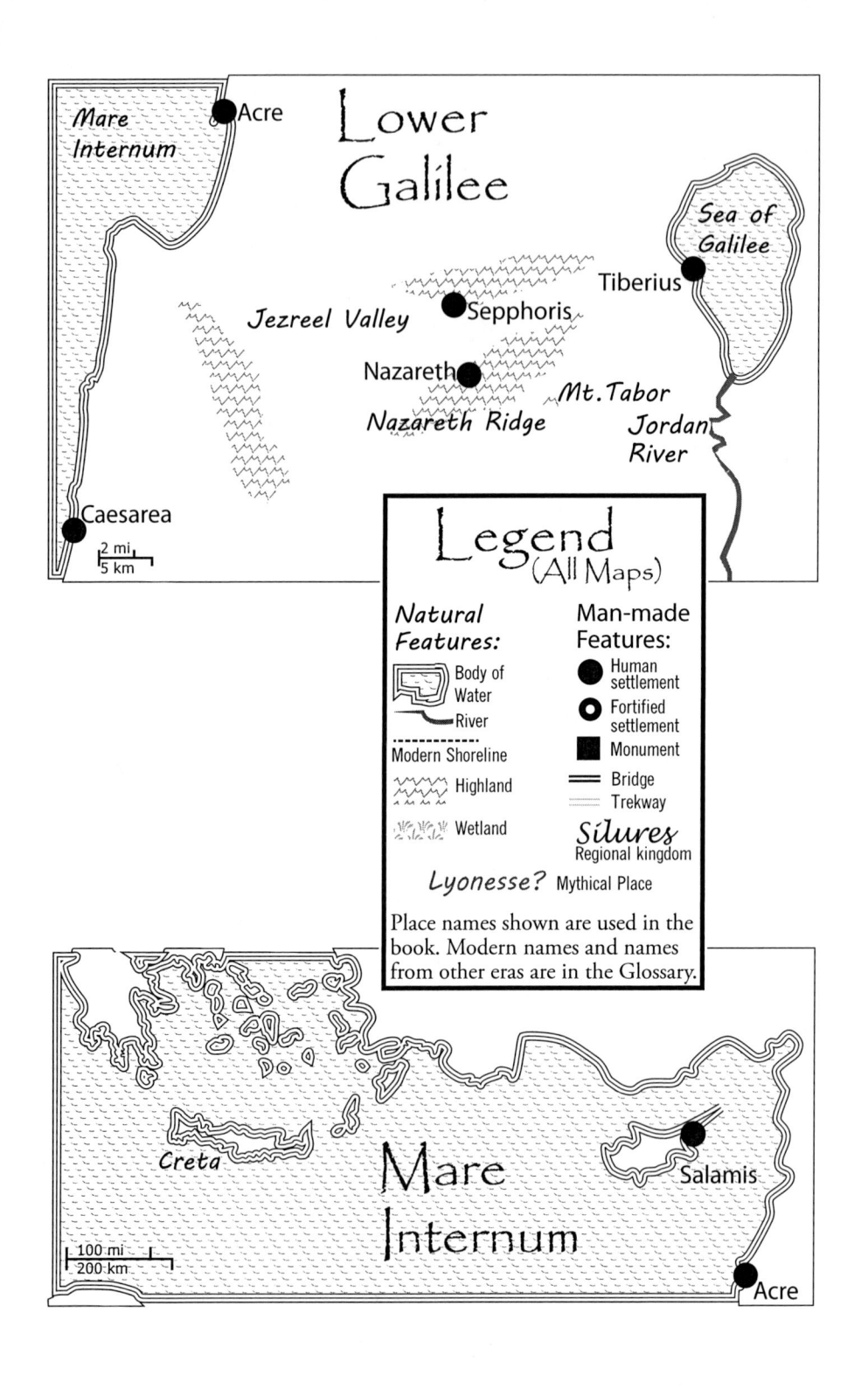

- Mare Internum
- Acre
- Sea of Galilee
- Tiberius
- Jezreel Valley
- Sepphoris
- Nazareth
- Mt. Tabor
- Nazareth Ridge
- Jordan River
- Caesarea

2 mi / 5 km

Legend (All Maps)

Natural Features:
- Body of Water
- River
- Modern Shoreline
- Highland
- Wetland

Man-made Features:
- ● Human settlement
- ○ Fortified settlement
- ■ Monument
- Bridge
- Trekway

Silures Regional kingdom

Lyonesse? Mythical Place

Place names shown are used in the book. Modern names and names from other eras are in the Glossary.

Mare Internum

- Creta
- Salamis
- Acre

100 mi / 200 km

Part 1
The Journey to Britain

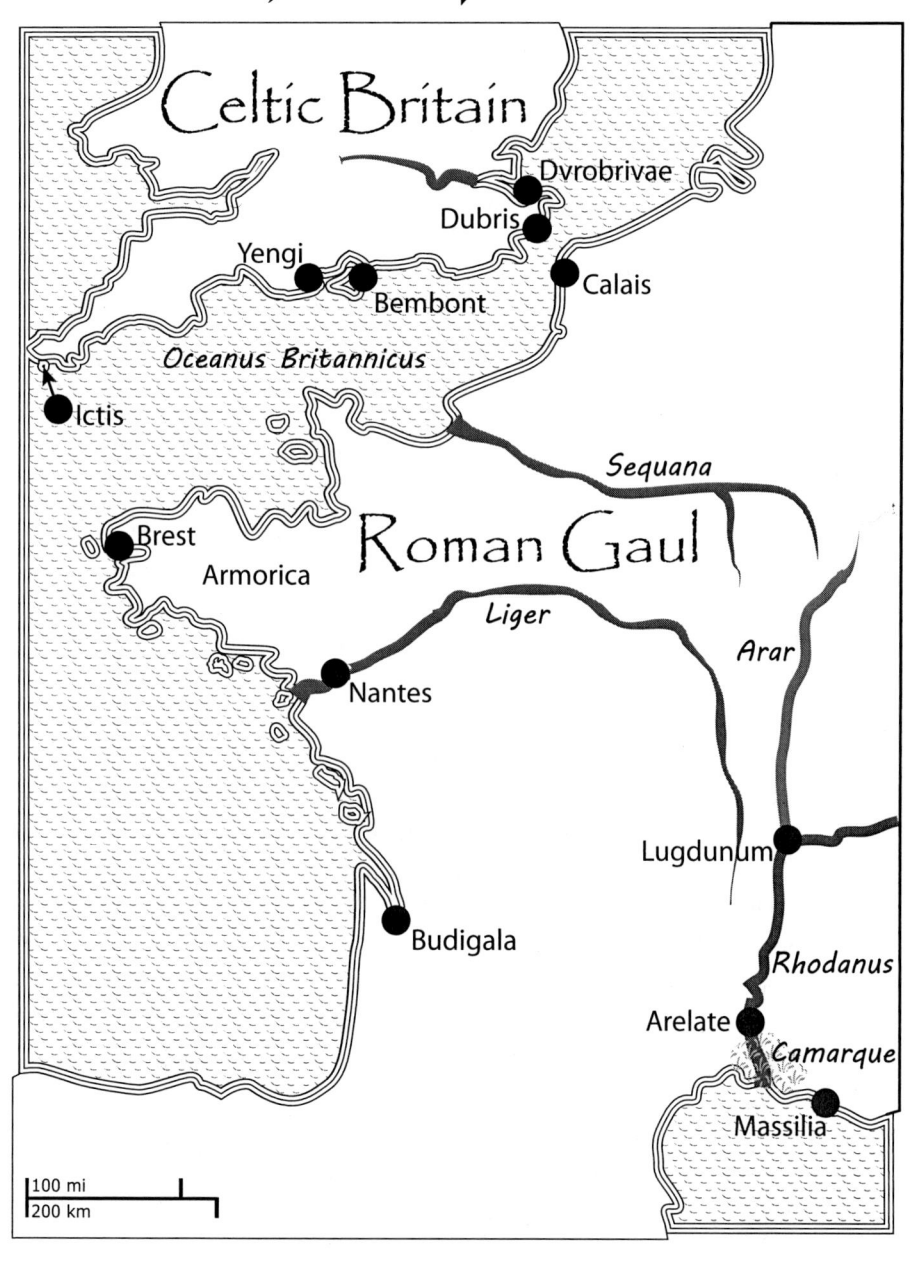

Prelude

St. Hilary's Parish, Cornwall, A.D. 1997, during the reign of Queen Elizabeth II of England

Dad grimaced at Ned's flip-flops. Ned thought they were quite sensible, but Dad thought them too casual, even for the family's summer holiday in the peaceful Cornish village.

"Look, Mum," said Ned. He had crouched for a closer look at a plaque at the base of a headstone. "Dad, I've found the strangest thing!"

"Not so loud, Ned, we're in a churchyard," said Mum. "People won't appreciate your disrespect."

Ned held himself back from saying the first thing that came to mind—that most of the folk in the churchyard were in no state to mind. "But Mum, this old headstone is so odd," he said instead. "And it's got a boy on it!"

"Now Ned, what on earth are you fussing about?" said Dad. "And do control your voice. Your mother is right, we're on consecrated ground."

As Mum and Dad approached, Ned read the words aloud: "F. T. O'Donoghue, Priest, died March, 18, 1881." Although more than a century old, the polished plaque was relatively easy to read, in stark contrast to the more timeworn features of the headstone itself. "There's a priest buried here, under a carving of a boy. Why would a priest have a headstone with a boy on it?"

"Here, Ned, let's be sensible," said Ned's father, with his usual knowing air. "This old thing is only a Celtic cross. Certainly they've told you about the Celtic church at that horribly expensive school we're sending you to. Really, now, it is not a boy at all. It's Jesus being crucified—simply a very old crucifix." He turned to Mum. "Where does he get that insensible curiosity? I'm sure it's not from my side of the family."

For his part, Ned thought he was being sensible. He might be only thirteen years old, but why shouldn't he be curious? Such an odd old headstone presented a mystery that wanted solving. "It looks like a boy," said Ned, "and he seems to be alive and happy. He's fully dressed, too. Jesus on the cross is always mostly naked."

"That's just because it's so primitive," said Mum. She always agreed with Dad.

As his parents started to drag him away, an old priest rounded the corner and addressed them warmly. "So, I see you've found St. Hilary's finest treasure." The cleric's face was timeworn and wrinkled, but he seemed to be getting around well enough.

"Vicar, how do you do?" said Mum. "We're so sorry to be such noisy tourists trampling around your peaceful churchyard."

"Yes, do forgive us," Dad said, giving the priest a smile and a sensible handshake.

"I am sure the dead love the noise of the living." The priest winked at Ned. "I'm Father Michael Walters, vicar here at St. Hilary's. I welcome you to our parish, and I hope you will join us for Mass tomorrow morning at 9:30."

"Oh, yes, Father, we do adore the simple ordered worship of these country parishes. We would be delighted," Mum said.

"We are actually somewhat high church in this parish. I hope you don't mind a few smells and bells, as they say. Though we are still Church of England."

Following a bit of small talk, they settled into a silence. Ned took the silence as his chance. Looking from the headstone to the old vicar, he posed his question slowly, as if a show of deliberation might ease his parents' annoyance. "Father Walters, is this a boy on this cross?"

"Oh, hang it all," muttered Dad.

"Yes, it is our Lord as a young man," said the vicar. "Right about your age, I would say. Such headstones are found all around this county." Father Walters paused. Perhaps he had noted Dad's displeasure. Nonetheless, he continued. "These tunic crosses, as they are called, date from around the tenth century. They remind us of a story many have forgotten."

Ned glanced his father's way. "What story?"

"Some people believe that our Lord's great-uncle, St. Joseph of Arimathea, brought young Jesus to this land. These crosses are considered to be reminders of that visit."

"But, Vicar, that must be just a fanciful legend," Dad blustered. "Invented in the Middle Ages by the church, to attract pilgrims and make a little money. Surely you'll agree, it is important for us to differentiate between established belief and fanciful, as well as insensible, legend."

The vicar kept his silence, though Ned detected a hint of a smile on the vicar's visage. Ned wanted to hear more, but he knew when his parents were through with a subject—and the vicar seemed to sense it, too.

Saying something about a bread pudding in the refrigerator at the bed and breakfast, Mum walked away.

Dad followed after, reminding her to douse the pudding with a bit of treacle.

The vicar and Ned were left alone for a moment. "It must have been quite an adventure," Ned said, "for Jesus to be here in this strange land with his uncle."

"It might have been life changing—or maybe even life making—for the young Jesus," said Father Walters. "Scripture tells us nothing about Jesus's life from the age of twelve to the onset of his ministry. Most people assume he spent those missing years in Nazareth, learning Saint Joseph's carpentry trade and studying. Your father is right that it would have been an improbable journey to take in those days, but remember that nothing is impossible for God." The vicar gave Ned a warm smile. "Never be afraid to ask questions, my son."

"C'mon, Ned," Dad hailed from the gateway. "We mustn't bother the kind vicar any longer. So nice to have met you, Father Walters. We look forward to seeing you tomorrow!"

Father Walters walked back into the church.

Ned paused, still examining the stone. He had more questions yet. He knew from school that the Romans did not invade Britain until well after Jesus's death. If Jesus had traveled to Britain any time during his life, he would have encountered primitive Celts and pagan druids.

Back then, no one would have made such a journey—all the way from the Holy Land to Britain, and back again—just for a holiday. What might have drawn young Jesus so far from his home, to travel among people who would have been so strange to him? And what is going on with this cross?

If it was made in the tenth century as the vicar said, why is there a plaque marking it as a headstone for a priest who died in 1881?

Ned turned to rejoin his parents. *Yes, Dad is right. The vicar's story really is quite insensible.*

But that boy in the cross puzzled him. He contemplated the carving again. *The boy has his arms spread, just like Jesus on the Cross, but he does not seem to be suffering. He wants something. He yearns for it. What can it be?* Ned thought about how he and his friends at school often conspired together. *That's it!* The carving reminded him of how they liked to share secrets. *What secret is this carved Jesus trying to tell me? I can ask the vicar to tell me more tomorrow.*

Chapter 1
What to Do About Jesus?

Jerusalem, A.D. 8, during the reign of Augustus, first emperor of Rome

Caiaphas

Caiaphas strode across the court of priests in the highest level of the temple, forbidden to all but clerics. The courtyard of priests was where they ritually slaughtered, washed, and cooked the lambs and other sacrificial offerings on the Sabbaths and holy days. Among the structures rising above was the House of God that housed the Holy of Holies, reserved to the high priest himself; and the less sacred but still awe-inspiring *Hekal*, the worship hall for all the clerics.

Caiaphas descended a broad stairway to the classrooms. Laymen were only permitted to gaze upon the temple structures above when they came to hand up their sacrificial offerings, but the classrooms were open to all the Israelite men.

Like the other Sadducee priests, Caiaphas wore a simple *ephod* as an apron over his white cloak, the hem of which was bordered with blue fringe. For the task at hand, this would be a sufficient display of his authority. No need to call undue attention to himself. His mission did not require him to display his role as one of the Sanhedrin, the governors of the temple.

Annas, the high priest and Caiaphas's father-in-law, had tasked him with investigating another false prophet. The people's hunger for deliverance from their Roman overlords was creating an environment in which such charlatans flourished, and lately they seemed to be popping up more than ever. Such thinking could be dangerous. Romans were ready to pounce at any hint of insurrection.

Usually, Annas sent a junior priest to chase a blasphemer away, but this time he had chosen to send Caiaphas. This would make sense if someone were spewing especially dangerous teachings, but how dangerous could this one be? This had to be some kind of a bad joke. This was merely a boy of twelve.

Still, Caiaphas would deal with the situation. A few strokes of the whip would correct the boy's impudence before he could do any real damage.

Caiaphas turned into the room used for teaching, stood in the back, and listened. He was soon amazed. Learned doctors, men who should know better, were listening with rapt attention.

The boy was not much to look at, a little tall and thin for his age, but not malnourished. He had an engaging face with a thin nose and lips, smiling and expressive. Locks of medium brown curls flowed to his shoulders and framed his face. His teeth seemed healthy, and all there; it was enough to make him suspect the boy might be the son of a rich family, but the meanness of his garments and the calluses on his fingers belied that notion. He wore only a simple off-white tunic, a prayer shawl, and a skullcap, with a plain pair of sandals on his feet. Well-worn though his clothes were, they were also well mended. His family must be of modest means, but not impoverished.

The boy certainly knew Holy Scripture; Caiaphas had to give him that. The more he listened, however, the more he caught on to the subtle and dangerous nuances in what young Jesus bar Joseph had to say.

"We are all called to be in God's service," Jesus declared.

So far, nothing wrong with that.

"Even as a child I am called to do his will, as the Psalms say. Today in this temple, as this beautiful morning light shines upon me, I am here because of God. There is hope for Israel. We will see the Messiah come soon, out of obscurity and from a poor family."

"But how can you assume he will be from humble beginnings?" asked an old rabbi. "We believe the Messiah will be great and powerful."

"The Prophet Isaiah said clearly that the Messiah will come from the line of Jesse," said the boy, "and that a branch shall grow out of his roots.

That family is no longer great in Israel. Therefore, it follows that the Messiah will come from obscurity."

A young rabbi then spoke up. "With respect, sir, the boy is right. What he says is in the beginning of Isaiah's prophecy."

The boy is clever, but it is dangerous for him to advance his arguments with Scripture. Heretics and blasphemers could twist many passages to deceive listeners. That was why interpretation of Scripture was the province of the highest of the priests.

"I come today as a messenger from far-off Nazareth. God is God of Love. We must know his love before we can love each other. We must disregard external representations and gaze within. This must be part of our preparation before we can be freed from Rome. We must love even those who are not Jewish, for they too are loved by God—"

"But young man, we Jews are the chosen people of the one true God," said a man in the crowd.

"We are the blessed flock of all nations," said another older man. "Do you not know that we alone are favored?"

"But, good sir, consider the words of the prophet Isaiah," said Jesus. "He says that the Messiah will save those people who have walked in darkness, and that even the gentiles will see a great light—for upon them hath the light shined."

The old man was left speechless for a moment. Then he whispered something to the man seated beside him.

"I fear the whispers of this place," Jesus said. "People, do not whisper—have faith that we will be saved. We must have hope, and I pray for those who whisper hatred and jealousy. We must know that the Messiah shall be conspired against when he is here, just as the Psalms say, and he will suffer reproach for God's sake because of this hatred. But then he will be exalted and glorified among all, and he will save Israel from her captors."

The young rabbi interjected again to say that Jesus spoke the truth from the book of Daniel.

The older rabbi shook his head.

It seemed to Caiaphas that the boy was not only using Scripture to advance error, but also that he meant to advance the cause of the rebellious zealots. Allowing such teaching in the temple would bring down the wrath of the Romans. Caiaphas nearly raised his voice to silence the boy, but his curiosity made him hesitate. He leaned forward to hear what else the boy had to say.

"The Messiah will bring love to all. He will be the salvation of Israel, sent by God, who is his father, as the Proverbs say. The Son will look to the Father and gain insight into his mission of saving this land. I am still a boy, and I struggle with growing and understanding. I only wish to become a better servant to God, so that I may glorify him. I wish all of you peace in the Lord."

What is that about the Messiah being the son of God? That was dangerous blasphemy. And the boy's words of peace only deepened Caiaphas' concern. *His words of love can easily hide from the ignorant the danger in his teachings, just as the sweetness of wine can hide poison dissolved within the same glass.*

Suddenly, an old man and a woman in peasant garb burst in. The man's sudden entry was odd enough, but it was the woman who caused everyone to look up in astonishment. Not only was it unheard of for a woman to enter these rooms, but she had not even bothered to cover her head. The woman appeared to be in her late twenties or early thirties—certainly old enough to know better.

"We've been sick with worry!" she said. "We've been looking for you for three days!"

So, these must be the parents—the carpenter and his wife.

Caiaphas crept closer to hear. She had regained some sense of propriety, lowering her voice to keep what she said to the boy between her and him.

The boy raised an eyebrow and sighed audibly as his mother kept talking.

What impudence! The boy had caused his parents such grief and worry. He should be begging their forgiveness. Under the laws of Leviticus, a disobedient son might suffer death.

The mother paused for breath.

"Why were you looking for me?" the boy said. "Would you not know that I would be about my Father's business?"

The mother began to weep at her son's words. Was this just the emotional release from the stress of the last three days, or did what the boy had said mean more to her? No one else in the room seemed to catch on, but to Caiaphas there was no mistaking the intention of the boy's words. He was talking of God as being his own father. *The boy thinks of himself not only as the Messiah, but as God's own son. What blasphemy!* Now Caiaphas understood. *Annas was right to entrust me with this task. This boy is dangerous far beyond his years.*

But Annas had instructed Caiaphas to investigate and report back—nothing more—and as the parents led Jesus away, Caiaphas thought it best to let them go. *I could have the boy whipped, but what good would that do? It would only make the little devil's blasphemy more subtle.* No, Caiaphas would report back as instructed, and Annas would certainly appreciate his wisdom in recognizing the danger the boy posed.

Most Pharisees served in the synagogues around the country, and the Sadducees served in the temple. The two sects were rivals, but there was common ground between them when it came to the danger of blasphemy and incitement to rebellion. Caiaphas would write to the Pharisee rabbi in Nazareth, asking him to keep an eye on Jesus.

Mary

After the family's return to Nazareth, life seemed to return to normal. Joseph found work in Sepphoris, the great city of Lower Galilee. Jesus was now old enough to be a real help to him, so except for Sabbath days they awoke before dawn to make time for the long walk to work.

Mary was always the first to rise to get the daily bread ready. Jesus would be next, joining Mary on the rooftop. With Jesus off with Joseph through the long day, Mary loved this all-too-short early morning hour that Jesus spent with her.

In the predawn hour, the darkness served to heighten the senses, and the rooftop was a world of sounds and smells—the chattering of the women on nearby rooftops, the dusty aroma of the desert carried on an easterly wind from over the horizon, and the scent of dung wafted by a local zephyr from the flocks' hillside pastures. In the birthing season, the interludes of stillness would be broken by the cries of the newborn lambs, but now Mary heard only the sound of her fist punching down the risen dough. As she punched it down, the dough released the subtle scent of yeast, something that her nose was trained to search out in the darkness.

In the first rays of dawn, she saw the mess of wind-blown flour all over her hands and clothes. It was no matter; the breeze would soon carry it away.

Jesus smiled to see her covered in flour. "Good morning, Mother. What can I do to help?"

"The dough is already formed," she said. "We have a respite to give the loaves a chance for the second rising."

They needed to put little into words as they waited.

After the second rising, as they moved the loaves to the oven, Jesus managed to dust himself a bit, too. He was too old now to cradle in her arms, but the flour on his face gave her the excuse to touch him as she brushed it away, and then he returned the favor. Mary easily could have washed her face and hands with water from the cistern, but she would sooner have dusted them both even more.

The surrounding landscape emerged now in the gathering light. They saw the Jezreel Valley, the breadbasket of Galilee, and the highlands devoted to the raising of sheep and goats that ate from the tough grasses and shrubs that grew there. Nazareth was situated on the high part of the ridge, broken by the gullies and sharp ravines eroded away in seasonal flooding that left little moisture behind. The land even in the dry highland was good; the shepherds would have thrived, if not for the burden of taxation. As a woman, Mary knew little of politics, but she could not miss the sight of distended bellies among the villagers, and Jesus often told her how he blamed the Romans for the suffering of the people. Fortunately, Joseph earned enough as a skilled carpenter to provide well for their needs, and Mary had the good sense to husband every coin he earned.

Mary would have been content to stay on the rooftop with Jesus forever, but he always had the presence of mind to gently break her from her reverie.

"Mother? Time to finish the breakfast."

⊱ ✤ ⊰

Jesus's thirteenth birthday came a few weeks after he and Joseph began working in Sepphoris. For the first time, they returned home early so they could spend part of the special evening quietly with Mary. She had a simple meal of fish and vegetables ready on the table.

"Is something troubling you, Mother?" asked Jesus, shortly after they started eating.

"No, dear."

"Your mother looks fine to me, son," said Joseph.

"Mother, I can tell when you are troubled."

Mary sighed. "I was just thinking that you should be reading from the Torah on the next Sabbath. You will be welcomed at the synagogue as a man who can be counted toward the *minyan*."

"If we say anything about Jesus's birthday," said Joseph, "it will bring up that old gossip about how you must have been immoral before our wedding. You and I know the truth about Jesus's conception, but this will only stir that ugly pot again. Did we not go through all that during our betrothal?"

"But since he started working with you in Sepphoris, Jesus has neglected his studies. Soon, he will grow taller, his voice will change, and he will grow a beard. Everyone will know he is well beyond the age for reciting from the Torah. They will think he is a simpleton."

"Oh, come on, woman." Joseph guffawed. "I have heard many things said about Jesus, some of them not very nice, but his being simple is not one of them."

"What do they say about me, Papa?"

"The rabbi says you drive him to distraction, bringing up every contradiction in Scripture."

"I only seek the truth."

"The rabbi gets weary when you challenge him, no matter how respectfully you do it." Joseph turned to Mary. "It's actually a good thing Jesus is away from the synagogue now except on Sabbath days. I don't think there is anything more he can learn there, and it would soon cause no end of trouble."

Jesus smiled. "Don't worry if people start calling me a simpleton, Mother. Papa is teaching me an honest trade, and we do well with it. No one will care whether I can read from the Torah or not if I can build and mend the things they need."

"Would you be content just to follow in my husband's footsteps, knowing what the angel Gabriel told me about you?" Mary asked.

"If that is God's will, then certainly I will be content, Mother. We have a good life here. I feel God will call me to something else, though I do not know when that will be. Until then, I can be content right here."

❦ ❈ ❧

Three weeks later, Joseph took ill. It started with a deep cough, but soon he was too weak to rise from bed.

Then the Sadducees came, two of the temple priests arriving all the way from Jerusalem.

"We've come to talk to Jesus."

That could only mean trouble. Sadducees did not journey such a distance just for a pleasant chat with anyone, much less a boy of Jesus's age.

"He's away," Mary said, glad to be able to speak honestly. Jesus had returned on his own to work in Sepphoris that morning. "What business can you have with my son?"

Their insincere smiles tightened the knots in her stomach.

"We merely want to talk," the older one said. "We'll return at a better time."

Late that evening Jesus returned, sweaty and covered with the dust of the road. Mary told him that the Sadducees had come to see him, and he snorted and sat near the basin at the door to wash his feet. "So?"

"You are oblivious to danger," she wailed, and plunked a basket of bread on the table.

"I am determined to spread the truth."

"The truth as you see it."

"To anyone who will listen." He sat on a cushion at the table.

"Jesus, you are old enough for the authorities to treat you as a man. Even though you have not recited from the Torah, they can punish you." She saw nothing but truth and childlike innocence in him, no matter how much his wisdom belied that innocence. But not everyone would agree with her.

Mary needed help, and there was only one place to find it. She persuaded her husband Joseph to write to her uncle. Mary's uncle had the same name as her husband, so they usually identified him by his hometown: Joseph of Arimathea. Her mother's youngest brother, Uncle Joseph was only five years Mary's senior, so he seemed more like a cousin or older brother to her than an uncle. Growing up as children, they had played together on family visits. Her first taste of tragedy had come the year before her own betrothal, when Uncle Joseph's wife had died in childbirth. They were so close, she had felt his pain as her own.

With each passing day, Mary watched the road for a messenger bearing a reply from Uncle Joseph. She sensed approaching danger, a feeling of something ominous in the air of Nazareth. The people of the village seemed to draw silent at her approach. Even the rabbi avoided her. Her husband Joseph was far too ill to travel now, much less take Jesus and her away from danger, as he had taken them to Egypt so many years ago when the monster Herod slaughtered the babes. Now duty called upon her to tend to her sick husband, no matter what. They were all stuck in this place as the wolves circled in.

The day after the Sabbath, Jesus remained in Nazareth as the work in Sepphoris had stopped for a few days. Mary gave her husband some soup and then came out of the house to look up the road again. In the distance, two figures on horseback rode toward the village. Their horses' hooves raised clouds of dust, obscuring their appearance. Mary ran to find her son. This had to be the Sadducees returning.

She found him in the village square teaching, with some of the other village children squatting at his feet. Older passers-by scowled, evidently wondering what sort of mischief Jesus was implanting in those innocent heads.

She grabbed his wrist. "Come quickly."

As they began to scurry inside the house, Mary looked up the road one last time. She could now recognize her uncle Joseph. The second rider must be his son, Daniel. In tears, Mary hugged Jesus.

As her uncle and cousin alighted, she exclaimed, "Oh, Joseph, thanks be to God. You're here at our hour of need."

Daniel scowled when his father told him to stay outside with Jesus while he went inside to talk to Mary and her husband. It was hard to tell that the boys were related. Jesus's curly brown hair would never darken to match the coal black strands that fell straight from the crown of his cousin's head. The green color of their eyes was the only feature they seemed to share. Still beardless at fifteen, Daniel was turning into a strapping young man. Although his movements betrayed the awkwardness of that age, muscles were filling out his body.

"So, shall we make mud pies again?" Daniel asked Jesus, with something of a smirk.

Jesus silently folded his arms.

Daniel continued, "We heard you caused quite a commotion."

Mary could not stay to listen for more. Uncle Joseph was inside the house and waving for her to follow.

In the darkened side room where Mary and Joseph shared their bed, the two Josephs greeted each other. It was a humble home, but clean and tidy. Jesus's bed occupied one corner of the main room, which the family also used to cook and eat their meals. Joseph's workbench sat idle. In another corner was a small oil lamp table and a chair that Jesus used when studying.

"I'll talk things over with Uncle," Mary said, "and we'll wake you before deciding anything."

Seemingly satisfied, her husband slumped back in the bed.

Uncle Joseph opened his arms as he turned back to the main room and embraced her. For a brief moment they were once again childhood companions.

"Your husband's letter was waiting for me when I got home yesterday," Uncle Joseph began. "I came as quickly as I could."

"Thanks be to God. I fear Jesus is in danger."

"Haven't you told him to mind his tongue? He is far too young to be preaching on Scripture."

"You don't understand what it's like with a child such as Jesus. In most ways, he is gentle and obedient. Look at his bed. He has made it up perfectly ever since he was three; I have never even needed to remind him. When it comes to matters of Scripture, though, he is convinced that he knows the truth and must share it with the world. He cares not for any words of danger. God knows I have tried." Mary began to weep. "The Sadducees came to question him. I told them he was away, but what can I tell them next time? Some people of the village seem hostile, and I fear they will betray us when the Sadducees return. Something must be done with Jesus quickly, but I know not what."

"The time is even shorter than you think," Uncle Joseph said. "My friends among the Sanhedrin told me much in confidence. Annas is losing support among the Sanhedrin. His son-in-law Caiaphas's influence grows, and some say Caiaphas will replace Annas as high priest."

"What does that have to do with Jesus?"

"Caiaphas heard Jesus preach in the temple, and he is convinced that Jesus is dangerous. Your rabbi has been sending reports to him, too."

"What danger does Caiaphas think Jesus can be? He is only a boy."

"It matters not the reasons for Caiaphas's fear of Jesus," said Uncle Joseph. "Perhaps he is only using the boy to make his name as an enemy of blasphemers. Whatever his reasons, the Sadducees will come again, and they will not be put off next time."

How could the priests see her child as such a threat?

"I have it on good authority, " said Uncle Joseph, "that Caiaphas has alerted the temple guards to detain Jesus if he returns to Judea."

"All this for fear of a child!" Mary sighed. "What are the Sadducees waiting for?"

"Their authority is limited to Judea. They must go through King Herod Antipas to do anything more than investigate in Galilee. But even now Caiaphas has Antipas's ear."

"Maybe we should get Jesus away."

"I have already taken steps to do that. The time was too short to write back and ask you. I instructed the captain of my ship to depart from Caesarea and make for Acre. It will be easier to meet the ship there with Jesus. We will have to stay off the roads through Galilee as much as we can and avoid Sepphoris."

"Will he be safe once he crosses the border into Syria?"

"Jesus may gain a short reprieve, at best. Acre is a den of intrigue, with Jews, Greeks, Arabs, and Phoenicians all suspicious of each other. Caiaphas is sure to have his spies among them. The authorities in Acre could very well send Jesus back if they get word he is wanted in Judea; the Roman legates do favors like that for each other all the time."

"Maybe you could take Jesus to Antioch or Damascus. As soon as my husband recovers, I can travel there from time to time to look after Jesus."

"I'm afraid, dear Mary, that you do not understand the Romans as I do. Beyond Judea and Galilee, your son would be directly under their authority. They tolerate religions that are native to the lands they conquer, if the followers refrain from criticizing their gods. But if Jesus is as willful on matters of Scripture as you say, he will find that the Romans care even less for those they consider blasphemers of their pagan gods than Caiaphas does for the blasphemers of ours. Nor can we count on the Jewish communities in those provinces to protect him; they look to the Sanhedrin for moral guidance. The next time Jesus gets in trouble, he would be far from any aid I might bring."

Mary collapsed on a cushion. "So, what is to be done?"

Uncle Joseph paused. "I think it is best if I take Jesus with me beyond the authority of the Romans until he is fully of age. I will leave soon on a new expedition, and I do not expect to return for two years. He can accompany Daniel and me to the Isle of the Britons."

"The Britons?" gasped Mary. "But that is so far away. And aren't the Britons savages?" Her stomach knotted.

"The Romans tell many lies about them. In the regions where I travel, the natives have been trading peaceably for centuries with Greeks and Phoenicians long before the Romans extended their rule beyond their city limits. King Solomon himself used British lead and tin in the building of the first temple."

Britain? That was on the other side of the world. She resisted, but Uncle Joseph patiently convinced her that there was little choice; every alternative she suggested would be far more dangerous for Jesus.

Mary woke her husband to explain that they must send Jesus away.

He listened carefully. "Jesus is no longer a child," he rasped. "He has insight into Scripture far beyond his years, and even ordinary boys become men at his age. This decision must be his."

Mary and her uncle walked outside. They expected to find the two cousins wrestling or engaged in some other rough play. Instead, what they saw made them hesitate at the threshold, momentarily dumbfounded.

There was Daniel, down on his knees at Jesus's feet, his hands clasped as if in supplication or prayer, gazing up silently at his cousin.

Jesus met his mother's eyes. "I didn't do anything to him," he said. "We were just chatting, and suddenly he stopped talking and knelt for no reason at all."

No longer was he acting the part of the audacious young teacher who dared to challenge the Sanhedrin. Once more, he appeared to Mary as the innocent child, shrugging, not knowing what to make of his older cousin's strange behavior, a child caught helplessly in an awkward situation.

"Get up, fool!" Uncle Joseph commanded his son.

Daniel remained silently in his posture of supplication before Jesus.

Then Jesus spoke in a shaky, awkward voice. "Listen to your father, Daniel. Get up."

At these words, Daniel emerged from his trance. Slowly, he rose to his feet.

Once they were all back in the house, Mary explained to Jesus that for his own safety he should leave right away with Uncle Joseph for Britain.

"Does Papa agree with this?" asked Jesus.

"Yes, but he insisted this decision is yours to make." Mary paused. "He says you are a man now."

"Come with us, Jesus. Think of what an adventure it will be!" said Daniel.

"With Papa so sick, this is hardly the time for me to be off looking for adventures." Jesus turned to Mary and her uncle. "On the other hand, I do not care about hardship or danger. My Father will protect me." Seeing Uncle wince, Jesus corrected himself. "I put my faith in God to protect me. But how can I leave you alone, Mother, to take care of Papa?"

"I won't be alone. Joseph's children will help care for him." Even as Mary said this, she realized there would be trouble on that score. Jesus's older half-brothers and half-sisters, Joseph's children by a previous marriage, honored and respected Joseph as their father. They would certainly do everything they could for him. But to them Mary was the stepmother. Still an outsider.

"Papa has many children," said Jesus, "but I am your only son, and what kind of son would I be if I left you at a time like this? The Sadducees said they just want to talk to me. Let us hear what they have to say. If I agree to what they ask of me, they may leave us alone."

"Perhaps you will find it harder than you think to agree to what the Sadducees want," said Uncle Joseph.

"It doesn't matter. If I must keep my silence to stay with my parents, I will do it."

"Daniel and I will stay in the village until I see this matter resolved."

"That is very kind of you, Uncle Joseph, but you are wasting your time. My mind is made up to agree to everything they ask of me."

Joseph

Uncle Joseph could not stay long at his niece's house. The Sadducees might be along at any time, and it would not do for him to be found helping Jesus. So, he went with Daniel to find a place to stay among the villagers.

That evening he remonstrated with his son. "What has gotten into you? You acted this afternoon as if your cousin is a god! He's only a boy."

"But, Papa, I saw it with my own eyes. A divine light glowed within him, and suddenly his body burned as bright as the sun."

"The only thing having to do with the sun is that you were out in it too long. Stop this talk at once. Can't you see how you frightened the boy?" Despite a tepid acknowledgment from Daniel, Joseph feared this would not be the last of his son's strange behavior.

Mary

The Sadducees were at the front door an hour after dawn. Jesus let them in. Joseph lay coughing in bed, while Mary sat beside him and applied damp compresses to his forehead. The Sadducees looked in on him and offered a prayer for his recovery. Mary and Jesus joined in and thanked them for their kindness.

With the unexpected pastoral duty concluded, the first Sadducee, Elimelech, began. "We come under the authority of Annas, the high priest of the temple. He has received reports of your son's teaching in the temple, and your rabbi informs us that Jesus has continued to interpret Scripture to anyone who will listen."

"Did I not speak the truth?" asked Jesus.

"Everyone was impressed by your knowledge of the Scriptures, but that is not the point."

"Pardon me," said Mary. "As a woman these things are so strange to me. I only see him as my child. Can you explain to me why learned rabbis such as you need to come all the way to Nazareth? Surely, the temple will stand regardless of what my son says."

"Not for long, if the Romans hear that we allow talk of a Messiah coming to free our people from their rule."

"I understand," said Jesus.

"There is also the question of spreading blasphemy, " said Elimelech. "Scripture is full of contradictions. It is one thing to read from Scripture, but we must leave the interpretation in the hands of the rabbis. That is the only way to avoid the spread of error among the people."

"If I stop talking about Scripture now, will I be able to become a rabbi when I get older?" Jesus asked.

"Certainly you can, if you study. But even rabbis must stick to authorized interpretations."

"Perhaps this is God's will. Now that Papa is ill, the time has come for me take his place and earn a living for the family."

Elimelech said, "You are talking like a man now."

"I will stop talking about Scripture and just read from it under the rabbi's supervision. I owe that to my parents."

"Explain the other point," said Pesachya, the second Sadducee. He had been staring at Jesus and Mary with uncanny intensity.

Elimelech sighed. "I am afraid we must insist on one more thing." He turned to Mary. "It is something you will need to do, madam, to ensure we have a permanent solution to this problem. It is in our instructions."

"I will do anything to be left in peace with my family," said Mary.

"Your rabbi picked up a story among the villagers. They say that Jesus was conceived within you by the spirit of God, and that you revealed your nakedness to no man."

"What must I do?" asked Mary.

"You must go with us to the synagogue on the next Sabbath. We will call on you before the congregation and ask if the story is true. You will respond that it is not."

Mary looked over to Jesus. *I will do anything to appease these men, if Jesus can stay. I don't care what the village thinks of me. But it will not work. Sooner or later, some woman will blame me for her husband's unfaithfulness, no one will believe anything I say, and they will stone me for adultery. My husband Joseph could die as well. Who will look after Jesus then?*

Jesus pounded a fist on the table. "If that is not the truth, then what do you think is the truth?" His voice quaked and his face turned red.

Mary had never seen such anger in her son before.

"We don't care who your father is," Elimelech replied. "Our only concern is ending this blasphemous talk about you being the son of God himself."

"My mother is not a liar, and she is not a whore, but that is what everyone will say about her. I agree to nothing if my mother must do this." Jesus abruptly got up and stormed out of the house.

Pesachya waited a moment for Mary to recover. Then he broke the silence. "You have no real choice. No one wants to put someone as young as your son on trial for blasphemy, but eventually the Sanhedrin will do so—through your king, if necessary. It's out of our hands."

"We can stay in Nazareth a few more days," said Elimelech. "We will give you both that time to think this through."

Mary found Jesus just outside the village, looking over the Jezreel Valley. No words were necessary. Uncle Joseph was right; the Sadducees were demanding too much. Jesus must go, and he would not return for some time. Jesus became once more as a child, upset to be leaving his mother.

"Do not worry, my child." Mary embraced him. "This will be an exciting voyage for you. You will come back to us with many stories." *There is no other choice.* She wiped the tears from her eyes. *He must not see the pain this separation brings to my heart.* She could only pray that Jesus's heavenly Father, as well as Uncle Joseph, would look after him.

The two walked back to the house to gather the few things Jesus would take with him.

Husband Joseph's skin had a white pallor and his legs wobbled, but he managed to get out of bed.

Jesus ran to him, and the two embraced.

"I love you, my son. Respect your uncle and learn much from this trip. Be a helper, and know that I am praying for you. God will care for you."

Jesus softly replied, "I know he will, Papa. I shall be praying for you, too."

"I cannot wait to hear all your adventures." Joseph smiled, though his sadness showed in his eyes.

Jesus walked to the corner of the room and removed the flooring where the gifts of the three magi had been safely hidden since the time of his birth. He brought them to Mary. "You must use these to provide for yourself and Papa while I am gone."

"I have money saved, and those are divine gifts for you. I could never—"

"Mother, how else can you and Papa live if he is sick and I am gone? Who knows when I will return or when Papa will be able to work again? As your son, I should be working to support the family. I cannot leave here without giving you this. If you cannot accept it for yourself, then accept it for Papa's sake—and mine."

"Never forget my love is with you." Mary embraced Jesus again. "There is danger for you here in Nazareth, and we do not know who is waiting to inform the Sadducees of your movements. You should go to Uncle Joseph now on your own. It would attract attention if I went with you, and you need to be inconspicuous as you make your way to him."

Joseph

A short distance outside Nazareth, Uncle Joseph rounded a bend in the road and pulled his horse up sharply. The Sadducees and their men had laid their plans well. Up ahead, a temple guard and two of Herod's soldiers blocked the road. Daniel was following with Jesus holding on from behind on the same horse. Joseph tried to signal for his son to stay back, but Daniel reacted too slowly, coming to a stop alongside. Joseph watched helplessly as the party ahead of them quickly mounted their own horses.

Daniel spun his horse back toward Nazareth and galloped away.

Joseph hesitated. Surely, other soldiers and guards would be in Nazareth by now—they had to be trapped in between. Flight was hopeless, and later the Sanhedrin and Herod would take an attempt at escape as an admission of Jesus's guilt.

Joseph shouted to his son to turn back again, but it was no use. Quickly he gave chase, only to see his son's horse swerve down one of the deep ravines that sliced through the Nazareth Ridge.

Hoping to draw the pursuers in the wrong direction, Joseph galloped past, back toward Nazareth.

It almost worked.

But then Joseph heard a shout from behind. Turning his head, he saw that the soldier had drawn his horse up short at the top of the ravine, alerting the temple guards that they were going the wrong way. The other two turned back quickly to give chase after the true quarry.

Joseph trotted to the top of the ravine and watched helplessly.

The pursuers were skilled in riding through rough terrain in pursuit of bandits. Daniel had the advantage of a head start, but the pursuers quickly closed the gap. They would capture Daniel and Jesus before the boys reached the bottom.

The soldier was practically alongside Daniel in the narrowest part of the ravine when his horse stumbled and fell as he tried to grasp Daniel's reins. The gap between the ravine walls was too narrow for the other two to avoid his horse, and they were going too fast to stop. The flesh of man and beast collided into a single mass of bloody gore in the all-too-narrow space as Daniel made good his escape with Jesus.

God be praised! A miracle!

⁂

A few hours later, as he waited by the ship, Joseph saw more soldiers approaching with the port master. Someone must have recognized him and gotten word to an agent of Caiaphas in the port. But where were his son and Jesus? Should he try to get the vessel away as soon as possible, or should he stay? The search of the vessel was just about complete, and no contraband—human or other—had been found. Joseph looked over the small crowd next to the ship and recognized a Pharisee, one of the local rabbis, in deep discussion with the port master. It would attract suspicion if the vessel failed to leave once cleared to do so. Joseph had to give the Sadducees credit for enlisting such a network of allies so quickly from the rival sect.

Just as the search ended, Joseph saw Daniel turn a corner and make his way down the dock. Joseph wondered what his son had done with Jesus. He could not ask, as everyone on the narrow dock would hear.

"I have posted your letter to Seculus, Papa," Daniel said. "We can go now."

They had left Seculus at their last port of call, and there was no letter to him. Joseph thought about the incident when Daniel had knelt down in front of Jesus and wondered if he should trust his crazy son, but he knew that he had no choice but to take the cue to go.

Joseph turned to the port master and requested clearance to leave.

"This man was seen harboring a fugitive," the Pharisee said. "We have the report direct from our informer in Nazareth."

The port master stroked his beard thoughtfully, while he considered. He had the authority to hold the ship indefinitely.

"Your information is wrong," Joseph answered. *The harbor master looks like he's about to give in to the Pharisee. I had better make it clear there could be a price to pay.* He addressed the port master: "The vessel has been searched and there is no contraband. We are about to miss the tide. If we do, I will demand damages. That is my right, under the law."

The port master turned to the Pharisee and puffed up his chest. "What do I care about your local matters? My only duty is to enforce the trade laws of Rome."

"Herod Antipas may not rule Acre," the Pharisee replied, "but there will be trouble if you knowingly allow someone to leave this port whom the Tetrarch wants detained."

"Herod ordered the detention of a boy of twelve. Clearly, such a boy is not on this ship." The port master waved a hand toward the vessel. "You have no order to detain anyone else. The vessel is free to sail." The port master walked off, ignoring the continuing entreaties of the Pharisee.

"Set sail!" cried Joseph.

The sails filled, and the vessel slipped away from the dock.

As soon as they were out of earshot, he turned to his son. But before he could ask, Daniel anticipated his question: "Jesus is on the *Trumpet of Gideon,* bound for Cyprus. I booked his passage as the boat was leaving. We can meet him there."

Joseph smiled. His son might be crazy, but he was learning to find his way around a port. Daniel would have had to bluster his way through booking that passage for Jesus, even though he was hardly of age to do so. *I will make a fine merchant of him yet.*

Chapter 2
A Gift of Tongues

Nehemiah

Nehemiah regarded the sea with the wary eye of a seasoned sea captain. Since he had left Cyprus, the winds had been fair. To the untrained eye, this would look like another pleasant day of mostly blue sky with broken clouds, but the lingering redness in the morning sky spelled trouble.

Creta, over the horizon to the north, had several harbors offering safe havens, but they were all on the northern shore of that island. The sheer cliff faces along the long southern shore might as well be wolf fangs, ready to tear apart any craft unlucky enough to find that shore on the lee in a storm. No, there would be no making for land; they would have to keep their distance, so he commanded the helmsman to adjust the course away from that danger and gybe the sail. They would sail west as rapidly as possible, hopefully fast enough to get beyond the danger of the island to the north before any storm hit.

What strange events had led to the detour to Salamis. It almost seemed that Nehemiah's longtime friend had smuggled Jesus out of the country. Joseph was always a man of honor who paid his bills on time without raising spurious questions or quibbling with feigned excuses or protestations of bad fortune. Nehemiah's father had spoken well of the family when they first met as young men both learning their respective trades. It was no surprise to Nehemiah when he heard that the Romans had granted Joseph the Arimathean the honor of full citizenship, usually reserved to residents of Italia, and then the title of *noblis decurio*. But while Joseph made many friends in high places, he nurtured his friendships with the less fortunate as well.

The crack of the yardarm against the mast interrupted the captain's reverie. The gybe maneuver required the helmsman to turn the stern of the ship through the wind. The men had to slacken the bracing stays on the new leeward side to free the yardarm to swing back while the windward stays were tightened to support the mast. The timing was critical; in heavy wind, an unsupported mast could snap in an instant. Nehemiah was pleased that the hands stayed alert to keep the rig under control. He adjusted his balance as the ship heeled to the other side, and his thoughts returned to what Joseph was doing with the boy.

The business with the nephew was certainly strange. *Why would Joseph, of all people, set himself against the temple authorities?* When he had the chance, Nehemiah went to synagogues in the isolated Jewish communities scattered around the Mediterranean, but that was the extent of his piety. Joseph, on the other hand, was devout in adhering to all the inconvenient strictures of Jewish law.

Why is the boy such a concern? An edict of detention, evidently from King Herod Antipas himself!

Jesus seemed so harmless, just a skinny waif. Nehemiah had first seen him playing with other children on a dock as Nehemiah's ship sailed into Salamis to pick him up. He had seen the stronger boys push Jesus into the water, but the boy quickly emerged laughing. He had seemed so much like an even younger child, jumping across the docks and waving exuberantly to greet Joseph and Daniel once he spied them in the approaching ship.

Nehemiah felt a slight pull on his cloak. At first he thought it was just the wind, but there it was again. Nehemiah turned to find the boy himself tugging gently.

"Shalom," the boy uttered once he saw he had the captain's attention. "And peace in the Lord!"

The greeting sounded a bit pretentious coming from a youth, but Jesus's warm smile dispelled that thought quickly. "Shalom," Nehemiah replied. "What brings you up on deck?"

"I felt a change in the weather and the course of the ship."

The lad is indeed observant. Nehemiah explained how he had altered course to avoid the danger of the lee shore to the north with the threat of a storm coming.

"But the storm will come from the south," Jesus responded. "We cannot get past the island in time. We should be heading even further away from it as fast as we can."

Nehemiah looked at the boy dubiously. How could he possibly know such things? Passengers often expressed curiosity about the ways of the seas and the workings of his ship, but not even Joseph had ever presumed to offer him advice on the running of it. Wordlessly, he started to walk away. But after a few steps he turned to look back. Something about the boy piqued his curiosity. The merry look in his eyes gave him the appearance of utter childlike innocence. Yet at the same time, he bore a haunting look that betrayed an unnerving sense of confidence in his perception.

"Be at peace, Captain. My Father will protect this ship," said Jesus.

No, the boy is not being impudent. He attaches himself to the Arimathean because he is away from his own father. He expects Joseph to look after him as his own father would. He must idolize the father he left at home, and now he thinks that Joseph must have some strange power from his father to protect everyone.

Unable to think of anything to say to help the boy, the captain smiled kindly and went about his business.

Within hours, clouds filled the sky, descended, and became an angry dark gray. While the clouds came in from the east, a freak wind hit the ship from the south, just as Jesus had predicted. The waves broke around them. It wasn't supposed to happen this way; the southerly wind always filled in gradually.

The unexpectedly wild wind rose up before they had a chance to reef the sail. At least initially, Nehemiah had no choice but to run with it even though it took the ship racing towards the dangerous shore to the north. With full sail, turning at all into the powerful wind was no option; a broadside blow of wind and quickly mounting wave would certainly capsize the vessel to its more immediate destruction.

Nehemiah ordered his two hands to climb the rigging and reef the sail. He watched the two men get up there, stand on the footropes, and strain trying to no avail to pull in the cloth against the force of the wind.

"Can we go up and help?" Daniel was already drenched from the spray. He clutched the rail to hold himself upright on the swaying deck. Jesus was in a similar state right behind him.

Nehemiah weighed his options. With the helmsman needed to help him control the steering oar, there was no one else left except Joseph. None of them knew the ways of the sea, but the boys stood a better chance than the older and heavier man did. "Make sure you hold on for your life; there's no turning back if you fall in. Stay as close to the mast as you can."

"No!" shouted Joseph as he clumsily worked his way toward them.

"I have no choice. We are all doomed if we don't get that sail reefed." Nehemiah took one hand off the steering oar for a split second and pointed to the rigging. "Go!" he shouted to the boys.

Nehemiah felt for his friend, but the steering oar took all his attention. He caught only glimpses of the boys making their way across the swaying deck and then gingerly up the rigging. Pulling together, the four now on the yardarm slowly managed to pull in the middle section of the cracking sail. With less pressure on the steering oar, Nehemiah soon was able to pay more attention to them. At first it went well as they shifted left to bring in that portion of the sail, but with the sail still not reefed to the right, the rig was now unbalanced, and the ship began to sway even more. The captain and helmsman had to struggle harder to control the ship's course. Nehemiah's muscles quivered at the strain.

He stole another glance, but that was all it took to see the mistake. The experienced men should have stepped behind and around the boys, but instead they were all moving in unison along the yardarm to the right to reef the last section. Jesus would be out the farthest with Daniel alongside him, just as the unbalanced yardarm would be swinging through the air most wildly. Even on deck, the experienced captain had difficulty holding on to the steering oar as the deck rose and fell. It had to be far worse up above. He tried shouting but was soon choking on bitter seawater. The mounting wind swallowed his words anyway.

"Look," the captain barely heard Joseph shout.

"God help him," Nehemiah muttered when he took a chance to see. Jesus had lost his footing and was holding on with his hands to a single line as the yardarm pulled him through the air over the water. Daniel managed to pull the younger boy up to reach the footrope with his feet. The men finally stepped around the boys and moved to the outside. All too slowly, they were able to reef the last section that they had dropped while the boys were struggling just to hold on.

With the sail reefed, Nehemiah turned his attention to the battle for sea room from the dangerous shore. He turned the boat up into the wind as much as he dared. Even with the sail fully reefed, there was too much force on the rig to bring the ship fully broadside to it. Beyond that, the ship would slip downwind even more when heeled over on its side. The more the ship turned up into the wind, the more Nehemiah was blinded and choked by windblown seawater. He steered mostly by the sound of the creaking planks; as they sounded louder he knew he had to ease the strain on the ship and its rig by bearing away downwind. The two hands relieved the exhausted helmsman on the steering oar, but even though Nehemiah was equally exhausted, he remained there to guide them as they fought for every yard of sea room. Inevitably, the raging wind and sea carried them along to the north; turning the boat into the wind as much as they could only slowed their approaching doom.

Hour by hour the devilish wind continued to blow. Drenched and tired to the core, the crew fought on. Late in the afternoon, the ragged coast appeared through the crashing waves and mist—but then Nehemiah saw something that gave him hope. A rocky promontory jutted out from the shore and curved around to their right. They had just enough sea room that they might make it around the point. If they succeeded, the point of land would shelter them from the raging sea and wind, but there was no more time or distance to lose.

"Gybe-Ho—Now!" Nehemiah shouted and grabbed the steering oar to steer the stern through the wind and put the ship on a course to take them around the point if they were lucky, or else onto the rocks even faster.

In the raging tumult, one of the hands did not hear the captain and did not understand what was happening fast enough. The stay needed to support the mast on the new tack was not made fast. As the boat's stern came through the wind a thundering crack rang out, followed by the crash of the sail and its spar. Now at the mercy of the wind pushing it from behind with a useless steering oar, the stricken vessel tore its way toward the threatening shore.

All aboard—captain, crew, and passengers—stood transfixed as they helplessly awaited their doom—all aboard save one. The voice of a boy came through the storm. Jesus made no effort to shout over the roar of the wind, but his voice rang out clear as a bell. With a look of peace and confidence on his face, he was singing a psalm. In the old melody of King David, he chanted an ancient tune most on deck recognized: "The Lord is my shepherd; I shall not want. . ."

A ray of sunshine broke through the clouds and cast its light upon the kneeling figure of Jesus. The clouds parted further, and light enveloped the vessel. Rapidly, the waters calmed.

Cries rang out from all on board. "The Lord be praised!"

Jesus continued to pray, this time in thanksgiving.

Nehemiah turned to Joseph. "Your nephew will be a great prophet."

Daniel, standing close enough to overhear, said, "No, he is already more than any prophet." He turned to his father. "There is a divine power and light within him. That is what I saw with my own eyes in Nazareth."

Joseph shuffled back a step. He looked at his son wide-eyed and guffawed. "Do not presume to compare anyone to Moses, Isaiah, and the other great prophets!" Joseph paused. Little by little, he recovered his composure. "Let us just be grateful that Jesus is a good devout boy and that God heard his prayers."

The crew managed to erect a piece of the mast and jury-rig a patch of sail to it. Soon they beached the vessel on a small patch of sand. Sage bushes dominated the landscape, and there was nothing suitable from which to fashion a new mast. Nehemiah knew that impressive stands of cedar grew on the eastern end of the island, but that wood was too soft. Nehemiah and Joseph located a blacksmith in a nearby village. Joseph paid him handsomely, and within two days, two iron collars bound the broken mast back into place.

With fresh prayers of thanksgiving, the crew launched the ship back into the sea.

The rest of the voyage passed quickly in fair winds. Within a fortnight, the vessel passed south of the boot of *Italia*. A few days later, they sighted the shore of trans-Alpine Gaul and then the mouth of the River Rhodanus.

Jesus

With the sails securely stowed away, the donkeys on the towpath pulled Nehemiah's vessel along the *Fossa Mariana* canal that ran several miles from the sea up to their destination in the port town of Arelate. One of the hands led the donkeys while the helmsman steered. Nehemiah sat with the boys on deck. For once, he did not seem to have anything to do.

"This land seems so wet," said Jesus. "I vaguely remember Egypt being like this when the Nile flooded, except it was much hotter."

"It gets even cooler as we go further north," said Daniel. "Even in summer the sun doesn't beat down all the time like it does at home. You will see the land get more fertile up ahead. It's like the Jezreel Valley across all the flat lands and hills in Gaul and Britain. No deserts anywhere."

"We will be passing some farms, when the land gets a bit more dry and firm," said Nehemiah. "This swamp is known as the *Camarque*. Some of the farms graze cows and horses on this soggy part, but that's about it."

The boys started pointing out the eagles, hawks, and harriers flying through the air. Here and there, they spotted muskrats swimming in the water or making their way across drier patches of earth. "I have never seen such creatures," Jesus remarked.

Farther along, the swampland turned drier, and farms with lush crops began dotting the landscape. Then the farm plots merged, separated by fences. The yellowish-gray color of the fences seemed unnatural against the fields. Jesus did not say anything about them at first. *It must be a strange color of paint the Romans use in this climate. I never saw the Romans use anything like it back home.*

Off in the distance the boys spotted livestock grazing, and they picked out turtles and more creatures swimming and crawling close by. They approached a section of fence close to the waterway. "Whoa!" Jesus suddenly exclaimed. "Did you see that, Daniel? These fences are made of bones." Jesus spotted a skull in the mud. "They are human bones!"

"Those would be the Cymbri," said Nehemiah. "They were Gauls slaughtered by the thousands when the Romans came to this province more than a hundred years ago. It was the handiwork of a general named Marius. He's the same general who built this canal to bring supplies to his troops up in Arelate."

"Why make fences out of bones?" Jesus asked.

"They had one hundred ninety thousand dead Gauls on their hands," Nehemiah answered. "That's just the soldiers killed in two battles. The rest, even the women and children, killed themselves rather than be taken as slaves. There were too many to bury, so the farmers used the bones to make fences."

"It's like something out of Ezekiel," said Jesus.

"Are you going to prophesy to these bones?" Daniel asked. "I don't know how dry these bones are; they probably stayed a little damp this close to the swamp, actually."

"Don't be funny, Daniel. I don't think these bones are from the Lost Tribes. It just seems so brutal the way the Romans killed so many people and then used the bodies. The lives of the slaughtered do not seem to matter to them. I think it's important to know that while our people suffer under Roman oppression, we are not alone."

"That's all very interesting, Jesus." Joseph strode purposefully across the deck to join them. "However, I will thank you to keep such thoughts to yourself while we make our way across Gaul. We are crossing Roman lands ahead, and such words can put us in grave danger. We are only an hour or so away from Arelate, and I will have some business with the legate. He is a good and decent man, but never forget that he is first and foremost a Roman and proud of his country. I cannot afford to offend him."

Joseph

Joseph led Daniel and Jesus up the brick pathway that led to the home of his friend Septurius, the legate of Rome. A fine dommus, the home had iron bars on the windows. Joseph greeted the porter who guarded the vestibule, protecting against thieves, beggars, and any other urban horribles who might threaten or offend the tranquility of the interior.

They were shown to the atrium. There, marble and bronze statues surrounded the *impluvium* at the atrium's center. Out of the baking sun, the air felt cooler and fresher, almost as if a patch of pleasant countryside had been transported to town. As the Romans put it, *rus in urbe.*

Daniel showed Jesus around among the statues, also pointing out the ducks, swans, fish, and all manner of aquatic plants depicted in the mosaic floor.

Jesus looked up at the rectangular patch of open sky. "Uncle, why is part of the roof missing?"

"To allow rainwater to fill the pool," Daniel answered before Joseph had a chance. "That's why they call the pool an *impluvium.*"

"It's quite impressive with rainwater falling in," said Joseph. "It's something to see at night in the light of the oil lamps."

"I bet it splashes on the floor a lot," said Jesus. "I guess the Romans need to keep their minions busy with the mopping."

Joseph raised an eyebrow in warning. "Remember what I said aboard the ship?"

"I'm sorry, Uncle. I will just stand behind you and Daniel. I will be quiet as a mouse when we meet your friend."

Septurius strode into the atrium and embraced Joseph. Merchants of lower social rank were required to wait and then, when summoned, approach the legate as he sat behind a table on a raised platform in his office. But as a noblis decurio, Joseph was entitled to the courtesy of having the legate come from his office and greet him in the atrium. Besides, the two were longtime friends.

"Greetings, my friend," Septurius said in Greek.

Only a thin purple border on his white toga signified Septurius's office. The simplicity of his garb was a marked contrast to that of Joseph. Romans were not put off by distant travelers appearing in native dress, so Joseph had on his best cloak, a subdued shade of red with gold fringes at the hem and at the ends of the wide sleeves. It was loosely draped over his shoulders and open in front, revealing the long white tunic bound with a gold-colored sash around his waist. His skullcap was light green, with its turned-up edge revealing a gold-colored lining.

"Daniel, how you've grown over the winter," said Septurius. "What has it been, eight months?" He turned back to Joseph. "So, my friend, how long will you be in Arelate?"

"Just a few days at most, to hire a wagon team and possibly trade some of my olive oil for other goods," Joseph replied. "I need to see what wares the local craftsmen have." Joseph took the legate's cue as the two continued in Greek. *Clever of him to forgo Latin for this occasion.* That showed a bit of culture while also keeping the conversation private within the earshot of household slaves.

"Ah, you're in need of trinkets. You must be off to trade with the Britons again."

"Yes, but it is becoming a sorry business to deal with the Cantiaci tribe around Dvrobrivae. They know how much Romans dislike sailing across open seas, and they occupy the only place on the other side of the *Oceanus Britannicus* that you can reach while staying within sight of land. So, they take advantage by exacting heavy tolls. On my last expedition, I went out to a place called Yengi. Have you heard of it?"

"Isn't that the old Celtic trading port on the southern coast of Britain? They still export slaves from there, don't they?"

"Yes. Some merchants also go there to pick up iron ore. They find it lying around the beach."

"There's not much money to be made in iron," Septurius said. "And you don't have armed retainers to control slaves. Jupiter knows you would need them. I tried purchasing a Briton earlier this year, and the cheeky bastard struck another slave. I had to sell him off to the workhouse at a great loss. If he had done that to a freeman, I would have been forced to have him crucified. I'd have lost my entire investment."

"I go in search of more profitable metals," Joseph said. "A little tin will strengthen ten times as much copper into a strong bronze alloy. When I was in Yengi last time, I came across a chieftain who had several large tin ingots that he didn't know what to do with. I bought them for a song. I paid heavy tolls to the Cantiaci and several other tribes just to bring the ingots through their provinces back to our ship. It cost me more for the tolls than for what I paid for the ingots in the first place. Nevertheless I made a nice profit selling them in Judea."

"Yes, I have heard that it's a sorry business dealing with those British kingdoms."

"But looking around this room, I am reminded of how the good people of Rome love bronze. You have a lot of bronze items right here, and you cannot make bronze without tin. Even with the tolls, there's money to be made from tin if I can locate a reliable supply, and even more profit if I can figure out how to avoid the tolls."

"I see where you are going with this, and you may be onto something. There are many places to get iron and copper, but few places to get tin." Septurius paused. "You know, I might be interested in making an investment if you need capital for this venture."

"I am not far along enough to take your money for that—I must first secure the supply. This is an exploratory voyage, but there will be ample opportunity for investment if it works out. In the meantime, I was wondering if you might be interested in exporting a partial shipload under our usual consignment terms."

Septurius glanced about the room. "Let's discuss that tomorrow."

"Very well, we'll talk business tomorrow. But now, before the day wanes, I must be off to find rooms at one of your local inns."

"Nonsense," said Septurius, "I will not hear of it. There is plenty of room in my home for an old friend, and as legate of this city I command it." He laughed and turned to Daniel. "You seem to be old enough for your own room now." A slightly stocky, pimply faced boy of about fourteen approached as Septurius continued addressing Daniel. "You remember my younger son, Longinus?" Septurius looked at Jesus and then turned back to Joseph. "I will have the slaves make room for your servant boy, too."

Joseph turned to Jesus and saw the reason for Septurius's mistake. Between the rush to get him out of Galilee and the quick stopover at Salamis, there had not been any time to obtain decent clothes for the boy. He was still dressed like a peasant, in the same worn homespun cloth in which he left Nazareth, except that the voyage had taken its toll in the form of several large tears in the fabric. Daniel was turning red, but Jesus smiled. Joseph quickly explained their relation, though not the reason for the boy's abrupt departure from home.

Septurius beckoned Jesus forward. "Terribly sorry, I had no idea…"

"Sir, there is no need to apologize," Jesus said. "You were quite correct; I am indeed a servant, of my God and my people."

Septurius let out a hearty laugh and slapped Jesus on the shoulder. "Well said, lad!" He turned to Joseph. "With a wit like that and such a sense of public duty, I bet your nephew will be a consul in Rome someday."

"I see that the town prospers," Jesus said. "I saw on the walk here from the ship that you have started building an amphitheater and a chariot circus. You must rule here with wisdom, and the emperor will surely recognize that soon."

"Oh, he's good!" Septurius remarked to Joseph with a grin. Then he responded to Jesus. "Actually, the citizens here have Julius Caesar to thank much more than me. He's the one who stripped Massilia of its possessions and gave them to Arelate after Massilia took the wrong side in Julius's war against Pompey. As for me, Arelate is likely to be my final posting—but a long one, unless I do something either phenomenally stupid or great to get the attention of my superiors. Nonetheless, life is good here, and I have no complaints. As legate of Rome, I maintain the peace and see to it that the taxes are collected. Arelate is an important port, but it is not even a regional center of the province. My jurisdiction ends at the town walls. A posting such as this is not given to men of strong ambition."

Joseph smiled. *Perhaps I was too hard on Jesus earlier, on the ship.*

Daniel

There was something unsettling about the way Longinus kept glancing over to Daniel and Jesus as Joseph and Septurius wrapped up their conversation. Daniel detected a hint of a smirk that the boy managed to conceal from his father.

Septurius broke out in Latin as he turned to his son. "Be a good host now, and show these young men to their room. You will look after them for the next few days while they are our guests."

"But, Father, what of my lessons?"

"You can put those aside for a few days. As far behind as you are, I doubt it will make much difference."

Now it was Daniel's turn to conceal his smile from his own father. Seeing Joseph beginning to raise his eyebrow, he feigned a cough and brought up his hand to conceal the lower part of his face.

"Good. That's settled then. "Now that you have this unexpected holiday, I am sure that you and Joseph's boys will become great friends." Septurius turned to Joseph. "Come; allow me to show you to your room."

"Follow me." Longinus led them toward the rear of the house. The walls here were adorned with fresco paintings. A peristyle colonnade leading to the bedrooms surrounded an interior garden under an open roof.

Daniel now had to share the room he would have had for himself, but he did not mind. It was large and magnificently appointed. Longinus left to give them a chance to freshen up for dinner, and a slave stayed behind to attend to them. Daniel had made a fool of himself by teasing the household slaves the first time he had visited Septurius' household, but Jesus did not appear even to be tempted.

A few minutes later, Longinus returned with a tunic in his hand. "Father said to find something more suitable for you to wear than those rags. Here, I've outgrown this, but it probably fits you." He tossed the garment to Jesus and folded his arms. "Yes, that should do fine. You're a little young to wear a toga, and you're not really Roman." Longinus smiled and left before Daniel had a chance to say anything.

"I don't know why he's so full of himself when he still wears the *praetexta*," Daniel said once they were alone.

"Do you mean that broad purple stripe on his toga?"

"Yes, Roman boys trade it for a plain white toga *virilis* when they reach fifteen or sixteen. It is a big celebration. I just do not like the way he looked at you all high and mighty."

"He's a Roman. His country rules the known world, and we are from a conquered province. Of course he is going to look down on us. Look around this room. Back in Nazareth my family shares one small oil lamp to guide us through the darkness of the night. Here they have enough lamps in just this room to turn the night into day. By the way, what is going on with Septurius? He seemed secretive about dealing with Uncle Joseph."

Another young slave came in bearing Daniel's bag.

Not wanting strangers going through his things, Daniel signaled the slave to leave it on the chest. "It's too bad you didn't get a chance to bring anything from home. I'm sure Papa will get what you need now that we have a few days here." Daniel got up and began sorting out his clothes. "Anyway, Papa explained Septurius's story to me the last time. He comes from an aristocratic family, but he is not as rich as he appears to be. This house does not belong to him; he just gets to use it because of his position. The statues are all copies; there is not one Greek original among them. He only receives a modest salary, but he is expected to live on a grand scale to represent the wealth of the Empire. Aristocratic Romans in government service are not supposed to be involved in commerce, but many have no choice."

"Is it against the law?"

"No. It's just something that isn't done. Aristocratic Romans are supposed to live off their estates. Dealing in commerce is not wrong or illegal, but it is something an enemy would make use of. Even Senators in Rome conduct commerce, but they do it secretly through an intermediary." Daniel pulled out a blanket that needed folding.

Jesus started to get up to help his cousin, but the attending slave beat him to it. "Septurius is putting a great deal of trust in your father."

"That's how Papa makes his fortune. Everyone he deals with knows he can be trusted. That's why they made him a citizen and then a *noblis decurio*," said Daniel. "I was watching you earlier. You act as if you have been a Roman accustomed to this luxury all your life. Aren't you impressed at all with the marvels the Romans created?"

"All I see are the graven images of false gods and the fruits of oppression."

Daniel signaled to Jesus to mind his tongue. He had no idea what the slave might report to his master if he understood their Aramaic. He judged the youth to be about three years his senior.

Jesus suddenly commanded the slave in Latin to draw the bath water in the room next door. The two of them were now truly alone for a few minutes.

"You seem to be born to this life, Jesus," Daniel said. "You commanded that slave as if you were born true Roman."

"Hardly. I just wanted to get rid of him and get in the bath. Don't forget that our hosts are the Romans who rule our lands and use us, Daniel. Proud as they are, we should learn their weaknesses so that one day we can free our people. Look over there. Instead of painting a picture, framing it and hanging it on a wall, they painted the frame on the wall and then painted the picture inside. They seem to be afraid a guest might steal a real framed painting off the wall."

"Actually, I think they do it that way so that the host is not embarrassed into giving paintings away when their guests praise them."

Jesus laughed. "Don't you see, cousin? These people are weak. Yes, they have great wealth and they have their legions, but they have no strength of character. Septurius cannot stand up and say that he needs to conduct an honest trade, so he does it in secret. They cannot be seen to appear ungenerous to their guests, so they actually paint their pictures on the wall to make sure that making a gift of them is not an option. There is no great Roman civic virtue. Everything is only about maintaining appearances."

Daniel looked at his young cousin, a thin waif undressing for the bath. *I cannot believe how perceptive he is, and only thirteen.* Jesus hardly looked the part of the military leader who was destined to smash the legions of Rome, but then Daniel thought of the heavenly light he saw within Jesus back in Nazareth. He lowered his voice. "Are you the Messiah who will free our people?"

"I don't really know what work God has for me. I am just a boy," Jesus replied. "I pray for guidance every day. The only thing I know for sure is what my mother told me of how I was miraculously conceived. I do hear and feel things that I cannot begin to explain. Certainly, I want to save the nation of Israel and free our people, and…" his voice quavered. "I always see myself in the prophecies of the savior. It is a vision that stays in my head. I wish I understood more. I feel in my heart that God has chosen me as his instrument, but sometimes I feel struck by madness. I just pray that God will give me the wisdom to know his will and strength to do it; I must not fail him."

"But there is nothing God cannot accomplish through you," Daniel responded earnestly. "Think of how he used David as a child to slay the mighty Goliath with a single slingshot."

Jesus paused before he spoke again. "I feel more connected with you right now, Daniel, than I have ever felt with anyone. Some of what I confided in you I haven't even told my mother. I don't think I have ever put my feelings into words quite like this, even in my own head."

They looked at each other in silence. As if in a trance, Daniel recalled the vision he had seen back in Nazareth, of Jesus with the divine light shining within him. Daniel felt Jesus reach out and touch him. The gentle touch moved Daniel with great power and brought him back to

"I enjoyed reading Caesar's description of the native Gauls, particularly the druids," said Jesus. "Oh, good morning, Longinus."

Septurius turned to his son. "You should really take a cue from Jesus here. It's amazing how much he picked up the last night from Caesar's annals, and his Greek is perfect, too."

"But, Father, Greek is so hard—"

"Perhaps a druid teacher might work out better for you, Longinus," said Jesus. "They don't write anything down. The students just memorize everything they say."

Longinus felt his face turning red as his father broke out in laughter. Just then, the old Jew walked in, took his seat, and engaged Longinus's parents in a conversation about the marketplace. Daniel was listening, which gave Longinus his chance to scowl at Jesus. *What's with that sneaky beggar? He must know I am going to find a way to hurt him, but he just smiles back.*

The three boys were soon left to their own devices in the villa. The old Jew left right after breakfast for his business in the market. Father left in the middle of the morning to judge a lawsuit. Mother stayed busy with her attendants having her hair done and getting dressed through most of the morning, but she was off in her litter by midday, carried by several slaves to pay social calls. Early in the afternoon, the three boys engaged in some foot races around the peristyle garden. Longinus did not mind losing to Daniel that much, since he was the oldest and strongest. But the shame of losing to the frail younger boy irked him. No matter how he tried to tease and antagonize him, Jesus took it in fun.

Longinus got an idea as he recovered his breath. "Do you guys want to go outside? It's pretty safe as long as we take a slave to guard us in the street."

"Sure, why not," Daniel agreed. "You coming too?"

Still recovering his breath, Jesus nodded yes.

Longinus suggested to Daniel that the two of them change into tunics, just as Jesus was wearing already. Longinus knew which slave he wanted to take with him. He picked out a strong young man of eighteen, but Longinus did not pick him for his strength and ability to defend them in an attack. The young man had been given to him on his fourteenth birthday, and the slave knew that Longinus could have him whipped severely at any time. He could be counted on to back up any story Longinus gave his parents.

The cursory tour of the forum and the circus went quickly, and then Longinus led the group out through the city gates and down a path toward the river.

He stopped at a patch of meadow in the middle of a clearing. "The ground is level and covered with grass here. It's a great place to wrestle. What do you say?"

"Sure," said Daniel. "Sounds like fun."

Both Longinus and Daniel knew a crude form of wrestling that featured strength moves. Although Daniel was older by a year, Longinus was a bit heavier. Daniel had the height advantage. The two wore each other down to the point of exhaustion with neither gaining a clear advantage. Jesus stood aside, cheering on the best moves that each of them made.

It took some time, but Longinus finally found himself on his back, pinned. He clenched his fists in frustration. He did not care about losing to the older boy. That loss was not important to him. With the match over, Daniel was giving no sign of leaving him alone with Jesus and the slave boy.

"Here, get up, Longinus." Daniel extended his hand.

Longinus noticed Jesus smiling. *I wonder if that beggar even realizes what I plan to do. Surely, he cannot think I just forgot about the way he showed off and embarrassed me in front of Father this morning. I warned him, but he did it anyway.*

"I have to take a leak," said Daniel. "Be right back."

Longinus watched as Daniel concealed himself in some bushes. It was far enough to take time for Daniel to run back. Jesus looked distracted by something, but Longinus did not care what it was. He already had his story worked out, that Jesus begged him for a chance to wrestle, too. He would say that he thought he was going easy on the smaller boy, not meaning to hurt him at all. He took his opportunity and charged.

The next thing Longinus knew, he was flat on his back. His backside throbbed in pain.

"Are you all right?" Jesus stood over him. "Awesome move! Is that Roman-style wrestling, to come at your opponent when he isn't looking? I like it; it keeps you on your toes."

Daniel came running up. "What's going on?"

"Longinus and I wanted to wrestle, too. I hope you don't mind. I thought the two of you were done."

"He could have killed you. He's twice your size."

"Not really. Some Greek kids back on Cyprus showed me how to handle a bigger guy coming at you. You brace yourself and use the force of his power against him. They called it throwing your opponent." Jesus extended his hand to Longinus. "That was great; shall we have another go?"

Longinus shook his head no, as Jesus helped him to his feet. He glanced at the slave who had seen everything; he was hiding the lower portion of his face with his hand, but Longinus knew he was trying to conceal his laughter. He will pay dearly for that later, and so will Jesus.

Daniel

In the afternoon of the next day, the boys again had the house to themselves. In the morning, Longinus had led the cousins through the rooms, pointing out the religious themes in the statues, frescoes, and mosaics. Mainly, he wove the tales that glorified Rome and its gods. Then they had exhausted themselves with more races around the garden. Longinus then had the idea of taking lunch in the *triclinium* room off the atrium. They would have massages at the same time. Daniel wondered if it was a good idea for them to use this important room; it was where the Romans feasted their guests, and they were all hot and sweaty.

"Don't worry about smelling up the room or leaving a mess," said Longinus. "Everyone is gone but us, so there are plenty of slaves to clean up before Father or Mother return."

Daniel had to admit that he felt grand reclining on one of the three immense couches. One slave began serving him lunch while another began working his shoulders. The room was magnificent. The wall fresco featured an image of a god racing across the sky in his chariot, and Daniel's thoughts returned to the earlier tour among the deities depicted in statues, mosaics, and frescoes. "You have so many gods," he said to Longinus. "That's Apollo, isn't it? How do you keep track of them all?"

"We don't have so many civic gods. Just Jupiter, Apollo, Mercury, and the rest. We pray to them in major feasts and public occasions in the public temples. Jupiter is the greatest god because he makes men healthy, rich, and prosperous."

"So, do you pray to the god you want something from?" Daniel asked. That smacked of irreverent self-interest.

"Sometimes, but mainly it is just the offering of a sacrifice. Did you know your father will be taking some linen to Britain on consignment for my father?"

"Yes, but we are not supposed to talk about it." Daniel grunted as the masseur dug into his deltoid.

"I was just making the point that Father will offer a sacrifice to Neptune in hopes of keeping the linen safe across the blue ocean. We also have ancestor gods who deserve worship and respect. Then there are the household family gods—the *vesta* guardian of the hearth and the *penates* spirits of the storeroom. As a family we sacrifice most often to our household gods—"

"Sacrifice?" Jesus broke in. "In the house?"

"Yes, at the *lararium*, the altar in the kitchen that I showed you earlier. We keep the libation bowl, incense box, and sacrificial knife there, all ready to go. But getting back to the civic gods, I like Mars most of all, because he seems so Roman—"

"But how can this be? With so many gods, aren't some greater and others lesser? And if so many gods are necessary, how can any one of your gods be perfect?"

Daniel did not like the sound of this. He raised himself up on his arm and signaled the masseur to stop for a moment. "Jesus, it's rude to criticize the religion of our hosts while—"

"No, it's fine. I want to hear what Jesus has to say."

"How is Mars so Roman then?" Jesus asked.

"*Parcare subjectis et deballare superbos.*"

"To spare the vanquished and humble the proud. What does that have to do with anything?"

It's something that my tutor made me memorize. It sums up how we Romans see ourselves, and I'm sure Mars would say the same thing.

"Oh, that's rich," said Jesus. "I saw on the way here how you Romans made fences of the bones of the Cymbri women and children, as well as their warriors. Is that what you mean by humbling the proud?"

"They aren't so proud now, are they?" said Longinus. "The Gauls around here now do fine."

"Yes, that's where the 'sparing the subjected' part comes in, doesn't it? You only spare the Gauls because they pay your taxes. I bet they were doing just fine before the Romans came."

"We civilize the barbarians," Longinus shouted back.

"Yes, like you civilized the Gauls by killing millions and enslaving millions more. That's what I got out of Julius Caesar's account the other night. You should try reading it."

"Stop it, both of you." Daniel knew that this was getting out of hand. Jesus was getting personal, both of them were shouting, and Longinus was flushing with his anger.

"Roman armies have conquered the world," said Longinus. "They will never be defeated."

"Roman armies are nothing to the power of the one true God. Our God of Hosts will sweep them away just like he humbled almighty Pharaoh. There is always hope for Israel, and our people will be free of you when the Messiah comes as prophesized in Scripture." Jesus got up and stormed out.

"I'm sorry," Daniel said. "He doesn't know what he's saying."

Longinus just smirked back.

Daniel glanced around the room. The slaves were standing with their mouths agape. There was no undoing the damage now. Word was bound to get back to Septurius, and there would be hell to pay.

❧ ✤ ☙

Later that evening Joseph came into the room and pulled his son outside. "How could you be so stupid as to let this happen?" Despite the low volume of his voice, the rage came through. "I just got a good talking to from my best Roman client."

"I'm sorry, Papa—"

"You have no idea how lucky we are that Septurius happens to be a kind man! If he wanted, he could have Jesus on the cross and both of us in prison. To the Romans, that was both treason and blasphemy!"

"What will he do?"

"Nothing, but that's no thanks to you. He said he was just warning me for Jesus's own good, and he was absolutely right to do so."

"I was going to tell you. I tried to stop Jesus, but he and Longinus started going at each other so fast. I'm sorry. I should have tried to stop it sooner."

"Yes, you should have."

Daniel could only nod his agreement; his shame left him speechless.

Joseph turned to leave. Then he abruptly turned back to his son. "There was one other thing. When Septurius was relaying all the things that Jesus had said, I tried to think of something to change the subject. I told him that he must be proud of his son's progress in Greek for him to understand all of these things from Jesus. For some reason this only seemed to annoy him, and he told me that Longinus has made no progress at all since the last time we were here. At first he seemed to think that I doubted his son's word, and after I told him this wasn't the case he insisted that Jesus must have spoken these things to Longinus in Latin."

"That's true, Papa. The three of us have spoken Latin amongst ourselves since the day we arrived."

"But Jesus's parents told me Jesus couldn't speak Latin. They were worried about him traveling through Gaul like that; it was one of their biggest concerns. They told me that Jesus learned Aramaic from the family and Hebrew from the priests. And somehow he managed to teach himself Greek well enough to have intelligent discussions with scholars passing through. But they were clear that he knew nothing of Latin."

"Maybe Jesus picked up the Latin speech from passing soldiers in Galilee without his parents' knowing."

"Yes, that is what I thought of while talking to Septurius. I guess the explanation I gave the legate was the truth after all!"

After Papa left, Daniel returned to the room that he shared with Jesus. The boy lay wide awake now. Evidently, he had overheard what Joseph said. Jesus looked up at Daniel. "It's true, you know."

"What's true? That you picked up Latin from Roman legionaries in Galilee?"

"I had never spoken a word of Latin before we got here."

"Then, how—"

"I am not like other people, Daniel. I know that, and you seem to know it, too. I feel as though I carry hundreds upon hundreds of languages in my head. When I hear a new language, all I need to do is listen for a minute to figure out which language it is. I already know all the vocabulary and grammar. It is not something I try to do; it just happens."

Septurius

The next day Septurius watched as the last of Joseph's cargo was hoisted into the carts. With a wave, he wished Joseph and his party Godspeed as they left. Then he turned to contemplate the figure of his son wandering off in the distance. Septurius was anything but naive. He well understood that Longinus must have provoked Jesus and then turned upon him. It was a nasty trick that bore ill for his son's character and future.

Chapter 3
A Problem with Prophecy

Joseph

Roman roads were engineering marvels, but the hard paving stones were uneven. The cart-wheels jolted and squeaked over each one, and the road grated upon Joseph. He tried to fashion a cushion, but no matter where or how he sat or reclined in the cart, he could not escape the jolts and vibrations. Neither Jesus nor Daniel seemed to be bothered, but for Joseph the passage north through Narbonne Province in southern Gaul was agony.

The road up the valley of the Rhodanus River north from Arelate traversed easy low hills suitable for the use of horses. The Roman engineers who laid out the road system did so with an eye to the efficient movement of troops, however, not the needs of merchants moving goods, so the roads went straight up hills when possible. If the grade could be surmounted by cavalry and infantry, they did not build switchbacks that would have eased the load for draft animals pulling carts. The Roman-style harness did not help, as it tended to cut the windpipes of horses when the strain of the load became too great. While horses did well pulling carts across flat land, they struggled on inclines. A few of the hills slowed Joseph's baggage train, but they were not so steep or numerous as to require ponderous oxen unaffected by the harness.

The load was relatively light for a trading expedition. Joseph still had some amphorae filled with olive oil from Judea, although he had sold most of that in Arelate for a modest profit. He could offer the remainder to the Britons as a curiosity, but they preferred their native butter and pork rinds as cooking fat. Some of the money from the olive oil went to purchase pottery and other household items that now lay carefully packed away in straw on the carts. There was always a market among the richest Britons for the latest designs and patterns from the Romans. Rugs from Asia were bulky and heavy, but Joseph had a few of those because he knew the intricate patterns would fascinate and delight the Britons. Spices from the Orient traveled easily. But Joseph's main stock-in-trade was yet to be purchased; what the Britons craved more than anything was wine. Wine and the amphorae vessels to hold it could be bought farther ahead; there was no need to burden the carts now.

As the baggage train made its way up the valley, Joseph gazed upon the River Rhodanus running a parallel course to the left. Whenever possible, merchants in the Roman Empire replaced their pack animals with boats to carry their goods at a fraction of the cost, but the current of that river ran fast on its way south to Arelate. Such a course would be favorable in bringing metals back from Britain, but not going upstream.

Joseph's disposition improved as the baggage train neared the bridge across the Rhodanus into Lugdunum, the gateway to Lugdunensis Province. He looked forward to a much more relaxing barge trip north up the slow-moving River Arar tributary that joined the Rhodanus at the city. That would take them to a place near the River Sequana, which would carry them down to the *Oceanus Britannicus*.

As the cart turned a bend in the road they caught a glimpse of the city rising up all over the hillside in the distance. "There it is," exclaimed Daniel. "Lugdunum"

"I was just thinking: that is a curious name for the Romans to give a city. Who is this Lugh fellow?" asked Jesus. "The name does not sound Roman."

"It's not," Joseph said. "Lugh is supposed to be the greatest of all the druid gods."

"But didn't the Romans suppress the druids once they conquered Gaul?" Jesus asked. "Why would they name the provincial capital after one?"

"I don't know. Maybe the Romans just used the old Celtic name for this place before they realized its significance," Joseph responded.

"So, tell us more about Lugh," Jesus said.

"I'm afraid there isn't much I can tell you. On one of my father's expeditions, a Celtic man from Gaul described Lugh as the greatest of all druid gods, and that was it. Julius Caesar compared him to the Roman god

Mercury, but supreme among the druid gods as well. Anyway, we will be traveling on ahead in a few days with native bargemen, and perhaps they will be able to tell you more."

They descended a hill to the bridge. The difficult road portion of the journey across Gaul was almost over, but Joseph was still troubled. He pondered his prospects for making a profit on this expedition. The fastest money to be made was in the slave trade, but Joseph was no trader in the misery of other human beings. What else might he find in Britain to sell to the Romans at a decent profit if the tin should not work out?

Then there was the problem of Jesus. *He can be the sweetest boy imaginable. Whenever there is a chore that needs doing, I only have to ask him and then know that the task is as good as done. Never does he complain. Not even my own Daniel is as good-natured and obedient about his work.* But try as Joseph might to make Jesus understand how rash it was to incur the wrath of the Romans, he did not seem to understand. Every time Joseph talked to Jesus about how foolish it had been for him to argue with Longinus, Jesus would listen respectfully and then ask where he had spoken falsely. When it came to proclaiming God's truth as he saw it, Jesus either would not or could not grasp the concept of why discretion was necessary.

As the road turned just before the bridge, the city came into view again in a magnificent vista. "Jesus. Come here." Joseph reached into his bag and drew out the map.

The boy scooted closer. "Yes, Uncle?"

Joseph unrolled the map and handed it to him. "See there, the Rhodanus runs along the southern side of the city from the east, and that slow-moving river meandering down the western side is the Arar. And here is where they meet." He pointed from the point of confluence on the map to the one before their eyes. "That hill between the rivers is called Fourviere."

"What's that on the crown of the hill?"

"The forum." Joseph pointed out other landmarks on the hillside: the Roman mint and the amphitheater. And below, warehouses were visible on a large low-lying island at the confluence. On the right bank of the Arar lay a busy commercial district and port with offices and docks.

A renewed sense of awe struck Joseph as he pointed out the sights to his great-nephew. "No more than seventy years ago, this site was nothing but a small Celtic settlement. Now it is the center of commerce and Roman administration for all of Gaul. Trade from Britain and Germania passes through: wheat, wine, olive oil, and lumber." The traffic through the city was not quite as bad as in Rome, where merchant carts had to be banned from the streets until nightfall, but it was getting there.

Joseph spotted something atop Fourviere, and his heart withered. A small group of men worked at the high point of the hill just outside the forum—a place of execution that could be seen for miles around. Workmen busy at that site could only mean an imminent crucifixion.

But Joseph said nothing of that to Jesus.

The baggage train crossed the bridge into Lugdunum and around the Fourviere to another bridge that took them to the warehouse district on the island. While one group of workers stabled the horses, another unloaded the carts and stowed Joseph's goods in an available warehouse.

Dusk approached as Joseph led Jesus and Daniel back across the bridge to the commercial district at the foot of the Fourviere Hill. "There's no telling how soon we'll be able to hire a suitable boat to take us north on the Arar," he said, "but there's no need to retain the hired horses and carts any longer."

Up close, Lugdunum was a foul, overcrowded place. Occasionally one could spot a rich person clutching rose petals to his nose to mask the stench of the open sewers. The poor lived in the overcrowded tenements that rose eight stories high. Joseph often heard news of fires breaking out in the top floor garrets where the poorest of the poor resorted to dangerous charcoal braziers to ward off the drafts and dampness from the leaky roofs.

Joseph and the boys soon settled into an inn. It offered nothing like the luxury of Septurius's *dommus*, but it was clean. The food and wine were a welcome relief from the scant but overpriced offerings of the inns on the road north from Arelate, and they would sleep in real beds for the next few nights and have a room to themselves. So much nicer than the vermin-infested common sleeping rooms they had shared with all sorts of men on the road. Going through Valentia, a town halfway between Arelate and Lugdunum, they had stayed outside in the rain through the night because there was only one common sleeping area in the inn for both men and women, and Joseph was not about to allow that. A good number of the women loitering near the inns appeared to be professional.

Joseph joined in the smiles and laughter of his son and nephew over dinner. It was a relief to be in a decent establishment for a change. But he was still troubled by the workmen he had seen preparing for the crucifixion.

The innkeeper brought steaming bowls of mutton stew that gave off an aroma of thyme and rosemary.

Joseph lowered his voice and asked about the workmen.

The innkeeper nodded. "A notorious case, sir. Two slaves struck their master in an attempt to escape. The execution is set for tomorrow."

"Have you ever seen a crucifixion, Jesus?" Joseph asked with a sad heart. He spoke in Aramaic in case of eavesdroppers..

Jesus responded in the same tongue. "Mother and Papa always told me not to look when we passed one. They said it would upset me too much."

"You must have stolen a glance or two." Daniel said. "Weren't you curious?"

"Of course I was curious," Jesus replied. "Sometimes I couldn't help but hear the victims crying out in pain, but I never looked. I always remembered how Adam's curiosity to taste the forbidden fruit brought pain and death into the world. So, no, I never looked."

"Under our laws and customs you are now old enough to be a man," said Joseph. "And it's time for you to learn how the Romans can bring down their wrath when anyone offends them. You will come with me tomorrow and watch."

"How can I disobey my parents?"

"They are not here. They entrusted your well-being to me, and the circumstances have changed. Jesus, you must now obey me in this."

"Very well, Uncle. I am sure you know best," Jesus replied. "But I do not understand. These men were slaves and they struck their master. Would not their punishment be death in any country?"

"Are you defending the Romans now?" Daniel asked of Jesus.

"This is different," Jesus answered. "We're not talking about pagan idols or taxes. These slaves are being put to death for rebelling against their master. Our people would have done the same thing even before the Romans came."

"You're wrong, Jesus," said Joseph. "There's more to it than just putting criminals to death. You will see tomorrow. Our people execute criminals, but never like this. The Romans don't execute only murderers, traitors, and rebellious slaves." Joseph looked directly into Jesus's eyes. "They also kill those who offend or blaspheme their pagan gods, and even those they merely suspect of holding a rebellious spirit against the empire."

Joseph exchanged knowing looks with his son. For the moment, Jesus was silent. Was the boy beginning to understand the danger his preaching could cause? Joseph could only hope so. He also hoped that what lay in store for Jesus to see on the morrow would drive the lesson home.

Despite that somber turn, Jesus seemed to lighten the mood as they finished eating. Soon the road-weary party made its way to their room where they slept soundly.

They rose early, but not at the first crack of dawn which was typically the rising time on the road. Joseph took the opportunity to assign readings to Jesus and Daniel from the scroll of Psalms that he carried with him—not that the boys lacked for religious learning. He did not want them wandering the city aimlessly.

Leaving them to their studies, Joseph went to the docks to check with the boatmen. Unfortunately, they were all out on river passages with none scheduled to return that day. This would cost him a day, but it could not be helped. He found the agent for the gentleman in Arelate who had rented the carts and horses, so at least that bill could be settled. He now had the rest of the day to deal with Jesus and would contact his merchant friends later that evening.

Daniel

Daniel looked up, wide-eyed, when his father returned. "You're back early, Papa."

"Yes, we have some extra time, so let's go refresh ourselves in the bathhouse." He clapped Jesus on the shoulder.

As any good Jew would, they bypassed the pagan temple at the entrance to the bathhouse where the other patrons paid their obeisance. Nevertheless, Papa was compelled to point it out. "It is hard to keep our laws when we travel among the pagans. They decorate all their buildings with idolatrous statues and images, and you cannot avoid them if you want to carry on any business with the Romans. Even though both buildings bear pagan decorations, the one over there is the temple we should avoid. This, for all its trappings, is just a bathhouse."

Daniel had seen this bathhouse and others like it during his travels with Papa across the Empire, but still he was awed by the magnificence of the arched spaces and the colorful mosaics. Even the furnaces that heated the water were marvels of engineering. This facility was available to all citizens of Rome passing through the city.

Jesus appeared unimpressed. "I see what you mean," he said, once they entered the hot room. "It would be easy to think we're in one of their temples, but it's really nothing more than Septurius has in his home. This is just a big public facility on a much grander scale."

Papa wandered off with another trader he happened to recognize through the steam, and Daniel turned his attention to his cousin, already relaxing under the hands of the masseur slave. Not wanting a massage himself, Daniel picked a spot on the side of the pool where he could relax in the warmth of the waters and still talk to Jesus.

Back in Arelate he said he saw himself as the savior of Israel. Does that mean he will claim David's throne?

"Will you bring luxury such as this to Jerusalem when you take your kingdom?" Daniel posed the question in Aramaic so the slave would not understand.

"I do not know. I can only tell you that I must carry out my Father's will. He favors the nation of Israel as his chosen people, but I don't know whether that means our wealth and power in this world must rival that of the Romans. All this luxury makes the Romans soft. They see themselves as invincible, but I see all this being swept away. Remember how King Solomon fell from the grace of God when sinful luxury entranced him. That will not happen to me."

"I wonder if you will be God's instrument to destroy the Romans. They are not all bad. They swept the sea of pirates and they give merchants like Papa protection."

"Israel will trade and prosper just as it did before the Romans. I am called to be God's instrument to free God's people and restore the house of David to its throne. It follows that the power of the Romans over our people must end, and Israel must be ready to pay a bloody price. I do not know what it will take to remove the Romans as a threat to Israel. The Messiah also is called in prophecy to be a light unto the gentiles, so maybe they too will see the way of God and live in peace with Israel before it is too late for them. If not, God will destroy them, and as his son I am prepared to be his instrument if he calls me to that task." Jesus waved off the masseur and entered the hot pool.

His vision of his Messianic destiny was not so different from what he had described in Arelate, but his tone was more certain. *He is so graceful and gentle. How can this boy believe he can brush away the world's greatest empire like dirt from his sandals? He's right that Israel needs its freedom; Roman protection comes with too many chains.* Daniel recalled his vision that day in Nazareth that brought him to his knees at Jesus's feet. *If Jesus is the Son of God as he has said, then anything is possible.*

Papa summoned them to the cold pool. The quick dip in the cold water closed the pores of their skin and refreshed them. Outwardly, Daniel felt renewed, but inwardly he felt a growing sadness as the time came for them to begin the day's business. It did not take long to dry off and dress. They left together and joined the gathering crowd.

The scourging took place sometimes in public and sometimes behind the army camp walls. Every stroke of those multiple thongs, each tipped with a metal hook and bound together into a single whip, would generate rivers of blood and rip flesh from bone. Inevitable death did not come easily at the hands of the Romans. He could not imagine what woe would betide the soldier who killed the victim before he suffered the cross.

Daniel had seen several crucifixions, but the sight of these two victims, already scourged and led out by the soldiers, shocked him. Blood streamed from their wounds, and they seemed eager for the death that would free them from their misery. The crowd jeered and taunted them.

Jesus had a look of cold determination to see the proceedings through, as Papa had commanded. Daniel remembered how Jesus, only the night before, had seemed to be at peace with the idea that rebellious slaves deserved death—but could Jesus really be the Son of God if he lacked compassion for fellow humans?

The soldiers forced the victims to hoist the crosspieces on their shoulders and carry them to the place of execution at the top of the Fourviere. The crowd followed, continuing to mock the condemned men. Slowly they moved. Whippings from the soldiers made the victims stumble. Clearly, the condemned would never make it up the hill encumbered with the weight of their crosses. Wanting to get on with their business, the officers conscripted two men to carry the crosses while the soldiers dragged the victims ahead. Daniel and Papa walked on either side of Jesus. They glanced frequently at Jesus, but Jesus did not flinch.

Finally, the procession reached the summit. Several soldiers held the prisoners' arms outstretched along the crosspieces as another soldier drove massive nails through their wrists. Like many others, Daniel turned away, but Papa held Jesus's head, forcing him to watch.

Daniel heard the sound of the hammer on the first nail, and Jesus screamed as if he were in mortal pain. No longer was he steeled to bear the sight. Jesus's body shook and trembled. He went deathly pale and fainted in Papa's arms.

Daniel ran to the soldiers' pail of hyssop, and they let him dip a rag in it. When he returned, Papa was slapping Jesus's face, trying to revive him. Quickly, Daniel shoved the rag over Jesus's nose. The strong vapors of the herb quickly revived him, but then a look of sheer horror came over him. With unnatural strength, Jesus pushed Daniel away.

Daniel staggered and fell on his rump.

"Curse you and that filthy rag! What are you doing to me?" Jesus shouted.

Daniel tossed aside the rag. Why would it hold such terror for Jesus? "Papa, please. He's seen enough." It was no use.

Papa hefted Jesus up. "He must see this for his own good."

Both victims had been nailed to the crosspieces. Their arms had been secured with ropes to bear just enough weight to prevent the nails from tearing through the flesh.

Once again, Papa forced Jesus to watch as the last nails were driven through their feet.

Jesus shuddered when the soldiers raised the crosses. He sobbed quietly.

For the crucified, the torment would drag on in a continuing cycle of pain. As the bodies sagged, the weight cut their breath, making them gag. Involuntarily, their legs straightened. This relieved the pressure on their chests, allowing them to breathe, but at the same time more waves of pain wracked their bodies as their full weight bore down on the rusty nails driven through their feet. When it looked as if one of them was about to drift into unconsciousness, the soldiers held up a sponge of hyssop liquor to revive him so he would continue to experience the agonies. *Jesus is right about these people. Not even barbarians are so cruel. They do things like this in their coliseums for sport too.*

Daniel looked back and forth between the victims and Jesus. His cousin's trembling increased. Jesus breathed—and almost gagged—in rhythm with the dying men. No longer a mere observer, Jesus seemed to share their torment.

"Papa, can't you see how Jesus suffers now?" exclaimed Daniel. "Is this not enough? Please, please let us take him from this place!"

Steeled to his purpose, Papa ignored Daniel's entreaties. The day wore on, and the midday sun drained the victims of their remaining strength. Jesus grew calmer, but he was still pale. Tears welled in his eyes, but he still watched, continuing to draw shallow breaths.

Finally, the captain of the soldiers muttered, "No point in waiting through the night. They won't survive it. End it now."

Yes, better to end this bloody business and ensure the criminals are dead so all can leave.

One of the soldiers brought forward an axe. He swung it, breaking the legs of the condemned. Unable to support the weight of their chests, they quickly suffocated, drowning in their own blood and phlegm. The soldiers left with the crowd once they determined that the victims were truly dead, but they left the bodies to hang, as food for the crows and as a warning to all.

Now that it was over, Papa tried to lead Jesus away, but Jesus just stood there pale and transfixed, gazing at the bodies. Papa hefted Jesus over his shoulder and carried the boy down the hill. Jesus lost consciousness on the way.

Finally, they reached the inn, and Papa settled Jesus in his bed. He remained ghastly pale, though his body burned with fever. Both Daniel and his father stayed at Jesus's side, draping his body with wet rags to cool his fever and offering up to God the most fervent of prayers.

Daniel could not bear to look at his father.

"What have I done?" Papa wailed, patting Jesus's hand. "Curse my stupidity. But for his own good I had to make Jesus keep watching."

At first, Daniel blamed his father, but he kept his silence. Daniel focused himself totally on his prayers for Jesus, occasionally running out to change the wet rags that cooled his cousin's body. As the night wore on, his anger at his father gave way to compassion.

"Look, Papa, the fever diminishes. He seems to be resting more comfortably. Get some sleep. I will stay with him and wake you if he gets worse."

"I'm so sorry, my son. I should have listened to you. I should have seen how the Romans' cruelty was affecting him. I don't know what I will say to Mary and Joseph if we lose him."

"We won't lose him, Papa. God watches over him. Maybe you did the right thing. Maybe Jesus had to see everything. Maybe that was God's will, and you were his instrument."

Papa embraced Daniel, and holding him tightly, he said, "I love you as no man has ever loved a son, and I have come to love Jesus, too. I cannot bear the thought of losing him now."

"I know, Papa. I understand. Now get some rest."

✾

Daniel awoke late the next morning to find Jesus sleeping comfortably in the bed beside him. He touched his cousin's forehead, and thankfully, it felt cool. His father was gone, probably about town preparing the next stage of their journey. Daniel got up and went to order food from the innkeeper, fish broth for Jesus and heartier fare for himself.

When Daniel returned to the room carrying a wooden platter, he found Jesus stirring—still pale and weak, but awake.

Daniel sat on the side of the bed. Jesus tried to say something, but too softly for Daniel to understand.

"Shhh! You had a terrible fever, and you're still weak. Don't try to talk. Just take some broth. It will help to restore your strength." Daniel spooned broth to his cousin's lips.

At first, Jesus was too weak even to swallow, but the broth gradually revived him. "What happened?" he asked. "The last thing I remember was watching the crucifixion. It seemed to be over. How did I get here?"

"You collapsed. Papa carried you from the hill, and then you came down with a terrible fever. Father was afraid we were going to lose you, but I knew that God looks after you, Jesus. I knew he didn't bring his son into the world just to lose him to a fever."

Jesus smiled weakly and reached for his cousin's hand. "I had a terrible dream. Well, it seems more than just a dream." Jesus began to cry. "I'm scared, Daniel. For the first time in my life, I'm really scared. Hold me, please."

Daniel hesitated. The notion of embracing his cousin felt awkward to him. But Jesus, sobbing, seemed to need the comfort of a human touch. So

Daniel put down the broth, took Jesus in his arms, and cradled him like a baby. Time seemed to stand still. Daniel dampened a cloth and wiped the tears from Jesus's face. "Would it help to tell me about this dream? What scared you so much?"

"It was more like a vision," said Jesus. "I saw myself as a man, maybe thirty years old. I was back in Jerusalem, outside the city walls. Your father was there, and so was my mother. They looked older than they do now." Jesus began to sob again, and once more Daniel cradled him in his arms.

"What was everyone doing in your dream?" Daniel asked.

Jesus gripped his cousin hard and whispered in his ear. "It was another crucifixion, but this time it was me. I was the victim condemned to death by the Romans. It was the most horrible thing imaginable. It was even worse than the crucifixion we have just seen. They mocked me. The Romans put up a sign on my cross that said 'King of the Jews', and they made me wear a crown of thorns. I even saw them casting lots for my garments."

For a moment Daniel was paralyzed with fear, but then he collected his thoughts. "This is just a nightmare, Jesus. You were upset after watching yesterday's crucifixion."

"No, Daniel. I have seen a glimpse of my future, and I can still see it now. It's more than a nightmare."

"Oh, Jesus, be brave. I know that God did not bring you into this world just to die on a cross, but you still must recover your strength. Here, take some more broth, will you? Then get some more rest. I will sing from the Psalms of David as you go to sleep."

"Yes, cousin. I will take some more broth now, and then hear the Psalms of David. I must turn to my Father for comfort."

So after Daniel had fed the rest of the broth to Jesus, he took up the scroll Papa had left with them to study. For hours he sang, as Jesus awoke and then almost seemed to drift off to sleep. But each time Jesus seemed to have fallen asleep, his eyes sprang open again. Daniel began to feel as though Jesus was searching to hear the right verse before he would allow himself the luxury of rest.

As the skies darkened, Daniel came across the thirty-fourth psalm. It seemed to bear the testimony of one who narrowly escapes death, and it was among those attributed to David. Daniel looked at Jesus. Was he asleep? His eyes were closed, but Daniel could not be sure. Though he was weary, Daniel began to sing. "I will extol the Lord at all times; his praise will always be on my lips." The psalm continued with praise for the Lord, and it told how the humble would be made glad and how the Lord heard the righteous and delivered them. Daniel continued toward the end of the psalm:

> The eyes of the Lord are on the righteous, and his
>   ears are attentive to their cry;
> But the face of the Lord is against those who do evil,
>   to blot out their name from the earth.
> The righteous cry out, and the Lord hears them; he
>   delivers them from all their troubles.
> The Lord is close to the brokenhearted and saves
>   those who are crushed in spirit.
> The righteous person may have many troubles, but
>   the Lord delivers him from them all;
> He protects all his bones, not one of them will be
>   broken.
> Evil will slay the wicked; the foes of the righteous will
>   be condemned.
> The Lord will rescue—

Jesus sat up, looking animated. "Stop, that's it!" he cried.

Daniel looked at his cousin, puzzled.

"Don't you see? They will not break my bones, Daniel. It is not just the psalm. I remember it that way in my vision. I never saw the Romans break my bones. That is the last thing the Romans do to kill their victims. God will hear my cries and deliver me from the cross before they get the chance! Surely, my Father will do that just the way he delivered Daniel from the lions and Jonah from the whale. Oh…won't it be glorious, Daniel? The Romans will see the power of my Father and the sight will strike them helpless with terror, just as Joshua's enemies fled in terror from the ark. And then I shall lead the armies of the righteous and sweep away the tyrants from our shores and restore the house of David to its rightful throne!"

Daniel's eyes filled with joyful tears as Jesus drifted off into a sound sleep. He remembered his vision of Jesus that day back in Nazareth, and the divine light he saw glowing within his cousin. Yes, it all made sense now. Jesus was the Son of God. He had to be the promised Messiah who was destined to lead the people of Israel to freedom.

Once again Daniel felt himself grow weak. He knelt humbly by the side of Jesus's bed.

It was late in the evening before Papa returned to the inn. Daniel was waiting up for him, and the two of them went to the common room to get something to eat and talk where they would not disturb Jesus's sleep.

"I saw Jesus was resting comfortably when I left this morning," Papa began. "He seems to be even better now. I knew you would take good care of him."

Daniel said nothing at first. Then he smiled. "Yes, Jesus is out of danger. Tell me of your preparations, and then I shall tell you more of Jesus. Do we have a boat to take us north up the River Arar?"

"We won't need one," Papa replied. "We will set out in a different direction. But let me start at the beginning. I was introduced today to a Greek merchant from Massilia. His name is Pirro. We have mutual friends in this city who trust both of us.

"Pirro has a valuable secret, but by himself he cannot exploit it. His family has suffered along with all the Greeks of Massilia. He has managed to eke out a meager living trading with the British Belgae for iron ore at Yengi. By himself, he cannot mount a proper trading expedition—he doesn't have the money. So he needs us."

"That's fine. But what can he do for us?" Daniel asked.

"Ah. That is where his little secret comes in. Do you remember how I told you about the ancient tin route that the Greeks and Phoenicians before them followed to the lost island of Ictis to trade with the Dumnonii tribe directly? My grandfather told me the tale of how he traded with the Britons on the west side of that island, before Julius Caesar conquered the Gauls."

"But isn't that just legend, Papa?"

"No, son. Pirro has been there. He described Ictis perfectly, exactly as my grandfather described it to me. And he told me the Dumnonii are just as eager to avoid trading through the Belgae and Cantiaci as I am. You see? We will travel the ancient tin route and profit both the Dumnonii and ourselves. No longer will we be at the mercy of the Cantiaci who monopolize all the trade between Britain and Rome and who squeeze to the bone both miners and honest merchants such as me."

"But doesn't all trade in Britain have to go through the Cantiaci?"

"That is not a restriction imposed by Rome. They just hate to travel across open ocean, so they are willing to pay the price to cross the *Oceanus Britannicus* within sight of land. Under Roman law, I can conduct my trade anywhere. The Cantiaci won't be gentle if they get their hands on us, and the crossing to Britain will be more hazardous where the ocean is wider—but those are the risks we take."

"Have you concluded your deal with Pirro, Papa?"

"Yes. He will receive one-third of the profit from this expedition and show me the route. That should give him enough to fund his own expeditions in the future. If this works, there will be plenty of trade for both of us."

"So where do we go from here?"

"We head west across the hills to the River Liger. The road will be steeper, but it is not far. Pirro and I have already hired oxen teams, and I have sent an agent ahead to hire a flat boat to take us downstream. We can buy our wine along the way." Papa paused and finished the last piece of bread. "So, tell me more about what happened with Jesus."

Daniel related Jesus's vision to his father, and how the prophecy in the psalm, saying his bones would not be broken, had comforted Jesus.

Papa bowed his head and shook it sadly. "Oh, you foolish boys! Do you think the Romans always break the bones of such victims? They do that only to hasten death when it suits their purposes. Sometimes the victim is left to suffer on the cross for days, and dies with all his bones intact. Do you have that scroll of psalms with you?"

"Yes, Papa. Here it is."

Papa turned to the twenty-second psalm, also composed by King David. He pointed out the middle verses to Daniel.

> Dogs surround me, a pack of villains encircles me;
>   they pierce my hands and my feet.
> All my bones are on display; people stare and gloat
>   over me.
> They divide my clothes among them and cast lots for
>   my garment.
> But you, Lord, do not be far from me. You are my
>   strength; come quickly to help me.

"Does this not set out the vision Jesus had of his crucifixion?"

Daniel silently nodded in the affirmative.

"There is nothing in this psalm that speaks of rescue from the brink of death. See this lament."

> My God, my God, why have y forsaken me? Why are
> you so far from saving me, so far from my cries
> of anguish?
> My God, I cry out by day, but you do not answer,
> by night, but I find no rest.

"I say this to you truly, my son. If Jesus's vision is true, the prophecy does not call for God to rescue him, but for God to be glorified in the end. If Jesus's fate brings him to the cross, he will come to his death there. As one who has studied the prophecies of Scripture, there is no doubt in my mind on this."

Daniel began to weep.

"But no one can know God's purpose in these things. Perhaps Jesus is destined for great things. Right now, I fear for the strength of his faith in God. Jesus's faith rests upon a slender reed, if he believes that God will rescue him triumphantly at the end. I fear for what will become of his obedience and faith once he learns his true destiny.

"But let that be between Jesus and God," Papa continued. "God will know when Jesus can handle that. He is not ready to learn this now, Daniel. Maybe God will let his purpose be known to Jesus and give him the strength and wisdom to handle the full truth when that time comes. Let us not be the ones to reveal to Jesus anything. Let him be at peace until God reveals the awful truth. Swear this to me, Daniel."

With heavy heart, Daniel swore to his father that he would never be the one to reveal to Jesus the true prophecy of actual death on the cross.

Chapter 4
A Perilous Passage

Joseph

Gone was the painful vibration of the road, replaced by the bobbing of the river. Joseph rested comfortably as the flat-bottomed barge made its way down the Liger River. Summer was just beginning, and everything was pleasant. The sun percolated through the treetops. Cool zephyrs moderated the heat, and when breezes failed, a dip in the water provided quick relief. Tethered to the barge by thirty feet of line, two horses plodded along the towpath; but with the slow-moving current pushing the barge along, the horses barely need to pull. Their hooves sounded a steady, reassuring rhythm, punctuated by the laughter of their eager riders, Jesus and Daniel.

There had been thunderstorms, sandbars, and several rapid stretches, but now nothing disturbed the tranquility of the lazy river. For the first time on the journey, Joseph could truly relax.

The sudden change of plans in Lugdunum had cost him some time and money, but that had been unavoidable. He still grimaced when he thought about the extra expense of rehiring and reloading the carts, but replacing the horses with oxen had been necessary; and once they reached the Liger River, Joseph had found the boatman ready to load up and go.

The hire for the barge, its captain, and the horse team had been cheap—a fixed price to take them all the way to Nantes at the river's estuary. Fish and game were abundant. Pirro was skillful with bow and fishing spear. The boys were eager to learn, and soon they were bringing in fresh fish and small game. Seeing to the slaughter and dressing of the game in accordance with Jewish dietary law gave Joseph something to do. For all practical purposes, time could stand still. If the trip took longer than expected, that was now the captain's problem, just as the captain stood to gain if they arrived earlier.

They were now in the land of the Three Gauls, the region Julius Caesar had conquered some sixty-five years before. Bacchus, the barge captain, was an enterprising and amiable fellow; short, heavy set, but muscular. Despite his Greco-Roman name, there was no mistaking his Gallic-Celt family origins; his Celtic dialect was unmistakable. It seemed that he had to play the part of a Roman because he catered to Roman merchants. His face was clean-shaven and his brown hair closely trimmed in the Roman fashion. That and the worn Roman toga made him look a bit absurd, as someone pretending to be what he is not. Nonetheless, he seemed to know every sandbar and rapid. Plying the steering oar from the stern, he certainly had the skill to steer the barge past these obstructions.

The barge had a relatively shallow draft to navigate through the sandbars and a much wider beam than the typical river boat, to make up for the lost displacement. The cabin at the stern was just big enough to sleep the three men. A tiled fireplace allowed them to build a small fire next to the cabin. For the boys they lay planks over the cargo, and on this deck set up a tent. Often as not, however, Jesus and Daniel slept under the stars.

One evening as they made the barge fast to the side of the river, Bacchus yelled to the boys, "Set the horses out to graze."

Crew and passengers enjoyed a dinner of freshly caught fish, which they ate together, with some bread and wine that Joseph purchased in the nearby village.

"You know, Daniel," Jesus said, picking up a piece of cheese, "our dietary laws remind me of my Israelite identity whenever I eat." He took a bite.

Daniel laughed. "Really?"

Joseph lifted the cup to his lips and sipped the wine. This was a perfect opportunity to test the boys' knowledge. "Does it not bother you at all, then, that we drink wine purchased from pagans? Is that not contrary to our laws, the traditions of our people, and the teachings of our rabbis?"

"But, Papa," Daniel said, "there are no Israelite winemakers to be found. We haven't been near any community of our people since we passed Massilia. Surely God will forgive us when there is no other way of finding drink for our meals. We cannot obey every single law of our people while we travel so far away from home."

"Aha. That's what I like to hear!" said Bacchus. "A Jew who thinks in practical terms at last." Pirro joined in the laughter, and even Joseph smiled. "I have not forgotten how we lost a day stuck on that sandbar because you and the boys would not help dislodge the barge on your Sabbath day."

"We cannot compromise the law of God, but I do not think drinking this wine actually violates it," Jesus said.

The law was not always clear, particularly for a Jew traveling among Gentiles. As a younger man Joseph had known Rabbi Hillel, who had risen from his roots in Babylon to become one of the *Zugot*, the scholars of the temple. Joseph had asked Hillel's advice about adhering to the dietary laws when on his travels. Drinking wine made by pagans had troubled him, as that was contrary to what he had been taught from the oral traditions of the fathers. Rabbi Hillel had set Joseph's mind to rest. It's all well and good for scholars sitting in Israel to say a devout Jew should purchase wine only made by Israelites, he had said; but a Jew traveling far from the community, needed to understand the basis of the law from the more fundamental Torah, the first four books of Scripture.

So Joseph challenged Jesus to see whether he understood. "How can you say that? Didn't the rabbi in Nazareth teach you from the scholarly traditions?"

"I know the rule from those traditions, Uncle," answered Jesus. "But traditions handed down by rabbinical scholars by word-of-mouth are not accepted as law by the Sadducees. Learned scholars developed these traditions over many centuries, but the Sadducees might say that accepting them as law runs against the book of *Deuteronomy*, which prohibits adding to or taking away from the law of the Torah. On the other hand, the traditions can help people abide by the Torah by giving them clear guides to keep them within the bounds of the law."

Joseph almost dropped his cup. Could the boy have learned Hillel's teachings?

"Does the Torah differ from the traditions on purchasing wine from pagans?" asked Daniel.

"*Deuteronomy* condemns those who drink the wine presented by idolaters in their false worship," said Jesus. "The traditions go further to say that we should not drink any wine from any gentile, not just a particular libation that has been offered in idolatry. When we are at home among our own people, it is an easy choice to follow the traditions to assure our obedience to the law. But when we travel so far from home, the only wine we can buy is from pagans, which the traditions did not take into account, so we can only ask the seller if the wine came from a temple of some kind. When we do this we are doing all we can to keep the scriptural commandment to avoid idolatry."

"But if your god condemns what you call idolatry, aren't you taking the risk that pagans might invoke their idols while growing the grapes or making the wine?" Bacchus asked. "That could happen in the vineyards of Greeks, Romans, and Celts alike."

"The sin of the idolater does not pass to the righteous man simply because the righteous man purchases his wares," answered Jesus. "Those condemned in the passage from *Deuteronomy* drank the wine of the pagan sacrifice itself, and that seems to me a direct participation in the pagan ritual. We cannot help it if a pagan decides to pray to false gods while making something to sell. Purchasing what he offers is not the same as participating in his false prayers."

"I don't know about your god," said Pirro. "He tells you what you may eat and what you may not eat. Then he tells you how you eat it. And even so, you still have to find a wise man to figure out what he wants. He seems very demanding." The way Pirro raised his eyebrow accentuated his crooked nose. He seemed like a thin shadow of a man. His coal-black hair was tightly wound in curls, and he had allowed it to grow out a little in the Greek fashion.

Jesus finished his wine. "Some say Israelites are the chosen people of God," he said, "not because we are so high but because we so are low. Only a humble people would accept such laws."

All except Joseph smiled at Jesus's words. Joseph was too flabbergasted. He had been listening in amazement. Rabbi Hillel, a learned rabbi, had taken hours to locate the relevant passages of Scripture and analyze them, yet Jesus needed only seconds, working from memory, to draw the fine distinctions among the nuanced words to analyze the problem. The old rabbi had agonized at the thought of going against the oral traditions, even to arrive at a deeper truth. Mary had said her son knew no fear when it came to proclaiming the truth as he saw it. *If Jesus was not even going to let the scholarly traditions get in the way of that, was there anything that would?*

After supper, Jesus cleared away the dishes while Daniel and Bacchus got the barge underway to make use of the waning daylight.

With the others occupied, Pirro approached Joseph. "Your nephew is quite a know-it-all."

"I am thankful that he is a good and devout boy."

"I saw the way you looked at him just now. As if he were some sort of elder wise man. Your son is almost fully grown, and you tell me that he's two years older than Jesus, but they act as if Jesus were older. Perhaps I should have negotiated my deal with the boy."

"My nephew is intelligent, and he has been well taught in Scripture. I do respect that, but I know he's still a boy. You need not concern yourself with Jesus. Just show us the way to Ictis, and there had better be tin for us to buy when we get there, like you told me." *How could Pirro be jealous of someone so young?*

"You need not worry about finding tin in Ictis." Pirro walked away to the other side of the barge.

Joseph was glad to be left to his own thoughts. *That Greek is beginning to annoy me.*

By now Jesus had finished with the dishes, had made his way to shore, and was riding with Daniel on the horses. Joseph walked to the bow. The boys were laughing and joking with each other. *They have become best friends. They look like any other boys right now, but Jesus is truly extraordinary. The Greek is right about one thing; Daniel looks up to the younger Jesus, when it should be the other way around. My son saw something in Jesus from the very beginning.*

When dusk fell, half a dozen bargemen drew their boats together in midstream. Bacchus greeted his fellow captains cheerily. The boys hobbled the horses alongside those of the other bargemen and returned to the ship.

"Why do we gather the barges like this every night?" Jesus asked.

Bacchus tossed a line to another boat, and caught the one thrown to him. He crouched to tie it to a bronze cleat. "Rafting the boats together protects us all. Safety in numbers."

"Might we be unsafe?" Jesus asked.

Bacchus stood. "Thievery is not unknown, lad. Living aboard ship minimizes the problem. And we'll take turns keeping watch overnight."

Daniel joined them. "Are there pirates?"

The captain laughed and walked to the opposite side of the ship. "Barges move too slowly. A pirate could never escape the Roman garrisons using that road." He pointed to the road that ran parallel to the riverbank.

Bacchus turned out to be a well-known storyteller. Several of his friends joined him, and his passengers gathered around the fire at the stern of his barge to hear another tall tale. Bacchus began with his usual protestations that he had no more stories to tell and was too tired to tell one anyway.

"Perhaps you could just tell us about Lugh for now," Jesus asked. "I've been wondering why the Romans would name their provincial capital after him when they despise the druids so much."

"I cannot tell you anything of what the Romans do, but I can tell you something of Lugh," Bacchus began.

He told the story handed down through the teachings of the druids of how the world entered its present age in the Battle of *Mag Turied*. In that battle, the *Tuatha Dé Danann,* gods who laid claim to the Celtic lands of Europe, and the previous inhabitants, a race of giants called the *Fir Bolg,* fought against each other. Allied with a different race of giants, the *Fumor*, and led by their King Nuada, the *Tuatha Dé Danann* gained the ascendency over the *Fir Bolg* in the First Battle, but then were oppressed by their *Fumor* allies, setting the stage for the Second Battle, in which the gods of the *Tuatha Dé Danann* freed themselves.

Bacchus focused on the eve of the Second Battle, when Lugh first appeared. "King Nuada prepared a magnificent feast, but decreed that all who entered must demonstrate a unique art. Lugh responded that he was a carpenter, to which the porter replied that a carpenter was already present. Lugh then ran through a variety of arts of which he was master: warrior, poet, healer, magician, blacksmith, and so on. In each case, a master of that art was already present. Lugh commanded the porter to ask King Nuada if there were any present who could do all these things. Although forced to admit that no such master of all arts was present, King Nuada subjected Lugh to several tests, all of which he passed, to the ultimate shame of the king. The king was compelled to stand for thirteen days before his own throne as Lugh sat in triumph. Lugh then led the *Tuatha Dé Danann* to victory in the final battle against the *Fumor,* in which King Nuada was slain."

The party listened with rapt attention. Then Jesus posed a question. "When he arrived at the banquet, was Lugh a man or a god?"

"He was both a god and a giant. His paternal grandfather was the greatest healer god of the *Tuatha*, and his maternal grandfather was a formidable warrior giant of the *Fumor*. He possessed the graces and powers of the *Tuatha* gods, while at the same time he could take on the great strength of the *Fumor* giants by raising his eyelid, just as his grandfather did."

"That seems very strange to me, maybe because I do not understand pagan religions," said Joseph. "In your tale the *Fumor* seem to represent forces of chaos and darkness. Yet Lugh is one of them while at the same time he is one of the enlightened *Tuatha*. It's like having a being who is both god and man. It is absurd; the God I know is all-perfect and all-powerful. Men, like giants, are imperfect and spiritually weak by nature. A true god could never be both."

"With respect, Uncle, our Scripture says otherwise," said Jesus. "In Isaiah's book of prophecy, he says a child and son will be born to Israel, whom he also calls the Mighty God."

Daniel perked up and gazed silently at Jesus. Then he turned quizzically towards Joseph, seeking confirmation.

Joseph mulled over Jesus's objection. "I remember that passage only vaguely," he finally responded. "I need to check the wording the next time I get hold of that scroll, although I am afraid that will not be for quite some time. But I know that there is only one true God. He cannot have a son and them both be gods."

"I'm not sure you want to test what Jesus said," exclaimed Daniel. "Remember what happened to King Nuada." This brought a round of hearty laughter from the entire company, except Jesus. He looked at Joseph, apparently deep in thought.

Bacchus was asked for another story. After everyone agreed that this would be the last story of the night, he told how the Celts had sacked Rome some four hundred years before.

Joseph knew the Roman side of the tale. The Celts had been established in northern Italy, and they launched a raid deep into Etruscan territory, part of which was newly conquered by the proud Romans. The Celts returned the next year in greater numbers to defeat the Romans and capture and sack Rome itself. The Celts withdrew with their booty and never returned, but the Romans learned the lesson and built the *Servian* Wall around their city.

The story from the Celtic side was far more colorful, full of tall tales of the heroes and cowards who turned the tide of war. But what really caught Joseph's attention was in how entranced Jesus was with the tale.

At its conclusion, Jesus leaned toward Bacchus. "Captain, do your people retain any hopes of regaining your former glory over the Romans?"

"Mind your tongue!" Joseph glared at Jesus.

His outburst not only cut off Bacchus from answering, but also seemed to dampen the mood of the other bargemen, who quietly retired to their own craft.

"I—I'm sorry…" Jesus muttered.

Wordlessly, Joseph dismissed the boys to bed.

It didn't help his mood to see Daniel pat Jesus's shoulder in a friendly show of support on their way to the bow.

Jesus must have known how his question might endanger them all if word got back to the Romans. Joseph was at a loss to understand his great-nephew. The boy was so wise on matters of Scripture, yet he seemed oblivious to the power of the Romans, rulers of the greatest part of the known world.

Had he forgotten the nightmare of his own crucifixion? *No, Jesus could not have forgotten his nightmare so soon. He must truly believe that God will save him from the cross of crucifixion to lead Israel to a glorious victory over the Romans.* Joseph reconsidered whether he should set the boy straight on this prophecy, but still was convinced this was a matter in God's hands. *My job for now is to get the boy to Britain and away from the authority of the Romans—as soon as possible.*

❧ ✣ ☙

As the Liger gradually wound its way westward, Joseph noticed that the country appeared less Romanized. There were still plenty of garrisons situated along the river to prevent any trouble and to ensure the collection of the emperor's taxes, but there were fewer Roman villas and more Celtic settlements. The river broadened as they approached the estuary, and then it became tidal and brackish, signaling the end of this peaceful leg of their journey.

There, on the north shore of the river, sat the bustling port city of Nantes, thirty-five miles inland from the sea. The river channel was both deep and wide enough for oceangoing sailing ships.

As soon as they alighted, Joseph felt the all-too-familiar pressures of time and money. Having seen them safely to the port, Bacchus's contract was now fulfilled. As soon as he found another customer going upstream, he would reclaim the use of his barge. If Joseph did not find a vessel to take them to Britain by then, he would need to hire space in a warehouse. Bacchus would likely find his task far easier than Joseph's—to find a vessel to take his party and cargo to the land of the Dumnonii in Britain.

Joseph was taken aback when Pirro said he had no idea where to hire a craft to take them to Ictis. Before Joseph had a chance speak, Bacchus offered to help, so Joseph left Pirro, Jesus, and Daniel to guard the cargo and followed the bargeman toward the forum. Along the way it struck him that they were in one of the farthest corners of the Roman world. Few natives here understood Greek or Latin; most spoke only the Gallic Celtic tongue, which Joseph spoke with difficulty. Without Bacchus, he would have been lost.

As the focal point of a provincial outpost, the forum turned out to be unsophisticated by Roman standards; but thankfully he found himself in more familiar surroundings where commerce was conducted in Latin. His worst fears were soon confirmed. The commercial notices had numerous postings seeking and offering charters back up the Liger by barge, and south along the coast. Some adventurous captains took their vessels all around Hispania as far as Cadiz. But not a vessel could be found heading north, and no captain he spoke to was willing to risk life and vessel, for any price, crossing the hundred-mile expanse of blue water from the northwest tip of Gaul to the western tip of Britain. They preferred to pilot their vessels close to the shoreline, where they could hope for refuge from threatening seas.

Joseph left Bacchus in the forum and made his way back to the barge. He resigned himself to the prospect of a long wait that would eat into his profits. He felt alone. In a day or two he would have no choice but to deal with the warehousemen, a thought that made him shudder. Even in the ports where he was well known, the warehousemen were in league with one another to fix their prices, and here he was a stranger. He would be at their mercy, and there was no telling how long it would take to find the sailing ship for their next leg. *Pirro said he knew the way to get us to Ictis. Did he not know that it would be hard to find a ship? Or did he decide to conceal the problem?*

As he approached the docks, he was not surprised to hear the familiar sound of the laughter of Jesus and Daniel as they dove into the river from the barge and splashed around. Two native boys their age had joined in the fun. It seemed harmless enough, though Joseph did not like the idea of strangers aboard the barge in a position to see the goods he carried. Then he noticed a native man on the barge talking to Pirro, and he wondered what his partner was up to. Pirro hailed him and excitedly waved him forward.

Pirro introduced Joseph to his newfound companion in Greek, a language all three of them spoke fluently. "This is Kendrick." Pirro pointed to the two boys playing with Jesus and Joseph. "Those are his sons. Not only is he the owner of a sailing vessel, but he sails regularly to western Britain, and he's looking for cargo and passengers."

Joseph narrowed his eyes at Kendrick, a sunburnt man with the scarred, calloused hands of a lifelong sailor.

Kendrick laughed. "You wonder why I don't seek out clients at the forum." He shook his head. "Roman merchants from here never expose their goods to the risks of an ocean crossing, nor do they care to conduct their commerce beyond the protection of the Empire."

"It's true," Joseph said. "Romans are unlike Greeks or Phoenicians in this respect."

Kendrick laughed again. "The Greeks revel in the uncertainties of ocean travel. But to the Romans, a trading expedition across open ocean leaves too much to chance."

True. The Romans tended to cross at the narrowest point, where in good weather they would stay within sight of land all the way. Joseph's plan to sail the ancient trade route across the *Oceanus Britannicus* defied this wisdom, but the opportunities in the west could turn out to be the competitive edge that would make him rich. "Are you Greek, then, sir?"

"No, I am of the Veneti."

"Ah! My grandfather often traded with your tribe."

"That would have been back in the days before Caesar, when we controlled the Atlantic trade routes to Britain," Kendrick said.

"Indeed," Joseph said. "May I see your ship?"

Kendrick allowed him to inspect the small but stout-looking sailing vessel, and the two agreed to terms. Joseph was delighted that Kendrick was ready to sail immediately, saving him the warehousing expense.

When Bacchus returned to his barge, Joseph and Kendrick summoned the boys from their play. Using a horse team and everyone's muscle power, Bacchus maneuvered the barge alongside Kendrick's ship. As they all pitched in to transfer the cargo, Kendrick marveled at the goods Joseph had accumulated. "I've never seen such valuable wares traveling to Britain by this route. I'll happily take a small portion of it in lieu of cash."

"Really?" Joseph lifted an eyebrow. "Why?"

"To use on my own account with the Britons." Kendrick winked, then walked away to supervise his crew.

"I told you I would get us to Ictis," Pirro whispered.

Joseph nodded. *Why did he not say he could find a ship before I went looking in the forum? It's no matter. Maybe he didn't want to say anything until he was sure.*

They stayed overnight aboard Kendrick's docked ship. Just before they went to the cabin to sleep, Joseph took a walk along the wharf with Daniel. "I wish I had known that Pirro had contacts among these native ship captains. It would have saved me a great deal of worry," he remarked.

"I don't think he knew anyone," Daniel replied.

"Then how did he find Kendrick?" Joseph asked.

"Actually, it was Jesus's doing. He and I were diving off the barge, and he invited the two boys to join us. We got to talking, and one of them mentioned to Jesus that their father owned a ship that often sailed to Britain. When Kendrick came along looking for his sons, Jesus took him to Pirro."

Joseph shook his head. The Greek was turning out to be a boastful oaf.

And Jesus...the boy was such a mystery. He was wise beyond his years, yet as playful and innocent as a child. *Now, once again, good fortune smiles upon us because of Jesus. But what if his dark nightmare is a true harbinger of things to come? The prophecy cannot be clearer; the path that Jesus may take to the cross leads to true suffering and despair of any rescue even by God, at least in this life. So, what will come of the love that the boy holds for God once he comes to understand this? Can anyone's love of God stand such a test?*

The next morning they set sail with a fair wind. The river widened into an estuary with several channels among its islands. Kendrick easily guided the ship through. After passing the last island they sailed down a bay some two or three miles across, an arm of the ocean reaching inland. They reached the mouth at midday.

As they turned to the northwest Joseph sensed something forbidding on the distant horizon. On the Mediterranean, he often looked out on the sea without seeing land beyond. But the land was always out there, in any direction except beyond the Pillars of Hercules. There was always the danger of storms, but at least the Mediterranean was well charted. It was a civilized sea, too, swept clear of pirates by the Romans.

Here, the ocean to the west was the great unknown. The wind was still fair, but it blew colder off the sea. The ocean swells were big for the wind, and even the stoutly built ship seemed frail now against the forces such an ocean might throw against it.

The passage appeared safe for the moment. Several harbors offered safety as long as they avoided the rocks of the ragged coastline. Islands along the coast could provide at least some measure of protection if wind and sea should threaten. But any protection from the land would end in a matter of days when they sailed past the headland that lay 150 miles ahead. Beyond that, there stretched one hundred miles of open sea between the tip of Armorica—as the natives called this far northwest corner of Gaul—and Britain.

Kendrick

The wind died down as evening approached. Kendrick gave the helm and the watch to one of his crew, and he paced the deck. Joseph's two boys were running all around the ship with their games, but he didn't care. For the moment, he just leaned over the rail and gazed out with a forlorn look at a wide protected bay that stretched another ten miles further into the distance. He cursed the fickleness of the wind. "Of all the places, why does the wind stop and leave me here?" he muttered. The next thing he knew Jesus was standing next to him.

"Why does this place make you sad?" asked Jesus.

Kendrick sighed. "This is the place where Caesar vanquished my people, when my grandfather was a young man."

"What happened?"

"For centuries the Veneti tribe controlled the Atlantic trade routes to Britain. Then Caesar came. Initially we submitted to Caesar, but soon we rebelled and slew his ambassadors. Caesar retaliated, destroying the Veneti fleet, killing all the men, and selling the women and children into slavery."

Jesus looked across the water. "So this is where Caesar destroyed the fleet of your people?"

Kendrick nodded.

"If Caesar sold all the Veneti into slavery, how is it you are free? Did you purchase your freedom?"

"No, my family escaped Caesar's wrath. My grandfather obtained shelter with relatives among the Namnetes tribe at Nantes. All around Armorica, survivors came out of hiding once Caesar left to wage his civil war with Pompey. Regional trade developed between Armorica and the Dumnonii area of Britain. The Romans left us alone—we were too insignificant for them. But the Atlantic trade route to the west of Britain is a shadow of what it once was. And every time I pass this wretched place, I think of my people's bondage."

The boy kept his silence for a few minutes. Finally, he said, "God will not allow your people to suffer forever."

How could a child think of offering platitudes to comfort a stranger? "What do you know of suffering?" Kendrick asked. "When have your people known the yoke of slavery?"

Jesus responded with a story of how his God led the people of Israel out of bondage in Egypt to the Promised Land, and how they remembered the bitterness of that bondage every year at Passover. He talked about the laws God gave the people of Israel through Moses and how they wandered in the desert for forty years until they finally arrived in Canaan.

As the boy told his story, the sun lowered to the horizon, and the wind picked up. Kendrick was so entranced by the tale that he scarcely paid attention as the cursed bay slipped astern, out of view.

Soon night had fallen, and Jesus took his leave to go to sleep. Kendrick found his mood much improved. He dismissed the helmsman and took the next watch of the night himself to be alone with his thoughts. He hadn't known much of Jews before; their concept of just one God seemed so strange. But Jesus's sincerity and empathy impressed him. Late in the night the helmsman returned to take back the watch, and Kendrick retired to a restful sleep.

The next day a fresh westerly wind arose from the ocean. Under reefed sails, the ship tore ahead through building swells on its northwesterly course parallel to shore. The motion of the swaying ship made the passengers sick, even though none of them had eaten since the day before.

Kendrick watched the sea with a wary eye. As expected, the skies clouded over, confirming his suspicions. Something was brewing out in the ocean and coming closer. Late in the afternoon, he gave the command to gybe the sails and turn the ship into the entrance of a harbor. They headed for Brest, the final haven before the last headland of Armorica. After that, they would have been surrounded by open stormy sea.

Brest was a lonely outpost. Four fishing vessels sat at anchor. There was no sign of a harbor master as there had been in Nantes and hardly any sign of Roman authority. The small market also was closed. The only inn in the hamlet overlooked the well-protected harbor from the foot of the second of two small hills on the northern shore, separated by a small stream. The one road, actually more of a pathway through Armorica, came to an abrupt end at the very doorstep of the inn.

Everyone on board helped to secure the ship alongside the small quay, as storm clouds gathered in the west. The party made it to the inn just as the storm broke. It was a small establishment operated by a peasant farmer and his wife, with two rooms to rent off the main room of their home. Kendrick knew the landlord, so the rooms did not come too dearly—fortunately for Joseph. The wife prepared some fish chowder with warm bread that soon restored their spirits and sated their ravenous hunger.

With thunder and lightning crashing outside, they huddled together in the two rooms. There was barely enough space in the beds for all, but no one complained. Even those who slept on the earthen floor were happy to be sheltered from the raging storm.

There was no let-up the next day. There was nothing to do but eat more chowder and stay warm around the fire. Kendrick was surprised when Joseph and the two boys passed on another serving of dinner offered by the landlady late in the afternoon. He was even more surprised when he saw them gather up their cloaks. "Where are you going? The storm still rages," he said to Joseph.

"Our Sabbath begins at Sundown, and we must keep it holy," answered Joseph. "If we do not board the ship now, we will not be able to embark until the Sabbath ends, even if the weather clears tomorrow. We will spend the night on board the ship, and you and the crew can sail with us already on board as soon as the weather clears."

"But why not wait to see if the weather clears in the morning, and then go aboard if it does?" Kendrick asked.

"Our people devote the Sabbath day to study and prayers," Joseph replied. "In our own land we do not leave our home on the Sabbath except to go to our temples. If we again make our home here tonight, we must stay until the Sabbath ends. So, tonight we make your ship our home, so you will be free to sail."

Joseph

As the sun went down, Joseph, Jesus, and Daniel prayed on board the ship. The cabin was not watertight in the drenching wind and rain. They did not try to light a lamp, and they were not about to risk damaging the precious scrolls in the wetness, so they recited psalms from memory and devoted themselves to personal prayers.

In the morning, Joseph awoke cold, damp, and stiff, to the motion of the ship moving down the channel back to the harbor entrance. Kendrick poked his head into the cabin to offer them some hot porridge. As the three of them came up on deck to eat and dry themselves in the warm sun, Jesus remained silent and thoughtful. He kept looking at the sky and the waves, and then he closed his eyes. Meditating, perhaps.

Even on the Sabbath, Joseph was not used to the loquacious boy being so quiet. "Why don't you say anything?" he asked.

"I'm not sure, but somehow I sense that this is just a short break in the weather, Uncle," said Jesus. "I feel another storm approaching from the ocean."

"That's nonsense," Joseph responded. "The day could not be finer for setting out to Britain. The sky is clearing, and the wind is fair. If the wind holds we may reach Ictus by this time tomorrow."

"I know what the sky looks like now, Uncle. I just sense something else out there. Should I tell the captain?"

"Let us mind the Sabbath and leave the sailing to the gentiles today," said Joseph. "Come, finish the porridge and let us get on with our Sabbath prayers and studies." Joseph smiled. The admonition was gentle. He rarely had to remind Jesus of his Sabbath obligations.

"Very well, Uncle. God will protect us."

Joseph and the boys recited their prayers and studied the scrolls as the ship sailed to the harbor entrance and turned northward. Every so often they took a break and got up to look around. They passed through a small chain of islands leading off to the west, and then they spotted the rose-colored rocky shore on the north side of Armorica. But by afternoon the land faded off in the distance, and nothing but blue water could be seen in any direction.

With the sunset, the Sabbath day came to an end. Joseph breathed in the fresh ocean air. He looked over to Jesus and said a special prayer of thanksgiving. They were finally beyond the authority of Rome. Jesus no longer posed a danger of trouble with the authorities. But he also well knew that while they sailed away from the yoke of Rome, so too did they leave behind the Empire's protection.

Kendrick

To cross one hundred miles of sea, Kendrick could count on getting his initial bearings for many miles by taking transits from familiar points on land. But as the land faded behind the stern, he steered by the sea swell. The daytime sun bearing was a crude guide at best. The undulating wave sets always had a pattern and rhythm from one direction or another. Sometimes during the course of a day a distant storm or wind might create a new wave set, but Kendrick's keen eye easily distinguished the different wave set patterns moving across the same patch of sea, as one waxed and the other waned, and thereby maintained a constant course through the day. The clear nighttime brought out the most precise beacons burning in the sky, and the captain reset his course by them.

The first sign of trouble to Kendrick that night was the obstruction of the stars. One by one they seemed to turn themselves off. Kendrick still expected to reach Britain in time, but then he looked up and distinguished the gathering storm clouds in the light of the half moon. They were coming in and descending on his vessel fast and furious from the upper sky. Meanwhile, the wind at the surface began to die, killing off his last hope of outrunning the approaching storm. Kendrick sounded the alarm and set his crew about taking down the regular sails and hoisting the sturdy storm sail.

The storm arrived at midnight with a huge gust of cold wind and rain slamming them from the west. Kendrick tried to maintain his northerly course. With the small storm sail, the wind was not too much of a problem. But then the seas began to build at an alarming rate. The ship rolled with the waves. Kendrick had no choice. A big wave could cause the vessel to founder if it caught him broadside, and the quickly building wind and waves forced Kendrick to run with the wind into the *Oceanus Britannicus*. The vessel was not in any immediate danger, since they had hundreds of miles to run with the wind before crashing on a lee shore; but they were now in the middle of the sea with no means of getting back to the course they had steered by attempting to sail in a constant direction from the northwest tip of Gaul.

Jesus

All through the next day, there was little rest for the crew. With every gybe, Kendrick called on the passengers to shift the cargo to keep the vessel balanced, but he was not about to entrust them with the sails or the steering oar. At first Jesus huddled with Joseph and Daniel in the hold. It seemed like the sensible thing to do. But one-by-one, seasickness in the cramped space forced them on deck to vomit.

Joseph and Daniel had quickly returned to the hold, but Jesus felt better in the open air, despite the frequent drenching.

The sea looked even more frightening than it had in that storm off Cyprus. The windborne rolling swells came in like moving mountains from the west, each one threatening to swallow the ship. Jesus had not seen swells nearly as tall in the other storm. He began to appreciate the sturdier construction of the Celtic vessel. The sails were made of hides rather than cloth to better withstand the chafing of the spars. The wood did not creak from the strain nearly as much. He remembered overhearing Kendrick tell Uncle Joseph that the wood was something called *oak*.

The vessel seemed to overtake the swells. Struggling at first against gravity, it slowly climbed the backside to the crest. After breaking through, the vessel raced down the wave face with a rush of speed into the looming trough. The crash of the forecastle into the next wave sent up a mountain of spray that drenched them all as the cycle repeated.

Jesus prayed at first for deliverance, but then he changed. Kendrick was weaving the course of the ship to take it across the wave some as they raced down each time. Despite the crazy speed, the captain looked like he had the ship under control, picking his way through the waves to minimize the crashes and strains on the boat while keeping it upright. Jesus prayed in thanksgiving for the stoutness of the vessel and the skill of the crew.

Before long Jesus went below to fetch the others. Uncle Joseph would not move. Jesus turned to Daniel and grabbed his hand. "Come on, you'll feel better above." He almost dragged the older boy topside. He suspected that it was only the reek of vomit in the cramped hold that caused his cousin to give in.

It took a while for Daniel to gain his balance on deck as the boat rolled rhythmically, but Jesus was now able to anticipate its movements. As Daniel continued to clutch the railing, Jesus braced himself at the foot of the mast. One of the hands shouted something to him and pointed to a safety line. Jesus saw how the crewman was secured and tied the line around his waist the same way. As the ship broke through the next crest, Jesus spread his arms. He held that position racing down the wave face and took the drenching from the next wave full force.

Before long, Daniel was standing beside him. The two of them began laughing and shouting. It was the wildest ride of their lives, and they were loving it.

The winds finally abated. They were able to open the hatches to air out the hold and then clean it up with sea water. Bone weary now, Jesus found a small space covered with straw between some casks of wine. Disturbed by the noise of the crew, he moved one of the casks to close the passage behind him and drifted off into a deep sleep.

He dreamed of a one-room circular house of a native Celt couple. The walls seemed to be made of some sort of crude plaster. The doorway and walls were decorated with all kinds of pagan idols, some of them evidently having been molded into the plaster of the wall itself when it was wet.

In his dream, a woman stood over the bed of a boy who appeared to be about eight years old. She cried as she felt the boy's forehead. The doorway to the house opened, and her husband entered. Jesus could see his face clearly; a lonely tear glistened on his cheek. The two of them talked in low voices to avoid waking their son. They spoke in their native Celt language, which Jesus had never heard before. After listening to a few sentences, he understood everything clearly.

"So, you are leaving," the woman in the dream said to her husband. "Rushwig will die of the fever before you return. This seems to be the same as the one that took his brothers, and I am too old to bear you more sons."

"Goodwife, mind your tears. Rushwig's fate is in the hands of the gods, and they may spare him yet. You know how to take care of him much better than I do. But I must go. Our stores that took us through the winter are almost gone, and we need money to keep from starving."

"I cannot bear to lose our last son with you gone," said the wife. "I cannot bear the thought of watching over his dead body alone."

"All of us may starve if I don't get some money," replied the husband. "Be strong, Glaida. You know I would give up anything for Rushwig or you, and you know that whatever happens, I will take no other wife."

The husband turned and left quickly. The woman once again cried over her son. Then she picked up a sharp knife and rubbed the blade gently across her wrist. She did not draw blood, but she seemed to be preparing for the worst. She turned her attention back to her son and gently stroked his hair. The fever still burned, but the son yet lived.

Jesus woke suddenly as a random wave crashed over the ship. He prayed for God to save Rushwig and to forgive the idolatry that surrounded him. Somehow, Jesus knew that his prayer was answered, and he fell back into a deep and dreamless sleep.

Dumrac

Someone must have warned the Dumnonii villagers, for the raid had not started well. Too many of their warriors were lying in wait. Empty-handed though he was, Dumrac the pirate felt lucky to make it back to his ship with his life, his freedom, and his band intact.

They were halfway back to their home on the Isle of Vectis when they spotted the prize. Dumrac could not believe his good fortune. An Armorican merchant ship, evidently blown off course by the storm. The trade goods would not be worth much—some blankets and pottery perhaps. But the people on board should fetch a decent price, more if they could be sold to the Romans.

The merchant vessel never had a chance. The two vessels had come upon each other suddenly as they steered around a rocky headland in opposite directions. Dumrac's vessel had a deep keel and a large fore-and-aft lateen sail. It could easily outdistance the merchant ship, particularly as the quarry tried to turn back upwind to get away. With its lug rig, the merchant ship could not sail into the wind nearly as well as the lateen-rigged pirate ship. The merchantmen knew better than to put up a fight .Soon Dumrac had the merchant vessel in tow with its crew and passengers in chains.

Dumrac sized up his captives. Too bad they were not Dumnonii. Slaves from Britain would have fetched a good price from the Romans. The captain appeared to be from Armorica, and the Romans never bought slaves from their own provinces. The passengers appeared well-to-do. Perhaps a hefty ransom could be negotiated with the family. If not, the young passenger and the two crew members could be sold in the hillfort market as laborers; they would fetch the best price. The others had a few good years of labor left in them, too.

Dumrac ordered the captives transferred to his own vessel, and he took stock of the captive cargo. He was amazed. It was no small prize of a poor Armorican trader, but a small fortune of fine wine, olive oil, spices, linen, and pottery. And then as they began moving the casks, they came upon another passenger fast asleep. Dumrac couldn't believe that the lad, a boy of maybe thirteen years, had managed to sleep through the capture. Then again, the merchant vessel was unarmed and hadn't really offered much resistance.

One of his band roughly kicked the boy to wake him up. The slave chains were on board the pirate vessel, but the boy was a thin and frail thing who clearly wasn't about to pose any kind of threat.

Dumrac laughed as the boy rubbed the sleep from his eyes and observed his unfortunate situation. But then the boy's eyes grew wide. "You!"

"So, who are you?" asked Dumrac with a laugh.

"I am Jesus Bar Joseph from Nazareth in Galilee," he replied, in the pirate's own tongue.

"Well, then, Mr. Jesus Bar Joseph," said Dumrac with a mock bow as his companions laughed louder. "My name is Dumrac, and we are honored that you come to us from such a distance. I am sorry we have no proper slave chain for you at the moment, but we will fix that as soon as we get you aboard my ship with the others."

"I know who you are," said Jesus. "You have a wife named Glaida and a son named Rushwig."

Dumrac was shocked into silence. *How can this boy know such things? But maybe he hadn't been asleep after all. The men well know the names of my wife and child; the boy must have overheard them speak the names earlier.* Dumrac sent his men back to the pirate ship as he grabbed Jesus.

"Let me go! You'll be sorry if you don't."

Dumrac laughed.

"Rushwig is gravely ill," Jesus whispered. "But God, who watches over me, keeps him alive. If you keep us as slaves God will see to it that your son dies, and then your wife will kill herself in her grief. You must give back the vessel and the cargo if you want them to live."

Dumrac gasped as if struck by a dagger. He had no explanation this time. Rushwig's illness was a closely guarded secret between him and his wife. Dumrac was a proud man, and he didn't want it known in his village that he could very well die childless. None of his men knew of the illness; he was sure of that.

"How do you know this?"

"God revealed it to me in a dream. You know you can't explain it otherwise."

"I must see that Rushwig is well."

"Very well, take us back with you. But you must leave me free to care for the others. When you see that Rushwig is well, you must release us, together with our ship and cargo."

So Dumrac allowed Jesus the run of the ship as he made his way back to his base on the eastern side of Vectis. Dumrac explained to his companions that it was easier to let Jesus take care of the captives than do it themselves, and it wasn't as if the frail thin boy posed a threat or had any means of escape.

Joseph

As he sat in his chains, Joseph was amazed once again that Jesus understood the Celtic language. He might have learned a few words from Kendrick's sons, but surely not enough for Jesus to speak as fluently as he did, and with the accent and idioms of the British dialect.

Jesus did his best to reassure them that the pirates would release them all, together with the ship and its cargo, at the next stop on the island.

Joseph hung his head in disbelief.

"I told you, Papa," Daniel said. "I saw the divinity in him that day back in Nazareth."

Jesus

The two ships entered Dumrac's lair through a narrow channel into a well-hidden swampy area. The pirate said it was called Bembont. The channel branched into several directions amid low-lying hills, offering a choice of hiding places. The native houses were concealed in a dry hollow at the foot of a hill that provided a convenient lookout for any threat from land or sea.

Just before their arrival, Dumrac grabbed Jesus by the arm. "I'll keep you as my own share of the booty, to avoid the necessity of putting you in chains with the others."

Uncle Joseph's party set foot on Britain not as traders but as captive slaves. As they made their way into the channel, Glaida waved happily to her husband.

Jesus sensed that Dumrac was stalling on his promise to release them all. Yet he said nothing as the others were secured in a latched-covered dugout hole for the night. He followed Dumrac and Glaida to their home.

Inside, Rushwig rested in bed. "Papa!" The boy embraced Dumrac.

The man put his hand on the boy's head. "No sign of fever?"

"None," Glaida said. "It cleared up yesterday."

Dumrac glared at Jesus, who nodded. Dumrac grabbed him and pulled him away from the others. "I cannot release the ship, its cargo, the others. It's too valuable of a prize. And it's not all mine to give away. My companions would turn on me."

"But—"

"Look, boy. I promise I'll never sell you or put you to any hard labor. All you have to do is be a companion for Rushwig. Surely, your god will see that as a fair exchange for the life of my boy, won't he?"

Jesus crouched against the wall and said nothing until the family had finished their meal. "Do you wish to hear a story?" he asked.

"Yes, please," piped up Rushwig.

Once again, Jesus related how God had brought his people out of bondage in Egypt. He got to the part where the boy prince of Egypt died after his father Pharaoh went back on his promise to free the people of Israel.

Rushwig put his hand to his temple. "Mama, my head hurts."

Within the hour, he was back in bed wracked with fever.

"I think God has answered your question about whether keeping me in a milder form of slavery is a fair exchange for the life of your son," Jesus said.

Dumrac glared at him, then glanced over to Glaida.

Jesus looked, too. The tears in her eyes were plain to see. He turned back to Dumrac. "I would never wish anything to harm your wife and son, but this is the work of my God, not me. You must let us go if you want them to live."

Without another word, Dumrac led Jesus out of the house and down to the dug-out hole. Fortunately, Dumrac's companions were still carousing and drinking mead to celebrate the capture. They couldn't hear Dumrac unlatch the heavy grate cover and swing it open, nor could they see the merchant vessel glide down the channel with all its cargo and crew. Just as they were about to pull out of range, Jesus fetched a bag of precious spice from the hold and tossed it to Dumrac on shore. "Sell this to feed your family," he said.

Joseph

As Kendrick's ship set sail to the west, all aboard gave thanks in their own way for their deliverance.

"Are we out of danger?" Joseph asked.

"We will be sailing past the land of the Durotriges," Kendrick replied. "They are a fierce and warlike people. In the days before Julius Caesar, their trading post at Yengi was the gateway to Britain. All that trade now goes to the east, and they resent any traders they encounter. We will find no welcome on their shores, but we can stay out of danger by keeping out to sea. Another eighty miles to the west, we will come to the land of the Dumnonii, who will welcome us anywhere further down the coast where we might need refuge."

Joseph turned to Jesus. "I am so sorry for bringing you this way. Your parents entrusted me with keeping you safe, and I have put you in great danger. I will come this way no longer."

"No, Uncle. Only God can keep me safe. Ever since we started down the Liger, I have felt the warmest feeling in my heart. I feel that God intends for you to prosper. I will pray tonight to ask him to show you how this voyage can be made in safety."

As the sun rose the next day, a rainbow appeared. It hadn't rained that night. And only Jesus and Joseph could see it.

"Uncle, that is the sign you need from now on. Sail out on the blue waters away from land only when you see the rainbow, and God will keep you safe."

Southwest Belerium

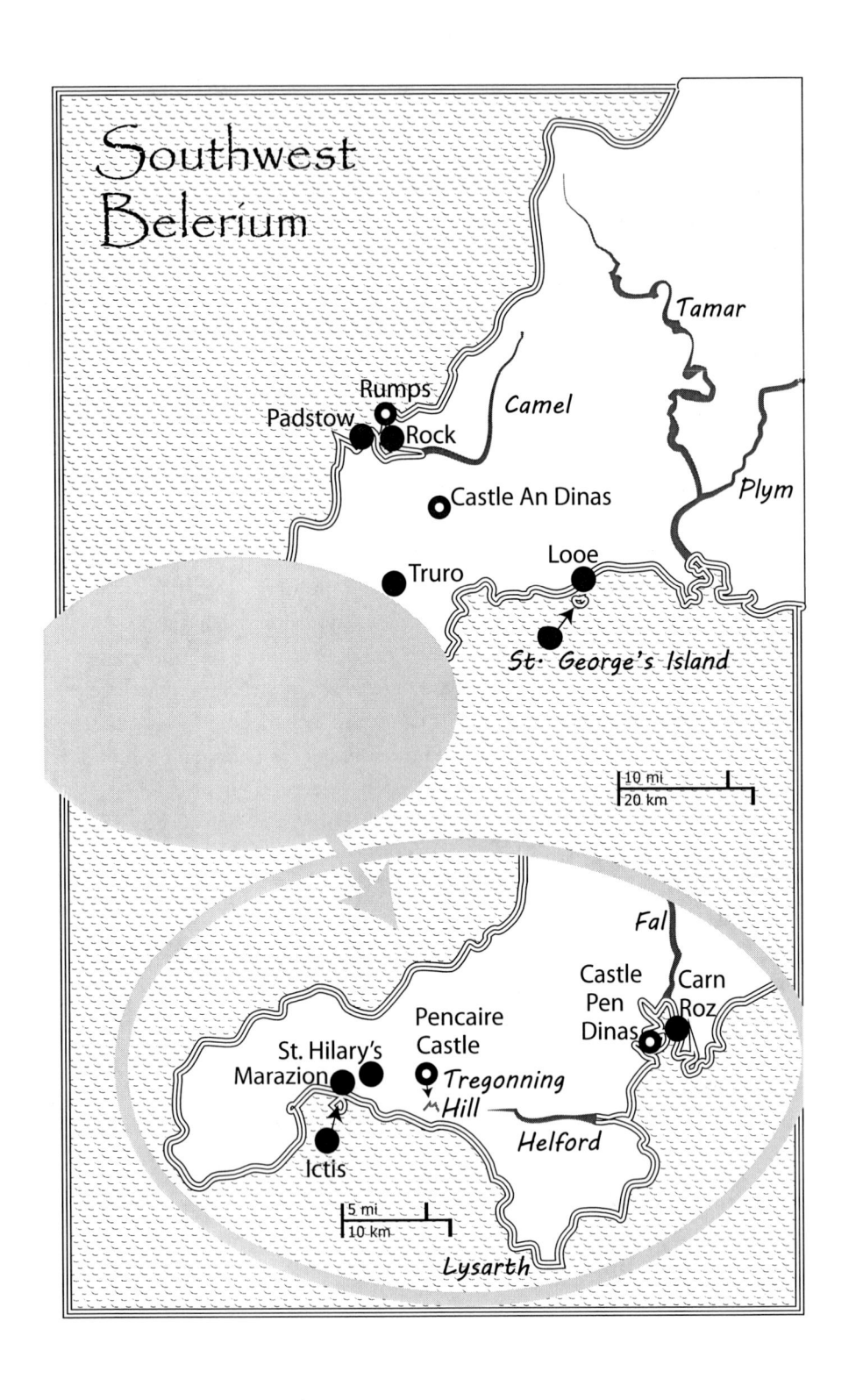

- Tamar
- Camel
- Rumps
- Padstow
- Rock
- Castle An Dinas
- Plym
- Truro
- Looe
- St. George's Island

10 mi / 20 km

- Fal
- Castle Pen Dinas
- Carn Roz
- Pencaire Castle
- St. Hilary's
- Marazion
- Tregonning Hill
- Helford
- Ictis
- Lysarth

5 mi / 10 km

Part 11
Growing in Wisdom and the Favor of God and Man

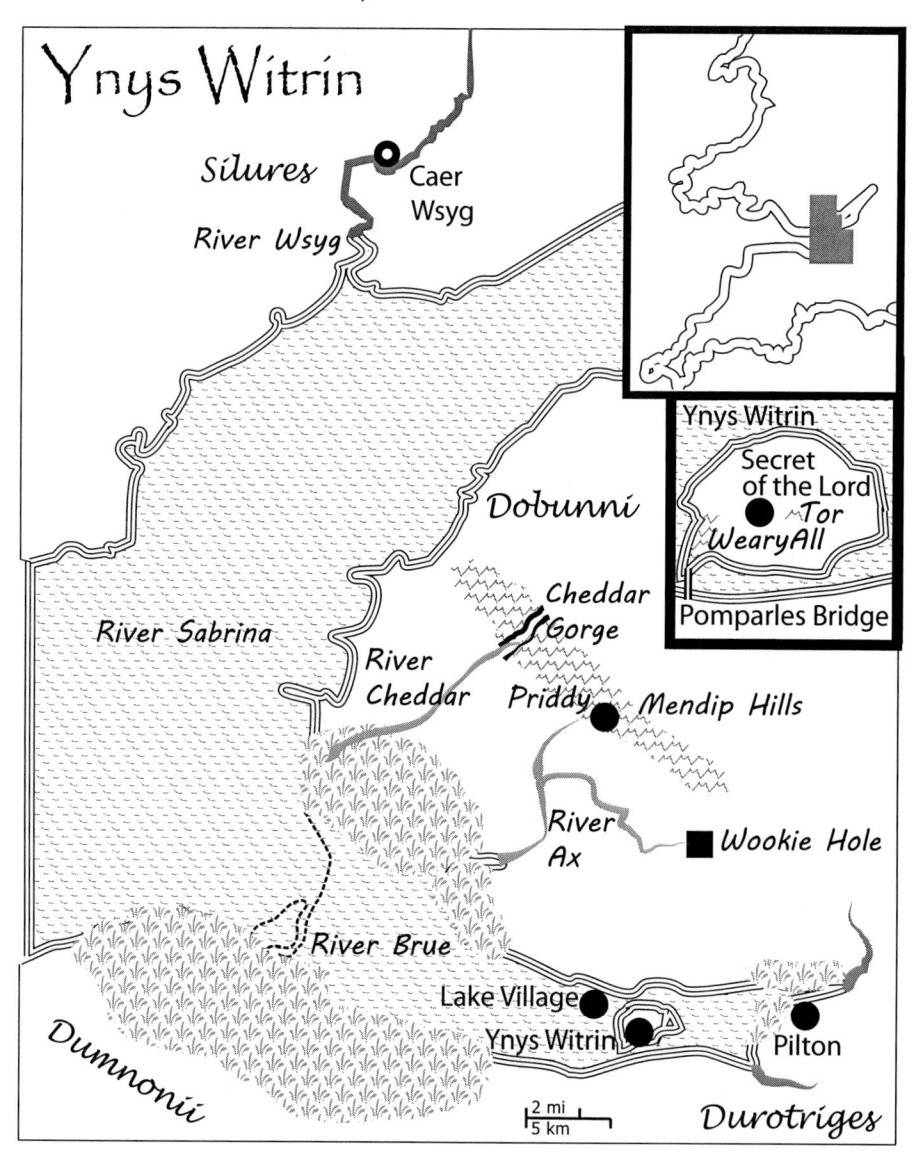

Interlude

St. Hilary's Parish, Cornwall, A.D. 1932, during the reign of King George V of England

"Bernie, I really do think it'd be best to keep it in storage—it's such a rare old thing, and best kept safe under the tarpaulin." Annie's tone was insistent, although she never raised her eyes from the white doily she was crocheting.

The vicar leaned back in his chair in the parlor and set aside the letter he'd been reading. No one knew when or how the old stone cross depicting the boyish figure of the Christ child had ended up in the vicarage cellar. Legend was that it had gathered dust there for several hundred years. "Well, it has lasted these centuries. I very much doubt it will wear away all that soon with a bit of rain and air, my dear," Bernie responded. "Besides, it's such a beautiful cross, displaying Our Lord in his childhood. Tunic crosses such as that are rare and shed light on an aspect of Christ that not many know about. It will be an excellent addition to our churchyard."

Bernard Walke had been vicar of St. Hilary's for some twenty years, and his parishioners had grown accustomed to his High-Church practices. He celebrated mass frequently and with reverence. He used the Book of Common Prayer, but emphasized all the sacramental elements of the service. He introduced incense and icons. To some outsiders the Anglo-Catholic orientation made the place unrecognizable as Church of England. He liked to think of himself as a gentle soul—a peace advocate both during and after the Great War. And his mail attested to a national following of the broadcast of his devotional plays from the parish on BBC radio.

Being on the wireless was all well and good, but the beautification of the church was a greater pleasure. After a parish-wide cleaning, he had come up with the idea of resurrecting the tunic cross from its dank cellar tomb and displaying it prominently along the path leading to the entrance of the church.

How troubling that his wife and greatest ally did not share his enthusiasm.

"Yes, but why are they rare, Bernie?" The question was rhetorical.

"Now Annie—"

"You know as well as I do that religious intolerance still exists, and those bands of sectarian zealots out of Plymouth—the ones that call themselves 'Kensitites' and 'The Protestant Truth Society'—are still doing everything they can to fight what they call your Popish ways." She shook her head, as the flicking of her wrist drew up loop after loop of white cotton thread. "They still come by to disrupt the services. They say they have a judgment authorizing the removal of the things you worked so hard to restore in the church."

"That case in the Consistory Court is nothing to be concerned about. They have no proper jurisdiction over the church. They just got some woman who never attends our services to claim that she is aggrieved by what she calls our stone idolatry." He turned to the next letter in his stack.

"You cannot keep ignoring the writs. The officer has been by several times this week trying to serve you."

"It's a matter of principle, Annie. The Consistory Court employs the language and forms of the old spiritual courts, but that continuity was broken and its spiritual nature lost when it began allowing appeals to the secular courts on spiritual matters. I will not plead before such a court or accept its judgment on such things." He sighed. "But I see your point about keeping that tunic cross in the safety of our cellar, at least for now."

෴ ✤ ෴

The next afternoon, Father Walke—as everyone but his wife called him—mounted his horse to take a pleasure ride up Tregonning Hill and treat himself to a view of the vast Cornish countryside. On clear days, one could see all the way to Land's End and Bodmin Moor. As he settled into the saddle, a young woman from the town ran up to the vicarage gates, shouting, "They've come, Father!"

He turned back. "Who has come?"

"The radicals!" she shouted. "They are in the church itself!"

Father Walke went pale as he realized who she meant. He ran to the church with a parishioner—the bell ringer—and attempted to enter the main door of the church. They found it barred from the inside, so they made their way around to the priest's door leading to the Lady Chapel. Father Walke pounded on the door and shouted, "Open up, this is the priest!"

The door cracked open, and the two were admitted—only to find themselves at the mercy of a thuggish bunch in workmen's clothes. The bell ringer made a dash for the belfry to ring for help, but three ruffians quickly restrained him.

"Oh, dear God!" Father Walke howled. Several men were pillaging the church, smashing the statues at the side altars. A pair of them toppled the image of the Blessed Virgin. All was a blur of havoc and desecration. Closing his eyes, he tried to take himself elsewhere, but could not. The crash and clatter of brass and shattered pottery assaulted his ears.

The only privilege the pillagers allowed him was that of taking the Blessed Sacrament to safety in the vicarage. As he walked by, a few parishioners, seeing what was going on as they returned from school or work, lined the churchyard path, kneeling and praying.

As I pass from the tumult of passion, the world of quiet faith is now out here with the people.

⚜

Crowbar Raid on a Church
Kensitites at St. Hilary
Ornaments Carried Off
Vicar a Prisoner

Dreadful headlines blazed across the front pages of the London papers. People countrywide and even overseas responded with a wave of donations in solidarity with Father Walke and his ravaged church. Postal money orders and checks began arriving in the mail within days. Throughout the week, the people of the parish used the funds to restore the church.

Carpenters and masons repaired the building. Other images were brought in as replacements for those carried off.

On the following Sunday, Father Walke led a Mass of reconciliation. Once again, the church was made cheerful with flowers. "We are eternally grateful to everyone from near and far who gave money or lent a hand to help restore our parish home," Father Walke declared during the sermon. His voice cracked with emotion, and he paused to recover himself. "It is surely the work of the Spirit that in a few short days our church is restored, nearly to what it had been. But I fear that the peace we have enjoyed these past years may be at an end. We must stand strong during this difficult time. We must not be afraid of those who despise us, and as Our Lord taught us, we must love our enemies as we love ourselves."

A special meeting of the parish followed the service. All semblance of order was dashed in the anger and frustration of the members. Many demanded a police investigation and prosecution of the outsiders. Others pointed out that prosecution would be difficult in light of the order of the Consistory Court that backed the raiders with some color of law.

"And what about poor Father O'Donoghue's headstone?" asked Matilda Lawrence. The frail gray-haired lady, the matron of the parish, hardly ever spoke. The pews fell silent, and all turned to listen. "I still remember him from when I was a girl. What did he ever do to deserve having his grave defaced?"

"She's right!" declared Tom, a burly miner. "They smashed his headstone to pieces. Surely, that Constancy Court—what is that anyway?"

"The Consistory Court," corrected one of the parishioners. "It's an old ecclesiastic court from the Middle Ages, run by the bishops. It doesn't do much of anything nowadays."

"Humph! Surely a court would not authorize grave robbery!"

"The court only authorized the removal of the listed objects from inside the church," said the lawyer. He was a vestryman from Penzance and a longtime friend of Father Walke. "The court only has jurisdiction over the interior of the churches; it has no authority over graveyards. I wouldn't call it grave robbery—a good case for grave desecration, though."

"My friends, we are losing sight of why we are here." Father Walke rose. "This is a house of peace. We come here to reconcile all men to God, even those who despise us. Besides, I'm sure that ruining the headstone was an accident. I saw the motor coach back into it while trying to turn around. The driver got out and apologized for the damage."

Father Walke's words only partly quieted the anger in the pews.

"At least they ought to pay damages," Tom muttered.

A number of people agreed.

Annie took a turn to speak. "Let's use the tunic cross from the basement of the rectory as a new headstone for Father O'Donoghue."

Bernie looked at his wife, a bit shocked. "If it had not been for you speaking up before the raid, that old cross could have been smashed to bits. These radicals despise anything that smacks of idolatry. I am so glad I listened to you in keeping it safe where it is. Why are you changing your mind now?"

"Too much has been destroyed," Annie replied. "It brings me to tears to think about it. They didn't just destroy our things. What we lost were symbols of our Christian faith that no money can replace. The tunic cross shows Christ as a child. Now most of all, we must be as children, and without fear, we need to trust in our Father. It is important to show this symbol to the people of our parish. We mustn't hide it!"

Bernie smiled. His wife's wisdom and sense of calm never ceased to amaze him. She was right.

A few parishioners spoke up, dead set against the idea, afraid of what might happen to the precious artifact if the raiders came back. Others were more interested in pursuing retribution. Nonetheless, the idea of using the tunic cross gained support as others chimed in.

"I can certainly keep an eye on the churchyard," the constable said.

"Besides," added the lawyer from Penzance, "the exterior is beyond the power of any future writ from the Consistory Court."

Some of the raiders came back to disrupt the services by singing their own hymns in an attempt to drown out the voices of the choir. The second Sunday on which this happened, the police came by to take names, and some were later convicted of brawling and violating an order of the King's Bench obtained by the lawyer from Penzance.

The raiders never returned after that. Maybe they feared the law was now on the side of the parish, or perhaps the they finally realized that they would only be stirring up public sympathy for the church, along with a fresh outpouring of donations, if they made the papers again.

≈ ✤ ≈

The new plaque of polished stone to mark Father O'Donoghue's grave had arrived a week after the Mass of reconciliation. Father Walke, wanting to wait for all the fuss from the raid to die down, held off from affixing it to the tunic cross. Parishioners still distraught from the raid and its aftermath called on him for more pastoral support. But Annie was not to be put off forever, and she kept reminding Bernie that he needed to get on with it. On the appointed day, it took three burly men to carry the tunic cross up from the vicarage cellar. Father Walke wanted to help, but the men said he would only be in the way.

Slowly but surely they carried the cross up the cellar steps, down the hallway, and out of the front door. The lead man carrying the base suddenly lost his footing, and the bottom of the cross fell to the pavement with a thundering crash. His scream rang out.

"Are you all right?" asked Father Walke.

"It only just missed my foot. What's this?" The man reached down and pulled out a loose chunk of the stonework. "I'm afraid my clumsiness broke the statue, Father."

"At least you still have your foot. I hate the thought of you being laid up and unable to work. Are you sure you are unhurt?"

The man nodded.

"In that case, can you chaps turn it over? Let's have a look at it… It's not so bad. The stone must have cracked over a period of time. We can cover the hollow in the base with the plaque when we cement it on."

The men took up the cross once more and carried it to a cart to be pulled by a donkey to the churchyard. The usually docile creature chose this day to be ornery. It made quite a sight and entertained the women watching as they hung out their laundry, to see the men try to cajole the beast along. Not even Father Walke's prayers seemed to help. It took a little girl running up and holding out a carrot to entice the beast forward.

It was the middle of the afternoon before they reached the churchyard. The men laid the cross on the ground face up and started mixing the cement. They were about to start applying it when Father Walke stopped them. "Can you men come back to finish up after you get off work Saturday? I've just remembered something I must do, before I…before I consecrate this cross, and I need to pray about it."

The men exchanged glances. They seemed to take the request as something strange at first, but they agreed to come back and finish the job.

༄ ✻ ༃

On Saturday they returned as promised. They did not seem to notice that someone had already cemented the new polished stone plaque over the lower front side of the base. They planted the cross upright in the ground and poured fresh cement around the base to keep it stable.

Father Walke thanked the men. Once they were gone he looked over the monument. The new plaque bore the words from the old broken gravestone: *"F. T. O'Donoghue, Priest, died March 18, 1881."* The tunic cross itself, with its poignant image of the Christ child, looked beautiful, even after so many centuries.

Alone with the relic, Father Walke knelt and felt around the edge of Father O'Donoghue's plaque. The seal had to be airtight, and it was. Months before, he had come across an ancient paper that one of the parishioners had found in a sealed bottle, in a box, in the cellar at the bottom of the old thirteenth-century tower. The writing was faded but still legible. *The Secret of the Lord,* it read in an antique script. Below that, a rubbing showed five horizontal lines intersected by dozens of cross marks. He had vaguely remembered seeing something like it, years ago, in an Irish museum—an old Celtic script called Ogham that dated from the time of Saint Patrick.

He had tried to track down a scholar to translate the writing, but with St. Hilary's being such an out-of-the-way place, he'd had no luck. And now, with the news his doctor had brought him the evening before the men hauled the cross to the churchyard, he was rapidly running out of time. Tuberculosis, the doctor had told him. The diagnosis meant that within a few days Father Walke would be in the sanitarium, forced to retire.

I pray I made the right decision. I felt the Spirit guide me to keep the secret safe again. Whatever the secret was, concealed in that ancient writing, he felt that it belonged with the carving. The hollow was just big enough to form the receptacle. Folded now into a small stoppered bottle and covered under the plaque and cement, the paper was safely ensconced within.

The fading light of dusk still illuminated the stone figure of the boy with his outstretched arms. Father Walke felt as if the boy, newly entrusted with the Lord's secret, now yearned to share it.

The Holy Spirit knows best. The secret will be revealed when the world is ready for it, even if I do not live to know it.

Chapter 5
The Tin Finder

Near the Celtic village of Carn Roz, A.D. 9, during the reign of Augustus, first Emperor of Rome

Kendrick

Kendrick guided his ship slowly westward along the southern coast of Britain. Fair winds had taken them swiftly past the hostile shore inhabited by the Durotriges, and they had finally reached the land of the friendly Dumnonii tribe, who inhabited the long peninsula known as Belerium that stretched westerly from the south side of Albion. It was still a long sail to Ictus, which lay close to Belerium's very western tip, and the prevailing wind had turned. Now it was from the west. The lug sail rig allowed for some progress to be made into the wind, but the ship sailed much more across the wind than into it, tacking from one direction to the other.

With a friendly shore to the north, it was no longer necessary to stay several miles out to sea. They caught a few glimpses of the shy natives when the boat stopped briefly for water at the mouth of the River Plym.

They proceeded slowly westward until midmorning of the sixth day from their launching across the *Oceanus Britannicus*. As he brought the boat around onto the other tack, Kendrick noted with satisfaction that he would be able to make the entrance of the River Fal.

Pirro came over to join Kendrick at his station on the steering oar. "It is a foul business sailing a ship into the wind, forever going this way and that."

"Aye," growled Kendrick. "It's like crawling up a slippery slope. And now we battle the tide, too. If I did not play the wind shifts to the best advantage, we would not make any progress at all."

"How far to Ictus? Can we get there by sundown?"

Kendrick pointed to the right where the coastline curved off into a distant mist. "You can almost see Lizard Head from here. It is about ten miles ahead, all of it upwind and against the tide. From there we will turn more to the northwest, but it will be another twelve miles to Ictus. If the wind veers to the left, we may be able to sail in directly on one tack once we pass Lizard, and make it to Ictus…oh, sometime tonight at the earliest."

Joseph had approached, listening. "That will not do," he grumbled. "The Sabbath begins tonight at sundown. I cannot conduct any trade until sundown on the morrow."

"It would be best not to arrive while my partner is indisposed," said Pirro. "The native merchants will not understand his devotion and will take it for rudeness. Besides, we are all weary of the sea and long to spend a day on dry land."

Kendrick smiled. "We will make for Carn Roz, just inside the harbor ahead. It is the village of my cousin Bannoch. He will feed us handsomely and find us comfortable beds. I long to visit him and his family." With his decision made, Kendrick beckoned one of his crew to take over the steering.

"Your cousin Bannoch sounds like a generous man," Joseph said.

"He's actually a very distant cousin. Bannoch's great-grandfather was the brother of my own great-grandfather. When he settled his family among the Dumnonii, the hill fort king granted him several hillsides on the east side of the harbor. Others of our people joined him later. This was before that dark day when Julius Caesar crushed the Veneti."

"Did they purchase the land?" asked Joseph.

"The Dumnonii are a simple people. They do not understand money. Their peninsula is even more isolated from the rest of Britain than Armorica is from Gaul. The community owns the land, and the people give a tithe from what they produce to the hill fort king in exchange for his protection. Farmers and herders barter with artisans for tools and goods. We will need to make a gift to Bannoch in exchange for his hospitality."

"Perhaps a roll of Roman linen from Lugdunum," suggested Joseph.

"Yes, that will do nicely," answered Kendrick. "The natives here turn flax into linen too, but it is much coarser than what we have. They will appreciate the lightness of your fabric."

The ship sailed between the headlands that lay astride the entrance to the River Fal. A magnificent harbor, it stretched four miles north and south and about a mile east and west. In most places, rocky cliffs fell to the shoreline, but here and there, flatter stretches, with beaches and tidal pools, offered an easier landing. Half a dozen creeks and rivers emptied into the harbor. Kendrick said that a network of navigable waterways reached miles further inland.

Looking to the west side of the harbor entrance, Kendrick pointed out to Joseph and Pirro a fortification atop the headland. Called Pen-Dinas, the headland was nearly an island, connected to the mainland by a narrow isthmus, protected by the steep slopes leading from the water's edge. The slope was not so sheer as to render an attack by sea impossible, but more than steep enough to weaken attackers trying to make their way uphill against a hail of arrows. Earthen and stone ramparts guarded the isthmus. "The hill fort consists of three ramparts laid out in concentric circles," said Kendrick. At the very top is a clear meadow, commanding a view far out to sea."

"That would not hold out very long against the Romans," observed Joseph.

"No, it would not," agreed Kendrick. "Most of the cliff forts in this land lie atop much steeper cliffs that are impregnable from the sea. Compared to most Celtic tribes, the Dumnonii are a peaceful people, although they don't shy away from fighting when circumstances call for it. The hill forts here are simpler structures than in the rest of Britain. If trouble threatens, the people bring themselves and their cattle to the hill fort. Most of the hill forts lack any supply of water or sufficient land inside to graze the cattle, so they provide protection only for a few days while the king summons help from his neighbors. Only a few of the elite warriors are in the king's permanent armed retinue; the men of the villages would do most of the manning of the ramparts."

"What about the people on the east side of the harbor?" asked Pirro. "In time of danger, surely they do not ferry their cattle across the water."

"They have a more traditional hill fort inland, on a small rise of land. The king sends his retinue back and forth across the bay to support both forts in times of trouble," Kendrick replied.

As the ship rounded the headland on the eastern side of the harbor, it turned north. This brought the wind to the beam, allowing the crew to break out the main square sail to good advantage. They sailed past the entrance of the Percuil River, which emptied into the east side of the harbor, and soon they heard shouts of greeting from the boys of Carn Roz, who recognized Kendrick's ship.

Kendrick sailed his ship into a tidal pool halfway up the harbor on the east side and brought it alongside a massive rock that formed a convenient natural quay. By now, the villagers had gathered along the shore to greet them.

As the crew secured the ship, Kendrick spotted Bannoch, a sinewy, mustached man standing with his wife, son, and daughter. Aside from the deference paid by the other villagers, the intricate bronze torc around his neck, his silver belt buckle, and his wife's silver earrings distinguished the family's station in life. Their work clothes, made of sturdy linen and wool, were similar to those worn by the other villagers, except cleaner. They all wore simple laced leather shoes.

Kendrick embraced his cousin. "Bannoch! I trust the season finds you well and prosperous."

"The gods be with you, my friend." Bannoch wore a checkered, belted tunic over dark brownish-red leggings. "You bring passengers. What brings them to our land?"

Kendrick introduced Joseph and the others. "They've come from a country far to the east, by way of the ancient Atlantic trade route."

Bannoch raised an eyebrow, but he said nothing other than to invite the party to his home to refresh themselves. Kendrick knew Bannoch was too shrewd to engage in a business discussion before he knew more.

Bannoch's son did not share the same restraint. The eleven-year-old had been among the urchins greeting them from shore earlier. Fedwig was a freckled, fair-haired boy. Undistinguished by any ornaments in contrast to his father, he nonetheless seemed to be confident of his station in life. Kendrick lifted him in the air, saying "Ah, Fedwig, how you have grown over the winter! I can hardly lift you."

"I am too big for that now," Fedwig replied, trying to maintain his dignity—to the amusement of all. "That will cost you a present!" True to his word, as soon as his feet were back on the ground young Fedwig began searching the captain. Despite Kendrick's protestations that he had forgotten to bring anything, Fedwig soon was grasping a fine new cowhide ball freshly picked from Kendrick's pocket bag. With a shriek of delight, he ran off into the meadow, accompanied by other boys, to play with it.

"Now, something for you, my dear Golia," said Kendrick to Bannoch's daughter, who wore a green tightly patterned sleeveless dress that reached a few inches below her knees. Kendrick pulled out a polished comb carved from bone. The girl was taller and more reticent than her younger brother, but her broad smile still betrayed her delight with the gift.

"You spoil them too much, Kendrick," said the wife. She hugged Jesus and Daniel, welcoming them. She was a strong woman with a kind, freckled face.

"Forgive me, Tilda." Kendrick laughed. "I cannot help myself."

"Come, let us retire to our home," said Bannoch. "Your passengers must be weary from their journeys, and I will not be having them thinking ill of our hospitality." With that, Bannoch signaled to the others that the excitement was over for now and that they should return to their daily tasks.

Jesus

Tilda proudly showed off the family home. It was similar to the structures that Jesus had seen in the pirates' lair, but instead of wattle and daub, the walls were of stonework integrated with the stone wall that surrounded the village proper. Although nothing was carved into the circular wall, pagan idols and trinkets hung from the rafters that supported the thatched roof. Animal-skin blankets covered a large bed for Bannoch and Tilda. Two piles of reeds were formed into crude mattresses covered with woolen blankets, evidently for the children.

A few of the villagers brought in more cuttings and quickly formed them into beddings. Tilda said that Kendrick and Joseph must take the big bed during their stay. Kendrick started to object, but it was useless to deny Tilda the chance to provide that measure of hospitality by giving up her own bed. The boys would sleep on the mattresses. Pirro volunteered to spend the night on the ship. Looking at Uncle Joseph, Jesus could tell Joseph was pleased for the chance to rest from his weary travels on a real bed.

Kendrick explained to Tilda that Joseph and his young charges could not eat pig or shellfish, but would be more than happy with any kind of mutton, beef, or scaled fish.

"But why do they deny the hospitality of the village? Surely, they do not think I would serve them meats with any harm in them," Tilda responded. Bannoch frowned but said nothing, evidently yielding to her position as undisputed mistress in matters of the home.

Kendrick shook his head. "It's no reflection on your hospitality. Jews must obey the commandments of their God from the east." He paused. "It is like the *geisa* imposed upon the greatest Celtic heroes. Remember King Connaire, who was forbidden to kill birds. He was not allowed to go south around Tara or north around the plain of Brega. He was forbidden to hunt the wild beasts."

"Yes, I remember what the druids taught me in my youth," Bannoch interrupted. "King Connair was like many heroes and kings who had so many prohibitions laid down on them that they could not possibly abide by them all." He exchanged looks with Tilda. This was becoming a matter of honor and faith beyond his wife's domestic authority; she would now defer to him. He withdrew his hand from his sword and smiled. "It is best to respect the obedience our guests render to their god. Otherwise that god might turn on us."

Pirro happened to be standing next to Jesus. "Did you follow that?" Jesus asked him in a whisper.

"Kendrick lost me when he started going into the Celtic legend," Pirro whispered in response. "The important thing is that he was able to appease Bannoch so quickly. The Dumnonii are incredibly gracious with their hospitality, but like all Celts they are quick to anger in response to any real or imagined slight. After a battle, they will even fight to the death in the banqueting hall if a warrior feels slighted because he is denied the best cut of meat—what they call the hero's portion."

"Very well," Tilda said. "I must go to the banquet hall to prepare for a feast tomorrow, in honor of our guests." She made a little bow toward Joseph, who nodded in return. "Golia, fetch some refreshments for cousin Kendrick and his friends."

"Yes, Mother."

Tilda left, and Golia turned to a little cupboard on the other side of the room and arranged bread and cheese on a platter.

"That looks delicious," said Jesus, "and I appreciate your hospitality. But I'm not hungry, and if you will excuse me, I'd like to explore the village." He turned to Uncle Joseph. "May I, Uncle?"

Joseph nodded his permission and said, "Yes, but don't wander too far."

Jesus leaned over to Daniel. "Shall we go explore?"

Daniel's eyes remained on Golia. "Umm. No. I'll stay here with…with Father."

Joseph did look weary. And perhaps Daniel was hungry.

As he strolled through the hamlet, Jesus stopped occasionally to ask people how they worked their various crafts. About a dozen round huts built on similar stonework sides as the chief's house made up the village proper within the confines of the surrounding stone wall. Other huts beyond the wall, where most of the workers appeared to live, had walls built from the same crude plaster construction he had seen in Bembont.

Most of the men and older boys had returned to their fields and herds across the hillsides. Those who remained in the village were mostly women, but a blacksmith and his helper worked on forging an iron plough tip in one of the stone huts.

A foul smell came from another hut, where a team of women tended a large, boiling pot. Jesus poked his head in and learned they were rendering water, animal fat, and ash into tallow for soap and candles.

In other huts, women worked spindles and looms, turning wool and flax fibers into cloth. A large, strong woman tanned hides while another made shoes. Some of the women worked outside, turning stone querns to grind whole grains into flour. In another hut, a woman brewed mead, which Jesus tasted and found rather to his liking.

Daniel

Golia placed the wooden platter on the low table in front of Father and asked a question in her unintelligible tongue. Daniel knew something of the speech from his previous visit, but the dialect he knew was from the eastern side of Britain. His skill was also wanting after his long absence.

Pirro said one thing, and Father another.

Kendrick tousled Golia's hair as if she were a boy, and then apparently excused himself, for he walked out.

Pirro sat cross-legged on the floor by the table and shoveled food into his mouth. Golia brought him a cup of wine. Mouth full, he grunted something that might have been thanks.

Golia turned her ocean-blue eyes on Daniel and said a single word.

"Umm...sorry?" he muttered.

"She asks whether you want some wine," Father said.

"Are you not having any?"

He chuckled. "Despite Jesus's reassuring teaching on the matter, no."

"Ah. How do I say 'no thank you'?"

Father gave him the Celtic words, and Daniel repeated them. He helped himself to a piece of cheese and found it turned to paste in his dry mouth. He swallowed a half-chewed clod. "Gah...Wa...water?"

Father translated, and he and Golia spoke for a minute.

She was perhaps fourteen, just on the cusp of maidenhood, with long flowing locks of golden hair rippling down her back. The hem of her dress left her slender ankles exposed.

"She has only wine and mead in the house, but will draw water for you if you want."

"Don't go to any trouble on my account. What's mead?"

"A drink made from fermented honey," Father said.

"Is it forbidden?"

Father thought about this a moment. Golia stared at them, wide-eyed.

"Under the circumstances, I think not," Father said. "You may have some, if you like."

"All right, then, I'd like to try it." He looked at her as he spoke, hoping his smile didn't look too foolish."

Father relayed the request, but when Golia turned to the table to fill a cup from a pot-bellied clay jug, Father leaned closer and lowered his voice. "Daniel, no flirting with the *goy*."

Daniel's cheeks burned, and he longed for the drink.

Jesus

The largest structure in the village was a well-used banqueting hall, constructed like the stone huts with a base of stone, but on a larger scale, with two circular rows of pilings supporting a framework for the thatch. Jesus passed this by and wandered further down the pathways of the village.

He found Kendrick greeting a strange-looking man dressed in pristine linen garments that were of a finer material than those of the others.

Unlike the other villagers, he showed no inclination to talk to Jesus, giving him instead a long stare before going on his way.

Kendrick stepped closer to Jesus. "That was Belenus, the local druid. Don't worry if he seems mysterious and unfriendly. All the druids are that way, particularly with strangers. They are supposed to be all-seeing and all-knowing, so they need to maintain an air of mystery."

"I read in Caesar's account that the druids counsel the Celtic kings. Is Bannoch required to consult Belenus?" Jesus asked.

"It goes beyond that. While Bannoch is the undisputed chief of the village, to the druidic way of thinking, Bannoch may act only in ways that are consistent with the plans of the gods. It follows that he cannot ignore or refuse the druid."

"So it seems the druids hold the real power. Kings and chieftains are mere figureheads."

"Not so. Although the kings are subject to the laws proclaimed by the druids, the druids must do as the kings and chieftains ask, unless they determine it is an impious thing. This mutual dependence between king and druid goes back to the beginning of the world, as the Britons understand it. Another thing that keeps the druids in check is the common belief in their infallibility."

"Doesn't that strengthen the druids' power?" asked Jesus.

"The people have been known to turn on the druids when they meddle in secular affairs, particularly when they are caught in errors. So they are usually content to leave it to the kings and chieftains to make the mistakes that are inevitable in governing—particularly in the conduct of wars and diplomacy or in planning the crops. Queer as it might seem, infallibility can be quite a burden."

Jesus paused to consider that. "I see your point," he finally said. Jesus was about to ask Kendrick more about the druids, but the captain put him off. "My ship is still tied up in the tidal pool. I must attend to it before the retreating tide leaves it high and dry."

Jesus walked out beyond the walls to a village common. There he encountered Daniel trying to understand Fedwig and Golia. Daniel leaned closer to Golia. "Sorry, again?"

She prattled on for a while about a Celtic game called "Hide-and-seek."

Jesus listened to the rules and translated them for Daniel. "Sounds a bit silly," Jesus muttered, "but Golia is very eager to play."

"It sounds like fun," said Daniel.

"Does it?" Jesus said.

"Come on," Daniel muttered.

Fedwig and Golia led the two strangers to their favorite spot, a small meadow on the edge of the forest that offered various hedges and trees for hiding. Fedwig began his count, and the others took off in different directions.

Jesus ran into the woods. With the voice of Fedwig fading behind him, he felt a sense of freedom and contentment he had never known before. There was something about this land of the Dumnonii that he could not put into words. His feet sprang across the soft ground. Maybe it was the smell of the wildflowers or the warmth of the afternoon sun. He looked back at the village with the smoke of its fires wending through the thatched roofs; they might be crude by Roman standards, but these were good-hearted and welcoming folk. They had no tax collectors; they did not even have money. As he looked over the rolling hills, he felt like running for joy as far as his legs could carry him.

In the distance, he heard Fedwig still counting away and turned his thoughts back to the game. He spotted the perfect hiding place behind some fallen trees and rocks. He jumped in quickly with plenty of time to spare.

A voice spoke softly in Hebrew, "Jesus, come out."

Jesus peered out between some leaves and looked for Daniel. That had to be him; Fedwig and Golia obviously did not speak Hebrew. But he wondered why his cousin was not speaking the more familiar Aramaic. "Go away, Daniel," he said. "This is my hiding place. Go find your own." Waiting for a few seconds, he heard and saw nothing.

"Jesus, come out," the voice called again.

Why would Daniel do this? Fedwig was almost at the end of his count, and Daniel's voice would surely lead Fedwig to discover them both. "Just go away," he said in a harsher tone.

"Jesus, come out," the voice called a third time.

This was strange indeed. It did not really sound like Daniel. Could it be Joseph? No, it did not sound like him either. Who else could it be?

Jesus's mind raced, and then he remembered a story from the book of Samuel. Samuel had been called when he was just a boy assisting the high priest around the Ark of the Covenant. Jesus suddenly realized to whom the strange voice belonged. Jesus got up from his place of hiding, went into the field, and said, in Samuel's words, "Speak, Lord, for your servant is listening."

Then God the Father made himself known to Jesus and took him back further into the wood.

When they paused at a clearing, Jesus stooped down to remove his sandals.

"Why do you do that?" asked the Father.

"Did you not say to Moses that he must do this on the sacred ground in your presence, Lord?"

"Yes, but Moses was a man. He was a great prophet, but nonetheless a man. You share my divine substance. Surely, you know that you are my true son, and there is no need for a son to stoop down to undo his sandals in the presence of his father. Come, and fear not. Let us talk as father and son."

"But how can I share your substance, Father? I don't know what that means, and I have no divine powers."

"Remember that you are also begotten of your mother, which now makes you of one substance with her as well. You are both fully human and fully divine. For now, most of your divine nature lies hidden from you beneath the surface. Your human nature is what you are most aware of and what other men see. But surely you must see things happening around you that are beyond the power of ordinary people."

"Yes, Father. I have seen the hand of divine power all around me. I saw it when we feared all was lost off the Isle of Creta, and suddenly a divine calm settled the sea. I saw it when the rainbow appeared to show Uncle Joseph how it would guide his way across the sea. But I only prayed for these things. I did not make them happen; you alone must have done that."

"That is true. Right now, your human nature governs, and you cannot avail yourself of the power to move the might of heaven. You can only pray like any person, but those powers lie within you, Jesus, and so much more. You will make the blind see, make the lame walk, and raise the dead. Eventually you will judge the souls of all men and rule my kingdom on earth. No mere human can wield these powers. To use them, your human substance must release itself and surrender to the divine substance within you."

"How am I to do that, Father?"

"First you need to grow in knowledge and wisdom. The hardest part is not in using divine power, it is in knowing when not to. Your divine power could end all your struggles and suffering, Jesus, but that would swallow up your humanity, and your incarnation among men would be meaningless. You need to live among people and struggle through life as they do, for that is why you came down from heaven and became flesh. This takes time, Jesus."

"You talk of my 'incarnation' rather than my 'birth,' Father. How old am I?"

"In your human substance you are thirteen years old, but you possess wisdom and knowledge far beyond your years. Even within the bounds of your human substance, you taught the great doctors in the temple at Jerusalem. That is merely what is on the surface. Your divine substance is infinitely greater; it has all the knowledge and wisdom of the ages, for in your divine substance you are the Word of God, eternally begotten by me before the beginning of time. In the divine realm, there was never a time when you did not exist."

"I suppose I should be trembling in fear right now. I am sure Moses did. Any righteous man would in the presence of God, but I do not."

"That comes from your unseen divine nature, my son. There is a special love between us borne before the beginning of all time that can never be undone. "

Jesus closed his eyes. *I have never known such peace as I now feel. How can it not be so when I bask in my Father's love?*

The Father seemed to be waiting patiently for Jesus to reopen his eyes before he continued. "Your divine knowledge and power lie hidden from the human substance which now governs your perceptions and actions as a human child. When you became incarnate as human flesh, you put aside your divine dignity—but even as a child you have spiritual gifts that will remind you of your divine nature and assist you on the path that lies before you."

"What do you mean by spiritual gifts, Father?"

"You have the gifts of tongues and the interpretation of tongues. Those gifts allow you to both speak and understand any language spoken on Earth.

"You also have a keen understanding of the physical world, Jesus. Already you have seen that at work on the seas. You will help your Uncle Joseph build his fortune while you are here in Britain, and your gift in sensing the physical world will guide you in your work. As you scratch the earth's surface to uncover its riches, so too will you be revealing to yourself more of your divine substance, which is hidden from you now.

Jesus felt so much emotion, so many contradictory feelings, welling up inside him, that he began to sob. "I am so unworthy. I have so many faults. How can I be divine when the God I know is perfect?"

"There is a reason for everything, Jesus, even in what you see as your faults. Your divine substance has always been perfect, but for now it is hidden. In your human substance, you remain a boy, and that now largely controls what you do and know. As you grow older, you will grow in knowledge and wisdom. Before the time comes for you to fulfill the purpose for which you became incarnate on earth, you will achieve the full measure of perfection in your human substance as well. When that time comes, your divine nature will come forth to abide within you together with your human substance in perfect harmony and unity of purpose. Until then, the divine knowledge and powers that abide within you will unveil themselves as appropriate to your stage in life—as a boy for now and soon as a man. Do not judge yourself harshly, Jesus. You are still far too young to assume the burden of infallibility."

Jesus paused to reflect before he spoke. "Kendrick just told me how infallibility is a burden to the druids."

"We are not conjurers of cheap tricks, you and I. There is much for you to learn from the druids, my son, but remember that their magic is false and the infallibility you speak of is only what foolish men perceive. True infallibility is not the same." The Father continued with a note of sadness. "Trust me in this: The burden of true infallibility is far greater."

"Father, if you are all powerful, all knowing, and all good, how can there be evil in this world?" Jesus asked.

The Father laughed. "You see, Jesus, when word about infallibility gets out, suddenly *everyone* becomes a critic, including my own son." He continued in a serious tone. "But do not worry about offending me. Jesus, as a son of man you cannot truly judge what is evil or good in the world without understanding my purposes. When I created the world, I created a perfect existence for man in the Garden of Eden, where death and pain did not exist; but I also granted man the power of free will. Through Adam, man chose the way of death and turned away from God and into sin. Jesus, you will be the hope for humankind. You will show a pathway for a world of imperfect people, and it will lead them to salvation, reconciliation, and a perfect existence—if they choose to follow it.

"Your path is not an easy one," the Father continued. "The time has not yet come for me to tell you everything I will ask of you. You will make choices of your own free will, just as everyone does. Before you come to fully know and understand the divine substance within you, you may even turn from me. You may doubt your own sanity. For if you do not struggle with your choices as all people must do, then they mean nothing. Do not let yourself be troubled by this. Now is the time that is set aside for you to learn and grow. In time, you will learn to surrender to your divine substance and bring it to the forefront of your existence. Then you will be ready to begin your ministry, which will lead the world to true freedom.

"Come, Jesus, let me show you something. Do you remember how Daniel knelt at your feet the day he came with Joseph to Nazareth?"

"Yes, Father. We all thought he was going crazy. Did you make him do that?"

"No, Daniel did that of his own free will. I merely showed him the divinity within you, like this." With that the Father created a small pond with its shoreline right at Jesus's feet, and he caused the surface to be absolutely still, creating a perfect mirror.

Jesus looked down and saw, for the first time, his image in divine glory.

Overcome by the shock, he fainted.

※

When Jesus awoke, he found himself in the hiding place he had picked out earlier for the game of hide-and-seek. It seemed so long ago now.

His talk with the Father must have gone on for more than an hour. Would Daniel be sounding the alarm to call out a search? He needed to find the others before that happened. Peering through the branches, he made out the figure of Fedwig searching around. Quickly, he stood up and waved. "Here I am, Fedwig; I am all right," he shouted.

Fedwig let out a sigh of exasperation. "You're not supposed to get out and shout like that. You're supposed to stay hidden and make me find you!"

"But I've been away for a long time. Wasn't everyone worried?"

"What are you talking about? I just finished my count. We were all together moments ago!"

Jesus looked up and noticed that the sun was still at the same angle as when the game started.

Now he understood. He and God the Father had talked outside of any concept of earthly time.

"I'm sorry, Fedwig. My head is a little out of sorts. I must have been on the ship too long. Please carry on with the others; for now I need to run."

As Fedwig stood dumbfounded, Jesus took off, running tirelessly and with unbounded joy across the fields until the men of the village began to return for the evening meal.

Joseph

The next morning, Joseph looked up from the scroll as Daniel continued to chant the verses from *Deuteronomy*. Once again, he spied Jesus looking out the doorway instead of at the sacred scroll. What was this? Jesus had always been devoted to the reading of Scriptures on the Sabbath, but ever since sundown, the boy's mind seemed to be elsewhere. He was about to deliver a gentle reproach when Daniel looked up from his reading, too. The two exchanged a look. Whatever was going on, Daniel appeared to know about it. So Joseph held his counsel for the moment and bade Daniel to continue the chant.

When Daniel reached the end of the passage, Joseph signaled him to stop and called for a break. Jesus got up and left. Daniel was about to follow when Joseph asked him to stay. "Why does Jesus let his mind wander from the readings?" Joseph asked. "Is he so ungrateful to God that he cannot keep this first Sabbath after our deliverance from danger and slavery?"

"No, Papa, he loves the Lord today more than ever." Daniel hesitated. He could see that Joseph expected an explanation. "Jesus told me last night that he was called by God."

"And what did God call upon him to do?"

Daniel sighed. "Nothing really—he's supposed to trust his feelings more to bring forth his divine nature."

"So, he now believes that he is God?"

"It's not quite like that. He said that he is both the Son of God and the Son of Man. He also said God revealed his inner divinity to him. He said there was more, but he was not ready to tell anyone yet. The way he described it was just like what I saw the day we came to him in Nazareth."

"Daniel, you make no sense. There is only one God, the creator of the universe. It is one thing to say that Jesus has the favor of God or even that he is a great prophet. But he cannot be divine like God. To be divine is to be God. God would not have a son and make him half a God!" Joseph sat down and buried his face in his hands. "I cannot believe he is such…such a blasphemer…"

Daniel's voice made him look up.

"I don't know how to explain it. I only know what I saw and what Jesus told me, and I believe him."

"Did he say anything about crucifixion?"

"No. He said God talked to him about who he was and how he came to be here. It wasn't so much a prophecy of the future."

"Your cousin never ceases to amaze me, Daniel. But I tell you this truly, that if his destiny takes him to a cross he will die on it, and I fear what will happen to his faith and love for God when he learns that. I remind you this is something we must never speak of to him. God will tell him when he is ready. You promised me that, did you not? It is all I ask of you."

Daniel nodded. "Yes, Papa, I remember."

"Very good. Stay here. I will find Jesus and talk to him now." Joseph left the hut and found Jesus leaning over a low stone wall and gazing out on the village and its fields.

"So, Jesus, must I remove my sandals? I have never walked in the presence of a divine being before."

Jesus broke out of his reverie and smiled. "Do so if you wish, but it does not matter, Uncle. You are a good man. Besides, I wouldn't know how to strike anyone down, even if I wanted to." With that Jesus turned back to look out over the view. "So—Daniel told you."

"Yes, I pressed him about what was going on when I saw you were not paying attention to your prayers."

"Don't be troubled. I was going to tell you anyway, and I am sorry about not paying attention to the prayers. I had much to think about."

"Were your questions answered?" Joseph asked.

Jesus laughed. Then he turned to Joseph. "I'm afraid that every answer leads to more questions. There is even more that is mystery to me now."

"Shall we return to our prayers?" Joseph gestured toward the house. "It is still the Sabbath, and the chanting of Scripture delights the heart of God."

"I think I have chanted enough from Scripture today, and I feel it would delight God even more for me to marvel at his work. That's what he told me to do—to trust myself." Jesus turned to look down the fields and over the tidal pool where Kendrick's ship lay aground on the mud. "Look at that, Uncle. Is not God's creation marvelous? He gives each creature what it needs, from the tiny worms in the mud to the chief of the village who welcomed us so warmly. This is a happy land, Uncle. The people are simple and primitive, but they are good of heart. They are not burdened by foreign oppression."

"They are pagans, though," said Joseph. "Surely, you know the druids lead these people into many superstitions. They have false gods for every tree and river."

"They are merely ignorant, and I don't think God is finished with them yet," said Jesus. "Surely, he will send them the message of truth and righteousness."

"Are you going to be the messenger to these people?" asked Joseph.

"Before yesterday, I would have said 'Yes, no question. Find me a druid, and my words of truth will slay his falsehoods,'" Jesus answered. "But now I see how little I really know."

Joseph was relieved to hear Jesus express humility and self-doubt. He would need to learn tolerance among pagans of all types. Perhaps a little less Scripture and more time for discernment would do him good.

Besides, Jesus was now old enough to be a man under Jewish law, and if he insisted that God was somehow calling him from prayer, who was Joseph to gainsay him? So, Joseph let him be and returned to continue the chanting of the prayers with Daniel.

Fedwig

As the sun began to set in the west, Fedwig joined the rest of the villagers at the feast of welcome in the common dining hall. It was a splendid affair with plenty of mead and pig meat. He could not sit with his father. Sons were not permitted to appear with their fathers at public affairs until they were old enough to take up arms. The Dumnonii were less rigid in this, but for big banquets, Fedwig was used to banishment to another table.

Kendrick presented the linen from Lugdunum. The gift was well received. As the meal was almost over, Jesus entered and watched from the side. Father soon spotted him and summoned him to take a seat at the head table. Fedwig observed Jesus as he begged off the pig meat and took only some hot bread, fish, and mead. These strangers in flowing togas and sandals who kept to themselves were mighty odd. This one could not even play a decent game of hide-and-seek.

The mead continued to flow well after everyone's appetite was sated. Then the men began the drinking songs. Jesus soon picked up on the choruses and joined in. After another song began, all the men suddenly stopped, leaving Jesus to finish the last chorus alone with Mother. At the end the company gave them a round of enthusiastic cheers, and Mother embraced Jesus in a warm hug. Fedwig laughed and clapped with the others.

During a lull, Kendrick regaled everyone with the tale of their escape from the pirates, giving much credit to the cleverness of Jesus. Soon there many calls for another song, and they pressed Jesus into service. Fedwig could tell that Jesus had taken a boastful pirate drinking song and changed the words into a lament. The audience, helped along by the intoxicating mead, found the combination of sad words and bright tune riotously amusing, erupting in wild cheers when Jesus finished.

As Pirro and Kendrick walked with his parents back to their hut, Fedwig trailed behind.

Father asked, "Was that tale about the pirates true?"

"I assure you it is," Kendrick said.

"Far too true," Pirro muttered. "That boy has some strange magic about him."

Does he mean to question Jesus's trustworthiness?

A stern look from Kendrick silenced the Greek merchant, but the mention of magic caught Fedwig's attention. He forgot all about Jesus's strangeness and inability to play hide-and-seek. Jesus was now his idol.

Jesus

The next morning, Fedwig, downcast, tagged along after Jesus as the travelers walked down to the ship. "You have to leave already? You just got here."

While Uncle Joseph and Daniel climbed aboard, Jesus turned back to Fedwig and clapped his shoulder. "Don't fret. I have a feeling we'll soon be back."

Fedwig grinned.

Kendrick and his passengers set sail on the tide. As they rounded the harbor entrance, a fresh following wind took them rapidly southwest.

Jesus watched with a longing gaze as the mouth of the Fal dropped astern. Then he heard Uncle Joseph's footsteps approaching.

"I hear you were quite in your element last night. Could not the son of God have waited for the end of the Sabbath before joining the pagans in their carousing? I thought you were going to spend the day contemplating God's creation," Joseph admonished.

Jesus smiled. "Come, come, Uncle. The Sabbath day should be a day of rest and joy. These people are God's creatures, too, and we were making our home with them. So, why is it not proper to join them for their communal banquet? Do we not eat among our own relatives at home throughout the Sabbath?"

"Tell me at least that you did not join in the libations to their gods."

"No, Uncle, I drank no toast to any pagan god. Nor will I ever do that."

Pirro

By early afternoon, they spotted a small rocky island that rose two hundred feet above the water. As they sailed across the bay and drew near, they spotted wagons making their way across a tidal causeway.

"Look, the merchants see us, and they bring their wares," said Pirro.

"Yes, that is Ictus." With the tide low, Kendrick sailed the ship as far as possible into a shallow cove between the island and the causeway that linked it to the mainland. Kendrick led his passengers on a short trek across the mud flat. But when they examined the merchant carts, they were disappointed. There were samples of various wares, principally grains, woven cloth and ceramics, but no metals of any kind. If they filled Kendrick's ship to the brim, they would not have enough to make the expedition worthwhile.

Kendrick was surprised to discover that his passengers had come this way in search of tin. "I wish I had known. I would have told you back in Nantes that the tin trade from Belerium died years ago."

Pirro swallowed to quell the bile rising in his throat. Joseph would consider him an idiot or worse.

Joseph glared at him, and then he turned to Kendrick. "I'm sorry. We didn't want the secret of the tin treasure getting out all over Nantes. That secret doesn't matter much now, and I wish I had put my trust in you, Kendrick."

"I saw the carts when I was here before." Pirro spoke fast. "All the Greek and Roman historians said this place was known for tin. They even named Britain the 'Casserides,' after the word for tin ore. I wasn't here to trade for tin back then. I had no reason to look in the carts. How was I to know? This is not my—"

"The damage is done," said Joseph. "I'm ruined."

Only one of the wagon merchants had ever sold tin, but he had sold the last of his stock to a Belgic trader a month before. The merchant explained, "When we sell tin to the traders from the east, it travels across the lands of many tribes before it reaches the Romans, and each tribe demands a share of the price. What the Romans are willing to pay does not leave much for us after those other tribes take their tolls. The only tin we sell is what can be panned from the streams, and that is running scarce after centuries of mining."

"Do you have some of the ore for me to see?" asked Jesus.

The trader produced a small, brownish-black, oily rock.

Jesus held the sample in his hand and felt its weight. Then he looked across the bay to the low-lying hills on the mainland. "I think this ore can be found all around us. We just need to know where to dig."

The merchant laughed. "You'll do a lot of digging."

Jesus turned to the men. "The Lord wants this venture to prosper. He will guide me." He pointed to a hill that rose to the east across the bay. "Let us go tomorrow morning. We will find tin ore by the evening."

The three men exchanged glances. Each must know what the others were thinking, but how could they say it? If not for Jesus, they would all be in a chain of slaves heading into some god-forsaken corner of this country.

"Give the boy a chance for a day," said Kendrick. With nods all around, the others agreed. It did not take much to secure a few picks, shovels, and hammers. The merchant agreed to bring them to the spot identified by Jesus at dawn the next day.

In the morning Kendrick landed the ship on the shore four miles to the east of Ictus. They quickly concluded the purchase of the tools, and they followed Jesus inland. "How far are we going?" asked Daniel.

"We have to get to the foot of the hill. That is where the best veins will be—a little more than a mile in," Jesus answered.

The cunning boy led them along a well-trodden trail to an enclosed hillside village. Once again, he weighed the sample rock in his hand and looked around. A hill fort was just up the hillside. Jesus pointed to a spot to the south of the fort's circular rampart. "We will dig right there."

"I know these people," said Kendrick. "Go on ahead, and I will have a few words with the village chief. That's his hill fort. It's called Pencaire."

Jesus swung the first blow with a pick. Daniel and Pirro joined in with shovels.

Kendrick soon returned with the village chief.

By early afternoon, they had dug five feet into the ground. By then, Kendrick had taken Jesus's place with the pick. As he swung it again they heard the sound of cracking rock.

Jesus grabbed a pick and took another swing. "Yes, that's it, I feel it now."

Soon they cleared away the dirt layer, exposing the bedrock. Jesus took a heavy hammer and swung with all his might. The rock broke cleanly along a fault line. Jesus took out the ore sample the merchant had given him, and he compared the sample with the rock his hammer had uncovered.

"Is it the same?" he asked, and Kendrick said, "It certainly appears to be identical."

The village chief was shocked that strangers had found the lode of ore so close to the surface, right under his nose.

Joseph was shrewd enough to close the deal. "Tell the chief we will give him an amphora of fine wine for each three cartloads of ore his people bring to Ictus," he said.

Kendrick translated, and the deal was done.

"Well, this wasn't quite what you expected," said Kendrick, with a laugh.

"Not what I expected," agreed Joseph, "but we have a supply of ore, and we know the Romans will buy the finished ingots. All we have to do is refine it and transport it."

"See, I told you there was tin—" Pirro stopped when Joseph gave him another scathing look.

He's still angry. He will give Jesus all the credit if this continues to go well, and he will forget that trade with Ictus was my idea. If it goes badly, he will blame me, not that precious nephew of his.

Chapter 6
Days of Awe

Joseph

This was not going to be the simple exchange of goods for tin ingots that Joseph had planned. He had expected to be well on his way back across Gaul by now with a cargo of tin, but it had fallen to Joseph and his own people to oversee mining and refining the ore. Some of them would need to stay behind for that.

Joseph gathered everyone in Kendrick's ship. He looked from one member of the company to the next. "We cannot trade profitably by just bartering with the merchants," he said. "Their supply of tin is too unstable, and they have little else we can sell at a profit in Gaul or anywhere else in the empire." Joseph paused for effect. "On the other hand, if Jesus can locate veins of ore, we have more possibilities. It does not take much to get the locals to dig the ore and bring it to a convenient trading post on the shore. All we need is a base camp where we can refine the metal and cast it into ingots."

Joseph looked at his great-nephew. "You seem to like it here among the Dumnonii." Jesus was smiling already. "I take it you wouldn't mind staying for a while?"

Silence fell over the group. No one doubted that Joseph could require the boy to stay, but it would work so much better if he had his heart in it. Jesus's smile turned into a serious expression as he considered the situation. Then he said, "Very well, Uncle, as long as Daniel is with me and we can stay in Carn Roz."

Daniel smiled. He had no objection.

Kendrick let out a great laugh at Jesus's feigned attempt to drive a bargain, and then he turned to Joseph. "You cannot find a better place than Carn Roz. The harbor and its streams take you right into the heart of tin country. It's also an easy sail on the ocean from Carn Roz over to here, or by sailing east with a good wind you can reach the mouth of the Tamar in half a day. That covers most of the places tin is found."

"Daniel will join you," Joseph told Jesus, "and we will make the base at Carn Roz if Bannoch will have you."

Daniel and Jesus beamed at each other.

"There's little doubt of that," Kendrick said. "Tilda would never forgive Bannoch if he refused the boys. We will need to give Bannoch something for supplies and protection, but it will not be much. The druids might have something to say about this, but we can deal with that."

"I can stay behind, too," offered Pirro. "I can help with the tin operations and look after the boys. Mainly, I can look through the villages to trade for the better weaves of cloth, pottery, and anything else we can sell for a profit in Gaul. There will be plenty of space left on Kendrick's ship for lighter goods, once we load on as much tin as we can."

In their first conversation at the tavern in Lugdunum, Pirro had made it seem so simple, as if the Britons in Ictus were eager to shower them with tin ingots in exchange for trinkets. If not for Jesus, Pirro's scheme would have led to Joseph's ruin. He could not blame Pirro for their perils at sea, but he had to wonder if Pirro had ever been to Ictus, as he claimed when he painted such a rosy picture. Nonetheless, Pirro was an experienced trader, and there was little to go wrong with the idea of using empty space on the return voyages to bring back staples and curiosities from Britain to sell to the Romans and Gauls. Joseph reluctantly nodded.

"What about you, Uncle?" asked Jesus.

"I have other commitments in Gaul and elsewhere. I cannot let my regular customers forget me. Besides, you seem to have a knack for finding tin, and there is nothing more I can teach you about it. I will leave the initial load of trade goods with you and Daniel. Use them to purchase the ore and anything else you need from the natives. I must do what I do best, which is to carry on my business and come back as often as I can with more supplies, wine, and other things to trade."

Elsigar

Fedwig burst into the clearing, out of breath.

Elsigar looked up at Fedwig, then glanced at the sundial and sighed.

The boy had arrived just in time to avoid punishment. The others were already seated on some logs. Why did the boy always try his patience so? It was just as his predecessor had told him: Nothing good ever came from Carn Roz. It seemed to Elsigar that Bannoch and his Dumnonii villagers hardly paid any attention to the druids at all. True, the Carn Roz villagers took part in the four great feasts of the year, but they treated those occasions as just another excuse for carousing and drinking mead. They went through the motions, but they did not seem to be true believers.

Elsigar still visited Carn Roz to judge the occasional lawsuit or criminal case because he was the only druid skilled in law—a *brithem*, in their language. For the most part, he left druidic affairs concerning Carn Roz in the hands of the novice Belenus.

"Today, we begin the study of potions," Elsigar said. "What do we normally need to work a valid spell, a curse, or a blessing? Come, Fedwig, surely you remember that."

Fedwig mumbled in response.

How dull this lad must be. Elsigar frowned. "You must pay more attention, Fedwig." Elsigar called on another boy.

"For any magic to work, the druid must be qualified. The druid must be present with the subject or something that he possessed. The druid must intend to work the magic, and the druid must perform the spell properly," the boy responded.

"Correct," Elsigar said. Only priests had the authority to perform magic. That was a longstanding law. He was about to differentiate the usage of potions when he noticed Fedwig scowling. "So, Master Fedwig, you don't seem to approve. Perhaps you would care to share your thoughts?"

"I have heard of magic performed by a visitor in our village, and he is no druid," Fedwig replied.

"Blasphemy!" Elsigar cried. He grabbed his cane and lashed out at the insolent boy. When Elsigar heard the tale of how Jesus had magically effected an escape from pirates, he was determined to speak to Belenus when he saw him that evening. Elsigar had to make sure that the novice would inform him if these visitors ever returned.

Belenus

Belenus waited with Bannoch's family and the villagers on the shore the next day as Kendrick sailed into the tidal pool. He had been surprised to see the ship return so soon, but he had Elsigar's instructions and had sent for the senior druid.

Belenus allowed Bannoch's family to greet the visitors, but when he heard Kendrick explain their intent to establish a base camp at Carn Roz, he knew he had to act quickly.

He raised his hand to call for silence. A hush fell over the villagers. All eyes turned to him. He pointed to Jesus. "Elsigar would talk to that one." Without giving the visitors a chance to concoct a story, he summoned Jesus to follow him.

Jesus turned to Kendrick and Bannoch, but they both indicated he had no choice but to follow. Belenus saw Joseph start to object, but Kendrick silenced him with a quick gesture. So Belenus set out with Jesus in tow, up the hill into the woods and then to a clearing where Elsigar awaited them. With him was his council, which included six other druids. Unlike Belenus, who wore ordinary clothes, Elsigar and his councilors wore flowing white robes and adorned themselves with gold ornaments. The midday sun filtered through the leafy canopy, intermittently causing the druids' golden visors to light up like haloes.

For several hours Elsigar questioned Jesus. He wanted to know everything about the journey to Britain, and more particularly all that had occurred of a supernatural nature. The boy maintained his composure and answered every question.

Once his questions were exhausted, Elsigar withdrew, together with his councilors, leaving Jesus in Belenus's charge. Without understanding the words, Belenus and Jesus could hear through the trees a heated discussion.

Jesus asked Belenus to explain what the councilors might be arguing about.

"I can only surmise from my training. I didn't see proof of any crime, so I doubt that many will insist on punishing you. The real issue is whether to permit you and the others to stay. It is not an easy question. Even if they believe you, some will say you are imbued with the influence of a powerful god, and that could upset the spiritual balance between nature and men among the gods we know. They likely will try to invoke fear of the wrath of our own gods."

"But since they argue, there must be another point of view."

"I imagine that others are saying that excluding you, and requiring the people to turn their backs on their long tradition of hospitality, would be a display of fear. They would say our gods are not so weak that they need fear the presence of another god from the east. Druids always seek knowledge, so some will want to learn the ways of your god."

"Why did Elsigar question me so closely on whether I practiced any magic?"

"That could be the deciding point. Having an outlander here invoking incantations and spells without druidic training would be a great impiety. It could undermine the spiritual balance we work so hard to maintain, and it would make the case for the fear mongers who wish to exclude you. But if you are simply the subject of a spiritual force, as you seem to say, then it becomes very difficult for them to argue against you. The gods bless or curse all men to some degree. If they believe you, the protection you appear to have from your god would actually work in your favor, particularly among those who are governed more by their quest for knowledge than by fear."

"How will they make the decision? Do they take a vote?"

"Elsigar is the only lawgiver among the councilors. He will decide one way or the other. He must first consult with the others and hear each point of view. Each has his own expertise: history, incantations, healing. The *faith*, the soothsayer, will speak after all the others have had their say. Then he will reveal the entrails and interpret them." The sound of arguing ceased from across the forest . "They must now be waiting on the *faith* to carry out the divination. It may not be long before we hear the decision."

"The waiting grows tiresome," said Jesus.

"You seem confident."

"I told the truth," said Jesus, "and God wants our voyage to succeed. I don't care about your incantations and divinations. God will show Elsigar the truth."

Elsigar returned with the councilors. They stood in stoic silence in a circle around the edge of the clearing, waiting for Elsigar to render his judgment. The fading sunset set their robes aglow and gave the proceedings an ethereal quality.

"I find no deceit in the boy," Elsigar began. "It appears he practices no magic. The escape from the pirates, the finding of the tin, and all that occurred beyond ordinary forces known to men came about through the acts of his god, not through any supernatural power invoked by him through any incantation, potion, or other magical art. Nor does he intend us any harm."

He turned to Belenus. "Keep an eye on the business the visitors conduct in the village. As long as there is no impiety in what they propose, leave it to the chieftain or the king to negotiate with them. Although these visitors do not believe in our gods, it is not impious to extend hospitality to strangers or to trade with them. Keep me informed."

Elsigar and the councilors solemnly left the clearing in single file.

Daniel

With no objection from the druids, it did not take long for Papa and Kendrick to conclude their negotiations with Bannoch. He was more than happy to take a modest share of Papa's trade goods in exchange for providing the needs of Pirro and the boys, as well as their protection. Fedwig was delighted that Jesus had returned so soon, and Tilda welcomed Jesus and Daniel into the family home to stay.

Daniel was still having a difficult time understanding and making himself understood, but the language he had picked up among the Cantiaci on the previous visit was coming back to him, and the dialect of the Dumnonii was starting to feel more natural. The way Golia kept laughing when he spoke made it clear that his tongue still marked him as an outlander.

Daniel glanced over his shoulder to make sure his father was still outside with the other men. He turned back to Golia. "I am sorry we're such trouble." She had seemed a little put out that she had to give up some of her space in the family hut.

"Oh, well it's... I didn't mean..."

He took a step closer, bowing his head close to hers. The top of her head didn't even reach his chin. "Are you sure? Perhaps I should sleep in the woods."

She giggled and nudged his shoulder. "Don't be silly." She bundled up the rest of the things from her pallet. "It's no trouble—"

"Golia!" Tilda called. "Come help with the dinner."

"Yes, Mama." She dropped her little bundle on the pallet she'd now have to share with her parents, and ran out before Daniel could say another word.

Papa left most of his trade goods in the village before sailing with Kendrick on the next tide, taking with him enough to conduct some trade in

Ictus. He left instructions for Pirro, Jesus, and Daniel to meet him at Ictus two days after the next Sabbath.

They took over an abandoned hut at Carn Roz as their base camp. Daniel worked with Jesus and Pirro to fix the roof and to construct a smelting furnace. The blacksmith fashioned a smelting pot from iron and offered instruction about the construction of the furnace. Fedwig and the other boys helped them gather clay for the ceramic furnaces, and Tilda arranged for the tanner to make the bellows from animal skins.

With the smith's guidance, Daniel and Jesus constructed a low cylindrical hazel-wood frame. They mixed clay with ground rock to make cement and covered the framework thickly. Holes in the bottom allowed for refueling and for inserting the bellows. The work was most intense for the first two days, but then they had an easy day, waiting as the smith helped Pirro to fire the ceramic structure of the furnace. The boys lounged on a hillside nearby. Daniel wondered where Golia was.

Fedwig was the first to get bored with watching. He ran off, returning with his sword. Not a sharpened sword, but more than a plaything. Cast of iron, it was weighty enough to teach the boy the proper handling of a weapon. Daniel watched with Jesus as the boy turned and whirled, thrusting his instrument at imaginary foes.

"Is there another sword for me?" Jesus called out.

Fedwig grinned. "Sure!" He ran off again.

Daniel looked at his cousin in shock. "What do you mean, Jesus? We are traders. We come in peace. Ours is not the place of war."

"Maybe not," Jesus replied, "but war is an art I must learn if I am to lead the Jewish nation to freedom someday. Besides, we are making our home here. If we look to Bannoch's people for protection, should we not be prepared to help as well?"

Daniel's heart pounded. He remembered his father's words about the prophecy of death that lay ahead for Jesus. "Papa will not approve."

"He is not here, and he need not know."

Daniel frowned and sat up straight. "You do not have to take up arms to free our people. Jesus, do not follow this path. It is the way of death. It cannot be your destiny."

Jesus looked sternly at Daniel. "You forget yourself, cousin." His voice dropped. "More than that, you forget who I am. Do I have to remind you how you got down on your knees at my feet because you saw the divine within me? Everyone thought you were crazy, but you were right. I am not only the Son of God; I am eternally one with him. God the Father has told me that, and he also told me I should trust my feelings. My feelings tell me that I must prepare for the day I lead our people from bondage, as their Messiah." Jesus paused, scowling. "I don't need your father to tell me my destiny, and I certainly don't need you for that."

"Was it not the hand of God, rather than the sword, that parted the sea for Moses?"

"The Romans might not let our people go, the way Pharaoh started to. You forget how Joshua, David, the Maccabees, and so many other heroes of our people fought to drive the heathen from the Promised Land."

Tears blurred Daniel's vision. He could practically see his young cousin suffering in crucifixion already. If Jesus were to lead an armed rebellion against Rome, then surely Rome would hang him on a cross. Jesus had to know that. But he expected God to save him. He did not expect to be forsaken there. "There is more that even you do not know, Jesus."

"Really? What?" asked Jesus, growing impatient.

Daniel shook his head. "I cannot tell you. Papa wanted it left between God and you. I promised not to say anything."

"Then don't! Keep your father's confidence, Daniel. At least he puts his trust in God. I won't ask you to choose between obeying Joseph's commands or mine." Jesus cocked his head while continuing to stare down his older cousin. "At least I won't quit yet. Just don't tell him what I'm practicing."

Fedwig returned with another sword. Jesus took it and imitated the moves he had seen the boy perform. Fedwig held up his own sword, and the two boys thrust and parried. Jesus managed to dodge a few of Fedwig's slashes, but then the tip of Fedwig's sword caught a corner of Jesus's toga and rent a gash, exposing his midsection. With another quick move, Fedwig placed the point of his sword against Jesus's throat. He smiled triumphantly.

As the two held that position for a moment, Daniel stood. "Perhaps it is better not to be a swordsman at all, rather than be a mediocre one. It would seem much safer that way."

"Oh, I give up." Jesus cast down his sword. "Confound this stupid toga. If we are to live with the natives we might as well dress like them. Let's go and see Tilda about proper British tunics." He turned to Fedwig.

"Don't worry. I'm just getting started. You will show me later what you know of the sword and battle axe, won't you?"

"Of course!" Fedwig beamed, obviously flattered beyond measure to have Jesus ask for his instruction.

With a sigh, Daniel followed Jesus in search of Tilda. Maybe they would find Golia as well.

Jesus

When the day appointed to meet Joseph at Ictus arrived, the smelting furnace was ready. Bannoch had sent word to neighboring villages that fine wine and spices could be had in exchange for cartloads of charcoal and limestone, and there was a good supply of those essential materials. All they needed was the ore.

Bannoch furnished a guide and a *curragh,* a narrow watercraft made of hides stretched over a woven framework, to take them to the headwaters of the Helford River. From there the guide pointed them in the direction of Ictus. It was a ten-mile trek across open fields. They joked of how they looked like proper British natives now, and whether Joseph would recognize them. Tilda had made up a full outfit with tunic and leggings for Daniel. Pirro declined her offer, refusing to abandon his toga.

Tilda held that Jesus was too short for leggings; it did not make sense to cut cloth for something he would soon outgrow. So she fitted him out like Fedwig with a belted tunic and laced stockings that left his knees exposed. Jesus did not mind; it gave him more freedom of movement.

They set out before dawn, and it was early afternoon before Ictus came into view. Looking across the water, they saw Kendrick's ship approaching from the distance. Waiting on the island for them were two ore-filled carts.

Pirro waded into the channel.

"Shouldn't we wait for the tide to go out?" asked Daniel.

"It's shallow enough. From the top of the hill, I could see the bottom almost all the way across," Pirro replied.

Behind them, the guide was shouting, but he was still out of earshot. "I think the guide may be warning of some danger," said Jesus.

"The tide is just as likely to be coming in. Joseph left me in charge, so I say we go for it."

Reluctantly, Jesus followed Pirro. Soon seawater swirled around his waist. His feet slipped from under him. "Daniel!" A wave broke over his head, filling his mouth and nose with brine. The current grabbed him and dragged him further from shore.

Pirro flailed and bellowed for help as well.

Daniel reached a secure footing and threw a line to Jesus, drawing him back just as the rising water was dragging him out to sea. Together they helped Pirro ashore. Laughing at the outlanders' antics, the Britons enjoyed the spectacle.

"The next time he says 'let's take a chance on the tide,' remind me to stay on shore," said Jesus to Daniel, laughing as the sun began to dry his clothes.

Kendrick brought up his ship. Pirro and the boys were delighted when they saw what he had lashed down to the deck: a sailing craft big enough to carry a few passengers and cartloads of ore.

Kendrick showed them how to work the mast and the sail. With the fore-and-aft lateen sail and larboards, the boat could sail much closer to the wind than Kendrick's ship. They could even bring the bow through the wind from one tack to the other rather than gybing it all around.

"Stay close to shore and keep an eye on the sky," Kendrick warned them. "If the boat goes over with a load of ore, it will sink. Make for land whenever the weather threatens, and reef the sail when you are caught in a storm."

Joseph had brought more wine and goods from Armorica to trade with the natives. "We're off," he said, as soon as Kendrick's ship was reloaded with staples bartered from the merchants. Turning to Jesus, he whispered, "I saw the rainbow just now!"

"Aren't you coming to Carn Roz?" asked Jesus.

"Time is money for Kendrick, his crew, and his ship," said Joseph. "This was supposed to be a few days from Gaul, remember?" Then looking to Pirro and Daniel, he continued, "Back in Gaul, the River Liger will soon dry up for the hot months of summer, but we will bring the best wine, spices, and anything else to be had anywhere in Gaul worth trading before winter sets in. Until then, use what you have to trade for the ore and make as much tin as you can. My fortune is now in your hands."

Kendrick's ship set sail for Armorica with Joseph. Jesus, Daniel, and Pirro set to work. They soon had the small sailing craft loaded with tin ore, but with daylight starting to fade, they decided to stay on in Ictus until morning. After watching the sails of Kendrick's ship disappear into the approaching dusk, Jesus took a good look at his companions. *Pirro's lack of good sense almost got us drowned, and Daniel is only two years older than I am. Without the counsel of Joseph or my parents, I am really on my own now.* Jesus prayed silently, and then felt better knowing that the Father would be with him.

At first light, the three set sail for Carn Roz. Arriving at midday, they unloaded the ore and with the village smithy's guidance, set about to prepare the first charge for the furnace. First, they crushed some ore into fine pieces. Then they washed it through several pans of water, allowing the heavier pure ore to sink to the bottom while pieces of lighter, impure rock settled on top. They also crushed some of the limestone and charcoal. By then dusk was upon them.

The next morning, the smith helped them determine the right proportion of ore, charcoal and limestone for the smelting pot. They lit more charcoal in the pit of the furnace.

"Heat it slowly," the smith advised.

The three took turns with the bellows. A few hours into the afternoon, the ore began to melt.

The smith peered in. "This is the critical stage. Skim off the slag. See it forming on top of the molten metal?"

After several hours the slag stopped forming, and they used a hoist to lift the smelting pot out of the furnace and over to a vat of water. Many villagers gathered around, watching. Jesus had the honor of tipping the pot to pour the molten metal into the water. With a loud hiss, the slow stream of metal solidified and cracked into knuckle-sized pieces.

As soon as it seemed safe, Pirro reached into the water and pulled out a piece. He tossed it to Jesus amidst cheers. Jesus let it drop to the ground, and everyone laughed. Finally satisfied that the piece was sufficiently cool, he picked it up. It was silvery white with a blue tinge and seemed quite soft for a metal. This was what they had come so far to obtain.

❧ ✵ ☙

Gradually, Jesus and Daniel built up their store of tin. Every week or so they melted down the accumulated pieces and cast a solid ingot.

From sun-up until the day's casting was complete, Jesus was an earnest craftsman, tending the fire with care and working the ore pot. Once the last of the ore was poured off, however, Fedwig was sure to be near with the training swords. Fedwig used his sword in the Celtic style, swinging in broad heroic strokes as if to single-handedly take on an attacking band of foes. Jesus tried to copy the style, but always met with disaster. This was not how the Romans practiced their swordsmanship.

The next time they sparred, Jesus joined Fedwig in a head-on clash of wildly swinging blades. He fell back a few steps. Sensing weakness, Fedwig rushed forward with a triumphant shout. Jesus watched for his opportunity.

Fedwig raised his sword high to deliver a mighty blow.

Jesus found his opening and made a quick thrust to bring his own sword up against Fedwig's throat.

Fedwig growled at losing to a novice.

Jesus clapped his shoulder. "You must be very good at your craft to teach it so well."

Fedwig laughed, and they went to join the others for supper.

Arriving at the dining hall, Jesus found the men of the village leaving. Bannoch pointed across the bay, and Jesus saw smoke signals. "Does that mean danger?" Jesus asked.

"The smoke would not be black if there was danger." Bannoch replied. "This gathering might be called at the behest of the druids, or perchance we are favored with a visit from a bard. I hope it is a bard; druids can be so tiresome. Come to think of it, it has been some time since the king has heard from a bard. Do you still have your Roman toga?"

"Yes, but won't that make me stand out?"

"It is better to stand out as a foreigner than to come dressed as a boy. The Dumnonii welcome strangers, but they do not welcome boys at gatherings of men. Dressed as you are, you would have to stay behind."

Pirro always wore his Roman toga. Daniel could have remained in his British garb, but decided to wear his toga, too. Jesus and Daniel changed quickly and reached the tidal pool just as the men of the village prepared to leave. Pirro brought a few amphorae of the best wine.

As their *curragh* pulled out into the bay, they spotted several craft coming from the entrances of the various creeks and rivers that lined the harbor. All the boats were heading to the hill fort on the other side. As they got nearer, men from the various villages began exchanging greetings and boasts across the water. Once they landed on the headland, they made their way to the top, where they found a whirlwind of activities, even as more men continued to arrive by foot across the isthmus and by boat from the harbor. Some were wrestling and sword fighting, as others watched. Mead flowed freely, but Pirro soon found plenty of takers when he began to offer the wine. Bannoch spoke to some men and announced that the cause of the gathering was indeed the arrival of a bard.

The hill fort king turned out to be an old man with a sparkle in his eye. Resplendent on his chair, he greeted the village chieftains and the principal retainers of his realm. Bannoch introduced the distant travelers. The gift of wine from Pirro was well received, and the king insisted that Jesus, Daniel, and Pirro take some of the best seats in the hall.

The meal began as the summer sun set. Venison was the main course. Jesus and Daniel were glad to partake, knowing they were not doing any great violence to the dietary laws. They had seen how the Celts slaughtered the animals and drained the blood. With mead flowing, the bard recited verses of praise for the heroics of the king. It didn't matter that these must have been tales from the king's distant past. Waves of hurrahs filled the hall as the bard continued, each verse furnishing a convenient excuse for the men to cheer their king and drink more mead.

The hall quieted as the men focused their attention on the bard. This was the serious business of the gathering; to hear the news. The bard sang of distant marriages, wars, and alliances. Although most of the focus was on the Dumnonii, there was also news from lands far and wide. The bard even had word from Rome; he praised Augustus's favorite great-nephew, the heroic Germanicus, and condemned the scheming Tiberius.

The men sat up straighter and listened most intently when the bard sang of raids against the other kingdoms of the Dumnonii. The high king of the warlike Durotriges tribe was ratcheting up his raids on the eastern Dumnonii along the southern shore. And from the north came word of a new menace: the Scotti from Eire were now plundering the northern shore of the Belerium Peninsula. Coming by sea, they could strike anywhere from the mouth of the River Sabrina to the western tip the Dumnonii homeland. True, the raiders had been beaten back for the time being, but not without a cost in lives. Many women and children had been taken away, to be sold to the Romans into slavery.

The bard finished his tales, and then came his chance to listen and gather the news from the mouth of the River Fal. Bannoch recounted the tale of how Jesus led the escape from the pirates of Vectis, and once again Jesus found himself singing the imaginary woeful song of the pirates, much to the delight and cheers of the company. The bard promised to spread word among the Dumnonii that the travelers staying at Carn Roz were ready to exchange wine, spices, and other trade goods for ore as well as for fine cloth and pottery, which Pirro was planning to sell in Gaul.

There was more drinking and carousing, but soon the native men were dropping on the floor or in the chairs, sleeping off the effects of the evening and snoring soundly. The three travelers joined them. The next morning the bard was off to bring news and song to another community, having been well-fed and comfortably housed for his efforts. Jesus and Daniel returned to Carn Roz midmorning and got a late start on the day's work with the smelter. They kept at it well into the evening.

Daniel

After a few weeks, the smelting became second nature to Daniel and Jesus. They soon figured out how to charge the furnace with just the right amount of charcoal, so they could leave it for hours without over- or under-heating. They made use of the additional time by riding horseback over the countryside with Pirro, getting to know some of the other villages. They alternated days, taking turns so that one of them could tend to the fire.

One day while Jesus and Pirro were away, Golia brought Daniel bread and cheese for lunch. He laid aside the map he was studying. "Come sit with me."

She put her tray on the ground and sat nearby. "Shouldn't you be tending the fire?"

"It tends itself, mostly. I'm just waiting for the ore to melt, to skim off the slag."

Golia nodded, her blue eyes looking everywhere but at him.

"You're bored with all this talk of metalwork, aren't you?" He took a bite of bread.

"No, no, not at all."

He scooted a little closer. "You're very kind to say so. And to feed me." He took another bite.

She giggled. "I can't let you go hungry, can I?"

He leaned closer. "Golia…you are…very kind."

Her eyes widened. Her voice quavered a little. "Am I?"

"Mm-hm." He kissed her.

When she leaned into him, he dropped his food and put his arms around her.

She clenched his shoulders. Then she pushed away. "Oh! If my father…" She stood. "I should go."

Daniel jumped up and grabbed her hand. "Don't. Your father—huh. Can't be any worse than my father."

"It's different for you. You're a man. Why would your father—"

"Never mind. Not important." He pulled her close and kissed her again.

Jesus

By the middle of summer, the lode of ore near Carn Euny started to peter out. By then Jesus and Daniel had trained a few villagers to run the smelter. This left Jesus free to journey with Pirro and Daniel as far the River Tamar to map out new lodes of ore in the southwestern lands of the Dumnonii.

Halfway through the Roman month of September, the first fresh hints of autumn stirred the air in the forests. It was the evening before the first of the Jewish month of Tishrei, the onset of Rosh Hashanah, the beginning of the New Year. Jesus and Daniel were back in Carn Roz to prepare for the holy day, a time for reflection and judgment.

Jesus and Daniel were cleaning up the smelter with the aid of their helpers when Fedwig ran up. "There's a sail in the distance," he cried out. "It looks like Kendrick's ship." With that, the boy was off to the shore to join the village urchins and greet the vessel as it made its way into the harbor.

"I hope Papa will be pleased," said Daniel, as the two looked over the stack of tin ingots. Pirro also had his horde of pottery and other export goods purchased from the surrounding villages.

"I am sure he will be," Jesus replied with a confident smile. "This should be enough to fill the hold of Kendrick's ship."

Leaving the remaining cleanup of the smelter to their helpers, Jesus and Daniel made their way to the tidal pool. They arrived just as Kendrick's ship pulled in.

"You have grown so quickly in a few months, Jesus," Joseph remarked as he embraced the two boys. "You're catching up to Daniel."

"I hadn't really noticed, Uncle, but I think you're right." Jesus nudged Daniel's shoulder. Daniel still stood a few inches taller.

"Come see all the tin ingots we have for you," said Daniel.

"Not yet. It's time to prepare for the holiday," replied Joseph. "There will be time enough to count our riches after we have accounted to God for our sins."

"That is how we should start the year," Jesus said.

Joseph greeted Pirro and Bannoch, but would hear no word about business. He had a letter for Jesus from his parents. Joseph's health was up and down. It was not safe for Jesus to return. The Sadducees were gone, but Mary sensed that the rabbi still reported on them. The letter carried as much love as any letter possibly could.

Once Jesus had finished reading, Joseph took the two boys away to spend the next few hours before sundown in contemplation, leaving Pirro to explain to Bannoch that this was just another custom of Joseph's strange god.

With sundown came the onset of the holiday, confirmed by a sliver of light from the new moon. They spent several hours in prayer celebrating God's sovereignty over all, and they continued after waking the next morning. In the afternoon it was time to perform the *Tashlikh*, the symbolic casting away of sins by throwing pieces of bread into a flowing stream. It was far from the elaborate celebration of the holiday featuring the sounding of the *shofar* or ram's horn in the temple and synagogues of home, but they were sure God would understand.

The day after, *Rosh Hashanah* marked the beginning of the Days of Awe. Though it was still the season for repentance leading up to the Day of Atonement or *Yom Kippur*, the law permitted them to resume their work. Only then did Joseph allow himself to view the ingots and trade goods that the boys and Pirro had gathered.

Joseph clapped his hands in delight. The hoard was certainly enough to fill the hold of the ship. He closed his eyes, offered up a prayer of thanks, and embraced Jesus and Daniel. "I didn't expect half of this. You two have made me feel that God has already inscribed and sealed me for a good year."

"Don't forget Pirro, Uncle. He has been traveling constantly among the villages to gather up the other goods for you to take back to Gaul."

"Of course, Pirro, you know this is still the season for Jews to reflect on our transgressions rather than count our riches. So forgive me if I seem a bit restrained. Thank you for looking out for the boys and for all your work."

The boys described their explorations for more tin, and Daniel explained about the villagers doing the smelting. "We can put new smelters into operation as fast as you can bring more wine and trade goods to pay for labor and supplies."

Pirro let out a sigh. He did not appear to be listening.

Jesus saw how Pirro looked distracted. *I feel sorry for Pirro. Even he must see that the profit from this venture will be in the tin and not his trinkets.*

The morning after *Yom Kippur*, Jesus finished writing a letter to his parents. Joseph had brought some scrolls of precious papyrus for Jesus and would take the letter all the way to Nazareth. The Arimathean was heading even further into the east this time, and he would not be back until the following summer, at the earliest.

❧ ✻ ☙

In the year that followed, Jesus continued practicing swordplay with Fedwig whenever he was at Carn Roz. By the summer of his fourteenth year, he could even challenge some of the men.

Jesus, Daniel, and Pirro had built their own warehouse for ingots and trade goods, and they had many smelters going, operated by hired workers. During the year, Jesus traveled through the land of the Dumnonii, finding more lodes of ore. He and Daniel arranged for its mining and its delivery to Carn Roz to be refined and cast into ingots.

Having hired men left Jesus plenty of time for sword drills. It also left Daniel with too much time for pursuing Golia—not that she ever tried to evade him.

Returning hot and sweaty from a day's practice, Jesus longed for a Roman bath. A dip in the stream behind the round hut he shared with Pirro and Daniel would have to do.

As he passed the hut, he heard Golia squeal within, "Stop it!"

He ran inside. Daniel stood behind Golia, his arms around her waist. He nuzzled her neck, and she giggled.

"What are you doing?" Jesus barked.

Daniel frowned at him. "Nothing. Just…playing. Right?" He tickled Golia's ribs.

"Stop!" She squealed again, finally twisting out of his grip. But she laughed.

Jesus closed his eyes a moment, sighing. "Golia." He looked at her. "I want to speak to Daniel—alone."

"Of course. See you later." Her hand trailed down Daniel's arm as she walked away.

"Your timing is awful," Daniel said.

"I think my timing was fortunate. This business with Golia needs to stop."

Daniel poured himself a drink of water from the pitcher on the table. "It's no concern of yours."

"Your father will be home soon. If he finds out you've been consorting with a *goy*—"

Daniel choked on his drink. "Consorting?"

Jesus folded his arms. "What would you call it?"

"It's nothing! Just…fooling around. It's no sin."

"Isn't it?"

"No. It's not. I haven't lain with her." He snorted and lifted his cup. "She wouldn't let me."

Jesus rolled his eyes. "You don't think it's wrong to lust after the beauty of a woman, 'or let her captivate you with her eyes,' as Solomon says?"

"I hadn't thought about it." Daniel dropped onto a stool.

Jesus scoffed. "Of course you hadn't."

"Look, O Perfect One, it's not that easy for us mere mortals."

"I'm just as human as you, Daniel."

"How can you say that?"

"It's hard to explain."

Daniel combed his fingers through his hair. "I know it's wrong to carry on with a gentile girl. But you can't understand the way she makes me feel. It's…" he clutched his hand to chest as if to hold his heart inside. "It's hard to explain."

"You know it's wrong."

Daniel shot up, knocking the stool back. "You can't preach to me. You have your secret, too." He gestured to the practice sword belted to Jesus's hip.

Jesus put his hand on the hilt. "That is totally different. This is something I must do to fulfill my purpose. The only thing you're trying to fulfill is your own lust."

Daniel made a fist and took a step back. Then he relaxed. "You have no idea what your destiny really is."

"And you do?" *He thinks Joseph knows something the Father hasn't revealed to me. But why would the Father reveal something to Uncle and not to me?*

"We've been through this before." Daniel righted the stool. "Papa told me not to tell you, and I'll honor his command. He'll be back soon for *Rosh Hashanah.*" Daniel stepped close, as if to emphasize that he still was several inches taller. "Just keep all this about me and Golia to yourself." Daniel pushed past him and walked out.

✤

Joseph returned not only with Kendrick's ship, but with three more as well. They were needed to carry back all the tin smelted during the year. He brought another letter from Jesus's parents. Papa had taken a turn for the worse, but Mother clung to hope. The gifts from the magi and the savings Mary had put aside in years of prosperity were seeing them through. It was still unsafe for Jesus to return. Jesus surmised that Joseph's condition might be worse than the letter described. The words of love were those that Mother would choose. Joseph must have been too ill to take a hand in the writing this time.

Jesus observed *Rosh Hashanah* with Joseph and Daniel as he had before. During the Days of Awe that followed, they loaded the ships. After a long, hot day of hauling ingots, Jesus walked alone in the woods.

God the Father appeared. "You have done well here in Britain," the Father began. "Your great-uncle is pleased, and so am I."

"Thank you, Father. I am happy to serve you."

"It is not me alone that you serve so well. Do you remember what I told you? How you and I share the same divine nature?"

"Yes, Father. I have thought of that often. But it only raises more questions in my mind."

"You wonder how it is that you can be God, while I am God. And still there is but one God."

"Yes, Father. Exactly."

"You and I are both one as God. There is but one God, and there always will be just one God, as I revealed to Abraham and Moses. My divine nature is poured into yours. It has been that way since before the beginning of all time. But, at the same time, you are not the Father, and I am not the Son. We are the same God in different persons."

"I hear what you say, Father, but I do not understand what it means. I seem to see and do on my own will."

"Like all people, you have free will. That is your human nature. Just as you are begotten of me, so too are you fully born of woman. You are both son of God and son of man. You are fully human, and for now that human nature makes the Godhead difficult for you to understand. It will always remain something of a mystery to other people. As you grow in knowledge and wisdom, it will become clearer to you. Your understanding will come from an unexpected quarter."

"I must be patient, then, Father."

"There is another facet of this Godhead. Do you not sense it?"

A dove descended from the sky. Jesus stretched out his hand, and the dove perched on a finger.

"I sense a source of joy and wisdom at times when I am most at peace, Father. It is not me, and it is not you."

"That is the Holy Spirit, my Son. It too is God and is always with you whenever you open yourself, even when I cannot be seen."

Jesus closed his eyes and inclined his head. He brought the dove slowly towards his lips and gently kissed its head. The dove cooed softly. After a few moments it took flight and slowly circled in the clearing.

The Father again spoke to Jesus. "You performed the *Tashlikh* last year. Do you remember what I said then? You have no need of any ritual to cast aside sin, for sin is what separates man from God. In our divine substance, we cannot be separated."

"But if I have free will, can I not be led into error?"

"Yes, but nothing can truly separate us, the way sin separates God and man. Even in your human nature, everything has a purpose. Your path will not always be clear, and you will make choices that you regret. But you will discover more of your divine nature, and we will be reconciled, no matter what happens."

"Should I stop taking part in the *Tashlikh*, Father?"

"You must make your own choice, Jesus. You will struggle just as all men do. You are the person of God who shares in the life of men, for that is your purpose in becoming incarnate."

With that, the Father left Jesus in the clearing.

A few days later at Yom Kippur, Jesus held back when Joseph and Daniel performed the Tashlikh.

Joseph raised his eyebrows. "Jesus?"

"How can I atone for sin, if I've not—I mean—I haven't sinned, Uncle."

Daniel glared at him.

"All men sin, Jesus," Joseph said. "Every one."

Oh, Father, Joseph will never understand.

Daniel cast his bread broadly across the water. "Of course, the man who's going to save Israel needn't perform the same rituals as we pathetic humans."

"Daniel, that was uncalled for." Joseph recited Scriptures from the book of Micah.

I thought a leader had to be greater than everyone else. Is it possible that first I have to be like everyone else? That I have to be humble and admit that I make choices I regret? Jesus tossed his bread onto the water.

As they walked home, Daniel strode ahead, leaving his father behind.

Jesus jogged to catch up. "What is wrong with you?"

"Not everyone is as sinless as you claim to be."

"Of course not. Look, I took part in the Tashlikh, didn't I?"

"Only because of Papa."

"And you. Daniel, I'm not trying to set myself above anyone. I just—"

"I'm not concerned with you! Why do you always think everything has to do with you?"

"Why are you angry, then? Don't take it out on me because you feel guilty about Golia."

"Why don't you mind your own business?" Daniel broke into a run.

~ ✳ ~

The day after Yom Kippur, Jesus handed Joseph a scroll to take back to Nazareth. "There is so much to say to Papa and Mother, so I have been writing some each day."

Jesus watched Pirro sail away with Kendrick and Joseph on the loaded vessels, back to Armorica. He would make his way back to Carn Roz on the next vessel heading from Armorica to Belenium. *Pirro says he must look to the sale of his own merchandise back in Armorica. He would do better to trust Uncle Joseph and look to what he can do here. He drinks too much of his own wine and then complains that he does not have enough to trade with the Britons. He gambles away most of what he has. After a whole year, he does not even have enough to fill the hold of a single ship.*

Jesus started another scroll that night.

Chapter 7
Rumps

Daniel

They rode out from Carn Roz in search of ore.

Pirro had insisted on tagging along, but Daniel and the others largely ignored him. Although he was older, the others were worldlier. Even Fedwig. It showed in their bearing and confidence as they rode, and in the sense they applied to business.

Jesus, riding in the lead, was now in his sixteenth summer. No longer was he a frail child. Years of sword practice with Fedwig had built definition in his muscles, and he had grown to a man's full height. As a swordsman, he was more skillful than powerful, combining the bravado of the Celtic technique for swinging a weapon with the intensity, focus, and discipline of a Roman. He was a fair match for any of the warriors. Daniel was older, but Jesus clearly was the leader. Even Daniel—*especially* Daniel—couldn't deny him that.

Fedwig's mark of manhood was his sheer size and strength. Younger than Jesus by almost two years, he was nevertheless taller and more stout. His participation in a minor reprisal raid on the Durotriges had secured his place among the warriors. Jesus surpassed him in technique, but Fedwig had learned from Jesus and remained an equal opponent with the sword. The battle axe was Fedwig's chosen weapon. Jesus and Daniel both loved his company and easy wit. Fedwig still regarded Jesus as his hero, but Daniel never felt any jealousy. How could he?

Although Daniel had hardly spoken of them since arriving in Britain, he had not forgotten two things about his cousin. The first was the divine vision he saw in Jesus that day in Nazareth; perhaps that was why he had willingly yielded so many of the prerogatives that were rightfully his as the eldest. The second was the dark prophecy of an all-too-real, painful, and shameful death by crucifixion. Even as Jesus had grown proficient with the implements of war, Daniel had tried to discourage his cousin without violating the oath he had given his father.

Daniel now sported a full beard. Back in Judea, a beard was the mark of a full-grown man, but the Celts, who shaved their faces, leaving only a thick mustache, thought it strange. Except for the implements of hunting, he never took up arms himself. In Daniel's opinion, the fields of war were filled with the corpses of mediocre swordsmen who would have fared far better not to have been swordsmen at all. He saw no point in joining them.

Daniel managed the enterprise in his father's absence, hiring and firing the laborers and negotiating for supplies and transportation, all of which Jesus was happy to leave to him.

Over the rolling hills along the eastern shore of the harbor and the River Fal, they rode.

"We can swim the horses across the river to Trellisick where it narrows just ahead," said Pirro.

"I think I will check the current, unless you would care to go first," Jesus replied.

Daniel and Fedwig snickered. Pirro would never be allowed to forget he had almost gotten Jesus and Daniel drowned, on that ill-considered wade out to Ictus.

Pirro had asked to come along and search for trade goods that would fill the leftover space in the holds going back to Gaul. It could only be kindness that led Papa to keep him as part of the expedition—so the fool could earn at least a modest living. His part of the business was flawed; although the Romans and Gauls liked Celtic artifacts, the more intricately decorated wares from other regions of Britain were more appealing to them. Constantly out to make a big score, Pirro lacked the patience to haggle effectively, and he often gambled or drank away what modest profits he made. Although he claimed credit for bringing them to Britain by way of the ancient tin route, everyone remembered how he had underestimated the effort required to get the tin from Cornwall.

Fortunately, the tide was slack and the horses swam the channel safely. The hills on the other side were easier for the horses, and they approached

Truro, a small community defended only by a single stockade, well before dusk. A sentry challenged them at the gates of the settlement, but Jesus and Daniel were well known, and were allowed to pass.

"That's strange, don't you think?" Jesus asked. "We've often come this way, but the entrance has never been guarded before."

As they rode on to the common, Daniel detected a sense of fear. Truro was one of the settlements among the Dumnonii with large courtyard houses. In the past, the entrances and windows had been open and, but now the travelers found them closely shuttered. The people, who had been most welcoming in the past, now averted their eyes.

"They fear the pirates from Eire," Pirro remarked. "The bards tell of raids in which they kill all the men and carry off the women and children."

"We have heard the stories, too." Daniel slowed his mount to allow Pirro to come alongside. "But we are not even halfway across to the northern shore of Belerium. Don't the pirates just raid along the shore?"

"The pickings along the northern shore must be growing slim," Pirro replied. "Perranporth is less than ten miles away. It's not too far for the pirates to get here and make it back to their ships in a day, if they decide to raid further inland. That is why the people now do not trust travelers."

Daniel nodded. For once, the man was making some sense.

Despite the shuttered homes elsewhere, they were lucky to find the inn still open.

Jesus

The next morning, Jesus looked over the land as they rode forth from Truro. "The spirit is guiding me to the north," he said. "That is where the best ore will be found."

"But that will take us into the greatest danger," said Daniel.

"Let us go first to Castle An Dinas," said Jesus. "King Uryen will know the latest news, and his hillfort is the most secure in all the western lands of the Dumnonii. We will need his permission anyway to extract the ore, and we can hire the workers we will need there."

"Won't the men be afraid to work the tin lodes if pirates are around?" asked Daniel.

"They face danger anyway unless they abandon their homes, and they still need to feed their families," said Fedwig. "The ore is heavy, and the pirates will not be able to carry it off that easily. Working the tin lodes may be the safest thing for them."

Jesus nodded and led them forward.

Dusk was approaching as they made their way into King Uryen's hillfort. Castle An Dinas was the largest and most secure fortification among the western Dumnonii. Three concentric rings of earthworks and gullies surrounded the perimeter, with each ring topped by a wooden rampart. Just as the hillfort was protected from an attack in strength, so too was it protected from stealth. Jesus and his group made their way through a series of switchbacks designed to force any attacker rash enough to attempt the entrance through a killing field of missiles coming from all sides.

Inside, the hillfort was a hive of activity, stretching over twenty acres. Grains were being stored in cellars, livestock were being settled, and artisans of all kinds were closing up for the night. The warriors retreated to the banquet hall, where the mead was already flowing.

The hospitality of King Uryen's hall was offered freely. Though Jesus and could be taken for Britons, Daniel stood out on account of his beard. Pirro, too, had long since adopted British garb, but had not fully mastered the dialects. Most of the chiefs there had dealt with Jesus and Daniel, and some even recognized Pirro. It was enough that they were guests of Bannoch and under his protection for the group to be made welcome at the tables.

Amongst the carousing, Jesus and Daniel quietly blessed their food and offered thanks to God. By now they had learned enough of how the Britons prepared food that sharing their meals was no problem, apart from occasionally having to decline pork or shellfish. Usually there were plenty of other offerings to choose from. They had to avoid wine, because it was sometimes offered up to the druid gods, but the mead never was, so that was safe to drink.

As the meal wound down, the drinking continued and the carousing grew louder. Jesus stood up, and the hall quieted. It was traditional and expected for guests to offer toasts and gifts. "My friends and I offer thanks for the warm hospitality of this castle and of good King Uryen," Jesus began. "May he live long for the peace and prosperity of the people!" Cheers rang out. "As a token of our gratitude, I bring some fine spice from the Orient."

An awkward silence filled the hall. Some of the men jumped to their feet and drew swords. Others calmed them down.

A man with a bent back and a disfigured face stood and faced Jesus. "You are a stranger to our ways, so you must be forgiven for your ignorance. It is a bad omen. Such a gift to someone who is sick implies that spices will be needed soon for burial."

"I am sorry. I meant no disrespect. We have come far and travel light. That is the only reason we brought spice. It travels easily."

The men in the hall relaxed their glares of shock and disapproval.

Then Pirro spoke. "We did not know King Uryen was ill."

Fedwig let out a groan.

Pirro's comment seemed to renew the anger in the hall. From the muttering of the men, Jesus realized that Pirro's explanation had implied that King Uryen's illness was of no concern in the wider world. He signaled Daniel and Pirro to remain silent.

The old man stood once again. "Perhaps you should have looked for our king before offering the gift. Nonetheless, I am honor bound to accept it on his behalf. To refuse even an ill-favored gift would be the gravest insult. That would tarnish the king's name forever."

Jesus looked to Fedwig. Perhaps some of the damage could be undone by withholding the gift. Fedwig seemed to read his thoughts but motioned for Jesus to get up and go to the old man. Evidently, withholding a gift, once offered, would only make the situation worse. All eyes in the hall were on Jesus as he approached the elder. From the burlap bag, he drew out several small earthenware jars. The old man snatched them from him

"I am sorry that my gift has caused sorrow. That was never my intention."

"Nevertheless, you have offended."

"We will leave you for the night."

"That would be wise."

"We will pray for King Uryen's recovery."

❧ ✾ ☙

The group stood outside King Uryen's banquet hall. "That went well," said Daniel. "You don't suppose we should go back in and see if someone will put us up for the night, do you?"

Pirro, oblivious to sarcasm, looked at Daniel with horror.

Jesus chuckled. Then he heard a man laughing behind him. He turned to face a tall British warrior. The man was in his late twenties. The gold torc around his neck indicated he was a man of some rank.

"I know you meant no harm or disrespect," the warrior began. "Grannus was too hard on you. For someone so obsessed with protocol, he should have remembered to offer you shelter for the night. Allow me to make up for his oversight. You must stay the night with my family."

Jesus made a little bow. "May I ask who offers such kind hospitality to ignorant strangers?"

"I am Fergus, son of Uryen."

"The king's son? You have more cause for anger than anyone in the hall," said Daniel.

"It takes a noble and generous heart to welcome into your home such as we, who have brought on such disfavor," added Fedwig.

"You flatter me and blame yourselves too much, my friends. In other circumstances the spice would have made a fine and worthy gift. I care little for omens. Come, we need to move along so my wife can prepare some beds before we lose the day."

Fergus's roundhouse was bigger than most, as befitted his station as heir to the king. His wife bade them welcome and started making up some bedding.

Fergus introduced another warrior, his cousin Tristan, who was a few years older than Daniel.

"How do you come to be living in your cousin's home?" Jesus asked.

Tristan leaned against the wall. "I was orphaned at a young age and taken in by King Uryen. Fergus and I grew up together, so I was pleased to join his household."

Jesus nodded. Such were the ways of the Dumnonii, opening their homes to livestock and all manner of guests, retainers, and distant relations.

The smoke from the fire wafted up through the thatched roof and set an eerie glow to the room. "Fergus," Jesus said, "would you please tell us more of Grannus?"

Fergus snorted. "Grannus is clever. He wormed his way to my father's ear with his flattery. My father became sickly and weak a year ago. Ever since, he has listened only to Grannus. He no longer accepts counsel from me or from any of the others who love him truly. And now, Grannus speaks for a king who knows not what is done in his name."

"On our way through Truro, we sensed great fear of pirates among the people," said Daniel. "But I see no sign of that here."

"The people have reason to fear. They know not where or when the pirates will strike. They come to our villages in the middle of the night to plunder, and leave with their booty before any aid can come. They kill the men and carry off the women and children. They take the livestock and put everything else to the torch."

"What happens to the women and children?" asked Jesus.

"I hear they are worked mercilessly in Eire. I also hear that the pirates have begun to sell them as slaves to the Durotriges, who in turn sell them to the Romans for a handsome profit."

"Can anything be done?" asked Daniel.

"I have begged my father and Grannus for a company of warriors to go forth and punish the pirates. But Grannus feels safe within the precincts of this castle, and he cares nothing for the miseries of the people. He would rather lose villagers than put any of the warriors at risk. It is cruel and stupid to keep ourselves safe within these ramparts while our people suffer."

"The castle seems safe enough," said Pirro. "I do not see how pirates on a raid would ever breach the walls. From the stockade you would see them coming at quite a distance."

"The castle is safe enough from raids," Fergus replied. "But I fear the pirates sense our weakness and indecision. The land in Eire is poor, and they must envy our fertile farms. They must be spreading word among their kings of how the Dumnonii are too fat and soft to attempt any resistance. I fear one day the Scotti will invade in strength. Once they establish a foothold, it will grow until all the Dumnonii are murdered or enslaved. Not even the south shore of our lands will be safe, and not even this hill-fort will withstand an extended siege."

"It sounds as if all the Dumnonii are imperiled—even my family's village at the mouth of the River Fal," remarked Fedwig. "I would join in to defend our lands if I had the chance."

Fergus exchanged glances with Tristan. "And glad I would be to have you fighting by my side, my brother. But the cold night comes on. Let us now rest."

A few hours later Jesus was disturbed in his sleep. He looked up as the waning light from the central fire filtered through the smoke to show

Fedwig fully dressed and gathering up his sword and battle-axe. Quickly, he followed his friend outside. "What's happening?"

"Go back to bed, Jesus. You're a guest of my people. This is not your homeland, and it is not your fight."

"What fight? I thought Grannus refused to send any aid to the countryside."

Fedwig sighed. "Fergus and Tristan organized a small group of warriors. No one's meant to know. They got word that a band of pirates just laid low the village of Padstow. The pirates appear to be camped there, so Fergus will lead his men in a reprisal. They woke me a few minutes ago to ask if I would join them. We must leave quietly. But this is not your fight." He walked away.

Jesus followed. "I did not learn the use of the sword to stand idly by while my friends are overrun in their homes. We have become as brothers, Fedwig. Where you go into harm's way, so do I."

Tristan walked up to them. "What is this? You are not a warrior. You're a merchant, Jesus."

Jesus swiftly drew his sword and, before Tristan could react, pressed the tip of the blade to Tristan's throat. "You were saying?" Jesus asked with a hint of a smirk.

Tristan backed away, hands raised in surrender. "I guess you know how to use that."

"This is wrong, Jesus," said Daniel.

Jesus turned and faced his cousin.

"Do not choose the path of war and death. It is not the path for you."

"These people fight for their lives and freedom." Jesus sheathed his sword. "The cause is just—as just as when David led our own people. It will prepare me for the time when Israel will battle for its own freedom."

"If you go, I go, too!" said Daniel.

"And what will I tell Joseph if the two of you come to harm while I am safely ensconced in this hillfort?" Pirro joined them.

Fedwig rolled his eyes. "We might as well bring the women, too!"

"There is no time to sort out who is gifted with the sword and who is not. Join us, if you will, any of you," Tristan pronounced.

"What is this?" Fergus came walking up. "We said we would take Fedwig—not every trader passing through."

"Jesus knows the use of the sword. He proved that just now." Tristan rubbed his neck. "The others insist on coming too. They know they do so at their peril."

A servant ran up to Fergus. "Your father sends for you. There is little life left in him. He is passing quickly."

"You must stay," Tristan said. "If your father goes, we will need a new king. If you are not here to stand, then Grannus will succeed your father to the destruction of all. I will lead the pursuit."

"Very well, cousin." Fergus clapped Tristan's shoulder. "May the gods be with you and protect you—and all the rest of you, too!"

Jesus exchanged glances with Daniel. He could have done without Fergus's appeal to his pagan gods on their behalf, but this was no time for argument.

Guided by moonlight, they rode slowly at first. Coming alone, and in pairs and small groups, the village warriors joined in. Coming to join them on horseback was a figure Jesus had not seen since the day Uncle Joseph established the tin refinery in Carn Roz. It was Elsigar, the druid. Jesus twitched.

"I thought we came to fight with arms," Jesus remarked to Fedwig as they rode together.

"We did," Fedwig answered. "The druids always come, too. They come to invoke the favor of our gods. The men will not fight without at least one of them present."

"My Father is always with me. I do not need any kind of priest to ride with me in battle."

Elsigar's eyes widened in astonishment when he saw Jesus. But then he turned to Tristan. "The gods will try us. They are angry that the king has denied aid to his people for so long, and angry, too, that he has avoided our counsel. But fortune may yet smile upon us before this business is done."

By now the company had grown to several dozen men. They spurred their horses into a gallop and raced toward Padstow. The full moon shone and cast long shadows across the moor. The wolves howled. The cold night wind roared. Onward they rode to their fate.

Elsigar

The devastation of Padstow awaited them. Smoke from the fires appeared all too quickly in the distance. Ghastly heads of dead men nailed to trees confronted them as they rode into the village. No house remained standing. There was no sign of women, children, or livestock.

Tristan shook his fist. They were too late to catch the pirates.

Then they heard crying: a girl was found hiding behind a tree. She would not speak. One of the men shook her gently, but it only made her cry more.

Some of the men ran up from the riverbank. "We found the pirates' boats," one of them said.

"They're still around somewhere," another muttered, "but judging by the number and size of the craft, we may be outnumbered."

Elsigar turned his attention back to the girl.

"Give her to me," said Jesus. "She has just seen her family killed or driven off." Gently he held her and let her finish crying in his arms.. She pointed across the Camel River estuary to indicate the pirates' next target.

"That would be Rock Village," said one of the men.

The mystery became clearer. "Of course," Elsigar said. "The smoke and flames of Padstow would have been seen from across the river, and the other villagers would have lined the opposite shore to cry out against the pirates." The fierce wind blowing off the moor stirred the estuary into a frenzy of waves. "The crossing is too hazardous, so the pirates will be on the march around the estuary by land."

With some gentle prodding, Jesus got the girl to confirm this. After killing the men and burning the houses, the pirates had left on foot with the women and children of the village.

Tristan pointed to the boats. "Set them on fire!"

"No, stay your hand," Jesus cried. He knelt, folded his hands, and prayed.

Within moments the winds were stilled and the waters calmed.

The men scattered the horses to deny them to the pirates and then set out in the boats.

Elsigar was the last one off the beach. He looked at Jesus with amazement. *He worked no magic, but his prayers to his god are full of power.*

THE MAKING OF THE LAMB

Daniel

They arrived in Rock Village an hour after dawn as the men of the village were making their last stand. The pirates charged in, expecting to scatter the few remaining villagers. Tristan's men leaped eagerly from the boats and attacked, surprising the pirates as they came running from the shore.

Jesus and Fedwig fought side by side. As Fedwig wildly swung his battle-axe, Jesus thrust his sword home again and again with precision. The combination created a killing zone as one pirate after another was caught in the middle and found himself unable to resist both fighting styles at the same time.

Behind them, Elsigar shouted incantations and brought down curses on the enemy.

Quickly, the battle turned.

Daniel was among the last off the boats. He wielded a battle-axe given by Fergus. Running to the village, he found the battle well under way.

The mass of fighting pirates parted for a moment, and Daniel saw the shackled women and children from Padstow. He charged through the gap and began smashing apart shackles with his axe.

The pirates broke off their attack and started to fall back. Those able to turn around saw Daniel freeing the last of the captives—their booty. With a shout, they charged toward him.

Daniel did not know what came over him as he turned and swung the battle-axe. The pirates drew back, not knowing what to make of this crazy bearded warrior. Their hesitation gave Daniel the moment he needed. He turned and ran for his life.

He collected the freed women and children on a hill beyond the village. They watched as the pirates fled into the countryside.

Daniel never expected to find himself the hero in any battle, but that was how he was greeted. Jesus and Fedwig both hugged him, overjoyed that he was safe. Even Pirro had made it out through.

As the sun climbed higher, Tristan burned the pirates' boats. Clouds of thick black smoke billowed skyward. Tristan propped his hands on his hips. "Whatever happens, this band won't make it back to Eire easily."

But the pirates did not fade back as Tristan expected. They stayed out of range yet still near the village, taunting the defenders with shouted threats and boasting that reinforcements would soon arrive. As dusk fell, the pirates lit a signal fire atop a hill. It would be seen for miles out to sea. The threats and boasts were anything but idle.

Tristan gathered his men. "We cannot hold this village if more pirates come. All must make for Rumps Castle. We have two horses.. We can mount two warriors to ride out and alarm the country for all good men to hurry to the castle. With a few dozen more, we can man the ramparts and hold the fort against thousands." He addressed the villagers. "Gather such food as you can carry. Do not linger to save your possessions."

"Which way is the castle?" asked Jesus.

Tristan pointed north. "We will stay on the shoreline so we can see by the moon."

Elsigar stepped forward. "That will bring you to the castle from the west. Rumps is a holy place, and it is forbidden for men at arms to approach from that direction. You must go through the forest."

"Surely the pirates will see us coming and wait for us in ambush," said Jesus.

"It would be a great impiety for men at arms to approach that way. It is the way of the evil druid Athirne," Elsigar replied. "But do not fear. I will turn the roots and trees against the enemy."

Jesus shook his head.

"It is pointless to argue," Fedwig whispered. "The men dare not offend the gods."

"How many of our men must die because of this superstition?" Jesus whispered back. But Fedwig was right. Tristan spoke to Elsigar about sending the women and children, at least, by the safer route, as they would not carry weapons. The druid reluctantly agreed to that.

The two riders prepared to leave. Elsigar whispered some final instruction to them.

Daniel shook his head in frustration. What further mischief could the old druid be about?

Jesus and Daniel approached Tristan. "We'll go with the women and children and help look out for them," Daniel said.

"I cannot allow you to carry a weapon if you go that way," Tristan answered. "It will be perilous. You must rely on stealth. If you are discovered you can expect no mercy from our enemies."

"It is more dangerous for us to offend our God by following the druid into the forest," said Jesus.

"I saw the power of your god when you calmed the waters of the Camel."

"I only prayed for that. I am no conjurer."

"Pray for us all to be safe this night, then, my friend."

"That I will do," Jesus promised.

At last the women and children were ready. Elsigar had brewed up a potion to put the youngest to a sound sleep so they would not cry out as their mothers carried them through the darkness.

Fortunately, the tide was low and the moon was full, allowing the women to find their way between the sea and the base of the seaside cliffs. Jesus, Daniel, and a few of the wounded men scouted from the cliff tops, signaling each other by hand and ever wary for any sign of the enemy.

The going was slow. Every so often an outcropping of cliff or an arm of the sea cut off the lower path of the women, and they had to double back to find a detour up and down the high ground. That was when they were most exposed in the moonlight. Even if the children made no sound, the men and women feared that the movement of their shadows might attract the attention of their foes across the vales.

Hour by treacherous hour the night wore on. They worked their way around the headland, and then they started to follow the shoreline to the east.

Pirro

Pirro had not been overly surprised when Elsigar pronounced the prohibition on approaching the castle the easy way. He knew of the taboos the druids called *geia*. Caesar had written that the Aeduen magistrate was not allowed to venture beyond the borders of his people. There were more examples in the legends. The greatest Celtic warriors were subjected to the greatest taboos. They could not kill birds, cross certain rivers, listen to certain harps, or bed certain women. Sometimes they fell victim to conflicting *geia*, leading to their demise. But Pirro was an educated Greek. He cared no more about druidic beliefs than he did about the Jews' God. For him it was a simple calculation. *Given the options, it is safer for me to march with the warriors. Jesus was right about one thing. That confounded druid will get us all killed.*

The men advanced through the unfriendly forest with wary steps. There was no point in attempting stealth. They could hear the enemy around them on all sides. The attack was inevitable, and it would be at the time and place of the enemy's choosing. All they could do was march on as Elsigar shouted incantations at the enemy.

With a shout from their right, the attack came. The pirates had chosen the place well. They had the high ground. Missiles rained down. A thrown stone hit Pirro' head. It was not a fatal blow, but it dazed him enough for Pirro to doubt his senses. He looked around trying to get his bearings. Something was not right. *The trees are moving!*

Jesus

"There it is," announced one of the women.

Jesus paused to look. In the first rays of dawn, he saw a curious formation. A promontory with three hills stretched a thousand feet into the sea. From the west, the entire promontory was faced with a sheer cliffside, rising at least fifty feet from the thundering waves. Three bands of earthworks, topped by ramparts and separated by ditches, stretched across the narrow isthmus. Unlike Castle An Dinas, there was no long perimeter to defend. No matter how many men the enemy brought, it would be impossible to concentrate more than a hundred of them at once against the ramparts in an attack from the land, and they would face a killing zone similar to Castle An Dinas in the maze of ditches leading to the entrance.

The way to the castle entrance being clear, they abandoned stealth and broke into a run. The few sentries let them through. The armory yielded spears, swords, and battle-axes. It felt strange to pass them among the women, but there were not enough men. They would be able to hold the ramparts for an hour or two if the pirates attacked in force, but they sorely needed Tristan's men to defend the ramparts against any sustained attack.

Fergus

With Elsigar nowhere to be found, preparations for the funeral of King Uryen went ahead under the supervision of another druid. Perhaps it was for the best. Everyone at Castle An Dinas knew how Uryen had earned Elsigar's displeasure by turning from druidism.

Fergus knew Grannus was already trying to ingratiate himself with the druids, but while the druids had a lot of influence, it was up to the warriors to elect the new king. The druids would have to confirm it, but could withhold that confirmation only on the grounds of impiety.

The future of the western Dumnonii hung in the balance. If elected king, Grannus would continue to ignore the danger. Fergus's chance to state his own case and bring the warriors to his side would come when he gave the funeral oration for his father. It would need to be a speech not only to extol the virtues of the late King Uryen, but also to inspire the tribe to defend itself. It must be a funeral oration worthy of remembrance. *Where is Tristan? He should be back by now.*

Daniel

The sea breeze ruffled Daniel's hair as he peered out from the ramparts. Waves crashed against the rocks below, but he could still hear shouts coming from the forest. Figures emerged one by one. Friend or foe? It was hard to tell from a distance. The British Celts looked much like the Scotti. As more men emerged, it seemed there were far too many of them. This could not be good. There was only one explanation. More pirates must have arrived to slaughter Tristan's men in the forest. Daniel and Jesus, along with the women and children, were next.

Wait! Could that be Pirro? It must be. No one else wears a tunic so awkwardly. That certainly looks like Tristan's horned helmet. Perhaps one of the pirates is wearing it as a trophy. But it still looks like Tristan.

Hope rose and then turned to joy as the men came closer. It was Tristan's band indeed, stained with the blood of a great victory.

Jesus and Daniel spotted Fedwig, and they ran out to embrace him.

"It was just as Elsigar said," shouted Fedwig. "He turned the trees against the pirates!"

For once Jesus stood perplexed. "That makes no sense!"

"Your friend speaks true." Pirro laughed. "I saw it with my own eyes—just—well—there was no magic in it, though."

"Is everyone mad? Trees don't take part in a battle," said Daniel.

"Actually, it's something right out of a scroll I read once," Pirro went on. "It was another history of Rome, by a scholar named Livy. As I remember, the Gauls once used the same tactic against the Romans. They cut a grove of trees just short of causing them to fall. A Roman legion came through and walked into the trap. The Gauls started pushing the trees over, and the legionnaires were caught among the falling timbers. They were surprised and slaughtered when the Gauls charged."

"Elsigar told the riders that the local men should do the same thing," said Fedwig. "Our men got to the forest first. It was obvious where the pirates would come at us, and we saw the obvious place to anticipate the attack—where the road winds around some rock outcroppings. The men prepared the trees, just as Pirro said. The pirates came along thinking they were laying this great ambush, but once the trees started falling on them, they were trapped. We must have killed half of them. The rest scattered."

"We're not safe, then? Why don't we hunt down the rest of them before they hurt anyone else?" Jesus asked.

"I'm afraid the pirates lit another signal fire," Tristan removed his helmet and ran his fingers through sweaty hair. "There will be more on their way. We heard them still boasting of it. We need to make ready the defenses of the castle."

Elsigar came along as they started back to the castle gates. "So, tell me, Jesus. What do you think of my magic now? Is it just superstition?"

Jesus raised an eyebrow. "The Lord works in mysterious ways." As the druid continued on his way, Jesus whispered to Daniel with a laugh, "That didn't sound half bad for a pagan, actually."

"I heard that."

Daniel could not help smiling at Jesus. *That is one sharp-eared druid.*

They spent the rest of the day organizing the defenses. More men arrived from the countryside. Some brought their women and children. Tristan shook his head. There would be many mouths to feed. They sent out warrior parties to scavenge the countryside for livestock and food. They burned anything they could not bring back to deny it to the enemy.

The training came next. The men were eager to defend their homeland, but most were peasants and craftsmen, unskilled in the warlike arts. Largely isolated, the Dumnonii tended to be peaceful, but that blessing was now a weakness. Tristan set his few warriors to drilling the newcomers. The best of them were given spears and bows. The others were told to gather up rocks to throw. There was no time to teach the wielding of a sword or battle axe.

Pirro chuckled. "I feel a little more useful now. It won't take much skill to hurl rocks down from the ramparts. I can handle that."

Daniel agreed with him.

During a rest break, Daniel and Jesus looked around. The cliff on which the castle stood was divided into two promontories, each pointing into the ocean on either side of a small bay no bigger than two hundred feet. A small hill crowned by a stockade sat on each promontory. The third hill was behind the fortifications across the isthmus, crowned by the highest stockade to form a citadel, connected to the ramparts by a stairway raised on posts above the ground. Between the three hills and the small bay was a depression that formed a natural amphitheater.

As dusk fell, Elsigar came up to them. "Have you noticed what makes this site such a holy place for us?"

Daniel looked around. "It is certainly an unusual formation. You could make an altar and conduct religious ceremonies for a thousand people in the amphitheater."

"Yes, we do that. The setting is quite dramatic. But there is a deeper symbolism. We come here to honor Lugh and Minerva."

Jesus, Daniel, and Pirro looked at each other blankly.

"The left-hand promontory is named Diancech," said Fedwig, "and the one on the right is named Balor."

"I am glad to see that you remember something from my teachings."

The others joined the druid in laughter. Fedwig blushed and looked at the ground.

"Do you remember old Bacchus, Daniel?" remarked Jesus. "The bargeman who brought us down the Loire? He told us a story about Lugh. Dianceth and Balor were Lugh's two grandfathers. One was a god and the other was a giant. It was from them that Lugh inherited his two natures—god and giant, So, I assume the two promontories represent the two natures of Lugh."

"Now for the three hills. Do you remember them, too, Fedwig?"

"I'm too big now for you to beat me if I mess this up, right?"

"Don't tempt me," the druid replied gravely, as the others smiled.

Fedwig pretended to be greatly afraid, and then he answered. "There's Morrigan atop Dianceth, and Bodbh atop Balor, and Macha here next to the gate."

Pirro chimed in. "Morrigan, the great sorceress. Bodbh, the great warrior crow. And Macha, the great queen. You honor the three persons of the druid's goddess, too, the one that takes after the Greek Minerva."

"Very good," said the druid. "You figured it all out."

"Hold on," said Jesus. "I think there might be something more. Let me see. Three hills represent three persons—one god. Two promontories represent two natures—one person." Jesus started looking around, and then he stepped back to take in the entire vista. His jaw dropped in amazement. "I've got it!"

"Got what? There's nothing more," said the druid.

"You missed the most important part. Everything is unified to the same purpose. There is only one fort, but each hill and each promontory plays its part in it. They are all the same, and they are all different. Just as there is only one God in three persons—God the Father Creator, God the Son of Man and Son of God, and God the Holy Spirit. The Father is God, the Son is God, and the Holy Spirit is God. They work one will. But the Father is not the Son, and the Son is not the Holy Spirit, and the Holy Spirit is not the Father."

Elsigar stared at Jesus. Then he turned to Daniel. "This is something of your eastern faith?"

"I have no idea," Daniel groaned. His stomach had shriveled into a knot.

Elsigar took a gold coin from his pocket bag and gazed at it for a moment. When Jesus asked about it, he said he would have to tell him another time. Without another word he put the coin back in his pocket and left them. Jesus went off by himself as well.

As Daniel, Fedwig, and Pirro continued exploring the fort, Daniel gave up trying to figure out Jesus's rambling. Perhaps he'd explain himself later.

Pirro said, "Caesar, writing about these cliff-side forts, said the Romans would exhaust themselves breaking through the ramparts at the cost of many men, but once they broke through, the Gauls would simply go down to the boats and find another promontory down the coast. Caesar made it sound very frustrating. But I don't see any way down to the sea from here."

"It's right over there." Fedwig walked over between the two promontories and pulled aside a small bush at the edge of the cliff. Pirro looked over. He could barely make out the trail of footholds leading down to the water's edge.

The rations that evening were small, unlike the Celts' usual bounteous fare, but Jesus did not come for the meager meal. Daniel finished his ration and went looking for his cousin. He found him on the inner rampart, staring out to sea. Daniel approached, but Jesus took no notice. "Are you still pondering the druid's riddles?" Daniel ventured.

Jesus finally turned to answer. "No, I have been pondering the riddle from my Father."

"You had me worried. This business about three gods, now—"

"One God in three."

"This business is not in Scripture. It sounded like you were getting it from the druids." Daniel leaned closer to him. "You're not becoming one of them, are you?"

"No. It's something my Father talked to me about."

"Back when we first came ashore in Carn Roz?"

"No. A little more than a year ago, right before Yom Kippur."

"You never said anything about it." Daniel drew back. *We've had our disagreements, but does he no longer trust me?*

"It was such a riddle; I did not know how to explain it. I wonder if I will ever fully understand it myself. The druid gods are false, but I think I understand our true God better from the way Elsigar described the workings of his."

He's crazy. Or overtired. "Come. We need our rest." The two of them turned. Another signal fire beyond the ramparts blazed across the night.

Tristan

The sea was draped in morning fog. Sentries summoned Tristan to the outer bank of the ramparts. The pirates huddled in groups around a string of campfires just beyond the range of the Dumnonii's bows. There were not enough of them to successfully assault the ramparts, but their ranks had definitely waxed stronger.

A shout rang out from the top of Morrigan. Off in the far distance, Tristan saw boats emerge from the fog. *Just as Fergus feared. This is no raid; it is an invasion.*

Tristan gathered the men. "This castle must not fall to the pirates! It would be the perfect foothold for them to start seizing the land of all the Dumnonii. We must fight to the last man."

The men roared their agreement. They knew the cruelty of their foes, and they expected no quarter from the enemy surrounding them.

"We must get word of our peril to Castle An Dinas. Someone must ride through the enemy lines." It would be a desperate flight. He couldn't assign that task.

Young Fedwig was the first to volunteer.

"I am lighter," Jesus shouted out. "The horse will go faster with me. I have a better chance of breaking through."

"Bravely said, my friend," Tristan responded. "But King Uryen was on the verge of death when we left. Your bravery will live long in song and story among our people, but for now they know only of the spice you gave, and Grannus will blame you for bringing an evil omen regardless of how the king fares. Fedwig will receive a kinder reception."

Tristan gathered a group of men just inside the gates. With a shout, they charged out at the nearest group of pirates where they were huddled around a fire. The diversion worked perfectly, drawing the undisciplined pirates and thinning their line. Fedwig rode forth a few moments later and found a gap. The men in the sally fell back to the gate, their work done. Two had fallen, and the pirates soon raised severed heads in triumph. *Fedwig is away through the first line, but will he fall into the hands of other pirates coming in from the shore? If he makes it to the castle, will the tribe be ready to defend itself?*

The hours trickled by. It seemed an eternity to the men, watching the enemy approach from the sea. Inaction gave rise to anxiety, fear, and doubt. The pirates already on shore began taunting and jeering.

Elsigar shouted back at them from the ramparts. "I cast the supreme curse upon you, just as Carpe did at the Battle of Mag Tured. I laugh at you and give you shame to such extent that your feet will quiver beneath you when you try to attack. Your sons will hang their heads in shame when they hear how you crawl on your bellies away from these walls. I invoke all the skills of my dreadful art."

The words of the druid had their effect on the enemy outside the gate. None among them knew how to counter Elsigar's magic. They fell silent and fearful.

The great host of the enemy came ashore at midday and formed up in ranks. Elsigar broke into a song, intricate in its cadence and melody. He sang of how he had fasted on the land overnight and held up the branch of the hawthorn bush. He commanded the hills to swallow him up if he should be in the wrong. Then he laid his melodic injunction on the foes. He commanded them to leave the lands of the Dumnonii in peace, lest all the pregnant women in their homeland miscarry and all those not pregnant have their wombs overturned so they would never bear sons. Any sons already born should break out in such ghastly festering sores and pimples that forevermore all women, even their mothers, would spurn the sight of them and the dripping pus, and those sons would curse the memory of their fathers to the end of their days.

The druid's curse seemed to take away the bravado of the enemy. But still they charged the ramparts. Standing atop the stockade, Elsigar took a deep breath, puffed out his cheeks, and blew at them.

"What does that mean?" Jesus asked Tristan.

"It's the druidic wind. It sows confusion on the enemy."

The first wave of attackers broke on the foot of the ramparts. Jesus drew his bow. Arrows flew as fast as they could string them—the enemy was packed so closely that aim made no difference. The enemy fell back and came again, this time with a great ram that they battered against the outer ramparts. Once again arrows flew, and the enemy fell back.

Tristan took stock. His men had nearly depleted their stockpile of arrows. The enemy was coming again with the ram. His trap was laid. Just as they reached the outer gate, he gave the signal to open it.

Thinking they had broken the outer gate, the pirates rushed through. Some attempted to climb the banks, but most flooded on through the maze of ditches until they found their way blocked by the inner gate.

Then the killing began. Molten lead, rocks and the remaining arrows rained down upon the hapless pirates. Their bodies piled up quickly. Few who entered the outer gate escaped.

Later that night, Tristan passed out a ration of mead to his men. As the defenders celebrated their victory, they heard the lamentations of the remaining attackers.

Daniel drank his bit of mead. "Do they lament more the fate of their dead comrades, or the sorrows they believe await them at home from the druid's curse?"

Daniel

The next morning, Daniel awoke well before dawn. The men were all sleeping on the terrace that overlooked the outer stockade. Sentries kept a watchful eye on the enemy lines arrayed against them on the mainland.

Pirro was missing from his spot. It occurred to Daniel that he had not seen Pirro since the previous day's battle. The casualties among the castle defenders had been light, and Daniel was sure that Pirro was not among them. So where could he be? The mystery made him uneasy.

Daniel thought he heard a muffled sound coming from the sea. He turned and looked that way. The moon was still almost full, but a patch of fog obscured the sight. He looked back at the sentries; they continued to face the mainland. He went up to one of them. "I think I heard something coming from Dianeth or Balor. I am going to look. Raise an alarm if I am not back in a few moments." The sentry nodded.

Daniel made his way toward the sea on the high side of the amphitheater, just below the citadel. He saw shapes moving through the fog as he got closer to the clifftop overhanging the bay between the two promontories. He hollered a challenge. The shapes stopped moving.

A voice answered back, "All is well." Pirro. At first Daniel was relieved. But this made no sense. Why would Pirro lead a group roaming around the fortress with no torch in the middle of a fog?

He shouted back. "What are you doing?" Then he heard the whistle of arrows, and he sprinted back to the ramparts. "The enemy is in the amphitheater!"

After a moment's stunned silence, one of the sentries beat the alarm drum. It took more precious moments for the men to wake up and get oriented. Their first instinct was to look for peril from the enemy lines outside the gates.

Tristan ordered warriors with swords and battle axes to defend the rear. The others were to stay alert to defend the outer ramparts.

With his sword in his hand, Jesus joined the warriors forming their line behind the ramparts. "Where are they? How did they get in?"

"Pirro has betrayed us," Daniel answered. "He's leading them up the hidden path Fedwig showed us."

"Get up on the ramparts, Daniel. The men there will need your bow."

Tristan jumped down and led the warriors in a charge at the still unseen enemy. Jesus met them midway through the amphitheater on the low side, opposite the citadel on Macha. The sentries guarding Morrigan, Bodbh, and Macha attacked the intruders from the rear. The amphitheater filled with the sounds of a pitched battle. Blade clashed against blade. Desperate men on both sides fought through the fog-shrouded darkness.

With the sound of battle close behind them, the men on the ramparts turned to face a new peril. The sound was unmistakable. The enemy outside the gate was preparing a fresh assault from the mainland.

The barest glimmer of dawn tinged the horizon. Daniel made out shapes coming at them from the outside. This time the enemy carried ladders. Someone had to get word to Tristan. Without swordsmen or axe-men to defend the terrace, the enemy only had to mount the ladders to take the ramparts. He ran to the spot where Fedwig had left his battle axe and grabbed it. He ran down into the amphitheater, swinging his weapon wildly.

Daniel landed the axe in the side of one enemy and in the head of another as he fought his way to Tristan. "We need warriors on the ramparts. They are coming with ladders," he shouted. Tristan pulled back from the fight. His men were beginning to push the enemy back, but there were no warriors to spare. Already several of his men had fallen.

More intruders were coming up the hidden trail to augment the enemy. The warriors were too few to be everywhere, but Tristan dispatched a half-dozen men back to the ramparts with Daniel. That would not hold the ramparts for long, nor did it leave Tristan with enough men to hold back the intruders in the amphitheater, as more of them kept coming.

Daniel reached the ramparts with the warriors as the enemy began to reach the defenders on the ramparts. Desperately they drew their blades and attacked, trying to gain the advantage as the enemy struggled up the last few steps. Men on the ramparts toppled some of the ladders, and the men hurling molten lead and missiles were doing heroic work. But more foes with ladders kept coming.

Jesus

The tide of battle in the amphitheater turned against them. Jesus and some of the others were driven back. Looking across the amphitheater, he watched in horror as an enemy axe cleaved through Tristan's skull.

The enemy was unstoppable. With no one in command, Jesus shouted for the men around him to retreat up Macha to the citadel. A half-dozen warriors followed. Making it into the stockade, they barred the gate.

Jesus looked over the stockade. The enemy had turned toward the ramparts. The bridge from the citadel to the ramparts would not stand for long if the intruders attacked the support posts.

The last gasp of desperation was upon them. At best, the fight behind the ramparts would turn into a general melee. Quickly and silently, Jesus prayed to his Father for protection and strength. Then he formed the warriors into a line, alternating the swordsmen with the axe-men. "Thrust your swords at the enemy like this," he shouted, showing them the Roman technique. "Let the axe-men take the swings. Now, men of the Dumnonii, let us fight. On to glory!"

With a great shout from the men, Jesus led a charge down the slope of Macha and into the flank of the intruders. The combination of swinging axes and thrusting swords threw total confusion into the enemy. Jesus's men linked up with the remnants of Tristan's band, who were all now on the defense. Jesus heard screams of dying men from the ramparts.

Suddenly, above the roar of battle, Jesus heard the horn. That sweet blast identified one warrior and no other. Off in the distance, it had to be Fedwig sounding it.

Fergus

Leading the host of all the western Dumnonii, Fergus and Fedwig rode up on the hillside overlooking the desperate battle. Onward they charged, sweeping the pirates from the face of the castle ramparts.

A desperate fight was waged along the terraces of all three ramparts, but some of the villagers managed to open the gates. Most of Fedwig's host rode through to turn the fight in the amphitheater, but some of them scaled the rampart walls to help slay the enemy still fighting on the terraces.

When Fergus's men came through, the intruders in the amphitheater turned their thoughts to escape. Some tried to jump from the lowest point on the cliffs into the sea, but most of those broke their necks or drowned. Others retreated to the top of Bodbh, which had fallen to the intruders at dawn. But now the defenders outnumbered the intruders. The slope of Bodbh was far too steep for horses, so Fergus's warriors dismounted and drove the remaining intruders up higher and higher on the rocky mount, hacking them down with their blades until the last of them was slain.

A few intruders started down the escape trail to the bay between the promontories, only to see from halfway down the cliff their boats dashed to pieces on the rocks by the waves.

Half an hour later it was over. Fergus found the lifeless body of Tristan lying in the amphitheater. He cradled his cousin in his arms, but he did not grieve for long. Tristan had died a heroic death—the most honorable death a warrior could hope for. He had surely passed to the Otherworld—the Celtic paradise.

Daniel

Limbs trembling with fatigue, Daniel sought out Jesus. Finding him alive and unhurt, he embraced him. They were stained with blood. Death and suffering lay all around them. They shut all of that off and simply released their emotions in each other's arms.

Finally, Jesus lifted his head. "Where is Fedwig?"

They searched the amphitheater, but their friend was not to be found. They searched the upper decks on the ramparts, but he was not there, either. Then they looked outside the ramparts, and they found him. A chance arrow had pierced his lung. It must have happened when Fergus's men were sweeping the pirates and their ladders from the ramparts.

Jesus ran to Fedwig's side and collapsed on his knees, weeping.

Daniel, unable to hold back his own tears, put a hand on Jesus's shoulder. Fedwig still breathed, but the wound was clearly mortal.

Chapter 8
Ynys Witrin

Jesus

As the day waned, Jesus prayed over his friend, beseeching the Father to spare Fedwig's life. Every so often Fedwig awoke. He would cough up blood whenever he tried to speak, so Jesus urged him just to rest. Jesus clasped Fedwig's hand and let his own eyes close. *Never have I felt such sorrow. He is my friend, and now I will lose him.* Jesus was startled to feel Fedwig loosen his grip, but when he opened his eyes, he saw that Fedwig was sleeping soundly.

Jesus watched while Fedwig slept. *He was so brave to ride out. I should have been the one to do it. My Father would have protected me, and Fedwig would be safe. I should have tried harder to persuade Tristan to send me.* Jesus gnashed his teeth. *I cannot undo what is done. I must think of something else before this sorrow drives me insane.*

Jesus turned his attention from Fedwig and looked around. The carnage continued. The victorious Dumnonii were severing the heads of their fallen enemies, collecting them as trophies.

Elsigar came by often but did not stay long. There were many wounded to attend to, some with real hope. Fedwig could not drink the tea made from mistletoe and other herbs that Elsigar administered to the others. The druid had to content himself with spreading mistletoe cuttings over Fedwig.

"Why do our warriors cut off the heads of the fallen enemies?" asked Jesus. "It's barbaric."

"Diancecth is one of our principal gods," the druid answered. "The Romans have compared him to Apollo, but he is more than that. He is the greatest healer. He boasted to Lugh at the beginning of the world that he could heal any warrior for combat the next morning as long as he had not suffered the severing of his head. Decapitating the fallen enemy assures our warriors that the enemy will not be healed to rise against us."

"If that is true, why do our own wounded still die? Fedwig's head still rests on his shoulders, like most of our wounded. Why can't you save them all?"

"I can only appeal to Diancecth. I am not Diancecth himself. The gods will heal who they will. But surely they will welcome all of our fallen into paradise."

"Don't you think it's a bit presumptuous to appeal to Diancecth to help our own fallen, while our warriors prevent him from healing our enemies?"

"Should we do nothing to prevent our enemies from rising against us again?"

"It's your religion—not mine," Jesus answered. "I can think of one time our ancestors fought against the Midians—more than a thousand years ago. One of our greatest leaders, Gideon, rounded up all the men he could, but he had only thirty-two thousand against one hundred thirty-five thousand Midians. God commanded Gideon to release most of his men, until he was left with only three hundred to face the enemy. At the end of the day, God gave Gideon the victory despite the odds, and he went forth and proclaimed that the glory was God's and not his."

"That is great faith to place in your god," observed Elsigar. "I suppose Gideon would have left the heads of his enemies alone, even if it meant that the gods might raise them again."

"Gideon served the God of Israel," Jesus answered. "But he would not have tried to stop God from healing his enemies."

"Our gods speak with many voices," said Elsigar. "It is hard to put complete trust in any one of them."

"I imagine that is so," said Jesus. "Gideon showed incredible faith by turning to God for strength, but our Dumnonii warriors think they find strength in stopping your gods from healing their enemies. In doing so, they reveal their lack of faith. It is no different from hypocrites among my own people who claim to follow God, but would never put their faith in him the way Gideon did. Even among my people, not many would fight among the final three hundred of Gideon's men."

While Jesus spoke, Elsigar fingered a golden coin he had removed from his pocket. He showed it when Jesus asked to see it. The image on the coin depicted a snake egg, with dozens of snakes curled around each other to form a ball.

"What does it mean?" Jesus asked.

"I will explain it to you sometime," said Elsigar. "For now, we have duty to attend to." The druid left Fedwig in Jesus's hands.

Jesus continued to pray for Fedwig, even knowing that hope was gone. Daniel joined him as soon as Fergus could spare him.

At midday, Fergus approached with a small company of men, including Elsigar, and interrupted their prayers. They were dragging a man whom they had bound and gagged. Bruises covered his face and body, and his clothes were ripped to rags.

Pirro.

Fergus shoved him roughly to the ground. "We found this coward hiding behind a bush. He deserves death for his treachery."

"I witnessed his treachery myself," said Daniel. "But why do you bring him to us?" He turned to Elsigar. "Aren't you the lawgiver here?"

"I am the lawgiver among the Dumnonii, but he is one of your people. It is up to you to pass judgment. It is your right and responsibility."

"But he is Greek, and we are Israelite," Daniel answered. "He is not one of the people of Abraham, Isaac, and Jacob. His gods are Greek and Roman."

"Your father brought him to these shores, and our people welcomed all of you and gave you our protection," said Elsigar. "It would be dishonorable for us to render a judgment of death while there is peace between us. We must turn to you and Jesus for justice."

"If I am to render judgment, I must hear him out," said Jesus. "Let him speak."

Elsigar loosened the gag, and Fergus pulled Pirro up on his knees. The Greek trembled.

"Daniel saw you lead the pirates up the hidden stairway into the fortress," Jesus began. "Do you deny that?"

Pirro shook his head no.

"Then why did you do it?"

Pirro looked up at Jesus. "What do you care about me? I am just the trinket guy. While you and Daniel make big money in tin, I get by with the crumbs."

"Uncle Joseph was kind and generous to you. Perhaps if you gambled and drank less, your earnings would have stretched farther. Wasn't it your idea to fill our half-empty hulls going back to Gaul with trade goods from the Dumnonii?"

"No one back in Gaul wants the miserable bits of cloth and pottery these people make. I hardly make enough on what I sell to cover what I bring back in trade."

"Couldn't you try anything else?"

"Oh, yes. I tried. I wanted to bring back the one commodity that would have made me a fortune. But your uncle wouldn't have it, even though there would have been plenty of profit for him, too. Just down the coast in Yengi you can get a fine slave for little more than an amphora of wine. But your uncle would have no part in it."

"My father would never trade in the misery of others," said Daniel. "He made that clear to you from the day you first met."

"Where does that leave me? I am just the trinket man, the fool. I know how you laugh and joke about me when my back is turned."

"What did the pirates offer you to betray us?" Jesus asked.

"They promised me three shiploads of slaves and men to keep them in line. I was to have my pick of the Dumnonii as soon as they subdued this backward tribe. I would have been set for life."

"You would have condemned us all to slavery and death!" Fergus eyes blazed with anger. He started to draw his sword. But Elsigar reached out and stayed his hand. "I lost Tristan," said Fergus. "Fedwig lies here dying. And there are dozens more." Fergus slapped Pirro's face hard with the back of his hand and then spat on him. "I think we've heard enough. Be done with him."

"Is there anything else you want to say?" Jesus asked.

"What's the use?" muttered Pirro. "My life is over. You despise me. You always have."

"Gag him," said Daniel. "I cannot stand to hear another foul whine from his lips." He turned to Jesus as one of Fergus' men reinserted the gag. "If anyone deserves death, he clearly does. What do you say, cousin?"

Jesus turned to Elsigar. "How do you execute a man who is condemned to death?"

"We usually just lop off his head. Sometimes he is strangled, but it is over in minutes."

"It is hard to see why the Romans call you barbarians. I have seen them do far worse." Jesus paled. *That vision of myself, on a cross.* He quickly recovered and continued. "You are all quite right; this man is deserving of death, and it is just that you should demand it. The Celtic method of ultimate punishment is mercifully quick." Jesus buried his face in his hands, and then he looked up, directly at Pirro. "Here is the judgment I pronounce upon this man. Take him from this place in chains and sell him as a slave. Let him experience one small part of the pain and sorrow he would inflict on others." Pirro looked shocked and he tried to protest, but the gag silenced him. "Let him live long, suffering in his slavery, working in misery and toil."

A hush fell over the warriors. Some glared in anger, for they wanted to see the severance of Pirro's head.

The druid spoke. "Your judgment is more terrible than anything I would pronounce. We do not hold with slavery, so he will find himself with some other tribe. He will live a year, maybe two at the most. Although you gave him life, it is nothing less than a slow and painful death. But the people will not accept your judgment unless they see him scourged." The druid held out a cruel whip. "Care to start?"

Jesus shook his head. "Do with him as you will, but take him away from me and keep him alive. I have seen enough death and pain these last days." Jesus nodded towards Pirro. "He's not worth the trouble. I must get back to Fedwig and pray for him."

Daniel stayed with Jesus and Fedwig as the others left. Mercifully, Fedwig slept, even as he grew weaker. They prayed over their friend for some time.

"Did you spare Pirro's life just to make his punishment more terrible, as the druid said? Or were you moved by compassion?"

"He certainly deserved death, but something held me back. Maybe it was the call of the Holy Spirit. Maybe he will yet serve some purpose."

"He is not entirely worse off than if you had sentenced him to immediate death, is he?" Daniel asked.

"No. He will have the chance to seek redemption with God."

"That sounds like compassion to me. But he is such a miserable creature; it's hard to see how he would ever deserve that."

"Let's leave that to God. I cannot call it compassion though. Fedwig will die soon because of him. Tristan is already dead. And he caused the death of so many others. I felt no love for him. It was just something holding me back. I wanted him to suffer. I wanted him dead, as much as any of those who called for his head."

They soon heard Pirro crying out in agony, as each surviving warrior and widow took a turn with the whip.

Daniel

The next day they made their way back to Castle An Dinas. They bore Fedwig with them in a litter, but his strength continued to drain away. Bannoch and Tilda were at the fortress to meet their son. The chance to say good-bye to him was small comfort.

The next few days passed in a blur. An impressive funeral was held for old King Uryen. Many recounted the inspiring speech of Prince Fergus, now the king. They heard how his eloquence rallied the warriors to ride forth when Fedwig brought word of the danger they faced at Rumps.

They were all victorious heroes now—the fallen and the living. The living gathered in the banquet hall each night, singing for Tristan and toasting his memory. They sang for Fedwig and exhorted their gods to save him.

There was praise, too, for Jesus. Long forgotten was the awkward gift he had brought for King Uryen. Daniel listened, content to be obscure, as bards regaled the listeners with songs of Jesus's deeds—how he had stilled the waters at the mouth of the Camel; how he had fought alongside Fedwig at Rock; how he had led the women and children to the safety of Rumps; and how he had led the daring sortie into the final melee in the amphitheater. Most of all, the songs celebrated the friendship of Jesus and Fedwig, companions in arms.

Jesus spent most of his time with Fedwig, whose strength was now almost gone. Tilda never left Fedwig's side. Bannoch stayed too, except to do his duty in the banquet hall each evening to help celebrate Fedwig's deeds and those of all the heroes. Elsigar came by regularly to refresh the mistletoe and recite his incantations over the dying boy.

Fedwig closed his eyes forever the day after King Uryen's funeral, dying in the arms of his mother on the third night. As he breathed his last, not even Tilda expressed sorrow, at least not in words. Her son had died the death of a hero. Tilda and Bannoch offered a prayer of thanksgiving to Sucellos, the Jupiter God of the druids, for striking hard with his mallet and giving their son the best of deaths. Surely, they said, the gods would welcome their hero son into the Otherworld, the vast plain of Celtic paradise where horses run free, orchards produce apples in all seasons, and celestial music, wealth, beauty, and fairy-like women abound.

"He suffers no more pain," said Jesus, through his tears, but he was not to be consoled. He rode way from the Castle to spend the rest of the day by himself.

The funeral procession started out for Carn Roz from Castle An Dinas the next day. Jesus rode alongside Daniel. Despite Daniel's best efforts to raise his spirits over the day-long journey, Jesus said nothing. He ate nothing.

They came to Carn Roz in the evening. Daniel looked down from the hill overlooking the village and let out a long sigh. He glanced over to Jesus to make sure his cousin noticed what he saw. They exchanged looks; there was no need for words. Kendrick's ship was waiting in the tidal pool. Papa was back. There would be hell to pay.

"What were you thinking?" Father shouted. It was the first time Daniel had seen him direct such anger at Jesus. "Your friend is dead, but I hear you are quite the hero, Jesus. I hope you're proud of yourself."

"And you!" Father pointed at Daniel. "You took part in the fighting, too. You must have known that Jesus was training as a warrior. You hid that from me!"

"Don't blame Daniel. I entreated him not to say anything," said Jesus.

"That would have been great comfort to your mother, I'm sure. Just imagine if you had been killed alongside your friend. I can still remember what I told her. Don't worry about Jesus, I said. Daniel will look after him." He paused, searching Jesus's face for signs of remorse. "You are only a few years older than when I brought you here as a boy of thirteen," he shouted. "And now I hear that you have killed many men and condemned Pirro to slavery?"

"Pirro betrayed us all, Papa. Jesus did what he thought was just."

"I suppose you think that makes everything just fine," Papa stormed. "I can hear what they will say about me now. Do business with Joseph, and he will sell you to the barbarians when it suits his purposes. If word of this gets out, I am ruined. For generations my family has built this business with the trust of our customers and suppliers. We are peaceful traders—not warriors. We keep the trust of our partners. That generally means having them sold into slavery is something we try to avoid!" He grabbed a plate and smashed it against the wall.

"But you know, Jesus. I do not care if you ruin me—not even if it ruins Daniel, too. I know what is going on here. You think you are the Messiah, and that one day you will lead our people to freedom, but you cannot win against the Romans. You will die an awful and shameful death. And I love you too much to bear that." Father laid his head down on the table and collapsed in sobs.

Jesus said, "Anything is possible with—"

"My father is not ready to hear that now." Daniel pulled Jesus to the doorway. "I will stay and look after him. You'd better go and leave him be for a while."

"I'm sorry, Daniel. I have brought great sorrow to your father. We lost Fedwig—"

Daniel took a step closer, his voice low and trembling. "We have been through a war, Jesus. There is always a cost to that. Our cause was just, and we were victorious, but there is always a cost. Go and stay with Bannoch and Tilda. I know how much Father loves you, and I am sure he will be himself in a day or two. I will come and get you when Father is ready to talk this out."

Three days passed before Daniel could summon Jesus back to Father, who greeted him with open arms. The two of them embraced.

"I'm so sorry I hurt you, Uncle—"

"Jesus, I said many foolish things in anger. I forgot how much you have grown in the last few years. You are no longer a boy, and you will determine your own destiny. I must accept that now."

"I cannot stay here in Carn Roz, Uncle. Bannoch and Tilda talk about their joy and pride in Fedwig, but I still sense their loss. I keep asking myself if I could have prayed any harder for him. I wonder why my Father did not answer my prayers. There is too much sadness for me now."

"You have finished your work here, Jesus. You and Daniel have done well, but you have already mapped enough ore deposits to last for several years. You have revived for the Dumnonii their lost art of smelting and refining. The time has come for the two of you to move on to another venture; come with me to Ynys Witrin. There is lead and silver to be found in the surrounding hills."

With the decision made, Father quickly reorganized the enterprise at Carn Roz, putting the native workers in charge of the mining and refining. While Father met with them, Daniel stopped in the storehouse to take an inventory of Pirro's goods. They weren't worth putting on the ship, but took up valuable space. He had to get rid of them.

Maybe one of the local merchants would take them off their hands. He turned to go and found Golia in the doorway. He grinned. "I thought you were avoiding me."

She folded her arms. "Me? You're the one who's leaving."

"Father insists." In truth, Daniel was as eager as Jesus to get away from the scene of their grief and explore someplace new. But he couldn't tell her that.

"You won't argue with him, will you?"

"What is there to argue about?"

"Nothing, I suppose." She sighed and dropped her arms. She crossed the room and placed one hand lightly on his chest.

He tried to pull her closer, but she pushed away firmly. "You've been very sweet, Daniel, and I'll miss you." She walked out, hesitating at the doorway. "Good-bye."

Well. That was easier than I expected.

Joseph

Some of the Celts had located lodes of ore on their own, but Joseph retained the maps that showed the as-yet-untouched lodes discovered by

Jesus. These secrets would be useful in later dealings with the natives, and they would give Joseph an advantage over any future competitors. The tin part of the venture would now resemble what he and Pirro had envisioned back in Lugdunum: He would come once or twice a year to Ictis or Carn Roz and buy finished ingots from the native Britons.

Kendrick took charge of loading his ship with sheep and stores of wine to take to Ynys Witrin. Jesus and Daniel worked with him as stevedores.

On the final night there was feasting and drinking in the dining hall. Bannoch brought in a bard for their entertainment. Jesus was touched to hear so many of his deeds recounted in the songs and poems. He wept when the bard sang of his friendship with Fedwig. Joseph looked up and caught sight of Tilda brushing away a tear.

"You have spent some years here, Jesus," said Joseph over a mug of fresh mead. "How do you feel about leaving?"

"I can think of only a few instances that have made my life really happy. Looking back, I would say that the first thing I remember is waking up early to spend time with my mother and help her make bread. Then there were the times that my heavenly Father drew close and spoke with me. Another thing has been my life with these people. They lead such simple and happy lives. The earth is good here and yields abundant crops. Even as they follow their misguided religion, they are free of oppression and taxes."

"The village has you to thank for its prosperity, Jesus," said Joseph.

"This place has brought me joy, Uncle, but I am constantly reminded of the loss of Fedwig. I feel the Spirit guiding me to move on."

They said their good-byes in the morning and Joseph saw the rainbow that only he and Jesus could see. Jesus and Daniel promised to visit often. Tilda embraced them both, as if they were her sons. She stayed on the shore waving for a long time as Kendrick's ship slipped away from its mooring in the tidal pool and sailed down the Bay.

Jesus

With fair tide and wind from the north, they made their way around the southernmost headland at Lysarth by noon and then crossed the wide bay past Ictis to the westernmost headland, which they rounded early in the afternoon. The wind took a westerly turn, allowing them to point the vessel along the northern coast of Belerium without tacking away from the land. The winds held until almost nightfall as they passed the mouth of the Camel and then Rumps Castle. Jesus and Daniel gazed silently toward the shore as the ship slipped past these landmarks.

With sundown came the Sabbath, so Jesus, Daniel, and Joseph devoted themselves to their prayers throughout the following day.

They awoke on the morning of the next day to find themselves anchored on the southeast side of a bay that stretched some ten miles across. This arm of the sea gradually narrowed to the mouth of the Sabrina, which flowed from the northeast. A thick fog lay over the nearby shore.

"We must await the tide," said Kendrick. "Ynys Witrin lies twelve miles inland, but we can bring the ship right to it. We may need to row if the wind changes, but it looks good for now. You will be able to see it as soon as the fog lifts."

"It sounds like you have been here many times before," remarked Jesus.

"Yes. The natives mine for silver. My family has come this way for generations to trade for it. I have been asking Joseph to bring you here to locate the mother lodes ever since you showed us your knack for finding tin. Where you find silver, you also find lead."

"What kind of people live here?" asked Daniel.

"This is a kind of no-man's land. It's a swampy area that makes it hard to define borders. And it lies between several tribes, so no one tribe can really claim it for themselves without angering the others. The lands of the Dumnonii lie to the west and southwest. The Durotriges and Belgae inhabit the lands to the south and east. The Silures come from the north across this bay. The Dobunni come from their lands on the south side of the Sabrina to the east. Many of the local people live in Lake Village. We will pass it on the way."

"Aren't the Durotriges warlike? I thought they raided the Dumnonii," Jesus asked.

"Ynys Witrin is a sacred spot for the druids. They come from all over on their principal feast days, and they keep the peace," Kendrick answered. "They have laid down powerful prohibitions against bringing weapons there. Not even the Durotriges dare to incur their wrath. Over the generations, the tribes have also found it mutually advantageous to leave the place as a neutral ground where they can trade freely no matter how they have fought each other elsewhere. Look. The fog is lifting and the tide comes in." Kendrick commanded, his crew to make sail.

The fog was still lifting as they crossed the low-flooded shoreline on the tide. Despite a fair wind there was hardly any wave action. "This area is called 'The Levels' because it lies so low and flat," said Kendrick. "We are sailing near the saltwater marshes that lead to Ynys Witrin. They give the place its name. 'Isle of Glass' is what the name means, and it is a good one. The plants and reeds on the bottom absorb the waves before they form."

The waters of the River Brue leading to Ynys Witrin were so unnaturally still, it seemed the ship was sailing on glass. They continued for another hour, making their way in the eerie fog as it continued to lift ahead of them.

"There it is, only a few miles ahead now. The fog has cleared from all but the very top of the Tor."

Jesus made out the strange shape of a hill that had emerged from the receding fog. It appeared to pop out of the Levels as if from nowhere. The solitary, massive hill seemed out of place on such a flatland, and its shape seemed to vary as they adjusted course to approach from a different angle. At times, it appeared relatively higher, at other times wider, but always, from any angle, as a perfect cone.

Closing his eyes, Jesus remembered his homeland. He thought of Mount Tabor and recalled feeling some of the same energy from that place. Like the Tor, Mount Tabor seemed to pop off the floor of the flat Jezreel Valley, but Tabor lacked the surrounding mist and glassy waters. Aside from a sprinkling of trees, Mount Tabor was little more than a desolate rock. But in this new place Jesus felt the abundance of living creatures all around him. The brackish saltwater marshes gave shelter and provided feeding grounds to countless kingfishers, egrets, snipes, and ospreys. Turtles made their nests in the mud. On the firmer ground were stately oaks, elms, and beeches. There would be foxes and otters in those woods. Jesus imagined that such abundance as this would be as endless as the circle of life itself.

They passed Lake Village on their left—a strange site, an entire village constructed on pylons rising from the glassy water. A platform supported fifty circular buildings. Like all the roundhouses of the Celts, the roofs were thatched, with smoke from kitchen fires wafting through the centers, giving the impression that the village itself was ablaze. Unlike the roundhouses of the Dumnonii, the outer walls of these were constructed entirely from wattle and daub, with no stonework.

Here and there, armed men patrolled the deck. Jesus pointed them out. "How can that be, if the druids prohibit men from bearing arms in the area?"

"Warriors can't bring arms in," the captain explained, "but that prohibition doesn't apply to the villagers. They need to hunt and fish and protect their homes."

The villagers waved to the ship, and several followed along in coracles, waterborne baskets large enough for two men and covered with animal skins. Others came in larger curraghs.

The captain said that the natives would take them to the village later that evening. "For now," he said, "we need to use the tide to get the ship to the island to unload the livestock for grazing."

A much lower-lying hill topped by a ridge seemed to reach out to them from the island. They grounded the ship on the beach and lowered the sails. "Welcome to Wearyall Hill and Ynys Witrin," Kendrick announced.

Jesus and Daniel helped the crew unload the sheep from below-decks to graze on the thick grass of the island, checking each one for the appropriate marking. The villagers on the island seemed to have been expecting them.

Jesus and Daniel hung back as Joseph presented his gifts to the king of Lake Village. They were well-received, and the king reciprocated with an offer of hospitality for the entire party. Joseph introduced them. "This is my son, Daniel." The king nodded. "And this is my nephew, Jesus."

"Is this Jesus Bar Joseph of Israel?"

Uncle Joseph looked taken aback, but responded affirmatively.

Word of Jesus's arrival spread quickly through the crowd. They gathered around and began touching him. Smiling and laughing, they rubbed his clothes, his hands, his hair, and even his face. Jesus stood wide-eyed, trying to smile and be courteous, but he did not know what to make of the unexpected attention.

The village king called on his people to stop. He addressed Jesus. "The bards have told us of your deeds among the Dumnonii. I am honored to meet you and glad that you will be staying with us."

"I am humbled by the kindness of your words and the reception your people have given me. I can only hope you will not be disappointed in me."

Jesus looked over at Uncle Joseph staring back at him, apparently bemused to find himself eclipsed in his reputation among the Britons.

They all got into two curraghs and paddled with the Britons to Lake Village. They entered the dining hall, the largest structure. It felt strange to Jesus to look down through the cracks in the decking to the water a few feet below. Lake Village had fewer warriors than the Dumnonii and more craftsmen. The feeling was subdued, with far less boasting over the meal than Jesus and Daniel had grown accustomed to.

As they made their way from the hall, Jesus looked up. The sun was setting behind the Tor. For a few moments, a glorious blaze crowned the hill. Jesus stood transfixed. Then he felt someone tugging his shirt. He looked down and saw a short Celtic lad, eleven or twelve years old, smiling up at him. He reminded Jesus of how Fedwig looked when they had first met.

"The best way to see the Tor is from the top at sunrise. If you meet me at the dock two hours before the sun, I can show you the way—if you like."

"I would like that very much. What is your name?"

"I am Brian, son of Eogen."

"I am pleased to meet you, Brian, son of Eogen. I am Jesus son of Joseph."

"Everyone knows who you are." Brian laughed. "Don't forget you need to be at the dock two hours before the sun—just the two of us."

"My cousin will feel left out. But I suppose we can take him another time. So, very well, just the two of us it is."

The next morning, Jesus stumbled his way around the dock. The fog was thick, and he moved with care so as not to fall in. He could not see more than a few feet ahead. He was beginning to wonder if Brian would be there, when out of nowhere the boy grabbed his hand and led him to the nearest coracle. The craft seemed tippy, but Jesus managed to hold his balance. As they paddled around the village, Jesus heard people up and about, lighting fires. Through the soup-like fog that enveloped everything, he could not see them, only the flames of their cooking fires.

Brian steered from the stern, and Jesus helped paddle from the bow. He wondered how the boy could see where he was going, but somehow he knew the way. They paddled past Kendrick's ship, stuck in the mud now at low tide. They worked their way upstream, and dry land seemed to enclose them.

Brian landed the coracle on the shore. "We'll walk from here."

Jesus followed Brian across a field. He could barely see the boy through the fog, even though he was but a few yards ahead.

"Come on, Jesus, let's run from here. We're almost there."

"Hold up, I will lose you in the fog."

"Just follow the sound of my voice."

Jesus heard Brian start to run ahead, and he tried his best to keep up. Brian called out to him, and before he knew it, he was climbing up through the fog. He called to Brian, but heard no response. So, he kept climbing. The Tor was covered with grass with no obstacles, so it was not hard for Jesus to keep walking while making his way upward at an angle to the top.

The thick mist suddenly cleared. He looked up and saw the Milky Way. And there in the starlight stood Brian, laughing.

"I knew you couldn't keep up. I figured you would get lost once I stopped calling."

"You little urchin! I'll fix you!" Jesus lunged forward, but the boy led him on a merry chase around the top of the Tor. It was all knees and elbows once Jesus finally grabbed him. Jesus was far stronger, but the boy was like a greased pig, always managing to slip out of his grip. Jesus stopped wrestling and joined in Brian's laughter. He lay on his back for a moment to look at the stars.

Brian saw his opportunity. He jumped on top of Jesus and sat on his chest.

"Do you give up?"

"Oh, you're such a rascal!" Jesus laughed and raised his hands in playful surrender. "Yes, I give up!"

Brian crossed his arms triumphantly. "Who's mightier than the hero of Rumps Castle?"

"You are, Brian."

The boy raised his nose, looking down at Jesus. "Don't you forget it!"

That was too much for Jesus, so with a quick shove he sent Brian sprawling on the soft grass. He walked over and gave the laughing boy a hand to stand up.

Brian pointed off in the distance as soon as he got to his feet. "Look over there."

It was just a tiny sliver of light at first—but then the light of dawn spread magnificently over the thick banks of fog that lay over the marshes so far below them. Here and there, isolated hilltops popped from the mist. Jesus could make out the ridge of Wearyall Hill, stretched out towards the sea. It seemed to cut upward through the fogbank like the handle of a spoon sticking up from a bowl of thick soup.

"Do you like to come here, Brian?"

"Yes!" Brian paused, as if a bit embarrassed. "I just wish I was taller, to see further." Before he could say another word the boy found himself sitting atop Jesus's shoulders. "I'm flying!" he shouted, spreading his arms as Jesus began jogging around. "It's like being a bird flying over the clouds!"

After a minute of this, Brian patted the top of Jesus's head. "It's time to go. The druid will thrash me if I'm late."

"We wouldn't want that." Jesus lowered the boy to the ground. "I had a friend who got thrashed all the time for being late to class."

Brian started walking down and Jesus followed.

"Hey, Brian!" Jesus shouted. The boy turned around. "Thank you. I had a lot of fun."

"So did I!"

"We should come back again when we have time to watch all the fog burn off."

"Sure. Any time!"

"Next time, let's bring my cousin Daniel."

"All right!"

"Just one thing. Don't lose me in the fog on the way back. I'll never find the boat without you."

"I wouldn't play that trick again." But Brian started running down the hill. Jesus rolled his eyes and took off after him.

Before long, Jesus found himself going through thick fog. But this time he heard Brian shouting his name with some regularity. The boy was taking him through woodland. From the sound, it sometimes seemed that Brian was going off in slightly different directions. Was some path taking him this way and that? Or could Brian be playing another prank? And then Jesus heard his name being called from off to the side, and the voice was different, as if Brian were trying to disguise it. The boy was definitely up to something now. "Come on, Brian. Enough of this foolishness! You're the one who's going to get the thrashing if you're late." Jesus started walking toward the voice; through the mist he began to make out a clearing in the trees ahead of him. Once there, God the Father revealed himself.

Jesus sighed.

"Is there something wrong, Son?"

"No. Well, actually, there is."

"You still miss your friend."

"Yes"

"And you ask yourself why I did not answer your prayers for him."

"I am not sure I would put it like that."

"How would you put it, Jesus?"

"What did I do wrong? How could I have prayed any harder for Fedwig? Maybe I should have kept that druid from practicing his superstitions over his body as he lay dying." Jesus started to cry. "Tell me, Father. What should I have done differently?"

"Don't blame yourself. You did nothing to anger me, Son."

"Would he still be alive if I had done anything differently?"

"That's not for you to know, Jesus. Some consequences people can foresee, and some they cannot. Right now, you are no different, in that respect, from other people."

"Why did you not answer my prayers, Father?"

"You must learn to suffer sorrows as all people do. You would not grow much if I solved everything for you. You must remember the story of Gideon that you told to the druid. He prayed hard while he gathered his men. What do you think he prayed for?"

"I suppose he wanted more men."

"Exactly. Instead, I cut his numbers. I did not give him what he asked for, but I granted what he needed. I heard your prayers, Jesus. This time it was not to be."

"You gave Gideon the victory, but Fedwig is never coming back."

"You are the son of God, Jesus, and your trials will be many. There will come a time when you will feel forsaken entirely."

"I don't see how I can ever truly be angry with you, Father."

"I know your feelings, even when you do not put them into words. Even now, you question why I allowed your friend to die."

"Friends die in war—that happens," said Jesus.

"But you say to yourself that if I am all knowing and all powerful, I could have saved him. You are reluctant to show it, but you are angry."

"I try not to be, Father."

"Don't blame yourself for being angry. I know what the loss of your friend means to you, but you have even greater trials ahead. Just know that you are always my son. No matter how much you are stirred to anger, nothing can truly separate us. Never forget that."

"When Fedwig died, I felt so alone. I reached out in my prayers, and you did not answer. I believe I could face anything if I had a way to talk to you when I need you—not wait for answers without knowing when they will come."

"People do not always get answers when they want them. Like all people, you have freedom of will, and it is up to you to discern my will as best you can and make your choices. If I came to you each time you called, would you not start putting each question in your life to me? I cannot let that happen. At the right time I will reveal to you what you need to know."

He does not want to say more about Fedwig's death. "I heard Uncle Joseph talk to Daniel about arranging a marriage for him. Daniel speaks to me about the Celtic girls and women, but I am sure he will go back to Israel to find a wife when he is ready. Will I be as other men in that way, too?"

"You have love within you already, Jesus, but it is the sacrificial and divine love you brought with you from heaven. There will come a time when you will look at anyone and know all their desires, and they will be able to hide no secrets from you. You will care for them deeply, more than you do for yourself. Some will feel the same about you, and you will not be alone. But for you, that is not a physical love as between man and woman; no woman who lacks our divine substance can share such a physical love with you. Taking a wife or not will be your choice, but you will know your desires when the time comes."

"Was it wrong of me to fight and kill for freedom, Father? Uncle Joseph was angry with me. I thought I did the right thing; the cause was just."

"It was as just as any war."

"I thought of the heroes of Israel who fought such bloody battles—Joshua, Gideon, David, and the Maccabees, to name but a few. Did they not fight as men of God?

"You protected the freedom of the Dumnonii—for a while. But nothing lasts forever. Not even the deeds of all those heroes made Israel strong enough to keep the nation safe from exile in Babylon or Roman conquest. Before long, the Romans will come to Britain, too. It will not be just a raid like that of Julius Caesar. They will come to stay, and the British will not defeat them."

"Is that future firmly cast, Father, or can it be changed?"

"It is not your mission to change it, my Son. You will return to Israel before that happens. But you can plant a seed of hope and faith among these people to steel them against their coming trials. Remember that David and Solomon were not only warriors."

"How am I to do that, Father?"

"Go among the druids. Learn from them. Teach them."

"How can I do that and keep the law?"

"Do not fear the law of Moses, my Son. Be guided by the Spirit instead. The law was written to help the people of Israel stay strong, but it is also written in Scripture that you will be a light to all the nations. The seed you plant here will never prosper if the farmer is afraid to dirty his hands. I know the faith is strong enough in you to sort out truth."

"Much as I have come to love these people, their religion is pagan and barbaric."

"There is more to it than you see, my Son. Keep to your own faith, but do not be afraid to learn from the druids and attend their festivals—as the Spirit leads you. They are an unfinished work."

"You gave Moses the law after he went up Mount Sinai through a cloud. You now lead me down through this cloud of fog and tell me not to fear that same law."

"You are the fulfillment of that law, but that's enough for now. Your uncle and cousin have need of you back in Lake Village. Follow the path to the water and follow the shoreline to the boat. Take the boat and do not wait for Brian; I will look after the child."

There was much unloading and planning to engage Jesus once he returned to the village. He was not surprised when Brian could not be found that night in the dining hall, as it was the custom of the Celts to keep their boys separate until they were old enough to fight. But many knew Eogen, Brian's father, and they directed Jesus to the house.

Jesus met the man at his threshold. "I come to ask after Brian. He took me to the Tor this morning, and we got lost. I want to make sure he returned safely to his mother."

The man looked at Jesus with sadness. "You are cruel to mock me so," he said.

"I assure you that I did not come to mock you, sir."

"You were not with my son this morning. My wife died in childbirth twelve years ago, and Brian died of fever last year. I buried him with my own hands."

Chapter 9
The Secret of the Lord

Jesus

Later that night Jesus stayed up to write another letter to Mary and Papa. Uncle Joseph would take it with him when he sailed with Kendrick the next day on the tide. Jesus did not want to say anything about fighting alongside the Celts, but he knew that Joseph would tell them. So he explained as best he could the justness of the cause and his sense of loss over the death of his companions, particularly Fedwig. He sent his love and told them how he prayed for Papa's health every day.

As the day wore on, Jesus and Daniel walked through Lake Village, catching glimpses of the vessel sailing away. "You know today is Beltane," Daniel remarked. "The pagans will be at the festival."

"I know. I was planning to see it," Jesus answered.

"You cannot be serious. They will be worshipping idols. It is against the law."

"I did not say I would join in their worship. I will only watch."

"Why do such a thing? We should use this time to devote ourselves to our own prayers."

"It is written in Scripture that we must be a light to all the nations. It will not offend my Father for me to study these people and learn."

"Have you spoken to him again?"

"I did. Early yesterday morning."

"And he approves of this?"

"It was his idea."

"You are a strange Messiah, Jesus. First you fight for pagans, and now you will join their festival. I'm just glad no rabbi will see this. I guess you waited for Papa to leave before you told me."

"It was one less thing to explain in my letter home. It will hard enough for Mother and Papa to hear about the fighting."

"You're right about that. Look. The curraghs are leaving. We had better get back to the dock."

Jesus smiled. "Are you coming with me, then?"

"Don't I always, Cousin?"

Jesus and Daniel alighted at the foot of Wearyall and walked with the people, weaving their way among the meadows of the island, then following pathways through a wooded area.

In a field, the native men and boys started their games and contests while the women and girls filled pots and lit cooking fires. It would be a feast of great proportion.

On the side of one field toward the Tor, sheep, goats, and cattle grazed in an enclosed pasture. On either side of the gateway were two large unlit pyres.

King Grengan of the Lake Village spotted them and approached with open arms. "Welcome, my friends. We did not expect you. We were told that Jesus bar Joseph of Israel never comes to any of the great festivals."

"This is our first time," Jesus answered. "From what I have heard, this must be Beltane, where you celebrate the arrival of spring."

"It is much more than that," said a woman's voice. Jesus and Daniel turned and saw a woman in the long flowing linen robes and the golden headdress of the druid priests. Her eyes seemed to pierce right through them as she gazed through locks of flowing blond curls that enveloped her head and cascaded below her shoulders. Her face had an ageless quality, neither youthful nor old. "We will reawaken the fertility of the earth from the dark months of winter. We will purify and protect the herds so they may graze the fields without coming to harm."

"This is Esmeralda, the druidess and keeper of the Tor. The Lake Village is under her jurisdiction," said Grengan. "And may I present Jesus bar Joseph of the nation of Israel and his cousin Daniel."

"We have heard of your many deeds among the Dumnonii, Jesus bar Joseph, and that you bring the ways of a strange and powerful god to these shores. We must take care that he does not upset the cosmic balance among the gods already here."

"The people of Israel believe there is only one true God, and he has given me many spiritual gifts," Jesus answered her. "He cannot be confined by anything you or I may do, but I promise you he guides me here to learn and grow in wisdom, not to overthrow your ways."

"True seekers of wisdom are always welcome among us," the priestess replied. She turned to Daniel, who appeared distracted. "Is there something wrong?"

Daniel came out of his reverie. "I'm sorry. We did not meet any female druids among the Dumnonii."

"Because they do not have any," she explained. "But any person who devotes themselves to the required course of study may become a druid."

"I would like to join some of the games. You don't think that would be idolatry, do you, Jesus?"

"Not at all. I will be along shortly." Jesus turned his attention back to the priestess. "Will you perform the ceremony by yourself?" he asked her.

"I am the only druid here, but the lighting of the great pyres of Beltane is always the province of the local king after druids make the appropriate incantations."

"I thought that there were always half a dozen druids at the great festivals, each with a special function."

"Yes, we usually work in councils except for times of imminent danger, but this is a small mission, and if it were not for the Tor, there would be no druid here at all. If you join us at Samhain, you will see dozens of druids from all over Britain. The Tor is a special place. It is the entrance to the Otherworld, and Samhain is the festival where the spirits of the departed join with the living."

"Do you believe that these spirits come out just at Samhain?" asked Jesus.

"No, they are around us all the time, but Samhain is the special time for us to commune with them," the druid priestess answered. "The days leading up to Beltane also remind us of those spirits. Both festivals mark transitions. Just as today's Beltane festival marks the awakening of the earth, so Samhain marks the preeminence of the spirit world as we put the earth to sleep for the winter. The two festivals mirror each other."

"It is interesting that you commune with the spirits of the departed. My people from Israel would fear them."

"We must be very careful when we deal with the spirits of the Otherworld," the priestess remarked gravely. "You can climb the Tor before dawn and watch the sunrise above the mists. Feel the energy and freedom that surrounds you at the top, but never walk down before the sun burns the mist away. If you walk down through the mists, the spirits will ensnare you to enter the Otherworld, and you will never be heard from again. That is for certain." The priestess paused and looked askance as Jesus suppressed an urge to laugh.

"I am sorry. I mean no disrespect. It's just that I have climbed the Tor and been down through the mist. It seems that I have avoided your Otherworld."

After an awkward silence, the priestess left him at the edge of the crowd and moved on.

Too preoccupied to look for Daniel, Jesus sat cross-legged on the grass. *Could there be any truth in her words? Did God appear in order to rescue me from Brian leading me into danger? Brian was so childlike and innocent, I cannot believe he intended to do me harm.*

Daniel came back an hour later and shook Jesus out of his reverie, trying to read his expression. "Still missing Fedwig?"

Jesus nodded. It was true, though it was not the primary reason for his distraction. They shared memories of Fedwig for a few minutes, but Daniel must have sensed that this only deepened Jesus's sadness.

"Let's join the log toss competition," said Daniel. "And later, the bow and arrow range."

Although they both acquitted themselves well, they failed to emerge as the prizewinners.

They walked around, partaking of the abundant feast laid out for all. There were songs and stories and blithe young girls who enjoyed flirting with Daniel. When dusk began to fall, everyone stood silently as Esmeralda began her incantations, invoking the spirits to rise up and grace the earth with fertility for the coming season. She invoked the spirit of fire to keep all the livestock safe and healthy as they grazed the fields. Upon her signal, Grengan lit first one pyre and then another. A tall pillar of flame roared high into the darkening sky on either side of the gateway to the stockade. To the cheers of the crowd, the animals, their eyes covered with blinders, were led forth between the purifying flames.

Esmeralda finished the last of her incantations. It was done. The earth was reborn and all the livestock purified. There only remained the free-flowing mead, dancing, and song that continued well into the night.

Daniel

The next day Jesus and Daniel set out for the Mendip Hills. The journey was less than five miles as the crow flies, they were told, but a direct route would take them over impassable marshland.

"You could paddle a curragh or coracle across the River Brue, and then double back up the River Axe," Grengan said, "or walk on drier land around the Tor across the Pomparles Bridge and then detour a few miles to the east near Pilton, but make sure you stay away from there."

"What's wrong with Pilton?" Daniel asked.

"We don't like to talk about it. Just take my word and stay away."

On Grengan's advice, they elected to walk.

As soon as they rounded the Tor, the rolling hills appeared in the distance. They skirted the headwaters of the Brue to avoid the wet bogs and then made their way northwest to the Cheddar Gorge.

The gorge cut through the landscape as if God had taken a mighty hammer and chisel to split the gently rolling hills. Jesus and Daniel walked along the bottom of the gorge beside a small river, but soon the river took a turn to the right where it emerged from the entrance to a cave, leaving the upper reaches of the gorge dry. Sheer cliffs exposed layers of rock that formed the side of the cavern. Rocky pinnacles loomed dramatically above the upper rim as the undulations in the cliff reached the hilly surface five hundred feet overhead. The other side of the gorge was not so vertical, but the slopes that broke through the cliffs were nonetheless quite steep.

At the entrance of the cave, a man was loading something into a small donkey cart. As Daniel approached, he could see a few wheels of cheese. They found miners working on scaffolds suspended on the sheer cliff to their right. Spotting the cheese maker's wagon, the miners began to clamber down for lunch.

Jesus fished in his pocket and brought out a few of the Roman denarii Joseph had left with them, as they were now in an area where the natives understood money. He gave the coins to the cheese maker, thinking he was buying just enough for himself and Daniel. Instead, he was offered most of the contents of the cart, which included a dozen loaves of bread, several flagons of mead and two wheels of cheese.

"What are we going to do with all this?" Daniel asked. "We cannot possibly eat this much."

"We can share it with the miners. There's hardly any left for them," Jesus answered.

"Feeding a multitude with a few denarii is a neat trick. You might find it handy one day," Daniel remarked.

Jesus scraped away the mold from one of the cheese wheels. "It's nothing. I just didn't know how valuable our Roman money was."

Finding their lunch laid out and paid for, the miners quickly took a liking to the young strangers. After the meal, the men let them climb around the scaffolding and gave them samples of the ore, pointing out the subtle difference between those that contained only lead and those that contained silver as well.

Daniel could see that Jesus was puzzled, weighing the two different ores in his hands. "Is there a problem?" Daniel asked.

"This is going to be harder to find than the tin. I cannot tell the difference between the ore with just the lead and the ore with the silver mixed in."

"But even I can see the streaks of gray once it's split."

"So can I, but I have to look at it. They have been digging in this gorge for centuries. All the silver at the surface has been found. We will need to crack through many feet of rock before we see the ore. It will take weeks for us to do that, and we could easily come up with nothing but lead."

"Cannot God lead you right to it?"

"I am sure he could, but I don't think he is going to solve all my problems for me. He wants me to solve things on my own. I am old enough to struggle as any man must."

Leaving the miners, they ascended the Mendip Hills and started to double back toward Pilton. About two miles along the ridgeline, they came to a small group of Celtic huts.. Smaller than a village, it was just a small band of farmers. The place was called Priddy.

The cousins looked out across the terraces below.

"Look," said Daniel, pointing toward the distinct shape of the Tor.

"I don't understand why," said Jesus, "but something about that hill gives me energy."

With that, the two decided to make themselves a home at Priddy, where they had the view of the Tor. As soon as the villagers learned that Jesus and Daniel had Roman money, they invited the cousins to build a hut nearby. Taught by the villagers, Jesus and Daniel took up the craft of wattle, daub and thatch over the next few days.

The wattle part was not bad. It was like building a fence at first. They planted posts in the ground in a circle, then soaked small branches and wove them among the uprights as if they were creating a giant basket.

The daubing came next. The villagers delivered the supplies—water, mud, straw and manure—and left the mixing and working of it into the wattle structure to Jesus and Daniel. With shovels, they mixed the first batch.

"This smells appalling," Daniel muttered. He kept his breathing shallow, but it didn't prevent the stench of cow dung from stinging his nostrils.

"My dignity is too strong for such things to threaten it." Jesus stripped off his tunic and dug right in.

The shovels were useless for applying the daub. "You've got to work the daub all the way through the wattle with your hands," explained the elderly fellow from whom they had borrowed the shovels.

The foul mixture had a way of sticking to them and everything they touched. Before long, they were covered with it. Jesus laughed.

Daniel looked up, his nose filled with the foul stench of their work. His misery was clear. That made Jesus laugh even more. Daniel swung at him and missed, and Jesus knocked him down. Soon they were engaged in an all-out wrestling match in the pit.

Soaked through, they wound up laughing too hard for Daniel to worry about the foulness. It was the first time he had seen Jesus really laugh since they had lost Fedwig. They exchanged looks, and it seemed to Daniel that Jesus knew what he was thinking.

When the work for the day was done, they made their way to the stream at the foot of the hill. The water cascading over their bodies soon washed away all the foulness of the daub, and they were refreshed. Then Jesus noticed a glint of something in the streambed. He picked up a handful of sand and gravel and playfully poured it from hand to hand. The shiny sparkle had to be a tiny grain of silver.

They spent the night with one of the Celt families and finished the daubing the next morning. Then they made their way up the streambed, searching for more silver grains to lead them to the lode. The grains of the precious metal were few, and the going was slow.

One day turned into the next. They worked through the streams. Time after time they took a wrong turn up one little streamlet and then another. Finally, they reached the source of a streamlet where the silver grains seemed to originate. It was in the middle of a small field.

"You know where the lode is, don't you?" asked Daniel.

"Yes, I can sense it now," Jesus replied.

"Let's start digging! Which way?"

"There are three lodes under this field, Daniel. And they are all deep beneath the surface."

"I don't suppose you know which of them have silver and which just have lead?"

Jesus shook his head.

Driving the shafts was backbreaking work. Day after day, from sunrise to sunset, they chipped away at the rock and hauled the chips to the surface. Using the stash of Roman money, they paid villagers to finish the thatching of their hut. Every night they came home to collapse into their beds. They started on the lode closest to the surface, but they found only lead. The second lode was equally disappointing.

They began working the shaft to the third lode at midsummer. It was the deepest. They had to keep stopping to brace the shaft with timbers. Finally, after weeks of digging, they reached the lode. Daniel swung the axe and broke away a piece of the light-colored rock. And there, in candlelight, they finally spotted the thin grey veins—the telltale sign of silver.

"We did it!" Daniel shouted.

"No, Daniel," said Jesus. "It was God. He is the source of all we have and all we are."

"But look how hard we worked. It shows in your muscles—and mine, too." Indeed, after the hard summer of toil, there was not a spot of fat left on either of them, and their hard muscles gleamed with sweat.

"I am sure it is part of my Father's plan for me, cousin. He challenges me more. I feel myself growing in spirit, not just physically."

"Do you know more of what he plans for you?"

"After all my talking to him, I know nothing more than I knew as a child. He will tell me when the time is right. But he teaches me strength. And that is what I will need if I am to be the Messiah for our people and lead them to freedom."

Daniel sighed. He wanted so much to tell Jesus what his own father had told him of the prophecy. But he remembered the promise he had made . *It is for God to reveal it to Jesus—not for me or even for Papa.*

❦

They covered the entrance to the shafts and bade good-bye to the farmers in Priddy. The wheat was coming to its full height, and the start of the harvest would be upon them soon. The cousins promised to return with more men, and added that they would be spending more for their supplies. Making their way around the marshes, they saw signs of the approaching harvest on every patch of cultivated ground. It would soon be time for Lugnasad.

It was Daniel's task to negotiate with Grengan, and Jesus made it a point to stay away, for the venture in Britain was still the family business of Daniel and his father. They needed an exclusive right to mine the field, before they could hire men and reveal the location to anyone. Daniel explained to the king how he and Jesus had toiled all summer to find the lode. Surprisingly, it took little convincing.

"Our men could use the work once the harvest is in," Grengan said, "and it will help secure the prosperity of the Lake Villagers." The royalty portion he requested as king was modest. "There is yet more silver to be found," he said, "and I know from the Dumnonii how your cousin Jesus's discoveries benefitted the people.

❦

The next day Jesus and Daniel paddled to Wearyall with the Lake Villagers. All about the field at the foot of the Tor the men held their games and contests. There was free-flowing mead and feasting. They took part in the games, and Daniel won the archery contest.

The women laid out an assortment of treats on a long trestle table.

"What is this?" Daniel asked a willowy brunette.

She smiled and cast her eyes downward. "Bilberries with biscuits and clotted cream, sir. It's important to share the bilberries now, because they are the first fruits of the harvest season."

"The offering of first fruits is important among my people, also." He helped himself to the sweet confection and answered the girl's questions about his people.

The young Celtic women were particularly eager to get Daniel and Jesus to sample a dish called "boxty." Just a griddle cake made with savory meal and milk, it seemed strange for it to take such priority, until they heard the older women chanting a folk ditty:

> Boxty on the griddle,
> Boxty in the pan,
> If you can't make boxty,
> You'll never get a man.

Jesus and Daniel couldn't contain their laughter.

A hush fell over the crowd as several young couples approached the center of the field. One by one, the couples turned their backs to each other and walked away. Here and there tears were shed by the man or the woman or a member of the crowd.

Esmeralda approached, greeting people. Daniel pointed to the diminishing group of couples still waiting their turn. "What is this ceremony about?"

"Those couples were hand-fasted in marriage at last year's festival, but it did not work out," she explained. "They can walk away from each other and try again with someone else at this year's hand-fasting."

"How does this hand-fasting work?" asked Daniel.

"You will see in a moment," said the priestess.

One group of young men and another group of young women then gathered on either side of a hedge. In the middle was a gate with two large holes slightly above head height. Although it appeared that the men and women were not supposed to see each other, most seemed to find ways to sneak a peek through the hedge or some opening in the woodwork of the gate, much to the amusement of the benevolent crowd. Then one of the men stuck his hands through the holes in the gate and one of the women on the other side quickly grasped them in hers. The gate was then opened and the couple embraced, showing their delight in the matchup that occurred by feigned chance.

One by one, the couples were united to the cheers of the crowd. Everyone seemed pleased with the pairings, except when several women grabbed for the hands of one particularly handsome young man at the same time.

As the crowd gasped, his evident intended ran off in tears while the usurper smothered the bemused bridegroom with kisses.

"No good will come of that marriage, I fear," said Esmeralda. "But one never knows."

"So…they try their hand at marriage for a year," said Daniel.

"It doesn't seem like much of a commitment," Jesus muttered.

"It's not so different from our ways, when you think about it," Daniel replied.

Jesus frowned. "How so?"

"A man can divorce a wife at any time by handing her a *get.*"

"But that is by the law of God, not some pagan ritual," Jesus interjected sharply in Aramaic.

Esmeralda looked taken aback for a moment. She couldn't know what Jesus had said, but the sharpness of his tongue was unmistakable. Her mood quickly lightened, though, as a gentle rain began to fall. Along with the people, she raised her arms and spread them in a welcoming gesture. "Lugh is with us this year," she said. "He will protect our crops from the storms until the harvest is all brought in."

"Is that why the festival is named for Lugh?" Daniel asked of the priestess.

"Yes, partly, but Lugh is also the one who dedicated this festival. He did so in honor of his foster-mother, Talantiu. She was the last queen of the *Fir Bolg*, the last race who inhabited this land before the coming of the *Tuatha Dé Danann*. She cleared the great forest so the people could sow the land with crops, but she worked herself to death doing that. She told the men at her deathbed to hold funeral games in her honor so the country would not be without songs. That is why Lugh dedicated this festival to her.

"There are some who say Talanltiu was a goddess herself," the priestess continued. "Her name means 'Great One of the Earth,' and this festival also goes by a name for the labors of childbirth. 'Brón Trogain,' we call it. It is this time of year when the goddess earth begins to bring forth the fruits of the harvest so her mortal children might live."

Jesus seemed to have focused his mind elsewhere. Esmeralda asked him if something was amiss. He answered, "I was thinking about her taking on the motherhood of a being with two natures, for that is what I have learned of Lugh—that he was of the substance of both gods and giants. It would be a little like being a mortal woman called to be the handmaiden of the Lord God."

"That's too far-fetched for me, I'm afraid." Esmeralda took her leave of them and continued making her rounds in the crowd.

As the day wore into evening, Daniel left Jesus to his philosophical brooding and joined in the fun. He was fascinated by the artists and entertainers, and especially the girls who came from far and wide. The crowd was rude and profane in its roaring, but it was all in good fun. Some women shunned Daniel, presumably for his accent or his beard, but far more were eager to enjoy a laugh and a dance with the archery champion.

Daniel and Jesus spent the night as guests of one of the Lake Villagers. Several times during the night Daniel awoke to a cry from his cousin or the noise of him thrashing about. It was so unusual for dreams to trouble Jesus; Daniel could only remember the time the fever had taken Jesus back in Lugdunum after he'd witnessed that crucifixion.

When will God set Jesus straight on his destiny? Jesus has found sparring partners among the Lake Villagers, and he still works on his swordsmanship whenever he has the time. Despite his deep sorrow for the loss of Fedwig, he seems as intent as ever perfecting his fighting skill to become the heroic Messiah of the Jews.

Daniel felt Jesus's forehead. It was cool to the touch, so at least it was not fever again. Jesus did not seem to be in torment this time, but he seemed very sad. Daniel could not make out what his cousin was saying. Here and there, he heard him say "Joseph," which was strange because Jesus always addressed Daniel's father as "Uncle." Then, for no apparent reason, Jesus smiled in his sleep and stopped muttering.

❧ ✳ ☙

Daniel looked across the hut to Jesus's bed. His cousin was already up, and Daniel could hear the sounds of the Lake Village coming to life. He found Jesus leaning on the deck rail and gazing into the mist that filtered and softened the morning sun.

Daniel approached and noticed a warm smile on his cousin's face. Jesus certainly appeared untroubled by his dreams. "There is something I must do here," said Jesus, "and I want to do it alone."

"Can't this wait?" asked Daniel. They were planning to return to Priddy with a small crew of hired workmen, to start extracting ore and building huts for the workers. More men would join them as soon as the harvest was in. "We won't have much to show Papa if we don't extract some ore before winter sets in."

"It's something I need to start now. It will take a few weeks. You will be fine without me. You are the one who organizes the workmen best; you don't need me getting in the way."

"Is this something God told you to do?"

"Not in so many words, but I feel called to do it."

Curiously, Daniel studied Jesus. *Whatever he's up to, he doesn't want to talk about it. There isn't any point in trying when he gets like this.* "Will I be able to find you if we run into a problem?"

"Grengan will know where to find me."

Jesus

Daniel left for Priddy as soon as he had gathered his men. After Jesus saw them off, he waited for the mists to clear. Then he set out in a coracle with some tools. He paddled to Ynys Witrin but steered to the left of Wearyall, landing at the outlet of a small stream that seemed to flow from the Tor. He followed the stream to its source in a spring at the foot of a smaller hill. It was a pleasant spot, with bees buzzing through a grove of apple trees. He found a tidy stack of seasoned wooden posts, which he had purchased from the villagers. This was not going to be like the hut they had built in Priddy. *I feel the guidance of the Spirit helping me make a structure that will last.*

He took his time digging post holes in a perfect circle. He drove each post into the ground, then carefully notched the upper end of each post the way Papa had taught him.

Jesus daubed the hut, after which he had several days of waiting for it to cure in the sun. He walked to Priddy to help with the mining. Daniel already had the operation well under way. At one point during their labors, Daniel paused. "I heard from one of the workmen that you're building a hut in Ynys Witrin."

Jesus kept his silence.

After a few days, Jesus returned to Ynys Witrin. By then the sun had cured the walls, and he was ready to construct the conical thatched roof. He cut trees for the upright beams that would rest on the wall and then rise at an angle to a high point above the center of the hut, where they would be gathered.

The next day Jesus started chopping down trees for the angled upright members. After cutting down several and trimming the trunks to form each upright piece, he cut a notch in the bottom ends to form the joint with a corresponding tongue he had carved into the exposed upper ends of the upright posts, which were imbedded in the wattled walls. He looked up from his work and was surprised to see Grengan leading a large contingent of workmen to the site.

"You're early," he said.

Grengan laughed. "It's our custom to gather from the surrounding villages any time a roof is being raised—we can finish in a day. We call it the 'roof-raising.'"

They marveled as Jesus finished the joinery to secure the roofing uprights to the wattle-work. It was more stable than the lashings the Celts used, which had to be redone from time to time as their buildings aged.

Grengan assigned a few men to help Jesus finish off the remaining uprights, while the others raised the structure. Within hours the framework was done, just as the women of the village approached bearing mead and food for all. For the next hour they feasted and sang, and then they began the thatching. Grengan organized the men into teams that began competing to bundle up the thatch reeds and secure them to the roof frames the fastest, as the women and children cheered them on. As the sun set it was done.

The next day, while the men went to work on their harvest, Jesus brought out several amphorae of wine from his stocks, and with the help of a few women he prepared a special feast. At the end of the day, the villagers gathered.

Jesus stood before them. "I want to thank you all for completing the roof."

Grengan scoffed. "It is unnecessary for you to go to all this trouble."

But the villagers, eager to partake of the feast, quickly shouted him down.

Jesus laughed and poured out the Gallic wine.

In the middle of countless toasts, Grengan rose. "What is the purpose of your hut, since everyone in your party is welcome to stay at the Lake Village?"

"That is the secret of the Lord," said Jesus. "But it will soon be revealed."

The name for the structure near the spring at the foot of the Tor quickly caught on among the villagers. When families passed by the lonely oversized hut on Ynys Witrin, the parents told the children it was called the "Secret of the Lord." Jesus spent several more days constructing interior walls and furnishings, including a large bed with a wattle platform. It was now the most grand and comfortable house on the island, but Jesus returned each night to stay among the Lake villagers.

Daniel

The harvest season began in earnest a few days after Jesus completed the mysterious hut on Ynys Witrin. Over several weeks, the people of Lake Village and the surrounding places raced to gather in the harvests from the fields before the onset of cold weather. Possible storms could lay the crops to waste if they struck when fruited stalks were rising high on the fields.

Daniel returned to the Lake Village for the peak of the harvest season. With all the workmen needed on their farms, there was nothing for him to do in Priddy. He walked on the deck behind the hut he shared with Jesus in the Lake Village. Sure enough, his cousin was back out on that little spit of ground that extended from the seaward side of the settlement and remained above the water at high tide. He watched his cousin for a while. Jesus gazed toward the sea, as if his vision could pierce the thick fog. Then he turned his attention to working the sand at the water's edge, using only his hands. Jesus had never told Daniel what the sand structure was, but over a few days it had taken a distinctly recognizable form. There was just enough clay mixed into it to hold the structure together. Eventually Daniel realized that it was a model, marvelously complex and fragile, of Jerusalem.

Daniel continued to watch Jesus, who didn't seem to be himself. It was a month now since he had left Daniel to his own devices to manage the mining operation at Priddy. First there was that mysterious structure that Jesus had built on the island, and now he was working on this sand castle. True, with all the villagers occupied with the harvest there wasn't much to be done at the moment, but this wasn't the first time in Britain where they had encountered a period where the smelting or mining had to stop when their helpers were needed urgently in the fields. That was usually the time for them to head out and explore. *Does Jesus even care anymore about the success of the venture?*

Jesus stared intently into his model. He shook his head as if something was not quite right.

The model was a crazy thing to build, Daniel thought, but what could be wrong with it? Everything seemed perfect, just as Daniel remembered David's City. Then suddenly, Jesus jumped right into the model and began tearing down the temple structure.

"What are you doing?" Daniel shouted. "You've been working on this for days. Now you're destroying it."

"I am making it what it should be," shouted Jesus. "This is the New Jerusalem, not the Old." Jesus tore away the highest section of the slightly hardened sand.

"But you're ruining the temple. What is Jerusalem without the temple? It's the house of God!"

"No. God is everywhere," said Jesus. He was working frantically on his knees in the section of the model where the temple had been, scooping away the remaining bits of the crumbled structure. "The New Jerusalem does not need a temple. I am the only temple the people will need."

Daniel's jaw dropped. He recalled his glimpse in Nazareth of his cousin in glory. "What are you saying, Jesus? Will you take the place of the temple as the center of worship for all the people?"

"I'm not the one who said that, Daniel. It was you." Suddenly, Jesus stood up and pointed out to sea. "Look!"

The fog lifted from the water like a rising curtain, and there—not more than two hundred yards away—Kendrick's ship came sailing in. Daniel gasped. His father wasn't due back for another month at least, but there he was, waving to them from the deck. *Who is that woman with him on the deck, and why does he have his arm around her so protectively? Has Papa remarried?*

The ship approached, on a course to make its landing on the Lake Village dock. The crewmembers shouted to each other, but the woman paid them no heed. She was smiling at Jesus. Daniel turned his head. Jesus stood in the hollowed section of his model, smiling back at her. Daniel looked back and forth between them as the ship came closer. No. His father was not bringing a new wife. He could recognize her now, though she looked older than he remembered. She was Mary.

Jesus ran to the dock as Mary walked to the gunwale. She was dressed in the simple, flowing dress she must have worn all the way from Galilee. She still bore herself with the grace that Daniel recalled from so many years ago.

Suddenly realizing that he had forgotten about his own father, Daniel raised his arm in a welcoming wave. Daniel ran after Jesus to the dock. Turning into the wind, the vessel approached the dock slowly. A crewman threw lines to shore, and some of the Lake Villagers pulled them in.

Jesus leaped across the gap onto Kendrick's ship and into the arms of his mother.

"Oh, Jesus. I missed you so much!" Mary murmured with joy.

Jesus kissed her forehead. He stood a head taller than her now. "It's been a long time, Mother. I missed you too."

Daniel watched and listened from the shore just a few feet away. This was no ordinary reunion. Daniel felt the energy of their souls rejoicing, as something inside them was made complete. They came ashore arm in arm as the crewmen made the vessel fast to the dock.

Suddenly Mary stood back. "There is something I must tell you, Jesus. Your father, Joseph, he's—"

"I know, Mother. He is with God now. I had a vision in a dream, just as he had those visions that led us to safety in Egypt and back home again when the time was right. I knew you were coming, and I have made everything ready."

So that's Jesus's secret—the secret of the Lord. Daniel smiled.

"There is nothing for me now back in Galilee," Mary continued. "Not with my husband gone and you here. You are everything to me now."

"Life is good here, Mother, and we will be happy. The land is fertile, and the people live free of empires and their cruel taxes. They are warm and generous."

"But they are pagans, aren't they?"

"When I first arrived in Britain, all I could see was their ignorance of the one true God. But the Father wants me here for a reason; both to learn from these people and to teach them. It's puzzling. Their priests give me ideas that launch me into a profound spiritual insight, and the next minute they just seem to know nothing but idolatry and their endless array of deities and demigods."

"Let me look at you. You have grown into a strapping young man. I will miss the boy who used to help me bake the morning bread on the roof of our house in Nazareth."

"There will always be time to spend with you, Mother," said Jesus. "We must bake bread together tomorrow morning. We don't do it on the roof here; the cooking fires are inside. But when we do that, I still can be as a child for a while. I will buy the flour and yeast from the natives."

Daniel felt awkward as mother and son embraced once again. *Perhaps I should leave them some time to themselves.* His thoughts turned to his own mother, even though he had no memory of her. *Did she ever hold me as a newborn baby in her arms, before she succumbed to the injuries from my birth?*

Suddenly Mary's embrace scattered Daniel's feeling of emptiness.

"Oh, Daniel, I am so happy to be with you, too. We will have time to get to know each other at last, and you will be another son for me! I must make room in my heart, for there are many who are touched and will be touched by Jesus, but there will always be a special place for you."

Daniel felt another arm join in the embrace. "Truly we are brothers now," said Jesus. "As you have shared a father with me, my mother now is here to share with you."

Papa had finished his business on the ship. Daniel quickly wiped his eyes as he joined him, hoping he didn't notice.

"Let's see that sand sculpture Jesus was working on," said Joseph.

Mary nodded her agreement, and they walked over to it. "It's beautiful. You captured all the details of David's City. Will you finish the temple?" she asked.

Jesus stood silent, as if for once he did not know how to answer.

"I think Jesus was just thinking of home," said Daniel. "With you here, we don't need anything more to remind us of it."

Joseph and Daniel stayed behind as Jesus took Mary to explore the Lake Village. "It has been four years now since I brought him to Britain," said Joseph. "And still he sees himself as the Messiah who will free our people—doesn't he?"

"Yes, Papa. That is why he keeps up the sword practice whenever we get away from the Tor. Since Fedwig died he has taken less pleasure in it, but whenever I try to discourage him he says that is his destiny. He says he must prepare for it."

"Does he still talk about conversations with God in Heaven?"

"He doesn't brag about it or volunteer anything to me. He just tells me things here and there, when they help him explain something."

"Like what?"

Daniel hesitated..

"Come, now, tell me," urged Joseph.

"After you left, he told me God wanted him to spend more time among the druids, even attend their festivals."

"I don't understand how he expects to ever lead our people. No righteous Jew will ever follow him." Joseph gestured at the model of Jerusalem. "I'm puzzled," he said. "He's made a perfect replica of the city, but why has he not made a model of the temple."

"He had created an exact image of the temple," said Daniel, "but then he destroyed it. I was puzzled, too, Papa, but now it seems to me that he may be right. The temple is only a work of man. Perhaps the real blasphemy lies in elevating such a structure above the righteousness and power of God."

"But is he joining with the Celts in their idolatry?" asked Joseph. "That's blasphemy and against the laws of Moses."

"If God tells him to learn from the druids," said Daniel, "why should he care what Moses said about it?"

"Has he said anything about his dream of the crucifixion?"

"You asked me to keep that to myself, and we don't talk about it."

"It is not for us to reveal to him the true meaning of that prophecy. That is for God."

"Could you possibly be wrong about that, Papa?"

"I wish I were, but I know I am not. If his fate leads him to a cross, then die upon it he most certainly will."

"Have you talked any of this over with Mary?"

"Of course not. She thinks Jesus can do no wrong. Though I did tell her about Jesus joining in that battle at Rumps. I'm sure it was in his letter, too. That worried her, but she told me only Jesus could discern the path his Father in Heaven intended for him."

Looking up, Daniel saw Jesus and Mary approaching. He was glad that their presence would end this conversation with his father. The four of them took some curraghs and paddled to Ynys Witrin. The hut Jesus built at the foot of the Tor was no longer so mysterious. It was to make a home for his mother. It did not bother him that Mary would sleep alone in the magnificent bed. She certainly was weary from her travels, and the rest of them were no strangers to the makeshift bundles of plant cuttings that served them for mattresses on the floor. Daniel smiled as he drifted off to sleep. It was as if each of them had been made whole.

Mary

It was still dark the next morning when Mary rousted Jesus from his bed. The dough left in the warm area near the fire had risen overnight. "It's harder to use the fire embers to raise the dough." She kept her voice low as the others slept. "I had to check on it a few times during the night. The dough will not rise if it gets too hot or too cold."

They went outside into the morning fog and found a place to work. "You don't really need to do this," Jesus said as they formed the loaves. "We can buy our bread in the village. You can sleep soundly through the whole night."

"Did you think I came here to get fat and lazy?"

Jesus laughed. "Not you, Mother. And we get to have this time together. We cannot buy that in the village."

Mary smiled as they went about their work. They did not need to say anything. They could work silently, in the joy of each other's company.

Jesus went inside to put more wood on the fire. As the flames came to life around the baking stones, he and his mother positioned the loaves for the final rising. Mary signaled Jesus to follow her outside again, where they could talk.

"How have you been, my son?"

"How do I seem to you?"

"I can see that you have come to love it here in Britain, but Joseph told me you lost your best friend in battle, and that has made you very sad."

"That's right. But you have also lost your husband."

"He was so sick at the end, and it was hard to see him linger in pain. I was ready when the end came. After that, there was nothing to keep me in Nazareth—certainly not with you so far away. I had enough money for the passage to Arelate. That's where Uncle Joseph happened to see me in the market, and he brought me here right away."

"I saw that in my dream, Mother—the dream I had when I started building this house."

"It must have been harder for you to lose your best friend when it was so unexpected."

"I suppose that no death in war should be all that unexpected," he answered. "Even so, Fedwig's death still grieves me to the core."

"Are there no other friends you can make here?" Mary asked. "And what of Daniel?"

"There are plenty of friends to be had, Mother, but no one can take the place of Fedwig. He taught me the ways of the sword, and we always had such great fun. I miss the way he could laugh at anything. He never seemed to know any fear, even when I first met him as a child. Daniel is wonderful, and I am so happy we will be real brothers now, but it's not the same."

"Surely, you must have made a friend somewhere. I remember how you befriended every child in the village back in Nazareth."

"Actually, there was one boy who reminded me of Fedwig. But I only met him once." Jesus told Mary about Brian and their excursion to the top of the Tor. He left nothing out, not even Esmeralda's suspicion that Brian was a spirit attempting to ensnare him in the Otherworld—nor that, by all accounts, he was dead. "I did not mean to engage with any spirits of the dead, Mother; he looked like a normal boy."

"It does not sound like he meant you any harm."

"He was so full of laughter and love."

"Then I don't think he was from that Otherworld at all," said Mary. "God told you he would look after the boy. Perhaps he was lonely in heaven, so God sent him back to share a few moments with you, his Son, to bring joy to both your hearts. He led you to God, which no unhealthy spirit would do."

Jesus hugged her. "Oh, Mother! What a wonderful way you have of putting things. You have brought that memory close to my heart, and I can relive it now forever."

Jesus

The final rising complete, Jesus and Mary silently retrieved the baking stones from the flames and set the risen loaves above them on a rack. Soon the hearty smell of baking bread filled the house as the sun began to rise. Joseph and Daniel stirred. Jesus and Mary exchanged many smiles that morning. Jesus remembered everything Fedwig meant to him. He would never forget his fallen friend, nor would he ever forget Brian. But Mother was with him now, and for the first time since Fedwig's death, he felt himself able to accept it in peace.

Joseph

The harvest was finished a few weeks after Mary's arrival, and both Jesus and Daniel returned to the mine in Priddy. Their workers began filtering back from the fields.

Joseph stayed behind in Ynys Witrin. The same morning the boys left, he began experimenting with the ore that had been extracted so far. Silver was harder to purify and refine than tin, and different types of ore called for variations in the techniques. It took Joseph several days to perfect the processes for working the silver from the ore.

Mary settled in comfortably, taking up residence by herself in the solid house Jesus had built for her. *Jesus should be taking on the responsibility of the man in her life. He's supposed to be the head of her household.* Joseph shuddered when he remembered how he had found Mary wandering the streets of Arelate. He could not bear the thought that she booked a passage on a ship from Israel and lived aboard the ship by herself among strange men. Back in Galilee, it was scandalous beyond measure for a woman to be away from her family for anything more than running errands around the village. When a woman lost her husband, it became the responsibility of the men in her family to look after her. In fact, if a brother or male cousin of Joseph were unwed, it would be expected that Mary would quickly marry that man. And if there was no man available from her late husband's family, the woman's almost-grown son would be expected to take on the role of head of household. *Jesus should be doing that now, but he treats Mary as if he were still a child. He even helps her bake the bread, which no self-respecting man would do.*

Joseph was even more surprised to see Mary venturing out among the villagers. She was not fluent in the native language, but she seemed to make herself understood. It reminded Joseph of how Jesus picked up languages with seemingly miraculous ease. The way Mary kept her head covered made her easy to pick out even from a distance as she walked among the native huts. Whenever he asked, she explained that she was visiting this villager or that one, bringing a bit of food to someone who was hungry or sick or perhaps just helping out with some spinning or weaving.

The Celts held to different ways, and it was not unusual for widows and unmarried women to live independently. *At least there will be no scandal in Britain. Jesus seems unconcerned to leave his mother living on her own. He didn't even ask me to watch over her before he left. That is normal for a Celt, but scandalous for a Jew. Has Jesus become too much of a Celt?*

⊱ ✠ ⊰

By the time the boys returned, the days were shorter and colder. They managed to bathe off the sweat and grime from the mine in the frigid water. Joseph knew what they would be about; it was the evening before Samhain, and the pagans would be celebrating the end of the harvest. He called the boys to follow him outside for a word; he did not want to grieve Mary with this.

As soon as they were out of earshot, he got to it. "So, did you return for the festival? Don't suppose for a moment that I don't know what happens tomorrow."

"We weren't trying to hide anything from you," Jesus answered.

"What about you?" Joseph turned to his son. "Surely you know better than to consort with pagans in their idolatry?"

"God wants Jesus to learn what he can from the druids, and also to teach them. That's what he told me, and I believe him."

Joseph wiped tears from his eyes as he looked from one to the other. "I do not know you any more—either of you. We are Jews. We live by the law. That is not something we put on for show among our people back home. It is who we are. It is what we take with us everywhere. You are both young men now and must choose your own paths, but just as you choose yours, so too must I choose mine." He turned to Jesus. "If you insist on going to that festival, I must give up on this venture. I must leave Britain and not return. You can carry on through Kendrick or I can bring you back to Galilee, if you wish."

"All of us are trying to determine God's will," said Jesus. "I can only tell you that he wants me to stay and learn from these people."

"God does not speak to me directly," said Joseph. "I know his will only through his laws in the Torah."

"I must stay with Jesus," said Daniel. "I do not speak with God like he does, but I know from my heart that this is his will for me."

"Perhaps all of us should pray about this," said Jesus. "Let us do that tonight and pray that God might give us all guidance."

Joseph spent a fitful night, dozing off, then waking up and trying to pray. *How can I pray for discernment when that can only point me toward strict observance of the law? If it does, there can be no backing down. The boys seem just as determined to follow God's will as they see it. I can give up the enterprise in Britain if I have to; I just cannot bear the idea of separating from Daniel and Jesus.*

By the next morning, Joseph had changed his mind about leaving. He didn't say anything else about going or staying on; he just refrained from any preparation to leave.

Jesus

The assembly was unlike anything Jesus had ever imagined. He, was with Daniel and Esmeralda at the Tor summit, spying across the country. In every direction, lines of men and women of all the Celtic castes approached. It was like a giant web of humanity moving into its center.

From the southeast came the Durotriges, led by warriors arrayed in their blue greasepaint. "Is it not forbidden for warriors to bring weapons?" asked Jesus.

"They bring only their war paint," said Esmeralda. "They leave their weapons behind before they cross the border."

From the north, the boats bearing the Silures from across the mouth of the Severn were coming up the Brue past Lake Village. Some were already discharging their passengers in the fields between Wearyall and the Tor.

And from the west came the Dumnonii. Jesus wondered if he would see any of his old friends. Most of these people would be from the area to the east of the Tamar, which was as far as the tin exploration had taken him. Perhaps some would make it from the western reaches toward Carn Roz.

Thousands had already gathered in the fields, and canopies with flags on top demarked gathering places for the various castes and tribes.

In the eastern field, each king had, for himself and his warriors, a magnificent canopy decorated with the tribal colors. "The biggest canopies are those of the Dobunni, the Dumnonii, and the Silures," Esmeralda explained. "But the smaller canopies you see everywhere are for the other delegations that travel further. Every kingdom sends a delegation and at least a surrogate if the king does not come in person."

In the western field the common people gathered for contests and games.

From the top of the Tor, the druids were easy to spot. Their golden headdresses caught the rays of the sun. They clustered together, wandering among the common people and the warriors in groups of five or six.

Elsigar

Elsigar led his troupe of druids among the canopies in the eastern field where the warriors and kings gathered.

News of the battle at Rumps had traveled across Britain, and it was a topic of much discussion. Old enemies such as the Dumnonii and the Durotriges talked about laying aside differences to meet the common threat of invasion. Not only were the Scotti a concern; ever since the raid by Julius Caesar, there was always the threat of invasion from Rome. As one of the heroes of Rumps, Elsigar found himself much in demand that day among all the delegations, particularly those who traveled farthest to Ynys Witrin.

As he moved on, he waved to another druid from the Belgae, an old friend he had studied with in Bangor when they were novices. His friend was instructing novices of his own now, teaching an old lesson the druids had taught since time immemorial: the Mabinogion, the story of the Cauldron of Bran. The theme of treachery of the Scotti from Eire made it quite relevant now.

"The cauldron was given to the king of Eire, Matholwch, by Bran as part of the marriage arrangements for Bran's sister, Branwen. But the king mistreated her and brought about a war when her family gathered an army from across Britain to rescue her. During the fighting, the slain warriors of Eire were brought back to life when they were cast into the water of the cauldron. Efnisien, the British hero, turned the tide of battle by hiding among the enemy corpses. The enemy mistook him for one of their own dead and tossed him into the cauldron. He destroyed the cauldron from within, at the cost of his own life."

Just as his friend was completing the story, Elsigar looked up and saw others listening in. He recognized the traders from the east. Daniel, standing next to Esmeralda, seemed casually interested, but Jesus was paying rapt attention.

Elsigar quietly walked around to greet them. "Jesus, Daniel. I knew you were near Ynys Witrin, but I never expected to meet you at a festival. Did you not tell us that our idolatry was an abomination against what you call the one true God?"

"We did not come to join in the worship," answered Jesus.

"Then why have you come?"

"God moved me to open myself and see what there is to learn from those who do not share the faith of my fathers. I am not sure that any religion is devoid of truth. Perhaps we will learn a way of looking at our own truth from a different perspective. Or maybe there will be some kernel of truth to be found, once many layers of superstition are stripped away."

"Did either of you find any kernel of truth in the lesson you just heard?"

"It was confusing," said Daniel. "There were so many names and different kinds of magic going on. I could not tell if any of them were supposed to be a god."

Jesus nodded. "Indeed, but I found one thing in the story very interesting. The waters of the cauldron could restore life to the dead warriors, but there was no suggestion they could prolong the life of the living. To experience rebirth, the warriors had to die in their own lives first. Somehow, that rang true to me."

Elsigar closed his eyes and pondered what Jesus had said. The Mabinogion was one of the deepest mysteries in the druidic teachings. It had always confounded even the most advanced novices, but Jesus had captured its essential meaning neatly and effortlessly. He opened his eyes and exchanged a knowing glance with Esmeralda. "Bran's cauldron was destroyed," he said to Jesus. "Can the waters of healing be restored to us?"

"Perhaps they can, in a different form. Our prophet Elisha used the waters of the Jordan River to heal Namaan of his leprosy. The man was a Syrian general. It could not be just any water; Elisha insisted that Namaan wash in the Jordan even though other streams were closer. So, I would say yes. There is special water that can heal and restore life, and it is not only for the Jews."

Elsigar eyed Jesus closely. *Our paths have crossed many times since that day my narrowly divided council decided this boy could stay because he practiced no magic of his own. Physically, he clearly has become a young man of some stature, but his insight is as sharp as any wise man.* Elsigar reached in his pocket and felt the old coin that bore the image of the snake egg. *Jesus displayed tremendous insight at Rumps, quickly discerning the significance of a God who existed in three persons and another with a dual nature. Now there is this fresh insight into the Mabinogion. There must be something beyond guesswork. The spirits run strong in him, but are they spirits that bear good or bear ill?* "Perhaps there is much both of us can learn from each other," said Elsigar. "I must discuss something first with other druids. Can you meet me here at Imbolc?"

"I don't see why not," Jesus answered.

"I will look forward to meeting you then." Elsigar nodded. He stayed with Esmeralda as Jesus and Daniel went off to explore the festival.

"You are thinking of taking him to Ynys Môn, aren't you?" asked Esmeralda.

"Possibly."

"Nothing can be hidden from him there. We will have no secrets left. It is not meet to bring a stranger, and it is dangerous."

"There is danger coming from everywhere," said Elsigar. "The Romans are meddling more in the affairs of our tribes in the east. They look for a pretext to invade. There is no safety for us in ignorance."

As dusk descended, they lit the pyres and torches. All were fed, rich or poor. Discussions and games continued into the night. At the appointed hour, they gathered in a multitude at the foot of the Tor for the closing incantations, which Esmeralda had the honor of making. She called to the spirits of the Otherworld. It was time for them to come out and put the world to sleep. The Celts extinguished all the fires as one. Except for the moonlight everything was in darkness.

But one light shone into the night. It seemed to promise the awakening of the earth in the spring. It came from the Secret of the Lord.

Part III
A Mission from God

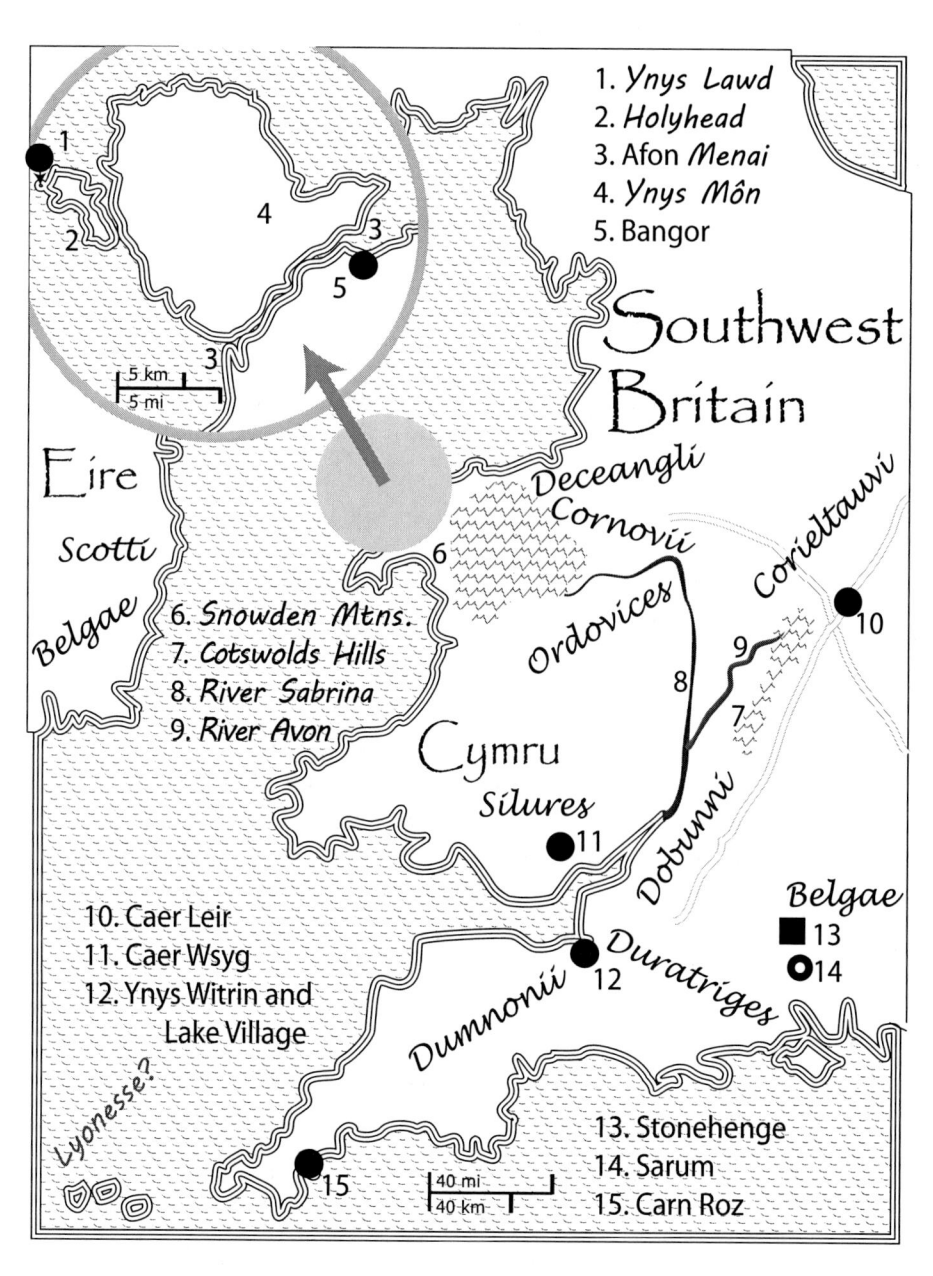

1. Ynys Lawd
2. Holyhead
3. Afon Menai
4. Ynys Môn
5. Bangor

Southwest Britain

Eire
Scotti
Belgae

6. Snowden Mtns.
7. Cotswolds Hills
8. River Sabrina
9. River Avon

Deceangli
Cornovii
Ordovices
Corieltauvi
Cymru
Silures
Dobunni

10. Caer Leir
11. Caer Wsyg
12. Ynys Witrin and Lake Village

Duratriges
Dumnonii

Belgae

13. Stonehenge
14. Sarum
15. Carn Roz

Lyonesse?

Interlude

St. Hilary's Parish, Cornwall, A.D. 1646, during the reign of King Charles I of England

Lieutenant Teague noticed the unusual marker at the town boundary. He had seen such things once or twice as a boy, when his father had taken him to the southwest. His horse walked on steadily, leading his men toward Saint Michael's Mount, a few miles ahead. That tall rock in the bay almost at Land's End would be their final fortified sanctuary from the Parliamentary pursuers.

"Are you all right?" he asked his commander, who rode beside him. The red sash over their thick leather coats signified their royalist allegiance. "You seem melancholy."

"I am so weary of this rebellion," the commander replied.

"Likewise for me. It will all turn out right, though. His Majesty is God's anointed. It is God's will that we shall prevail."

"What are you thinking? We beat retreats all the time. The north is gone, and there is not much left of the king's army after the battle at Naseby. We don't even know what happened to Prince Charles when Pendennis fell."

"Surely, he escaped. Even if the land is lost, he shall return when the country comes to its senses. But it will be hard on the people of Cornwall; most do not care for the Puritans."

"How can they, when the Puritans root out every trace of tradition in the church?" remarked the commander.

"Aye! I was just noticing that tunic cross over there. There is one near my home of Priddy. The vicar told me the tale of these crosses when I was a boy. They mark the story of how our Lord came to Britain in his youth. I wonder how long the Puritans will let it stand?"

"That is only fanciful legend," the commander remarked. "I fight for my king and the true faith—not for some folktale."

"My vicar taught that it was more than legend."

A cavalry officer from the rear rode up, looking panicked. "Sir, the Roundheads approach this way from the north, less than four miles off."

"Your orders?" Lieutenant Teague asked his commander. "Shall we turn round and attack these villains? Saint Michael will surely protect us!"

"The saint will protect us more once we are within his fortified mount on the island. We must double speed straightaway to Marazion, and hope the tide is out so we can make it across the causeway before the Roundheads come upon us."

The order was given and the company doubled its pace through St. Hilary Village. The local folk cheered them on.

As the men passed the church, Teague looked about. *It is a shame this church should suffer sacrilege. The puritans have no respect for the ancient traditions.* He dismounted and quickly entered the church to find the vicar.

As if ignorant of the rough world outside—or simply refusing to take note of it—the vicar was kneeling in the side chapel. As Teague approached, the priest turned suddenly. With a look of calm, he asked, "How close are they?"

"No more than four miles. We are ordered to Saint Michael's Mount, and I urge you to follow. You are truly in danger."

"And so is this church and all within."

"Also the old cross marker that bears our Lord as a child. You know how the puritans despise that tale."

"It is more than a tale," the priest replied.

"My vicar at Priddy often said that nothing in Christendom was as sure as the visit of Lord Jesus there."

"Go—go back to your regiment."

❧ ✤ ☙

Lying prone beneath the wild ferns in the field, Father Argall watched the Roundheads approach. The plain gray and black of their garments was broken only by the metallic shine of their armor. He prayed these men would stay far away from his sleepy parish, and especially from the church he loved so much. Dreading what might happen, he watched across the field from his hideout under the vegetation. The Roundhead cavalry approached and stopped. Two of them dismounted next to the cross.

Father Argall prayed in earnest, but he heard the officer say, "Brethren, here stands a thing of idolatry. We have seen these before, and I daresay they mock us in our attempt to save this land from the wiles of popery."

"You speak the truth, Captain," responded one of the surly retainers.

"Though we be in haste, we cannot deny the mission God has charged us with," the captain continued. "This is a papist crucifix, left by the evil monks who planted them long ago when their deception of this island began. We cannot tolerate such a symbol as this. It distorts the purity of true Christian faith."

"Enough of your rambling, Walter!" interrupted another officer, approaching from the rear division on horseback. "We are not here to be preached at. Smash the damned thing if it makes you happy, and let us get on with the slaughter of the royalist pigs!"

The captain ordered three of his men to topple the monument.

Once the statue lay on the ground, one of the young cavalrymen withdrew his axe and was about to swing at the image of the boy on the cross.

Father Argall charged from his hiding place with a wild howl, his black robe fluttering about him as he ran. Tears welled in his eyes. "Saint Michael—defend me in battle!"

His diversion worked. The young soldier dropped his axe and rushed ahead, reaching for the sword on his shoulder. Musketeers moved to the front.

"It's the papist priest, and he attacks us!" shouted the captain. "Fire!"

The vicar stopped in his tracks as the soldiers raised their muskets. The bullets from the fusillade tore through his body. He fell to the ground.

The parliamentary soldiers paused over his immobile form only a moment. They stripped the church of its ornamentation. They rode off in pursuit of the Cavaliers, leaving the dead priest and the tunic cross forgotten in the field.

❧ �քं ☙

"It will difficult to lift, but we must," said Jowan, the vestryman, to the men with him in the field just outside the village. They had found the granite cross lying on its side, with the image of the Christ child, arms outstretched. As they lifted it onto their cart, Jowan saw markings carved into its base that he had never noticed before. Somehow, they seemed familiar: a series of five lines with cross marks at different angles. The ravages of time had eroded the markings, but they were still visible, and he could feel them with the tip of his finger.

"We'd best be on our way," said one of the men. "The new Roundhead preacher will be coming anon, and it will not do for him to catch us with the monument."

Jowan withdrew his hand and helped the others secure the statue in the cart. Within the hour, they had it secreted in a cellar.

Then he remembered where he had seen the weatherworn image before. He walked back to the church, now a plain shell of its former radiance. The icons and reliquary, even the crucifixes, were gone, stripped away as graven images and symbols of popery. He turned to the sacristy and searched among the scattered papers left by poor Father Argall. He found a rubbing, evidently taken from the stone. It clearly showed the same five lines and hatch marks, and above the image were the words Jowan recognized as Father Argall's handwriting: "The Secret of the Lord."

It would not do for the rubbing to be found by the new preacher, so Jowan put it in a bottle and hid it in the cellar of the church tower.

Jowan lived to see the restoration of the crown. Every so often he stole into that cellar to gaze at the tunic cross. The boy seemed to be reaching out to him. The cross yearned to tell its secret, and he wondered what it was.

◈

Year by year, season after season, time took its toll on the stone even though the cross lay protected in that cellar. Moisture got in, then froze, and then thawed. Eventually, nothing of the markings was visible on the stone itself, but the graphite was inert, and remained. The worms that eat paper never found their way to the rubbing. No speck of mold or touch of flame got to it.

Chapter 10
Of Lepers and the Law

Ynys Witrin, A.D. 13, during the reign of Augustus, first emperor of Rome

Esmeralda

On the day after Samhain, when Elsigar and his councilors departed from Ynys Witrin, Esmeralda was on hand to bid them farewell. *The earth is at rest now, but Elsigar has allowed a menace to stay among us.* "Are you still resolved to allow Jesus to go to Ynys Môn?" she asked. *I cannot stop him from bringing the young outlander. The others respect him too much to listen to me.*

"Do I take it rightly that you would not approve?" Elsigar asked.

"Most definitely I would not. He has no respect for our gods, and he will bring down their wrath upon us all. Did you not see the light that was left burning through the night after our good people extinguished all theirs?"

"It came from the hut he built for his mother. But what of it? We know these people have their own faith."

"It is impious."

"It is not impious to offer hospitality to those who come from afar and allow them to practice their religion if they keep it to themselves."

"Elsigar, you were such a fool to let them stay when they first came to our shores. He has been practicing magic." *Maybe I went too far. He looks angry now. A druid such as Elsigar is not often called a fool to his face.*

"How can you say this? My councilors and I examined the boy when he first came to Britain and found him to be no practitioner of any magical art. Since then he has been nothing but a help to the Dumnonii. If not for him, the pirates from Eire would be knocking at your door.."

"He practices a mysterious and powerful magic. His god longs to conquer our own gods, and it will tear apart the balance of nature."

"How do you know this?"

"I heard it from his own lips just yesterday. He told me that he walked down from the summit of the Tor through the mists. How could he have avoided being ensnared into the Otherworld unless he had invoked a powerful incantation?" A look of consternation replaced the anger on Elsigar's face. *He's finally getting my point.* "You cannot trust him with the knowledge he will gain in Ynys Môn. He will use it against our own gods and destroy us all."

Elsigar paused, considering her words. Finally he spoke. "We knew from the start that Jesus is protected by a powerful god. That is not the same as practicing magic. Who does not ask protection from one god or another? We will see what happens when I return for Imbolc. Perhaps Jesus will have lost interest in our festivals by then. If he comes, we will sort it out. In the meantime, remember that I am not such an old fool that I cannot discern the practice of foul magic."

Esmeralda let out a gasp. *I have angered him too much.* Nonetheless, she opened her mouth to retort.

Elsigar cut her off. "Look to gain your own wisdom, woman, for you surely need it!" He turned and left.

"Elsigar!" she shouted after him.

The druid did not stop to listen.

Perhaps it is for the best. Imbolc is three months away, and the fool will not be around in the meantime to interfere.

Joseph

"Look outside. How pretty it is!" Jesus said to the others. He turned again to look through the doorway.

"The snow falls deeper here than the dustings we sometimes see in Judea," said Joseph. "I have seen it like this in parts of Gaul, but it doesn't often fall this deeply in Britain."

They were gathered in Mary's house. Outside, a midwinter storm had covered the field and covered the treetops in glistening white. Joseph had arrived the day before to winter with Mary and the boys.

"Let's go outside and run in the snow," Jesus said to Daniel.

Soon the boys were darting among the apple trees, pelting one another with snowballs. Mary came to the door to watch. "Thank you, Joseph," she said.

"It is I who should be thanking you. Your son has made me prosper."

"I never thought I would ever see Jesus so happy. He is a man now, but look at him and Daniel too, as they frolic. They are like children. But it's so cold out there; shouldn't they stay inside where it's warm?"

Joseph laughed. "They will come in when they feel the need." *She does not know the destiny that awaits her son. Should I share it with her?* Joseph gently held her shoulder. *No, she has been through so much, taking care of her husband for so long only to lose him. Even here, she doesn't get to see Jesus much. She deserves some happiness. I will not burden her with what I learned in Lugdunum. Jesus loves her dearly, but not even she can change the path he chooses. It is for God to tell her.*

"Is something wrong?" asked Mary.

"I was just thinking."

"Tell me what's on your mind." Mary smiled. "We don't keep secrets from each other."

She suspects something. What can I say? Oh, I have it. "Has Jesus told you about the new lode?"

Mary laughed. "The boys would never talk business with me; I am a woman, after all."

"Let me tell you. But it is something we must keep secret for a while."

Mary nodded.

"Jesus found another lode of silver ore. They have been working the first that they found last summer, and they have a lot of ore to work with now. But that first lode is almost played out. Anyway, we have to keep this secret until we make a deal with Grengan. Otherwise, anyone can come along and claim it."

"What do you do with the ore? It's just a lot of rocks isn't it? Are you taking all that rock back to Gaul?"

"It's far too heavy and bulky. We need to refine it here. The silver is tricky to work with. Daniel knows a little, but I am better at it. That is why

I am staying until spring, at least. We could sell the ore to other miners, but we make more money if we refine it ourselves and take it to Gaul. It's much easier to transport once we refine it into silver."

"Did you see this bronze vessel that Jesus made for me?" She led Joseph across the room to take a look. "It's beautiful, isn't it?"

Joseph smiled as he took the vessel in his hands. It was a typical Celtic vessel made of bronze, but with the Celtic patterns inlaid with silver; he had shown Jesus the inlay technique using silver wire. "So, this is what Grengan was talking about. He told me yesterday that the men of the village were making money over the winter crafting vessels for Jesus."

"Oh, Mother. You spoiled the surprise." Jesus walked in, pouting. Daniel came close behind.

"I am sorry, son. I didn't know it was a surprise."

Joseph turned to Jesus. "This will be great to take back to Gaul. It doesn't weigh very much, so it can fill our holds after we load up all the heavy tin and silver."

Joseph was left to his own thoughts as the conversation drifted off. *It's a bad business that Pirro never got a chance to do this. These vessels will sell anywhere, and this would have worked out so much better for him than the junk he was trying to sell. I wonder where he is. Is he even alive? His Celtic masters in the north likely have worked him to death by now.*

Joseph saw Daniel wince as Jesus went on about filling the space in the ships going back to Gaul. *Daniel must be thinking about Pirro, too. He believes Jesus is the Messiah, but how can that be since he caused Pirro to be sold into slavery? Pirro deserved his punishment, but it was a fate worse than death, and what kind of Messiah would be so lacking in compassion?*

Horshak

Horshak, the silver miner, called on Grengan in the Lake Village later that day. The two men embraced.

"I have not seen you since Samhain, and now winter is upon us," the village king remarked as he poured. "Come, have some fresh cold-brewed mead."

"Thank you. The cold-brew is the best. It just snaps on the tongue and says hello." Horshak laughed. "I drink to your health. May the gods protect you and your kin."

Grengan returned the toast. "So, how did the year go for you in Cheddar?"

"See for yourself. I brought your royalty." Horshak became serious. *He will be disappointed.* The miner opened a leather purse and offered up three small silver pieces.

"That's it?" asked Grengan.

"The silver ore becomes harder to find every year. And now my workers desert me. They all want to work for Daniel Bar Joseph." *He should be angry, but he only seems surprised.*

"So, you have come to complain."

"My family has worked the Cheddar Gorge for generations, and we have paid your royalty every year without complaint. We have worked alongside other miners who come to take the same silver we seek, but always that has been the way of it. And now you let a group of strangers set aside a field with the best ore for themselves. It is not just. It is not pious."

"It is not for the druids to say how I award mining stakes. The Cheddar Gorge is open to all who pay the royalty because everyone knows where it is. Daniel and his cousin located something new. They have brought prosperity to the village, and they already have paid more royalty than I get from you all year. If I let anyone dig up the silver that others find, no one else will go looking for silver again."

"They pay the workmen more than I can, because their ore is richer. Without workers my business will die."

"Find your own lode of new ore. It will be yours if you are the first to come to me with the discovery."

"This is not just. Esmeralda says the younger one uses magic to reveal the lodes of silver ore. It is impious for you to give him what he finds through dark magic."

"Many have seen them searching the streams for silver. From what I have heard, it seems like honest work."

This is not getting me anywhere. I must take this up with the druidess.

Daniel

Daniel and Jesus spent the next several days in Lake Village teaching more workers how to inlay the silver onto bronze. They joined Mary and Joseph on Ynys Witrin each evening. Joseph had a nearby hut where he spent his time experimenting with the silver ore to perfect the method for refining this particular variety. Mary spent her days out and about among the scattered native dwellings around the Levels and in Lake Village, calling on the sick and the hungry, bringing them comfort and aid. Although she knew only a few words and phrases, she managed to make herself understood well enough to offer food or a cold compress for the forehead of a child with a fever.

Late one afternoon as Jesus and Daniel paddled back to Ynys Witrin. A cold wind blew across the Levels. The smoke rising through the thatch of Mary's house on shore promised a warm respite, and the cousins redoubled their pace, paddling up the Brue to warm themselves at the fire.

At the entrance of the brook, they beached their coracles and began walking quickly. Jesus called out, but there was no answer from Mary or Joseph.

"Papa said he might head over to Priddy today to gather up more ore," said Daniel. "He said he might need to stay there overnight with our friends."

"And you know how Mother is," said Jesus. "She's always dashing far and wide to help the natives. Bless her. She was late getting back the night before last. Soon she will be staying out overnight as well."

"I am not sure Papa will approve of that. It would be scandalous in Judea for a woman to be away from home overnight without her husband."

"I realize that, but I think it is good for women to be independent. Look at the natives. Most of the women lead domestic lives, but some become druids and even warriors. Grengan said that is common among some of the tribes. Tell me, Daniel. If men can be free to come and go, why not women, too? Why do we say women are supposed to be so virtuous, and then we do not trust them out of our sight?"

"Can you imagine a woman leading the Sanhedrin?" Daniel laughed.

Jesus smiled. "We will never live to see that, cousin. But, one day, who knows? Whoa! What is this?"

They had reached the doorway of the house. Before them was a scene of devastation; mattresses and garments were torn to shreds and furnishings broken. They stood there for a moment, stunned. There were often raids and wars between tribes and clans, but in all their years in Britain they had never heard of thievery among the inhabitants of any village. Only outsiders would do such a thing.

Only the fire had been left undisturbed and still burned brightly in the central hearth.

"It's a wonder that they didn't torch the place," said Daniel.

"They were probably too clever to do that," said Jesus. "People would have seen the flames and raised the alarm. Leaving the fire gave them more time to escape. I will check on the money. You look for the map." Jesus dashed to the section of the floor where the money had been secreted and quickly discovered the awful truth. "All the Roman coin is gone!"

"At least the map is safe. I have it here."

"Has it been disturbed?"

"I don't think so."

"Praise God for that," said Jesus. "I will run up the Tor. Perhaps I can see them, and we will know if the brigands are escaping by land or by boat. Meanwhile, you raise the alarm. There will be some workmen in the farmhouses nearby. We will need all the help we can get, and horses, too! We have curraghs at the landing if we need them. Grab who and what you can and make it fast! Tell the men to come armed if they can."

"On my way!" Daniel shouted as they ran off in different directions.

The Stranger

A veiled figure pressed against the wall in shadow. Once the boys had gone, the cloaked visitor slipped inside. The map lay on a table, abandoned in their haste to depart. Slender hands braced themselves on the table as the stranger leaned over, studying the map intensely. Leaving it as it had been found, the visitor scurried out into the waning winter sunlight.

Daniel

It took Daniel some time to round up half a dozen men. He returned to Mary's house just as Jesus emerged from the doorway, brandishing the sword he had used at Rumps.

"At least the brigands did not get this," said Jesus.

"What do you plan to use that for?" Daniel asked. *He cannot be going to fight again. It is the pathway to pain and death for him. He must find another way. If only I could tell him why.*

"I saw the thieves from the summit. There were three of them, on horseback. They are halfway to Pilton. How many good men are coming with us?"

"Four are getting their weapons, and two are right behind me."

"How many horses?"

"The other men are bringing three." *What am I doing? This is so wrong!*

"With the one we have here and four in that field, we have a mount for each of us." Jesus mounted the horse that had been grazing nearby.

"Leave this to the Celts. We are guests in this prefect, outlanders under their laws. It is forbidden for us to wield any weapon here. That is their law, and we must obey it."

"They have robbed our home, Daniel, and left us destitute. Are we supposed to just hand over everything we have worked for?"

"I will not go with you, Jesus. This is the druids' sacred place, and they allow no one to draw weapons here. We all promised to live by that. They will hold us to that, no matter what. You know this."

"And when the time comes to free our people, will you tell me I break the laws of Rome? Someday that will be the whole point. It's a good thing you weren't around for the Maccabees to count on." By now all the Celtic men had gathered and were mounted. Jesus was about to turn his horse to lead the chase.

"Damn it, Jesus! That is the way of death for you!"

Jesus wheeled his horse around to face Daniel. "So, you are back onto this secret you cannot share?"

Daniel nodded.

"Fine! I told you once and I tell you again. Keep your secret and follow your own conscience. But I must follow the will of my Father as I discern it. I am sorry I questioned your loyalty, cousin. It was wrong of me. But there is no time to talk now. We're off!"

Joseph

Returning to Ynys Witrin, Joseph found Mary consoling Daniel inside the house. They told him about the robbery and how Jesus had armed himself and gone off in pursuit.

Must I be the instrument of this? Jesus is learning the art of war here in Britain. Sooner or later, he will return to Israel and make war on Rome, and that is his pathway to death. The prophecy cannot be clearer.

"Daniel feels so sorry," said Mary. "He feels he has betrayed Jesus."

Joseph turned to his son. "No, my son, you did what was right."

"But how will we go on, Papa? Now we cannot pay the workmen. We have nothing but a few sheep and some wine to give them."

"These people are not like the Dumnonii, son. They want their wages in coin."

"Should I have gone with Jesus?" asked Daniel. "He may be rash to pursue the robbers, but he is still my cousin."

"We are guests and traders," said Joseph. "Breaking the taboo against visitors taking up arms will only bring trouble."

"These people are kind," said Mary. "Surely they know that Jesus is only trying to defend our home against robbers. He hasn't threatened the peace between any tribes."

"The druids hold their superstitions even to the point of death," said Daniel. "When we fought at Rumps, the druids made all our fighters expose themselves to great danger because they held it was impious to approach our sanctuary from the wrong direction."

"I am sorry for all this," said Joseph. "Jesus has done well for us here, but I did not bring him to the Mendips just to make money." *I still cannot tell her about the prophecy. She is not ready.* "I was worried about him when I saw he was learning the art of war among the Dumnonii. I thought the druidic prohibition would keep him from taking up weapons if he stayed here. But Jesus defies the laws. Jesus will choose his own path, but I cannot stay part of this. I will send money and one more shipload of supplies from Armorica in the spring, but I will not return to Britain until Jesus turns his life towards peace. The two of you will be on your own with Jesus if you choose to stay with him."

"But Papa, how will we make it through the winter? Who will take our silver back to sell to the Romans?"

"God will provide, Son. He always does."

"If only Jesus had given God the chance," said Mary.

Grengan walked in. "I heard about the robbery, Joseph. Jesus is brave, but it is going to be a bad business when the druidess hears of him taking up arms in pursuit. Did they get everything?"

"All the Roman coin," said Daniel.

"That is nothing," said Joseph. "It will be hard getting through the winter, but we would have recovered the loss over time."

THE MAKING OF THE LAMB

"Jesus should be here any moment. I saw him with the men on their way back in the distance. It didn't seem like they were bringing back any captives."

"At least he is alive," said Mary. "Does anyone look hurt?"

"Bandits would be fast making their getaway. I doubt if Jesus and his men had much of a chance to catch up to them."

They heard Jesus approach and dismount outside. As he came into Mary's house, a shake of his head and the look of disappointment on his face were enough to convey that the chase had been futile.

Joseph frowned. "It was so foolish—"

"There is no time for that now," Grengan interrupted. "Esmeralda will be here soon." He turned to Jesus. "You took up the sword in pursuit of the brigands. Tell her you didn't have time to think when you went after them."

"I think we see who the brigand is." Esmeralda appeared in the doorway with two armed men behind her. "Seize him and the sword he still carries." She pointed at Jesus.

"He was only protecting his home," said Grengan. "He stole nothing, and he spilled no blood."

"Under our law, any outlander who takes up arms is a brigand, so that is exactly what he is." Her men seized and bound Jesus. She silently followed her men as they took Jesus away, to the sound of Mary's anguished pleas.

Esmeralda

At noon the next day, Esmeralda looked over the crowd assembled before her at the summit of the Tor. *Many braved the wind and cold to come. Jesus has the people on his side, not just his family.* Her men had bound Jesus to an upright stake. She drew her cloak tighter around herself to cut off the biting cold and wind. *Let's finish this before I am chilled to death.*

"The Tor on which we stand is sacred to all druids far and wide," Esmeralda began. "It is the entrance to the Otherworld. Every year at Samhain, druids come here to commune with the spirits of the dead and the living. Since time immemorial the area around the Tor and Ynys Witrin has been a sacred ground, neutral in any war between the tribes. It has always been the law that any outlander who takes up arms within this precinct commits brigandry. We have kept the peace only because no outlander has ever dared to defy our gods and break this prohibition. Until yesterday." Esmeralda turned to face Jesus. "Does the prisoner deny that he is an outlander and that he took up arms within the precinct of the Tor and Ynys Witrin? How say you, Jesus bar Joseph of Galilee? Do you deny it, yes or no?"

All eyes turned to Jesus, in hushed silence.

"I do not deny it."

Esmeralda faced the crowd. They must have known that Jesus could not deny the charge, and they all knew the law. Yet they seemed shocked. *They only just now fully realize the import of this offense.* "Who wishes to speak for the prisoner before I pronounce judgment?"

Grengan came forward. "You make it sound as if Jesus was the first to break this law, but that is not the case. True violence was committed against the home and kin of Jesus by the robbers who invaded our homeland. Those are the true brigands. Theft is unknown within this sacred precinct, but are we to imagine that the robbers entered his mother's home without arms? Are we to imagine they were anything but outlanders themselves?"

A murmur of approval arose from the crowd, but it ended quickly as Esmeralda raised her arm for silence. She grudgingly allowed Grengan to continue.

"All men of honor should defend their hearth and kin," he said. "Jesus is no brigand; he is only young and impetuous. When he saw how his mother's home had been robbed, there was little time for him to think. To have any hope of catching the robbers, he had to pursue them at once or not at all."

Esmeralda looked at Grengan askance. *Damn him to the dogs. He is beginning to make out a defense.*

Grengan had more to say. "Jesus broke the law, but he did nothing to threaten the peace. He has helped to bring prosperity to the people. He has defended us from the Scotti, who would have enslaved our women and children. He didn't spill any blood in pursuit of the robbers, and even if the pursuit had been successful, the only violence would have been directed against robbers who truly deserved to die."

The crowd cheered. "Silence!" cried Esmeralda. She turned on Grengan in anger. "Your words sound sweet, but they are impious! It is not for the outlander to decide whether to take up arms because he thinks his cause is just. If we allow that, then any tribe fearing invasion would seize this land as a buffer and let the blood be spilt here to spare their own people. Many are the kings in the lands around us who have subjected their own people to the horrors of war while keeping the peace around the Tor. What say we now to them?"

Esmeralda signaled to her man at arms that she was ready.

"People of Ynys Witrin and the Tor, draw nigh and give your attention," the attendant cried out. "Hear now the terrible judgment of the druidess. Let all men, women, and children take heed and obey the gods and their laws!"

Esmeralda raised her voice. "The prisoner admits he is an outlander who drew arms within this sacred precinct. Under the law he is guilty of brigandry, and the penalty is death!"

A stunned silence fell upon the crowd. Then there arose sounds of shock and dismay.

Esmeralda turned to the sun and clasped her hands in silent prayer. *Oh, how I wish I could make it so. If only it was so easy to rid myself of these outlanders, but I am a druid without a council, and I cannot impose a sentence of death on my own. I must do better than that. If I summon a council, Elsigar will come. He will want to punish Jesus, but then he will convince the council to spare that outlander's life.*

"On the other hand..." Esmeralda paused for dramatic effect and feigned a benevolent smile. "The ways of the druid are also the ways of compassion and mercy. The sentence of death is commuted. I banish Jesus bar Joseph from Ynys Witrin until the new moon and confine him to Pilton Hollow for the duration."

"But Pilton Hollow is infested by lepers," Grengan cried out. "You condemn him to a miserable fate!"

"I give him the chance for life." Esmeralda smirked. She raised her palms in a gesture of offering. "His fate is now in the hands of the gods." With that, Esmeralda descended the Tor with her men at arms bringing Jesus along bound behind her.

≈ ✤ ≈

Esmeralda walked slowly to the gate used to gain entrance to Pilton Hollow. *I dare not enter here.* Most of the children still appeared healthy, but they scurried back, away from the gate in fear of her approach. The disfigured townspeople stared at her. Their suffering was plain to see. She picked out men and women with faces and limbs that bore the telltale lesions and boils. In some of the advanced cases, the boils had erupted over the victim's entire face. She saw men and women lying about, overcome by the numbness and fatigue brought on by the disease.

But the fear was even worse than the effect of the disease. A victim could live with leprosy for years. Even after the boils or lesions broke out, it took years before the numbness and fatigue rendered the victim helpless. The druidess shuddered to look at the disfigured people. They were so pathetic and miserable. No wonder people claimed the disease caused limbs to drop off.

The elder of the village came forward to greet her at the gate. He was an old man, but he still bore no outward sign of disfigurement. Nonetheless, he approached slowly, in evident distress. His belly gave away the cause of his infirmity. It was distended from hunger, as were the bellies of all the villagers.

Esmeralda did her best to smile when the elder reached the gate.

"Are you reading the auguries today?"

"I will do that anon, after I take care of something else with you," she answered. *Why does the fool bother to ask for the auguries? The village is dying. No trader will sell them food, and they have nothing to buy it with. They are too weak to work their own fields. No other village will even accept their children as slaves.*

Esmeralda waved to Jesus, who sat in a caged cart, bound and gagged. "I am leaving this man with you. His family will bring his food and drink to the gate, and you are to take it to him. Do not let him come to the gate himself." *This will force Jesus to take his food and drink from the lepers.* "He has been sentenced to confinement in this village, and must not leave until I come to release him at the next new moon." *But once he eats from the hands of a leper, he will be confined as a leper himself until the auguries for the whole village turn good.*

"Why do you treat this man in this way?" asked the elder.

"He is an outlander who took up arms within the precinct of the Tor and Ynys Witrin. His fate must serve to deter others."

"It would have been more merciful for him to suffer a quick death."

"Do not question my judgments. I did what I must to keep the peace in this precinct." *I must also act to prevent the spread of blasphemy. Jesus talks of love for our fellow man and denounces our magical arts as superstition. If the people come to believe that, then they will have no need of druids.*

The guard released Jesus and brought him to the elder. Jesus remained silent.

Esmeralda prepared to take the auguries. She took a dove from its cage and held it close to her breast as she chanted the incantations. With a cut of her knife she took its life, and handed the carcass to her attendant. She continued her incantations as the henchman separated the entrails and spread the meat in a sacrifice to the gods over a fire.

The attendant returned the entrails on a plate, shaking his head in disappointment.

It took only a moment for Esmeralda to confirm the reading. The corruption of the entrails was unmistakable. "The auguries are poor. I must still warn the people of the danger that awaits them in Pilton Hollow."

Joseph

"Papa, you can't leave us!" Daniel barked.

A week had passed since Jesus's trial before the druid.

"I have prayed about this every day and night," said Joseph. "I thought Jesus would live in peace and turn from the path of war. Now I see how wrong I was. He will not change, and I love him too much to watch him continue on this path. Mary will not leave his side. You must choose whether to come with me or stay in Britain with Jesus."

"We can't continue without you!"

"You and Jesus are now men. You have found a rich lode, and I have shown you how to refine the ore. Traders come through Ynys Witrin all the time. Sell your silver to them. Sell them the lead, too." Joseph paused as Mary came in, returning from her daily trip to bring food to Jesus. "Selling your silver to strangers here will not be as profitable as if I took it to the Romans, but you can prosper. You could hire Kendrick on your own, but you will need someone to deal with the Romans."

"But Jesus is still held among the lepers."

"God will protect him," said Mary.

Daniel grabbed his collar as if to rend his garment. Then he dropped his hands and blew out his breath in a huff.

"I will send Kendrick back to you with a supply of Roman coin once I reach Armorica. I have been putting aside a share of our earnings for you and Jesus," said Joseph. "It is really your money—yours and Jesus's. Anyway, if we stayed, Kendrick and I would just be more mouths to feed. The Sabbath begins tonight, so I must get aboard the ship today. It would not be fair to delay Kendrick."

With a heavy heart, Joseph embraced Mary and set out for the curragh with his son. Kendrick and his ship awaited them at the Lake Village quay. A thousand emotions raced through Joseph's heart as he embraced Daniel. *Will this be the last time I ever see my beloved son?*

Yeager

Despite his status as village elder, Yeager took a turn bringing Jesus his food. "A woman brought you this. She said she was your mother."

"Your people hunger much more than I do. Feed it to them."

"Sooner or later you must take the food from our hands, and then you will be branded as a leper, too."

"That is not the reason. I can fast another day. Your people are hungry."

"You do not fear the leprosy?"

"God, my Father, will protect me."

"You only have one god? And he is your father?"

"Yes."

"You seem confident in your one god—as if you take it for granted that he will protect you. We have hundreds of gods—gods for everything you can think of—but they offer us no hope."

"I do not take him for granted. I am eternally grateful, and I offer my thanksgivings every day. I know that the one true God of my people loves me beyond measure and that all things are possible to him, so I have no fear."

"Are you sure you do not want this? It is good food, and it is yours, not ours."

"I am sure," said Jesus. The elder started to turn. "Hold on. There is only so much. Feed it to the ones who are most hungry, but not to those afflicted with the leprosy. Let us talk some more once you do that."

Yeager soon returned.

Jesus restarted the conversation. "I was struck by something you said before. Among all your gods, none give you hope."

The elder nodded.

"But there is always hope if you turn to the one true God and obey his laws."

"Obey what laws? We try to be good and honest men."

"I know, but there is something else I remember about this. It is in a book of our Scripture called Leviticus."

"Do you mean to say that your people actually write down the teachings of your god? That is something that even our druids dare not do. It is most strange for you, a brigand, to talk to me of the law."

"I bring to you the only law you can turn to with hope. Your own laws offer you none, and you are the one who has said it."

It took some time for Jesus to teach the elder the law of Leviticus for diagnosing the true cases of leprosy. It depended upon the type of lesion, whether it was depressed below the layer of the skin, whether hair grew in it and, if so, what color. In some cases the law called for victims to be isolated for a period of seven days to see if the condition was spreading.

"This is the hard part," Jesus continued. "When a man or woman is pronounced unclean with leprosy, you must turn them out of the village. They must live alone for the rest of their days, unless they are cleaned by God in his mercy."

"That is so heartless. Are we to abandon our mothers and fathers and children?"

"Yes, you must abandon the unclean. They will die anyway. All of the village will die soon of hunger if you do not cleanse it of the leprosy. You cannot save everyone, but you can save those who are clean. That is the law of Leviticus."

Jesus

Jesus awoke from a restless night with a chill. A mysterious flame appeared in the air in front of his face, but it illuminated nothing. Before he could speak, his Father revealed himself. "For someone confined among lepers, you seem in good spirits, my Son."

"How could I not be, Father, when God is with me?"

"I am always with you."

"I feel your protection all the time. As the psalm says, I can walk through the Valley of Death and fear no evil because you are with me. That is why I come to this place without fear. But it is so special when we really talk."

"These times are special to me, too. But there will come a time when we will be so united in purpose that we will know each other's hearts, minds, and wisdom without a word exchanged between us. You will see me in the godhead across all time and space, just as I see you now, for that is our divine nature. You will know my every thought and every desire—every one I have now, every one that I have had, and every one that I shall have in the future. While you share my divine substance, your human nature struggles with it. When your human nature and your divine nature become truly reconciled, you will know my heart at all times."

"Have I done your will, Father? Was I rash to pursue the bandits? Joseph thinks so. Was it right for me to share the laws of Leviticus with the elder, even though some here will truly suffer so the rest may live?"

"Do not let your heart be troubled, my Son. It is enough that you fulfill your destiny."

"You do not answer my question. I want to know if I am doing your will."

"That is something your human nature must struggle with, as all men must from time to time when they seek to do the will of their God. But there is something else I must lay before you now. It will be a mission that you may choose to accept or not."

"You already know that I will do as you ask."

"I knew across all time and space from the beginning of the world that this moment would come. I know the choice you will make, but it is your choice. You have free will as much as any man. Now, I am commissioning you to go on a mission. The druid festival of Imbolc will take place in a few weeks. Elsigar will be at the Tor."

"I told him at Samhain I might meet him there."

"You must do so. He will invite you to the school at Bangor and the island of Ynys Môn. It is the center of druid learning. Elsigar will tell you more of this. You will have many opportunities to teach the druids, but in that teaching you will learn the most."

"That will leave Daniel alone with Mary. Uncle Joseph has left us. They will need my help to carry on."

"Daniel too must have his struggles. He may survive without you or he may not, but he has his own life to live,. You must leave for Ynys Môn as soon as Elsigar makes arrangements for you. On the way you will befriend a companion who will guide you across Cymru to Bangor, which is on the mainland, and across a strait of the sea to the island of Ynys Môn."

"It will grieve Mother for me to leave her so soon after she arrived here, but I suppose you know that, too."

"There is one thing more. While you are with the druids, there will come a time for you to leave your studies to go further. On the west side of Ynys Môn you will cross another strait to a smaller island called Holy Island. Another whom you will meet but not befriend on the way to Ynys Môn will help you across. On the west side of Holy Island is yet another strait of the sea. That one very narrow but the most treacherous of all. You will cross that strait to the small island of Ynys Lawd. You must make that final crossing alone. Inside a cave on Ynys Lawd you will find a hermit, and he will teach you much. You will stay with him until he releases you. That is my will, my Son, but you have your free will, as much as any man. Will you do mine?"

"Need you ask, Father? Do you not know my heart already? But I would have you lay forth my destiny. Uncle Joseph seems to sense something forbidding in it that he does not share with me."

"All in good time, my son. Your human nature must first gain strength and wisdom. This is a time of deeper testing for you. We will not talk again until you are ready."

"I have so many questions, Father," said Jesus. But in that moment he realized he was alone.

Esmeralda

The wheels of the cart crunched on the ice as the druidess and her small entourage made their way to Pilton Hollow. She brought a caged dove—and two spare birds—to perform the augury reading. *I wonder why I take the trouble for this. The auguries will not change, and the town is doomed. The leprosy infects too many.* It was the first day of the New Moon, just three days from the gathering of the druids for Imbolc. Esmeralda allowed herself a smug smile. *Yes, Jesus is set to end his confinement in Pilton Hollow today, but he must have eaten from the hands of the lepers. All I need do is inquire into that, read the auguries, and then declare him unclean along with the others. Not even Elsigar will dare to get near him once he hears.*

The druidess stepped down from the cart, stopped at the town gate, and called for the people to bring forth Jesus. She waited patiently as the people gathered. *That is most strange. There do not seem so many this time.*

No matter. The badly infected must be too sick to come from their beds. I hate the sight of them anyway.

They brought Jesus before her.

"Have you consumed any food or drink brought to you from the hands of the townspeople?"

"Of course I have. You did not permit me to come to the gate and get my food from my mother. She had to give it to the townspeople, and they brought it to me."

"I must read the auguries over you. These people are unclean, and now you may be unclean as well."

"Do not perform your pagan rites over me!" said Jesus. "I am a child of the one true God, the God of my fathers. I do not brook with the worship of any other god."

"Have it your way, Jesus. Stand aside as I read the auguries for the town. You will share in their fate, as the auguries portend."

On her signal the attendant brought forth the dove. She slew it with one stroke of her knife and returned the carcass to the attendant.

It did not take long for him to separate the entrails and spread the meat upon the fire. He gazed upon them, and raised an eyebrow. He brought the entrails to Esmeralda. "The auguries are good," he pronounced. "No corruption of the entrails at all!"

"Impossible," the druidess shouted. She turned to the elder. "What magic have you allowed Jesus bar Joseph to perform?"

"There was no magic at all. He showed me how to examine the people for infection. We cast out those who were infected. It was a difficult thing to do, but Jesus said that was the only way to give the clean people a chance to live."

Esmeralda's finger quivered as she pointed toward Jesus. "You wicked sorcerer. You have cleansed the ritually unclean. There is no way to do that without magic. Elsigar shall hear of this!"

Elsigar

Elsigar traveled to Ynys Witrin alone, except for the company of his faithful horse. The countryside was shrouded in its wintry rest. In the last two days it had warmed just enough to melt most of the ice and snow, but the cold and damp caused dense fog to linger over the landscape, hiding the leafless trees in a dull, diffused shroud of white. He crossed the River

Brue to Ynys Witrin over the Pomparles Bridge. Its name meant *perilous*: a well-deserved name, indeed. He could not see the path through the thick mist, which forced him to allow the horse to find his own way to the other side. He knew the Secret of the Lord, constructed by Jesus for his mother, lay to the left of his course from the bridge to the clearing at the foot of the Tor, but he passed it without spying it through the vapors.

The fire appeared as a dim light through the mist and guided him to the gathering. Not many were yet in attendance, since the festival would not commence for another day.

Imbolc was considered the least of the major festivals. It was not the time for the multitudes to awaken the earth at Beltane, nor time to set the earth to rest as they did at Samhain. Set in the middle of winter, it was not keyed to any major event in the agricultural cycle, such as the commencement of the harvest that the people celebrated at Lugnasad. Although it was open to all, Imbolc was mainly for the druids to gather among themselves, a sacred time for contemplation and purification.

A dozen druids and emissaries were gathered around the fire. "I have been too long on the road today," said Elsigar. "The damp and the cold have chilled me to the core. The fire is such a comfort." Its heat enveloped him, brushing the chill from his hands and nose, though his bones remained icy.

"We are honored as always to have you, Elsigar." Esmeralda lifted back the gray woolen hood to reveal her face and flowing locks of golden hair. "I am glad our fire warms you, although I fear its power to purify our spirit is diminished this year."

"How can that be, sister?" *She has something dark to say.* "The flame of Imbolc has always purified the souls of those who partake in the feast—although I see that fewer of the people come every year. Would that more of the people knew of the power of purification from this flame." The wood crackled. The smoke stung his eyes, but the warmth was worth the discomfort.

"Not even the sacred fire can purify the souls of the impious, Elsigar. You have allowed an outlander to stay in this land, and we have suffered him to live in this precinct for almost a year. I know he practices a black and forbidden magic. He defiles the laws. Not even the fires of Imbolc will purify us in a season as foul as that which comes now at your hands."

"When Jesus came to Carn Roz as a boy, I too suspected he practiced magic," said Elsigar. "My council and I questioned him closely. Although he was the focus of many wondrous things, we found that he practiced no magical art of his own. I have come to know him well as he has grown in stature and mind. I am not surprised he would do things ever more wondrous—things that a druid might take to be the fruit of forbidden magic. But if he is the same young man, you are undoubtedly mistaken."

"I think not." Esmeralda related how she had confined Jesus to live among the lepers and how the auguries for Pilton Hollow mysteriously improved. "The elder of the village said Jesus instructed them in following the laws of his God. Jesus did not deny it. He healed this incurable disease by calling upon the powers of a god unknown to the druids. Surely that must be the practice of some dark magic."

"I will look into this."

"Do you still intend to invite him to Ynys Môn? What about his taking up arms in this precinct?"

"Jesus was only defending his home," protested Grengan.

"That was impious, but understandable." Elsigar turned to Esmeralda. "Confining him to live with lepers was cruel, but that now is over. As for the invitation to Ynys Môn, I do not know if he will even come tomorrow. He said at Samhain that he might, but maybe he will not. I will say nothing more until I speak to him."

The next day's dawn brought a change in the weather. The mist lifted and burned away early in the morning. Frozen dew clung to branches and twigs, creating an arbor of crystals high in the trees that lasted until the sun melted it. The summit of the Tor emerged into the bright sunlight.

Elsigar searched the faces of the new arrivals, mostly local people but also emissaries. *There will be more than a hundred, but they will not come in thousands as they do for the other festivals.* Then he spotted Jesus approaching. No longer a skinny boy, this was a stalwart young man with finely muscled arms and shoulders.

"Shalom. Peace be with you," Jesus said to him. "I pray your journey was not too hard."

"It was too damp and cold, but druids learn to abide the pains of travel as we carry our ministry far and wide across the land. We have some time before the festival starts. We should talk."

Jesus nodded.

"When I was here at Samhain you told a story of how Elisha used the waters of the Jordan River to heal a gentile of his leprosy. I hear you helped the elders in Pilton Hollow rid that village of its curse."

"I simply helped them deal with lepers under the laws of God." Jesus explained to Elsigar about separating the clean from the unclean, and how he had worked with them while he was in Pilton Hollow.

"This is set out in the laws of your god?"

"Yes, it is in the book called Leviticus."

"Did you use water?"

"Just to wash my hands when I was done. It was nothing like what Elisha did."

"Did you call upon your god?"

"I prayed to him, for the people. I prayed he would make them well."

"Did you use any spells or incantations?"

"Only a lot of prayers."

Elsigar closed his eyes and retreated to his own thoughts. *There is no guile in him. But he still admits that he teaches the people the laws of an unknown god.* Opening his eyes, Elsigar saw that Jesus was eating a crisp apple.

"Apple trees grow near my mother's house," said Jesus. "We used to gather many and put them away to last the winter. I love the way they grow all around Ynys Witrin. Here, I brought some more." He reached into his bag. "Have one."

"Thank you." The fruit was indeed delicious. *Can he know that for the druids, apples symbolize knowledge and wisdom?*

"Sometimes I wonder," said Jesus, "why this island is called Ynys Witrin?"

Elsigar shrugged, dumbfounded. "'Ynys' means 'island,' of course. And 'Witrin'? Well, what else would it be called?"

"I would call it Ynys Avalon."

"Avalon, indeed!" Elsigar savored another bite of his apple. Ynys Avalon—*the island of apples*—how fitting! *Apples, wisdom, and the Tor—how they all fit together.*

Elsigar took his turn through the afternoon leading the purification rituals, but most of the day he spent in silent contemplation. He looked over to Jesus from time to time, expecting him to be bored, but Jesus seemed to be enjoying his own quiet meditation. The more Elsigar contemplated how fascinated Jesus seemed by the apples, the more he realized he knew the answer to give to Esmeralda. *With Jesus, it is all about knowledge. He yearns to learn. He uses what he learns. That is how he rid Pilton Hollow of the leprosy. People have always feared such places because they fear to be infected. The law of his god is only common sense. When you cast out the unclean you save the clean. There is no magic in it.*

The festival concluded with the setting of the sun behind the Tor. Elsigar invited Jesus to come and study with the novices at Bangor and Ynys Môn. He wasn't surprised that Jesus accepted. What surprised him was that Jesus seemed to expect the invitation.

Chapter 11
A Chariot and Some Prodigals

Joseph

Joseph looked out over the choppy water as the ship approached the entrance of the Fal. Deep in thought, he did not hear Kendrick approach from behind. He flinched as the captain laid a hand on his shoulder.

"You have said hardly anything for the last five days, my friend," the captain observed. "Not since we left Lake Village, not even when we were caught in those doldrums. Usually, you're grabbing my ear constantly to get the ship moving. You are not yourself."

"I'm saddened, leaving Mary and the boys behind," said Joseph. "I meant what I said. I am not going back. So I may never see them again."

"I know you well enough to take you at your word, Joseph. I just will never understand why. All of us are doing so well."

"I will send you back from Armorica with money and supplies for the boys. You can carry on with them if you wish." *I cannot tell him of the path that leads Jesus to his horrible death on the cross.* "All I can say is that Jesus is on a dangerous path, and I cannot help him continue. I cannot stop him from remaining in Britain, but neither can I help him."

"It was impetuous for him to take off after the robbers, but he was defending Mary's home. The people would never have allowed the druidess to execute him for that. She only banished him for a few weeks."

Joseph smiled; then he became serious again. "It is not the Celts I fear."

"If you really need to be away from Jesus, why not continue working from Carn Roz and leave the boys in Ynys Witrin? Without you, the tin operation will fall apart. I cannot keep it going, but I could buy the refined tin from you every season and take it to Armorica to sell."

"I would need the maps Jesus made showing the ore deposits. He would be entitled to his portion of the profits I make here, so I would still be helping him stay in Britain."

"That would only be the case if he knew."

"Are you suggesting that I cheat Jesus out of his share? He's my own great-nephew!"

"Set his share of the profits aside, and give it to him when he returns to his homeland. If you did not stay, he would not get anything more from his discoveries, so it isn't as if you are taking anything from him. He is better off getting his share when he leaves Britain than not at all."

"I need to think about this." *Perhaps Kendrick is right. Jesus always said he trusted me to hold his share of the profits, and he has never asked for an accounting. Perhaps I should make everything I can here in Carn Roz and put aside a good profit for the boys.*

The wind was light, and it took most of the afternoon for Kendrick to work the ship up to Carn Roz. The tide was in, so he was able to land alongside the stepping stone on the edge of the tidal pool. Many of the villagers paused from their work to wave, and the urchins came out in force to greet them.

Joseph waved to Bannoch and looked over the village. They had three smelting furnaces now, and all were putting out smoke. *With the fields fallow for the winter, the smelter provides employment for the men. Maybe if I stay here we can get another furnace going in the mouth of the Plym. It would give easy access to the ore fields along the Tamar. Yes, Kendrick is right; there is more money to be made here, and the boys will be better off for it.*

With a good supply of wine still left, Joseph was able to barter enough tin to fill the hold of Kendrick's ship. Joseph decided to stay with Bannoch and his family in Carn Roz while Kendrick made the run to Armorica to sell the tin and withdraw some of the money Joseph had on deposit there. They agreed that Kendrick would then sail directly to Ynys Witrin to bring the Roman coin to the boys. It would give Joseph more than a week to think before Kendrick returned to Carn Roz.

Jesus

The trip down the Brue in the curragh was pleasant. Jesus was on the first leg of the trip from Lake Village, on his way across the mouth of the great Sabrina in Cymru. Spring was still more than a month away, but buds were starting to show in the trees, and birds were singing and nesting. It was certainly quite cool paddling down the river, but remarkably temperate for the winter.

Jesus was traveling with a passing bard who knew the way to King Cymbeline's capitol at Caer Wysg. Elsigar had arranged for this companion the day after Imbolc, just before the druid himself had set out on his return across Bodmin Moor to the lands of the Dumnonii. He had much druid business there and would travel by sea for the start of the Bangor school and meet up with Jesus in the spring. The bard would not be traveling further than Caer Wysg, but King Cymbeline was known for his hospitality and could be counted on to find another companion to take Jesus on the next leg of the journey.

The bard sat in front of the curragh. He seemed to be going through the motion of dipping his paddle in the water, without putting much force into the strokes. As one would expect of a bard, he tended to be talkative. He tried to press Jesus for details about the nasty business with Esmeralda, but Jesus demurred, thinking that it could only make more trouble in Ynys Witrin if word of what he might say ever got back there. Nor could Jesus talk about the silver find. The battle at Rumps was old news. By the time they reached the open water of the Sabrina, each had become lost in his own thoughts.

They paddled along the shore of the Sabrina, huddling in their cloaks as protection from wind and wave, until they reached the narrowing of the river estuary. Even using dry tinder and flints, the air was too damp for any fire to catch, so they spent a cold, restless night trying to conserve as much warmth as they could under their blankets.

In the morning, Jesus was wet, cold, thoroughly cross and miserable, and he found himself doing most of the paddling. God the Father had been quite explicit that he was not to tarry in Ynys Witrin, but he couldn't help wondering if it had been a mistake not to wait for spring. He was doing something that made no sense to him, simply because it was his Father's will. This was the first time his Father had given him a specific command. He was not about to disobey, but it certainly felt unusual. He knew what it was to obey his earthly parents, as well as Uncle Joseph for the most part, but their wishes seemed to make more sense.

Once they reached the shore of Cymru, they beached and hid the curragh. As they walked inland on a pathway across gently rolling hills, Jesus's heart was lifted by the freedom to move his legs and the warmth of the sun finally peeking through the clouds. He was in a decidedly better mood once they reached the entrance of King Cymbeline's hill fort at Caer Wysg. The gatekeeper first recognized the bard. When the bard turned and identified his companion as Jesus bar Joseph from Galilee, it was clear from the gatekeeper's look of awe that Jesus's reputation had preceded them.

Looking around the inner precinct of the fort, Jesus's first impression was that he was back in Lugdunum or even Jerusalem. The place was bustling with traders, merchants, soldiers, and functionaries all scurrying about their business. Jesus felt much more at a true center of a kingdom than ever among the Dumnonii.

The old bard brought Jesus before King Cymbeline, who was holding court in the banquet hall. The king patiently heard out each person in the queue of petitioners, before moving to the next. He was stout and advancing in years, but very quick-witted. He wore a heavy gold torc around his neck and gold bracelets on each wrist. His leggings were fashioned of leather. Otherwise, his clothes were simple British garb.

"Ah! The hero of Rumps is here." The king rose to greet Jesus once the bard had introduced him.

"Many fought as heroes to defend Rumps—many died. I cannot claim the credit," Jesus answered.

"I have heard other stories about you. They say you seek tin and silver. Is that what brings you to Cymru?"

"No, I am on my way to Bangor and Ynys Môn to study with the druids. Do you know Elsigar?"

"Yes, the archdruid of the Dumnonii." The king shrugged in a mock gesture of frustration. "I cannot say that I deal with him much. The gods bless me with my own druids to advise and consent to every little thing I do to assure that it is suitably pious."

Jesus smiled, as others laughed with the king. "Elsigar arranged to bring me here in the hope that you might assist me on my journey. I do not know the way."

"I was told you came all the way across the lands of the Romans, and that you do not worship our gods. I never heard of an outlander from so far away studying the ways of the druids. It takes twenty years to become a druid, you know."

"I am not trying to become a druid. I have been attending the major festivals of the druids to watch and learn. My own God inspires me to learn that there may be truths to be found in all religions."

"If that is pious enough for a druid as renowned as Elsigar, that is good enough for me! How are you planning to go?"

"I brought the bard across the Sabrina in a curragh. Elsigar said I should make my way up the Sabrina to its source and then cross the mountains."

"The Snowden Mountains are treacherous in winter. You will not want to make that journey now. Stay here for a few weeks and give the springtime sun a chance to melt the mountain snows." The king turned to one of his attendants. "Summon Guiderius and Arvigarus for me."

"I am afraid I have no coin to pay for my food and lodging. My family was robbed—"

"You are here as my guest," Cymbeline interrupted. "I would not hear of taking anything in exchange for hospitality."

Two young men came into the banquet hall and paused in the doorway. They were obviously twins, with identical open smiles on their freckled faces. Their eyes were blue, their flaming red hair hung straight onto their shoulders, and their upper lips bore faint traces of downy hair, as if they were competing to be the first to grow a man's mustache. Even their clothes were identical, except that one of them wore a slightly thicker gold torc around his neck.

"These are my sons, Guiderius and Arvigarus," said Cymbeline. "Guiderius came out of his mother's womb just a few minutes before Arvigarus, so he will rule this kingdom one day." When Cymbeline pointed to him, Jesus could see that Guiderius was the one with the thicker torc. "Arvigarus is studying the ways of the druids, and as luck would have it, he too is going to Ynys Môn. The two of you can go together. You will be a good influence on him." The king laughed, then let out a belch. "Just be careful he doesn't end up being a bad influence on you."

With that, the king dismissed Jesus and his sons. As the king's sons led him through the castle halls, Jesus noticed that most of the servants had tattoos on their foreheads. He asked what they meant.

"That is how slaves are marked," said Guiderius. "Haven't you seen that before? I thought you had been in Britain for several years now."

"I have been in the land of the Dumnonii and the precinct of the Tor. Those people do not keep slaves."

"They are marked like that so runaways can be spotted," added Arvigarus. "That mark is recognized all over Britain."

"What happens to runaways?" Jesus asked.

"They are returned, unless it's too far away," said Arvigarus. "In that case they are killed. It keeps them from running. Most slaves are put to work in the fields. Our father is the only man in the hill fort rich enough to keep slaves just for servants."

"And you use the slaves for tasks you should do for yourself," said Guiderius. "It makes you lazy and soft—just as you spend Father's money too freely."

Arvigarus took umbrage at his sibling's remark. They argued awhile, then burst out a door into the courtyard and drew swords. The contest swayed back and forth, but the advantage went to Guiderius.

Arvigarus, laughing, handed his sword to Jesus. "Let's see a demonstration of your skill."

The sword weighed heavy in his hand. The twins had used their swords to slash, while Jesus used his to thrust and parry as well. Nonetheless, Jesus had fallen behind with his practice, and his rustiness showed, forcing him to yield after a close contest.

Guiderius bellowed, raising his hands. "Victory! And over the hero of Rumps, no less!"

"I obviously need practice," Jesus said, handing the sword back to Arvigarus. "Perhaps we could continue swordplay every day."

The princes readily agreed.

Daniel

The spring leaves came in thicker, and the days waxed longer. Daniel was at the first silver lode near Priddy as the sun began to set. The few workmen willing to barter their labor had left for the day. Without Roman coin to pay the men, how could Daniel blame those who had stayed away? They had the spring planting to attend to.

Sweat and grime covered his body. Crawling through the shafts, digging, and carrying ore to the surface was backbreaking work. He wanted to lie down on the grass and sleep, but he could not. He looked over the pile of ore that had been brought to the surface. He picked up a small piece and threw it in frustration. All the ore he had at the surface was hardly enough to fire the smelter. The lode was done.

Daniel gritted his teeth. Without enough workmen, there was no point asking Grengan about the new lode Jesus had discovered. He was stuck.

And then there was the news that had arrived from Grengan earlier in the day. Esmeralda was starting to complain about Aunt Mary. Her house was too close to the Tor. It was impious, she said. Grengan thought it was silly, and he said he could handle Esmeralda and look out for Mary. Nonetheless, Daniel was reluctant to leave his aunt alone almost a day's journey away in Ynys Witrin.

Where is Kendrick? Papa said he would be bringing a new supply of coin from Armorica. But where is he? He should be here by now. I cannot do anything with the new lode until he gets here, and the first lode is finished. The natives will not keep feeding us indefinitely if I cannot make anything. Tears streamed down Daniel's face. He felt overwhelmed and alone.

Jesus

A fortnight after Jesus had come to Caer Wysg, the arrival of the next bard was the occasion for yet another feast. *King Cymbeline must be rich indeed if he can afford to buy all this food and drink. This is the sixth feast I have been to.*

Still, it was always fun to be among the Celts as the mead flowed freely. Jesus ducked just in time, to the cheers of all, to avoid a bone thrown by an inebriated guest. He was getting on well with Guiderius and Arvigarus. His swordsmanship had returned ; he could beat the princes almost all the time now.

He took a turn leading the men in raucous song as the good king laughed and belched above the sound of all the revelry.

Jesus finished the song and looked over to the king, who was no longer laughing and belching. He was listening intently to a messenger. Then he summoned Jesus and the two princes.

"I've just received word from the north," Cymbeline began. "I am again betrayed by Belariux. The Cornovii say he has stirred up war between them and the Ordovices. The upper reaches of the Sabrina are closed because of the fighting. Arvigarus, you must go by way of the Avon and then the Great Trekway. Take Jesus with you to Caer Leir. Imogen will welcome the two of you, and Postumux's people will know when it is safe to venture through the Snowden mountains."

"But Caer Leir is so far out of the way," said Arvigarus. "It is more than halfway across Britain, Father."

"It is the only safe passage to Ynys Môn. It will take you through the lands of the Dobunni, the Corieltauvi, and the Cornovii, all tribes that are friendly to us. You should leave in the morning. With the detour to Caer Leir, you are late for the start of classes as it is."

Arvigarus tried once more to protest, but Guiderius grabbed him by the arm and pulled him away. "Stop arguing and start packing." Jesus followed the brothers to the kitchen, where Guiderius tossed each of them a satchel and opened a pantry.

"Who is Imogen?" Jesus asked.

Guiderius took down a clay jar. "Our older sister. She's married to a warrior named Postumux. They live among his people on the northeast side of the Midlands."

"And Belariux?" Jesus asked, "Why does his action require us to leave?"

Guiderius peered into the jar and returned it, taking down another. "He's a former courtier of Father's. He was falsely accused of treason." He handed his brother the jar. "Dried beef. Wrap that in cloth or something." He turned back to the pantry.

Jesus turned to the bowls of fruit lining the sideboard and started stowing some in his satchel. "If he was falsely accused…why did your father say he was betrayed?"

"The falsehood was ages ago, when we were infants," Arvigarus said. "In retaliation for the accusation, he…he stole us away and brought us up as his own." He snorted, shoving the packet of dried beef into his bag. "We lived in a dank cave in the hills between the Ordovices and the Silures."

"How did you get back?"

Guiderius brought a box from the pantry. "Imogen found us…" He shook his head. "It's a long story. We were almost fully grown by then, completely unaware that we were the sons of the king."

"How very strange," Jesus said, "to have been raised by a man not your father…and yet not know who your real father was." *Come to think of it, I felt something like that growing up. but somehow I always knew who my real Father was.*

They nodded solemnly, their expressions mirrors of one another.

"Bread," Guiderius said. "There's a couple of days' worth."

Jesus wrapped the loaves and put them in the satchel with the fruit. "So Imogen brought you home to your parents?"

"To Father," Arvigarus said. "Mother had died long before" He had found some cheese and wrapped it. "Father's second wife wanted her son Clotten to marry Imogen, even though Imogen was in love with Postumux, but…" he glanced at his brother with a crooked grin. "We took care of Clotten."

Guiderius snickered.

Jesus hesitated. "What do you mean?"

Arvigarus tucked the cheese into his satchel. "Belariux, Guiderius, and I found Clotten while hunting. He insulted us, and Guiderius beheaded him."

Jesus raised his eyebrow.

"We gave him fair warning," said Arvigarus. "He was too thick-headed to back off."

The Romans had written about the hot-tempered Celts, and he had seen with his own eyes how quick they could be to draw weapons. But usually someone backed off before matters turned deadly. Celtic warriors were generally tactful in defusing such situations and getting back to their carousing.

"You would have done the same thing," said Guiderius.

"That is not the way of my people," said Jesus.

Arvigarus sighed. "Belariux recognized Imogen as the king's daughter. He came with us to the hill fort. At first, Father rejected Imogen because she had defied his wishes in betrothing herself to Postumux. And then Guiderius admitted he had killed Clotten, and that drew Father's ire."

Guiderius snorted. "A bit." He pulled a water skin from a peg and filled it from one of the mead casks.

"Our stepmother died shortly thereafter," Arvigarus said. "Then we were reconciled to the king and restored to our rightful positions, and Imogen married Postumux."

Jesus looked from one prince to the other. "I thought my life was complicated. How long has it been since you were restored?"

"Just about a year," said Arvigarus. "There's a lot more. Like how our stepmother tried to poison—"

"Please stop. I'm getting a headache," Jesus interrupted. "But what happened, that Belariux is a threat now?"

"Father pardoned him for stealing us," said Guiderius. "Since then, he's been away on some business with the Ordovices. No telling what he's been up to with them."

"I would think such a crime would call for severe punishment," Jesus said. "Your father is very merciful."

Arvigarus tied the flap of his satchel closed. "Too merciful, it seems."

※

In the morning, the twins parted with many hugs and some tears, but Jesus understood why Cymbeline was separating them. They could not both be king. Arvigarus needed to take another path, by immersing himself in the ways of the druids.

Jesus and Arvigarus mounted a sail on a jury-rigged spar on the curragh, and the wind from astern carried them up the Sabrina, which steadily narrowed as they made their way upriver. As they traveled, Jesus told Arvigarus about his upbringing as a Jew in Nazareth, the Romans' domination of Israel, and the expedition to Britain with Joseph and Daniel. He did not mention that he was the son of God or his destiny as the Messiah, but he revealed his uncanny knack for finding ores and for picking up languages.

By nightfall on the second day, the river had begun to twist and turn among the low hills that rose higher toward the northeast. This made the sail impractical so they began to paddle.

The next morning, as they paddled upriver through the land of the Dobunni, they passed many homesteads and farms, but no large settlements. Small sheep grazed in the meadows.

"The farmers don't seem to pay us any notice," Jesus said.

"Why should they?" Arvigarus replied. "The Dobunni are peaceful farmers and artisans. They have some warrior garrisons, but none round here."

They finally reached a settlement on the fifth day after leaving Caer Wysg. "It gets harder from here," said Arvigarus. "That's the Avon, where we're going. We'll have to portage the curragh."

"I did plenty of portaging with the Dumnonii when we searched for tin lodes," Jesus said.

"So you know it's a lot of work."

The settlement at the junction of the rivers turned out to be a market town. "We need supplies, but what are we going to do for money?" Jesus asked.

"No bother," Arvigarus answered. "My father gave me a good supply of Dobunni coin."

"Uncle Joseph told me that some tribes in Britain make their own coins, but I thought that was only in the southeast, where tribes trade directly with the Romans. Can I see one?"

Arvigarus opened his pouch. "Coin-making started to the east, but the Dobunni picked it up. My father is thinking of making coins, too, though it's just as easy for him to use the coins of the Dobunni." He dropped a coin into Jesus's palm.

Jesus was surprised to see that the small silver coin bore the name *Anted*. "Is Anted a ruler of the Dobunni?"

"Yes, he is the high king for all of the Dobunni."

"These are Latin letters. Are the Celts learning to write?"

"The ones that come in contact with the Romans are. The druids do not like it, but it is not impious unless someone writes a curse or anything about the gods."

The houses, built around open courtyards, were larger and more sophisticated than anything Jesus had seen in Britain before. A few even had upper stories. The merchants' stalls took the form of daub and wattle huts, but some of the merchants operated from rooms in their courtyard homes. Arvigarus easily replenished their supplies, not even bothering to haggle.

On their way back to the river, they came upon a house that smelled quite foul. Shouts and cries emerged from within. Jesus looked into the courtyard. It was the establishment of the local slave trader.

Men, women, and children sat in the main room. Jesus walked among them. Most did not wear chains. These were the docile ones, he presumed, sufficiently restrained by the tattoos on their foreheads and the knowledge of the fate that awaited them if they tried to run.

The slaver crossed the courtyard. He smiled as he approached, but Jesus waved him off.

"This might not be a bad idea, after all," said Arvigarus. "We could use some help with those portages."

"We can manage the portages," said Jesus. "Let's get out of here."

Just as Jesus reached the street, he heard his name called from the courtyard. He turned to see a thin, emaciated figure emerge from one of the back rooms. His ragged tunic was pulled down from his waist. His sides bore the unmistakable red marks and blood of a recent whipping, and Jesus could only imagine what his back might show.

He was gasping for breath, whimpering more than speaking. He stumbled towards Jesus with an outstretched arm. "Jesus, I knew it was you when I heard your voice," the wretched creature gasped.

The slaver raised his whip. "Get back, slave. This man is not going to buy the likes of you."

"Hold on." Jesus put his hand on the slaver's arm to stay the whip stroke.

The miserable creature fell to his knees as Jesus approached.

Jesus looked into the man's face. "Pirro, is it you?"

"Please, young sir," said the slaver. "You do not want to purchase this one. He's all worked out. I bought him at one of the mines, thinking I could put some muscle on him and sell him, but he is too disobedient and lazy. I am just about to give up on him. I will probably kill him tomorrow as an example to the others. Come, take another look at the good slaves I have. Good teeth, strong arms, fair prices."

Jesus paid no attention to the slaver. He stared at Pirro, shaking his head. The memory of his treachery, his whining, his pathetic condition—it all filled him with disgust. Finally, he turned to the slaver. "I am sorry to disturb you. I have never been to a slaver before. I do not have any money."

Jesus turned away and walked out to the street. Arvigarus hurried alongside, asking whether he was all right.

With tears streaming from his eyes, it was obvious he was not.

Behind, in the courtyard, Pirro's anguished cries waned further and further into the distance.

Arvigarus

Arvigarus could tell something was still troubling Jesus when they arrived at their campsite on the riverside. Although he was going about the preparations for the night, he kept his teeth clenched and did not talk. "What is that slave to you?" Arvigarus asked.

"I did not want to speak of it," said Jesus, "but I will tell you." He sat cross-legged on the ground and told Arvigarus about Pirro's history with Jesus's family and his treachery at the battle for Rumps. "They said it was up to me to pass sentence upon him. I sentenced him to be sold into slavery. I see, now, that I sentenced him to a living death."

"But for the traitor of Rumps? The sentence was just," Arvigarus protested. "His life should have been forfeited for his treachery."

"That is what my head tells me. I still feel so angry with him. Somehow, though, I did not have the heart to take his life at the time, but I ended up sending him to a living hell, and now he will die anyway."

"You cannot blame yourself, Jesus. You did what you believed was just."

Jesus shook his head. "Did your father kill Belariux for kidnapping you? That would have been just, but he showed mercy."

"And look what has happened. Belariux has betrayed my father again. That's why we have to go so far out of our way."

"There are many who deserve to die, and yet live. Sometimes, those who deserve to live are visited with death. So what do we say to those who should have lived? I was angry, perhaps justly so, but I should not have been so quick to deal out death, even a living death."

Jesus

The next morning Jesus awoke to the sound of a cracking whip. In the fog of waking up, his first impression was that it must be a sound from the settlement—a farmer dealing with an obstinate mule, perhaps. Then, recognizing Arvigarus's shout, he turned to look.

"Oh, good! You're awake." Arvigarus tossed the whip to Jesus. "You take it, he's yours."

"What?"

"The slaver was right. This slave is useless. He's lazy."

Jesus looked over to Pirro, whimpering close to the cooking fire. Then he turned back to Arvigarus. "How...?"

"You were so unhappy last night. So I went back to the slaver after you were asleep. I woke him up and bought the slave. Now, I am giving him to you. He's a gift."

"I don't want a slave."

"Kill him if you like. You mustn't refuse the gift, though. That would be an insult. You do not do that to a Celt, particularly a prince. Remember what my twin brother did to Clotten after he was insulted by him."

Jesus put one hand to his neck. "Suppose I think he has suffered enough, and I want to set him free."

"He belongs to you now, and you can do what you like, but with a slave's tattoo on his forehead, that's not possible. The first warrior who sees him walking loose will kill him as a runaway. That is what I would do. If you want him dead, just kill him. Practice your swordsmanship on him."

Jesus gave Arvigarus a look of exasperation. "I don't want to kill him. I don't want to get beheaded for insulting you. And I certainly do not want to be nice to him. I did not ask for this—"

"Master." Pirro had walked to Jesus's side.

"What do you want?"

"May I pour you some mead to have with breakfast?"

"Fine, why not. I will have some mead."

"See, it's not that bad," Arvigarus remarked. "He's a slave; just use him. It's what people do."

"I have a really bad feeling about this. I wish he would just go away."

Joseph

Joseph spent a restless night as the guest of the king of the Pencaire hillfort, on the summit of Tregonning Hill.

It was at the foot of this hill that Jesus had made his first discovery of tin ore. Back then, almost four years ago, it had all seemed so simple—in the beginning, anyway. Jesus had been safely beyond the reach of the Romans, and his knack for discovering tin was going to make them all rich. But then the scriptural prophecy had led Joseph to despair for his great-nephew's future. He had hoped that bringing Jesus to Ynys Witrin would turn the boy toward peace, but Jesus seemed as convinced as ever that he had been called as King David's Messianic successor.

Joseph lit a candle, and unfolded Jesus's map. It indicated another untapped lode of tin. Joseph had already arranged for the hillfort king's people to dig out the ore and bring it to Carn Roz. Kendrick would be sailing from Carn Roz on the morning tide to meet him at nearby Ictus, but Joseph still had not decided where he wanted the captain to take him.

More than a month ago, Kendrick had left him in Carn Roz to consider the possibility of running the tin operation without letting the boys know. He had expected Kendrick to take only a fortnight to retrieve a portion of the coin deposited in Armorica, deliver it to the boys in Ynys Witrin, and return for him in Carn Roz, but fourteen days had turned to twenty and then thirty with no word.

By the time Kendrick appeared, spring had banished the chill of winter. That had been several days ago.

Kendrick explained that the Roman port master in Nantes had held the ship for a petty bureaucratic inspection that took days to complete, and that then the ship had been caught in doldrums on the route to Ynys Witrin.

The only good news was that he had delivered the boys' share of the Roman coin to Daniel, who sorely needed it.

Jesus was no longer in Ynys Witrin or even in Priddy. He had left to study with the druids in Ynys Môn. *Why would my fool of a nephew leave his mother and run off with the pagans? How could he expect Daniel to look after her in Ynys Witrin, run the mining and oversee the smelting operation in Priddy on his own?*

And now the first lode of silver-bearing ore had played out. A rival miner was digging quite close to the second untapped discovery. Kendrick told him how Daniel suspected that Esmeralda, the local druidess, was in league with the miner. She was spreading word that Mary's presence so close to the Tor was impious. *Yes, my fool of a nephew really left everything in Ynys Witrin in a sorry state.*

Jesus was gone, and Daniel needed help. Joseph was needed back in Ynys Witrin, yet he agonized over whether to return. With the enterprise headed for ruin, shouldn't he be more concerned about his own son's future? But if he went back, Jesus would find out sooner or later. That would enable Jesus to stay and carry on down the path of war and his own destruction. Joseph loved Jesus too much to help bring that about. He folded the map and blew out the candle.

Lying in bed, unable to sleep, Joseph prayed silently to God for guidance, but he received no answer. He mulled over his options. Should he leave Britain forever? Have Kendrick take him to Carn Roz and stay there to manage the tin operations? Or maybe hire Kendrick's ship to take him back to Ynys Witrin?

After a while, Joseph threw off his blankets and paced the room. Jesus had always told him he should watch the sunrise from the top of the Tor. Tregonning Hill was not quite the same, but it would have to do. The vista from the summit took in Mounts Bay and Ictus, and one could see all the way to Bodmin Moor. It was certain to be spectacular in the emerging light of dawn. So why not take it in? This could be his last chance before leaving Britain forever.

No one was stirring as Joseph made his way by the light of the moon, first across the hillfort enclosure and then across an open field beyond the gates. Fog hung all over the countryside. It was just as Jesus had described. Joseph stood alone, with a seemingly solid ground of fog at his feet. He looked up and marveled at the stars.

It must have appeared at first as just another star, nothing special, one among millions. But then it descended from heaven, quite slowly, even majestically. Every so often it went off on a loop or a turn, but it always seemed to be approaching. Dawn gradually lightened the rolling banks of fog. But this star did not fade into the waxing light of the sun like all the others. As it came closer it took on form. But not solid form, for it was fashioned in flame. A chariot of fire.

Joseph fell to his knees and bowed his face to the ground.

From the chariot, a voice spoke. "You are created in the image of God, and you must bow to no one but God. Rise, Joseph, for I am not God. I am merely his prophet."

"Elijah?" Joseph rose to his feet.

"I am he."

Joseph made out the ancient figure alighting without singe from the chariot. "And I have been sent to you, for it is not for you to see the face of God even though he has heard your prayers. Your faithfulness to the law has earned you the love and favor of God, and you have earned rewards beyond measure for that. But Jesus speaks true that God wants him to learn from the Britons and to teach them. Do not doubt Jesus when he tells you he is doing his Father's will, for he will not deceive you. Abandon him not, even if you think he breaks the law, for you have your own part to play as Jesus grows in wisdom and in the favor of God and man."

"Am I to bare my soul to Jesus?" Joseph asked. "There are things I have seen in his future and have kept from him."

"There will come a time when Jesus will look into your soul and see everything. No mortal will be able to hide anything, and all desires will be known to him. But you are wise to let God determine the time when Jesus must learn what he is yet unready to know. Jesus will determine his own path when the Father enlightens him."

The mist burned off in the sunrise, and all the places and villages took solid form below. The sounds of the awakening hillfort made it clear that people would soon be out and about. "It is time for me to go. Fare thee well, Joseph." The prophet climbed back into the flaming chariot and ascended into the sky, just as the retreating mist parted like a curtain to reveal the summit of Tregonning Hill.

The decision before Joseph was now an easy one. *It seems to be God's will that I should rejoin Mary and the boys. I must return to them as fast as Kendrick's ship can take me.*

Joseph paused only briefly to consider the deeper implications of what Elijah had said.

Am I such a stubborn old fool that it takes a second coming of Elijah to convince me I might be wrong about Jesus—about his consorting with pagans, but more importantly about the path he is taking? It would be so much better to be wrong than to be right in this.

Jesus

Now with Pirro, Jesus and Arvigarus made their way up the Avon through the lands of the Dobunni. On the second day away the settlement, Jesus noticed a field on the side of the stream. It was an hour before sundown. He turned from the bow, where he was paddling, to address Arvigarus in the stern. "I need to make camp before the sun goes down."

"We can still go another mile upstream before it gets too dark. I am sure we will find another campsite."

"The Sabbath begins for me at sundown. I must devote myself to my prayers."

"Very well, I suppose we can make up the time tomorrow," Arvigarus answered.

"Not during the day. The Sabbath continues through sunset tomorrow. I cannot do any work. That includes paddling."

"What about him?" Arvigarus pointed to Pirro, who sat in the middle between them. "He can do your share of the paddling."

Pirro groaned and mumbled something about how weak and pained he still felt from the ill-use he had received in slavery.

"He'll be no help with the paddling," said Jesus. "It is much more demanding than sailing with the wind. You will exhaust yourself if you try to do all the paddling tomorrow on your own."

"It's been two days. He has not done anything. He just sits while we do all the work. Now he mumbles about being weak, and you give him another day off. Anyone would think he was the master and you the slave."

"He was hardly able to walk yesterday. Don't you remember he spilled half the mug of mead all over me?"

They beached the curragh and scouted for a clearing. Pirro moaned in pain and then walked slowly to a big log, where he sat.

"I would have whipped him for being so careless," said Arvigarus, "but I understand what you said—that putting him to work right away would weaken him too much. I even understood this morning when you relieved him for another day because his injuries were still festering. But now you are not even waiting to see how he fares tomorrow before you give him yet another day off. I can't make sense of that. All he has to do is mumble a complaint, and he gets out of any work, while we take care of him." Arvigarus grabbed the whip. "What he really needs is a dose of this." Arvigarus flicked the whip in Pirro's direction.

"Whether he is injured has nothing to do with this," snapped Jesus. "I agree he may be feigning injury, but tomorrow is the Sabbath day. The Lord created the world in six days, and on the seventh day he rested. In the law of Moses, he commands us to rest on the Sabbath day and keep it holy."

"That's what you said when you told me you could not help me sail on the Sabrina. That is the law of your people. But this man is Greek. He does not even believe in your god, much less follow your god's laws."

"But I believe, and I follow his laws," said Jesus. "And the law in Scripture clearly states that when we keep the Sabbath, we must keep it as a day of rest, not only for ourselves, but for our servants and slaves as well. Let's set up camp before the sun goes down."

Arvigarus gestured at Pirro. "I don't suppose you might trouble him to give us a hand?"

Pirro was already approaching. "Of course, Pirro is always ready to serve his master and his friend." But then, halfway toward them, he began limping.

Jesus and Arvigarus looked at each other and raised their eyebrows.

The next morning Arvigarus told Jesus he was going to visit a nearby village. Jesus tried to devote the day to his prayers, but he found it hard to concentrate. Pirro gorged himself on the food Arvigarus had left. He should have served his master first, but Jesus decided he did not care. He meant to fast that Sabbath, anyway.

Pirro came to Jesus and mumbled some appreciation for his kindness.

"I do not want to be kind to you," answered Jesus. "Your treachery cost the lives of many good men." His voice swelled. "How many children lost their fathers because of your greed? How many wives lost their husbands? I sentenced you to be sold into slavery because it was the kind of slow death you deserved, and I would do it again. I thought I was rid of you. The prince buying you was not my idea. I never wanted to own any slave, least of all you. I would have left you with that slaver, and you would be dead by now if Arvigarus had not bought you, so you can thank him, not me, for your miserable life. I do not even want to look at you!"

Pirro remained silent.

Jesus sighed and continued more calmly. "When I saw you at the slave dealer's, I was glad I did not have any money. I could not have bought you even if I had wanted to. I walked away thinking you were going to die, and I was glad it was out of my hands.

"I wish I knew what to do with you now, but I don't. Maybe I should cast you aside and let you be caught and put to death as a runaway slave. But it seems to be God's will that you continue to have a hand in my life, for good or ill. I cannot give you back to Arvigarus without gravely insulting him, I don't have it in me to be a proper slave owner, and you are too emaciated and lazy for me to sell you. There doesn't seem to be any way to set you free while you bear that tattoo. So, there you have it. I am bound to you just as much as you are bound to me. Don't ever thank me again for being kind to you, because I am not. Now, go away and leave me alone."

Arvigarus returned shortly after sundown. He appeared self-satisfied over dinner. "So…did you have a good time in the village?" Jesus asked.

"I actually do not mind that we had to spend an extra day here on account of your Sabbath thing."

"What did you do?"

"I hired one of the town's lovely wenches."

"Huh?"

"Sorry, I would have asked you to join me. We could have taken turns."

Jesus scowled, his face heating. "No, I would not have joined you."

"It was great, but you obviously do not approve. Why not? I paid her well, and I think she enjoyed it, too."

"It's really not my business. But you're right. I do not approve."

"What's wrong with it? She makes money, and we both have a good time."

"I don't know. Maybe she just tells you she has a good time, but she tells that to everyone because she needs the money. Maybe her family is starving and she is letting you use her body because she has no choice. What about her reputation? Who will ever marry her?"

"I wasn't the one who told her to sell her body. She already had her reputation before I even saw her today."

"Who will provide for your child if she has it?"

"Who cares? If she doesn't have my bastard, she is going to have someone else's."

 "Do you still have any of your father's money left?"

"Enough to make it to Caer Leir."

"Then what?"

"My sister will give us what we need from there."

Jesus rolled his eyes.

"What's wrong now?"

"That is not the point. Your father gave you money to see us all the way to Ynys Môn, not for you to show up at your sister's house as a beggar. I remember what Guiderius said, and he was right. You spend your father's money foolishly—first to buy a useless slave, and now to hire a whore."

At first he thought Arvigarus might react violently. Then he saw that his words had hit home. Arvigarus appeared to be ashamed.

"I am sorry, this is not my business," Jesus said. "As Jews, we are taught to be chaste outside of marriage. Let's have some mead and go to sleep."

The mead loosened them up. By the time they retired for the night, Jesus and Arvigarus were laughing and joking again. As much as Arvigarus could be a rogue, he was never mean spirited.

As they paddled up the Avon over the next days, the portages became more frequent. It was bad enough that Pirro seemed to go through the motion of paddling rather than putting any effort into it. Jesus could pretend not to notice. But the portages were worse. It was impossible to ignore Pirro's laziness when he seemed to take the smallest possible load on his own shoulders while Jesus and Arvigarus struggled with the boat and the larger sacks.

Finally, they reached a point where the river became too shallow, so they abandoned the boat and started eastward on foot. Weighed down with their supplies, they came to a steep escarpment. Jesus took the lead on all fours with Pirro in the middle and Arvigarus bringing up the rear.

As he started up the path, Pirro suddenly cried out in pain. "My foot! It's injured." They waited a minute to see if it would improve. "I'll never make it up the path if I have to carry anything."

"That's it. I've had it." Arvigarus pulled out the whip. He worked it relentlessly over Pirro's backside.

Pirro cried out loudly enough to be heard all through the river valley. His punishment over, he looked to Jesus.

"What are you looking at me for?" Jesus said. "I am not a slave driver, but that does not mean I have to be nice to you."

Without another word, Pirro picked up the packs he had dropped. He suddenly seemed able to carry his share of the load without a problem.

Daniel

Daniel sat by Mary's bedside in her house on Ynys Witrin and applied cold compresses to her forehead. The days had turned to weeks, and still there was no sign that her fever was breaking. It had started a day after Kendrick had brought the Roman coinage.

Everything had been going so well, until the autumn. They were working a good lode of silver ore and had found a second that they alone knew about. Jesus's technique for working the silver into Celtic patterns on the bronze ware created a unique medium that certainly would sell well among the Romans. The first shipload sent back to Armorica was sure to return large profits.

But everything had gone sour in the space of only a few months.

Workmen for a rival miner, Horshak, were digging all over the hillside where the new lode was located. Daniel was stuck; he could not hire workers, and he could not ask Grengan to reserve the area without proof that he had a working mine on the new lode. The lack of Roman coin had prevented him from hiring workers. Kendrick had finally appeared with a new supply of money, but Mary had fallen ill the next day, and Daniel could not leave her to supervise the operation.

Esmeralda had to be working against him. *Word is out that she claimed Mary lives too close to the sacred Tor. Grengan says he will defend Mary, but I'm sure there is going to be trouble.*

Daniel felt weighed down, as if all that un-mined ore rested on his shoulders. His aunt was in danger, and he could not leave her in the hands of strangers, no matter how friendly they were. He could pay people to look after her, but that was not the same as having family there. *I would never be able to explain to Jesus why I was a day's journey away in Priddy if Mary were to die.*

Jesus

Finally, they reached the house of Imogen and Postumux in Caer Leir, the main settlement of the Corieltauvi tribe on the Soar River. Their home was similar to the courtyard houses Jesus had seen in the lands of the Dobunni. Jesus and Arvigarus shared a large, comfortable room. The best part was that Pirro was out of sight, relegated to the slave quarters. All they had to do was wait for the snows to melt in the mountain passes, which would take them through the final leg of their journey. Postumux's allies among the Cornovii tribe would let him know once the passes were safe.

It appeared that the noble families of Caer Leir were trying to emulate the Romans in their daily life. The community's common hall was largely the province of the craftsmen and lower ranks of the warriors. Jesus and Arvigarus frequently made their way there to join in the boisterous revelry. Imogen and Postumux led a different social life, inviting upper-class friends to dinner parties and being invited back in return. As the hero of Rumps, Jesus often found himself a sought-after guest.

One night Jesus and Arvigarus attended one of these dinner parties with Imogen and Postumux. Arvigarus regularly spent his sister's money in the community brothels, a fact Imogen was obviously aware of but did not allow to be mentioned in her presence. But this night she insisted that her brother join them.

The host had hired a traveling bard, who asked the company if anyone had a story to request. The host turned to Jesus, the honored guest from across the sea. "Please, sir, you make the first request."

At first Jesus was at a loss. Then he asked the bard, "Tell the story of how Caer Leir got its name."

The bard made a little bow. "The community was named for a king of the Corieltauvi who lived many hundreds of years ago. His name was Leir, and he ruled for sixty years. He had no sons, but he did have three daughters: Gonorilla, Regau, and Cordeilla. He loved the three of them, but Cordeilla, the youngest, was his favorite.

"As he grew old, Leir thought to divide his kingdom among them and find them suitable husbands. But doubting his daughters' worthiness, he tested them by asking each whether she loved him the most. The two eldest daughters answered in flowery language to assure him they did, and he granted them each one-third of his kingdom.

"Cordeilla, the youngest, answered plainly, 'Father, can any daughter love her father more than duty requires? Whoever pretends to do so must disguise real sentiments under the veil of flattery. I have always loved you as much as any daughter can love her father, but I will not pretend to love you more.' This greatly annoyed Leir, so he disowned her and married her to an outlander, Aganippus, a king of the Gauls.

"When Leir in his old age came to be infirm, his elder daughters and their husbands rebelled against him and deprived him of all authority. Reflecting on how he had fallen from grandeur, Leir travelled to Gaul to find Cordeilla. He had little hope of assistance from her but sailed anyway. He sent a messenger to tell Cordeilla of the misery he had fallen into. She hired a retinue for her father and provided him royal apparel and food. Restored to his station, Leir met Cordeilla and Aganippus with honor and dignity. Aganippus brought an army to Britain and restored Leir to his kingdom. Leir died three years later and was buried in a great vault in the city he had founded."

The guests applauded and cheered when the bard finished his tale, and Jesus joined in. Later, when they returned to their room, Jesus brought up the tale again. "I think that is one of the best stories I have heard from any bard in Britain."

"It's nothing special." Arvigarus sat on the edge of his bed and removed his shoes. "I have heard it many times."

"It reminds me of something from the Scripture of my own people. Long ago, judges ruled my people like kings. Just as King Leir starts out with the full love of his most loving daughter, the people of Israel start out in a state of grace with God. Just as Leir turns from that true love because he is blinded by the flattery of the unworthy daughters, so too do the people of Israel turn from God, abandon his laws, and fall away into sin. Both Leir and the people of Israel become miserable and unhappy. For Leir that meant poverty and dishonor; for Israel it meant defeat in war and slavery.

"Both Leir and the people of Israel come to their senses and hear the call of the true love they have so recklessly abandoned. They despair of ever finding forgiveness, because they have proven to be so unworthy, but nonetheless they repent and reverse course. Leir goes to his daughter. The people of Israel appeal to God for a judge to lead them. Are you with me so far?"

Arvigarus nodded, though he seemed to be paying more attention to putting on his nightclothes.

"Now, here is the part I really love. Cordeilla does not give even a hint of rebuke for her father's wickedness and cruelty. Her love is so great that she immediately restores him to full honor and dignity. So too is shown the greatness of the love that God has for his chosen people. He never abandons his people on account of their wickedness, but he raises them up and restores them to grace. It happens time and again in the days of the judges, when he hears their cries and raises a new judge to lead them out of misery. It becomes a continuing cycle of God's grace, the people falling away, then hearing God's call and turning back to him, and then the magnificent return to grace. I think Leir's story is so powerful because it makes this cycle part of someone's life. It is beyond Scripture and history."

Arvigarus looked at Jesus in silence.

Is he totally confused?

Finally Arvigarus spoke. "You would take a story from Britain back to your homeland to teach your Scripture to your people?"

"I don't know for sure. I have been preparing to lead my people to freedom from the Romans. But yes, perhaps I will use this story if I am called to do so. I would have to change some elements, though. I do not think Jewish people are ready to look upon a daughter as a godlike figure, above a father who represents the sinfulness of man."

"How would you change the story?" Arvigarus asked.

Jesus sat on the edge of his bed and thought for some time. "I would reverse the role of the child and the father. I would have the sinfulness of man represented by a son who is by nature a spendthrift—a son who is prodigal. Leir is somewhat prodigal, foolishly giving away his kingdom on account of the flattery of the older daughters." Jesus gazed at Arvigarus and continued. "I might have the son fall away because of profligate and immoral living, spending all he has on harlots and that sort of thing."

"So I would be the scamp of your story." Arvigarus laughed. "Fair enough. Who would inspire the forgiving character?"

"I am thinking of your father. He lost you and your brother when you were infants. When the two of you returned years later, he welcomed you warmly, and he even forgave Guiderius for killing the stepson he favored as Imogen's suitor. Somehow, I can see him giving you half of everything he has and welcoming you back with total forgiveness after you waste it all away, as I have no doubt you would."

"I am not that bad. Shouldn't Guiderius be in the story, too?"

"Yes, there is room in the story for an older brother. As I recall, Guiderius does not approve of the way you spend money. I can see him serving your father after you take your share of the inheritance and leave. He might find it difficult at first to understand why your father would eagerly welcome you back and restore you to a station you might not deserve. But eventually he will understand, once the father explains his happiness in finding a son whom he had given up for dead."

Arvigarus snorted and climbed into his bed. "You talk much about forgiveness, Jesus. What about Pirro? Could you ever forgive him?"

Jesus thought again before he answered. "That will be hard. He caused so much death and suffering, including the death of my best friend. I do not see that he has ever tried to turn his life in a different direction as Leir did, do you?"

"He only thinks about himself," observed Arvigarus.

Jesus hung his head. "I am starting to feel some pity for his misery, but that is not the same as forgiveness. He was my uncle's business partner—nothing more. I cannot say I ever really cared for him."

Joseph

From the beach, Joseph gazed out to the flat, motionless, endless sea. He gnashed his teeth thinking of the last few days. He agonized over the terrible, foolish mistake he had made. In his haste to get back to Ynys Witrin, he had neglected to wait for the rainbow that would assure safe passage over the seas. A tempest had caught them in its grip and driven them onto a reef where Kendrick's ship now lay wrecked.

Kendrick's two sons, old enough to serve as crewmembers, whittled away at wood as if they did not have a care in the world. It was small consolation that they had made it alive to this small island. There was a little fresh water, and they could catch fish from the sea.

Joseph wondered if the sun had affected the captain and his sons. The captain seemed delirious, claiming they had discovered the mythical Island of Lyonesse. It was supposedly an abandoned land once joined to Belerium, but reputed to be nearly consumed by the azure sea.

Kendrick seemed oblivious to an obvious but inconvenient fact about mythical islands. When one wrecks one's ship in the process of discovering such a place, its mythical character tends to diminish considerably the prospect of any rescue.

Chapter 12
Bangor

Jesus a messenger from the Cornovii finally arrived to say the Snowden Mountains were passable.

Jesus, born and bred in a desert land, would have disagreed. The vales hundreds of feet below were touched by the emerging green of spring, but the mountain passes remained a world of swirling white and gray, gripped by a cold, damp, biting wind that cut through their cloaks. Clouds wrapped the mountains, sometimes obscuring the trail so they had to pick their way cautiously upward.

As Jesus, Arvigarus and Pirro made their way up a narrow escarpment, the way was sufficiently clear. But more than a hundred feet ahead, there was nothing to see but a thick milky veil streaming by in the gale. Jesus and Arvigarus sat on snow-capped rocks at the summit, waiting for Pirro to catch up.

"How many more ridges are there?" Jesus asked.

"There is a long vale ahead and then one more ridge after that. We will reach that by midday tomorrow. Then we'll descend through the vales to Bangor."

"It is nearly six weeks since I left Ynys Witrin. We will be several weeks late getting there. Elsigar must have arrived by ship already and started the classes without us."

"That cannot be helped," said Arvigarus. "We had to wait for the weather and then go through these mountains to avoid the Ordovices."

Pirro stumbled to the top to join them. "It is cruel of you to burden me so." He lost his footing on a patch of ice and slid back twenty feet, spilling the contents of his pack over the slope. He caught himself on a branch just in time to save himself from hurtling over a precipice. Pirro looked up at Jesus and Arvigarus. "I'm hurt," he shouted. "I think I've sprained my ankle."

"Clumsy oaf!" Arvigarus drew the whip and descended rapidly toward Pirro.

"Wait," Jesus shouted, coming after him.

Arvigarus turned to face Jesus. "He's faking an injury again. He's not even carrying his share of the load. A good dose of this will fix him, just as it did before."

"Whipping will not solve anything," said Jesus. "We need to gather up the supplies before the cloud blinds us."

Arvigarus glared at Pirro, letting him know he would be dealt with later. By the time everything was gathered and repacked, they had lost half an hour, and the thick mist was closing in again. The descent from the summit proved treacherous, slowing them further. It was not until early evening that they reached the valley floor.

"My back is so tired from the climb, Master. My feet, too," Pirro complained. "You make me carry so much."

"Your load is the same as ours. Help us gather wood for the fire," Jesus answered. "Then you can rest for the night."

"You are coddling him again," said Arvigarus. "He needs that whipping I promised earlier."

"We will have no more of that," said Jesus. "Starting tomorrow, he carries nothing more than his own food and supplies. If he keeps up, he can come with us. If not, he takes his chances on his own."

"What kind of choice is that?" said Pirro. "The natives will kill me if they find me on my own."

"I cannot do anything about it. The Celts put that tattoo on you."

"You were the one who had me sold. You knew it would be worse than a death sentence."

"It was nothing less than you deserved." Jesus turned and began gathering twigs. Many heroes died on account of your treachery, and my best friend lost his life."

"What choice did I have?" Pirro sat on the ground, making no move to help. "You didn't want me in the tin business, even though I was the one who led your family to Ictis. Didn't your uncle tell you it was my idea back in Gaul to open up the ancient tin route? But no, once we got to Britain the tin business became all about you. I became Pirro the dealer in trinkets, the junk dealer. Even the Celts laughed at me."

"You misled Uncle Joseph. You told him the natives would have plenty of tin to sell. Your lies would have bankrupted my uncle if I had not found the ore. Even so, my uncle was more than fair to you. We all had to figure out our role in the venture, and you decided to become a merchant of the native wares, because you knew nothing about tin. Nobody forced you. And then you betrayed us to the pirates."

"He deserved death." Arvigarus started chopping a branch into firewood.

"Yes, he did."

"He's no use as a slave. Just kill him now."

"I can't."

Arvigarus stopped chopping the firewood and gave Jesus a stern look. "You've told me about how the Romans dominate your homeland of Israel, and how it's time for your people to rise up and throw the Romans out. If you Jews are going to manage that, then you and your people are going to have to be willing to use some violence. The way you led the warriors at the battle at Rumps, shows that you may be the sort of leader your people need. But you don't seem to have the stomach for it."

"Maybe I am not cut out to be that type of leader," Jesus said. "The Dumnonii make do without slaves. The law given to Israel by God allows for slavery, but maybe it is time to end it."

"The Romans own slaves, so why shouldn't your people do so if the law of your god allows it?" Arvigarus asked.

"I have seen Roman cruelty more terrible that that of the wildest Britons, and I do not know why we call one civilized and the other savage." Jesus realized Pirro was being discussed as if he weren't there. *That must be how it is with slaves.* Jesus turned back to Arvigarus and continued. "I see the hopelessness in Pirro's eyes, and I know it will be there as long as he is a slave, even if I treat him kindly. I feel bound to him now, even more than he does to me. I never wanted a slave. I never expected to see him again. Now I cannot get rid of him without causing his death. He deserves to pay for his crimes, but I cannot bring myself to take his life."

The next morning they broke camp and continued through the vale toward the last ridge, with Pirro carrying only his own share of the food. By midmorning, Jesus noticed he was falling behind and waited beside the trail for him to catch up.

Pirro stumbled and struggled with his load. His injuries might be feigned, but Jesus could see that his body was drawn and weak from the cruelty he had suffered at the hands of masters before him. Even before Pirro reached him, Jesus began to unload his own pack and discard most of his food.

When Pirro came up, Jesus expected another complaint, but Pirro just looked at him quizzically. "Give me your supplies," Jesus said. "I will carry them for you. If you fall behind again, I will leave them on the side of the trail for you. Don't let Arvigarus see this. Just carry your pack empty."

Pirro complied without saying a word.

We are now within a day or two of our destination, and I can make it without eating or drinking. Pirro is too weak to fast. This time I can be the one to do without.

Horshak

Horshak waited at the edge of the clearing for Esmeralda to finish her incantations before the small crowd of worshippers. His workers had been digging around Priddy in search of a lode of silver ore, without success. He could tell she had noted his presence.

"Have you found it yet?" Esmeralda asked him..

"I had my men digging all over the Mendips first. That was just a ruse to make it look like we were searching without a clue. Then I had them start at the spot you indicated, digging trenches and pits for a hundred feet in every direction. We found no trace of silver ore."

"I saw their map, and it was clear," Esmeralda said. "It showed the River Cheddar coming out of the hillside at the foot of the gorge. It indicated a spot three hundred feet up the valley and then fifty feet up the western slope. There was a big X labeled 'the lode.' How could you have missed it?"

"I tell you, there is nothing there to miss. There are no grains of silver in the nearby creek, and my men have dug in every direction. They have gone down twenty feet, even though the map said the lode is fifteen feet below the surface. Perhaps the map was an intentional fake?"

"I saw that map with my own eyes. It was not laid out the first time I went into the mother's house. I left the house as soon as I heard Jesus and his cousin coming, but I could tell they were busy searching. I found the map when I went back in after they left. They must have searched to see if it had been taken."

"I cannot keep paying my men to dig, if we do not find the lode soon."

"These outlanders are tricky," said the druidess. "They come to take our minerals and pollute the minds of the people. Keep your eyes open. They probably have a new supply of coin to pay for workers. Don't let them get to the silver before you do."

Elsigar

Elsigar studied Jesus, who looked a wreck. "You're late."

Jesus explained how he and Arvigarus had crossed the mountains. No wonder he looked such a mess.

Like all druids, Elsigar was a creature of enigmas, but of all the people he had encountered in his long years as a druid, none was as enigmatic as this young outlander. Even as a boy, Jesus had been childlike in his innocence and yet mature in his wisdom. Jesus often showed extraordinary kindness, and yet now he was the owner of a slave—the very man he had condemned more than a year before. No doubt that punishment was just; it was also terrible.

Once Jesus and Arvigarus had told the story of their journey, Elsigar said, "You've missed two weeks of classes. Nevertheless, Arvigarus, you will join the third year *fuchloc*." It was too bad the prince had to be lumped with younger students, but it couldn't be helped. "Jesus, you will be in the *anruth* class."

"Why is he ahead of me?" Arvigarus said. "We're about the same age."

"You missed many years of instruction after you and your brother…" Elsigar paused, then said, "While you were away from your father's house. But Jesus has studied elsewhere."

Elsigar nodded to the slave. "He'll work with the servants of the school. No student may be attended by a personal servant or slave. This is a place of disciplined study, not a place for coddling the rich."

"That suits me well, sir," Jesus said.

※

Early the next morning, Elsigar walked into the hall, sniffed the air, and snorted.

"Problem, sir?"

He looked back to find Jesus behind him. "This place is confining."

"It's a fine hall."

Their feet padded quietly across the flagstone floor. "A druid belongs in the outdoors, where he may be at one with the gods of forests, glens, and streams. We druids have no love for temples or monuments."

"But what of the henges and stone circles? I've seen them all over the British landscape."

"They were constructed in an age long past, before the discovery of the secret of iron and before the coming of the *Tuatha Dé Danaan* from the isles of the north. We respect those structures as the holy places of the people of the older age, we preserve them, and occasionally we conduct rites among those ruins. But we do not emulate them with structures of their own." His eyes roved over the beams above. "This hall and the others in the school are exceptions, constructed of necessity to protect us from the weather." Elsigar reached his place. "Now take your seat. I hear the others coming."

A dozen novices, mostly men in their twenties but also a few young women, sat attentively before Elsigar on their mats. Elsigar called his class to order. "For the benefit of our new arrival, I will repeat what I said two weeks ago. You all have much to learn. Anyone may try to become a druid. Kings and warriors entrust their children to us for their education, but few stay the course.

"Over the next several months, the other senior druids and I will assess your progress. For those we select, we will start the final and most challenging phase of training." These students were all members of the noble stream, a ranking among the novices that took nine years of study or more to achieve. "By now you have mastered the telling of many legends, but rote memorization will not be enough to advance to the degree of *ollamh*, and then move on to your specialized training. Now you must show you can think like a druid."

He paced in front of them. "Today, we are joined by an outlander, and he arrives just at the right time. We will be talking about the very elements of druidic faith and belief, the transits through which gods and druids transform and regenerate the energy of the cosmos. We will see how these transformations link all people to the same elements, and thus in turn link them to the cosmic realm of the gods."

Jesus raised his hand. "That is very interesting, but what does that have to do with me? As you know, my people believe in one God."

"I am not yet sure if this involves you or not," Elsigar replied. "We will see. I will first ask the class to identify these elements and explain how they figure in our teachings. After the class discusses each element, I will call on you to tell us if that element has any comparable significance in your Scriptures. Perhaps we will see that we have more in common than you think. Perhaps not."

"What are Scriptures?" asked one of the class members.

"My people are blessed to have Scripture, which is the written word we live by," Jesus answered. "It has the law of God and the story of the relationship between God and his people. It also has psalms, which lift our hearts and console us in times of triumph and calamity. Our great prophets wrote down Scripture, with inspiration from God."

One young man turned to Elsigar, wide-eyed. "Committing matters of faith to writing. Isn't that…strange?"

Another student chimed in, "Some of the Cantiaci and the surrounding tribes in the southeast of Britain learned writing from the Romans."

"That's for business," said one of the star pupils. "For matters of faith, it's an abhorrence. Writing something like that gives it an unholy permanency."

"Isn't there danger of empowering an error or a curse," one of them asked, "to allow the writing of any druidic doctrine or teaching?"

Elsigar said, "We want to explore areas of common belief, but there will be many areas of difference between ourselves and the outlander." He cleared his throat. "Now: the elements I am looking for are four in number. Name them."

He rejected several possibilities offered by the class: wands, potions, mistletoe, and so forth. "These are certainly implements of the druids, but they are not the transits themselves that connect us to the cosmos. Anyone else?"

Finally one of the men in the back said, "Fire."

"Explain yourself," said Elsigar.

"We mark the two poles of the Celtic year with fire at Beltane and Samhain," the student said. "Beltane in particular is the feast of fire and light. The name for Beltane itself refers to a purifying fire. The druidic fire we make requires meticulous preparation of each pyre, with the logs assembled precisely. We follow the same prescriptions that the druid Mog Ruith gave to his assistant in the Siege of Druim Damghaire. The same preparation is made for the fire that puts the earth to rest at Samhain."

Elsigar nodded. "Yes, fire transforms everything. Even when the *Tuatha Dé Danann* arrived from the isles of the north, they burned their boats as they transformed themselves." Elsigar turned to Jesus. "Does fire play a role in your Scripture?"

"Definitely," said Jesus. "Ever since the days of our first prophet Abraham, my people have burned offerings to send them to God in heaven. Scripture records that God used fire, along with brimstone, to bring down wickedness. He even appeared to Moses in the form of a burning bush. So, in many ways, fire connects man to God."

"Can we name another element?" said Elsigar.

"How about wood? It is consumed by fire," suggested another student.

"Yes, but wood is not a basic element. What would you say, Jesus?" Elsigar asked.

"In our book of Genesis," answered Jesus, "we learn that God brought forth trees bearing fruit on the third day of Creation, but that was along with grass and herbs, and all of those things come from the earth. So, I would say that earth is more fundamental as an element. Before he made trees, God made the dry land appear, and he called it Earth. Men often fashion their works from wood, but wood is weak and fragile. Our greatest laws are the ten commandments that God gave to Moses in the form of tablets carved from rock. Even man himself was formed from dust of the ground."

"Interesting," said Elsigar. "Who can give me an example from our druidic teaching in which earth is an element?"

One student related how one of Lugh's magicians claimed he could throw down mountains until their tops rolled on the ground. Another student added a tale from the Courtship of Etaine about how Oengus obtained the help of the *Tuatha Dé Danann* in clearing a dozen plains and in hollowing out twelve river valleys, all in a single night.

"That sounds like something from the book of Isaiah," said Jesus. "In his prophecy of the coming of the Messiah, he says that every valley shall be exalted and every mountain and hill shall be made low. There shall be a voice crying in the wilderness to prepare the way of the Lord, to make straight in the desert a highway for our God.

THE MAKING OF THE LAMB

"I think I can name another of your elements," Jesus continued. "I remember you blowing air upon the pirates from the battlement of Rumps Castle."

"That would be an example of the druidic wind," Elsigar replied. "Can anyone tell us where the element of air is found in our teachings?"

Another student answered that the druid Mog Ruith used the druidic wind to turn his enemies to stone with the assistance of the gods in the Siege of Druim Damghaire. Others speculated that gods and goddesses often took the form of crows and swans because the air was a mysterious realm where only sacred beings can move about.

"Are there examples of this element of air in the Scripture of your people?" Elsigar asked Jesus.

"In the book of Genesis, after God formed man from the dust of the earth, he breathed into his nostrils to give him the breath of life. In the book of Job, God himself took the form of a whirlwind."

"We've named fire, earth, and air," said Elsigar. "Who can name the final element?"

The students quickly settled upon water. They talked about sacred thermal springs and how various springs, wells, and fountains were known to purify and cure in both the spiritual and physical planes. Jesus responded with a story of the prophet Moses parting the Red Sea. He also spoke of how the Spirit of God moved upon the waters of chaos at the time of Creation.

"That is good, but you have left out the greatest teaching about water as a spiritual element," said Elsigar. "Remember the story of the cauldron of Bran Vendigeit and how it brought cadavers back to life." He turned to Jesus. "Do you remember that discussion at Beltane?"

"Yes, I remember," said Jesus. "I told you then that the story reminded me of something from my Scripture, when Elisha told Namaan how the waters of Jordan would cure his leprosy. It could not be just any water; it had to be the waters of the Jordan. The legend of Bran's cauldron takes the point further, because the soldiers first had to die before they were reborn in the cauldron."

"As I recall, you said that point rang true with you, but it did not seem to come directly from your Scripture."

"I have tried to think about that since," said Jesus. "I am not sure how anyone can be born again. We cannot go back into the womb of our mothers."

"The womb is only how we are born of the flesh," said Elsigar. "We do not need the womb of our mothers to be born again of the spirit. Perhaps that is something your Messiah will show your people when the time comes." *Now I've given Jesus something to ponder.*

When Elsigar dismissed the class, Jesus lingered. "I am glad I was inspired to come. When I first arrived on these shores, I thought that druids were nothing more than pagans. I see now that we can learn much from each other."

"Maybe we need each other even more than you think," said Elsigar. "Bran's cauldron has been destroyed, but you say your people have a river of holy water. It seems to me they have no idea how to use it."

Joseph

Kendrick and his sons held the craft as Joseph waded out from the shore. It was a crude structure of reeds, branches, and pieces of wreckage, lashed together with vines. At first Joseph had thought Kendrick had taken leave of his senses, when the Armorican captain had begun to gather up pieces of driftwood, and carved joints to bind them without so much as a nail. Joseph had to give Kendrick and his sons credit: they had fashioned a craft—more a raft than anything else—with only the few knives they had kept on their persons through the shipwreck.

Kendrick had erected a crude rig with a small square sail made from their rags. With only a small oar carved from a branch to steer by and no keel, they would be at the mercy of wind and wave. For now a fair wind blew from inland, but would it take them to a more hospitable shore? Would they die of thirst in the middle of doldrums? Would the fragile craft even hold together through the pounding of waves? Kendrick had certainly done as well as any man might, but he made no promises.

It was madness to go, but it would be madness to stay, too. As he stood in the water next to the craft, Joseph closed his eyes and prayed for protection. When he reopened his eyes, he knew at once his prayer had been answered. A rainbow spanned the distant horizon.

THE MAKING OF THE LAMB

Daniel

Daniel applied another compress to Mary's forehead. The fever was not as bad as the day before, but she was still pale and weak. He had Roman coin to hire workmen now, but she was far too ill to care for herself, and he still felt obliged to stay at Mary's bedside.

He looked up and saw a Celtic woman at the doorway. He smiled at her. This was the first visitor since Mary had taken ill.

"I am Tomzica," she said. "I came by to ask about Mary. I have not seen her for more than a week. I hope you don't think that I am intruding, but I was worried."

"Come in. She is sleeping deeply. I don't think you will wake her."

The woman came in and sat on the bed. She put her hand on Mary's forehead. "The fever does not seem so bad."

"It was much worse a few days ago. I was afraid of losing her. She's been getting better, but she is still very weak."

"You didn't tell anyone she was sick?"

"I did not think of it."

"Men! Humph! You are always too proud. You think it is shameful to have sickness in your family."

"I wasn't trying to keep anything secret. I was just so busy taking care of her—"

"Yet how is anyone supposed to know if you don't tell someone? We wondered what had happened to her. She lives in this house so far away from any neighbors, and we thought she just wanted to be by herself. We never can tell what you outlanders might be doing, and no one wanted to intrude. Here, give me that compress. This is woman's work."

"But she's my family, my responsibility—"

"Just as it was up to me to take care of my little girl. Mary was an angel, coming by every day when my little Guinevere fell ill."

Within a day, a stream of women from the surrounding homesteads were taking turns at Mary's bedside. Daniel began to feel useless, but also relieved. The next day Mary was staying awake, talking and laughing with her visitors. She was clearly in capable hands.

With the crops planted in the surrounding fields, most of his workmen were ready to come back, and now Daniel had the coin to pay them.

"I'll be in Priddy," Daniel told Tomzica. "You must send for me immediately if Aunt Mary takes a turn for the worse."

"*Tsk.*" Tomzica shooed him out of the house. "Of course we will. Now go about your business."

Daniel's heart lifted as he gathered his men and supplies and started toward Priddy. All he had to do now was gather samples of the ore, and Grengan would grant the claim.

The villagers in Priddy seemed pleased to see Daniel return with his men. They told him that Horshak's men were digging near the discharge of the Cheddar from the nearby cave. *Good for Horshak, he must have found another lode.*

Later, though, one of his men pointed out someone spying on them from the nearby woods. Daniel thought better of setting out immediately for the lode site he and Jesus had discovered the previous season. Instead, he took a few trusted men and headed out to do his own reconnaissance of Horshak's work.

Daniel soon had his answer. Horshak's dig was nowhere near the discovery Jesus had made. But this was no coincidence. Daniel could tell why Horshak's men were digging in this place. Someone had seen the map, but they had not understood it.

Leaving his men to prepare their huts for another season, Daniel took a horse and galloped off. He was soon in Grengan's house in the Lake Village, pleading his case.

"I tell you that Horshak is spying on us, ready to steal our rightful claim. His men are watching us. If I bring my men to the site, Horshak will have his men digging right next to us."

"I cannot grant your claim until I see the ore samples," Grengan replied. "Those are the rules we set, to be fair to you outlanders and to my own people. You must bring me the sample first."

"But I can tell that Horshak saw our map, or maybe someone else did and told him what was on it."

Grengan waved his hands helplessly. "I am afraid that's a claim you need to take up with the druidess."

"Esmeralda! You can't be serious!"

"I know she has no love for you or your family. But if you accuse Horshak of spying, it is out of my hands. That is a matter for the druid, not the king. And one other thing: you had better be prepared for a trial by combat, with Esmeralda as the referee."

"I would have to fight Horshak?"

"That is our way."

Daniel rolled his eyes. "It's our discovery, but Horshak has more men. He'll reach the ore first if he starts digging alongside us, even if we have a day's head start."

"I have an idea for you. You should fast against him. Call on him with the power of the fast to stop spying on you and leave you to work on your claim without interference."

At first Daniel thought the idea was crazy, but Grengan explained the ancient Celt custom for seeking redress from a wrongdoer. *What do I have to lose?*

The next day, Daniel was back at Priddy. He let his workmen go but told them to be ready to return soon. He then walked boldly to the site where Horshak's men were digging. They looked up from their work as Daniel took a seat on a nearby log. He waited for the men to get back to work. Then he started laughing and jeering at them, saying that there was no silver, and how they were working for a thief. One by one, Horshak's men looked up at him, listened, and then went back to their digging.

For the rest of that day, Daniel took no food or drink. Nor did he eat or drink on the next day or the day after. Horshak's men did not respond directly to Daniel's taunts, but they began to look more embarrassed every day.

Viktrica

Viktrica tried not to be too obvious as she glanced at the outlander sitting serenely on the mat next to hers, waiting for the class to begin. This Jesus bar Joseph fellow from Nazareth, a town she'd never heard of on the far side of the Roman Empire, was quite the enigma. He had been with the class now for nine nights. It was odd how he insisted on devoting himself to his prayers every seventh day, when everyone knew there were nine days in a week.

And why would his people blindly obey a single god? Jesus himself had told the class about how this god had left his people to suffer captivity and slavery many times at the hands of the Egyptians, the Babylonians, and others. He tried to make the point that this one true god of his had actually redeemed his people, even parting the sea for them, but what kind of people would follow a god who made them suffer across so many generations? In the druid pantheon, no god would ever abandon for so long the people who sought his protection, lest they turn to another patron deity.

Whatever the quirks of his religion, this Jesus was certainly handsome. He must be past the day of his *aimsir togu*, the seventeenth name day when a boy became a man; but he was the hero of Rumps, already the subject of tales from the lyres of bards from far and wide. Such heroic youths needed no rite of passage.

Viktrica was a few years older than Jesus, but that did not stop her mind from wandering to thoughts of sharing the intimacy of her body in his bed. Would he be the virile stallion or the gentle lamb? Either way, she meant to have him.

Viktrica looked up. Elsigar was looking right at her as he called the class to order. *I am finished if he reads the thoughts in my mind. Can a druid with his powers really do that?* She sighed with relief as he turned his attention to the class.

Elsigar began to talk about Gargantua, the druid deity known to the Celts as the father of all. "Julius Caesar called him the Jupiter god, but Jupiter was no Gargantua," he said. Elsigar did not pause to review Gargantua's mighty deeds, which everyone knew. Instead he asked about his true nature. "Who was Gargantua's mother?"

Viktrica raised her hand. "That would have been Gargamelle."

Elsigar called on another student. "And what does that name, and even the name of her son, suggest to you?"

"The names are based upon the word *gargam*."

"Curved thigh?" Jesus asked.

The other student explained, "Both Gargantua and his mother are lame."

"Excellent," Elsigar responded. "And yet, in tale after tale we find that Gargantua is the most powerful of the gods. He swings a club that kills with one end, even as he can use it to restore life with the other. His magic harp, which he alone can play, has within it all the melodies of the world, and he can use it to slay men even as he plays its music for the wonderment of all. He is the fiercest of warriors, even among the gods. Just the sight of his virile member, standing forth long and erect, brings fear to the hearts of his enemies and unbounded pleasures to women."

Another student raised his hand to comment. "Gargantua's powers are a striking contrast to the deformity of his legs, but he is not alone among the gods in possessing strength through weakness and deformity. The all-seeing Odin has only one eye. Nuada, the god who distributes plenty, has only one arm."

Elsigar asked, "Is there a lesson in this for mortals?"

The class fell silent.

Even Jesus looked perplexed.

Then Genofi, the youngest student in the class, raised his hand. Though little more than a boy, he was something of a prodigy, advanced far beyond his years. "I think there can be strength in weakness. Perhaps those weak in the flesh can be strong in the spirit, and those strongest in the flesh might be weakest in the spirit."

"The ultimate weakness of men lies in death," Jesus said. "You surely would not suggest that we kill ourselves to become strong."

"Not at all," Elsigar answered, "but Genofi speaks truth." He looked from face to face, making sure he had every student's full attention. "You are now ready to share in a secret of the druids. You must not share it with anyone until the world is ready."

"But Jesus bar Joseph is an outlander," a student cried out. "He does not believe in our gods. How can you share such a secret with him?"

"I have known Jesus since he came to our shores," said Elsigar. "Since he was just a boy. There is no deceit in him. If he promises to keep the secret, it can be revealed to him."

All it took was a nod from Jesus for Elsigar to continue. "When the world was young and new in its formation, there lived a king. He taught the *Tuatha Dé Danann* even before they left the middle of the earth for the isles of the north. He was blind in both eyes, and yet he could see all: the past, the present, and the future. Every day, when the *Tuatha Dé Danann* came to him for their instruction, he would be casting his line into the stream to catch fish, so that is how he came to be known as the Fisher King.

"He taught the *Tuatha Dé Danann* many secrets about the foundation of the world. To this day, most of them are shared only among the archdruids, but you are now ready to learn one of those secrets concerning life and death. It is obvious that death springs forth from life, but it is not so obvious that life in the spirit springs forth from death. Consider the case of a seed. It brings forth new life, but to do so it must die in its first life and rot in the ground. In the same way, we can be born in the spirit."

Viktrica saw Jesus weeping beside her.

Elsigar looked at him. "What's wrong?"

Jesus sniffled. "I'm reminded of Fedwig, my best friend…who died at Rumps."

Without thinking, Viktrica extended her hand and wiped away the tears. "Do not let your heart be troubled," she said. "The death of your friend is nothing but a veil, a passage to a new life in the Otherworld. Rejoice for the time that was given to you to share with him, and know that he had a good heroic death and is happy now in the life of the spirit beyond its veil." For a moment they looked into each other's eyes, and time stood still. Viktrica shared that moment with Jesus in a way that satisfied her to the depths of her womanhood, for in that moment each of them cared for the other more than themselves. But as the moment passed, she experienced a gentle sadness. Unlike other men, Jesus bar Joseph had no lust for her in his flesh.

Elsigar was going on about rebirth in the life of the spirit. "The Fisher King left the *Tuatha Dé Danann* with many prophecies, some yet unfulfilled. The Celtic people of Britain have yet to experience many troubles and waves of invasion."

Jesus nodded. That was the story he told of the Jews, too.

"But there is hope," Elsigar said, "for the Fisher King prophesied that in the midst of the oncoming troubles, Bran's cauldron will be transformed into a vessel of rebirth. The Fisher King promised it would be restored to a righteous warrior."

Jesus

The next day, the whole school assembled for the crossing of the Afon Menai to Ynys Môn. The ferry was several miles from the school, where the strait was at its narrowest. From the school grounds, the waterway had looked like a river, but Viktrica said it was a strait of the sea. "The currents are treacherous and often unpredictable," she said, "driven by winds and tides flowing in from both ends at different times. The Swellies—"

Jesus laughed. "The what?"

"The Swellies—the currents. They create whirlpools and whitecaps, but the shortness of the distance gives us the greatest chance of making it across during a short period of slack water."

Elsigar's teaching continued in the open air as they waited to make the ferry crossing. Jesus wasn't able to join Arvigarus, because they were still in separate groups, but he waved a greeting. Jesus was not happy to see Pirro waiting with the servants. He had been spared the sight of him since their arrival at Bangor.

The hours wore on until the ferrymen announced that the time had arrived for the crossing. Then it was all a rush as the ferrymen made their best speed across the water and back, taking as many at a time as they dared while the slack water lasted.

Finally, they were all gathered on the other side just as whitecaps and whirlpools reappeared in the water.

The island was quite flat and mostly covered by open fields, unlike the hilly mainland with the Snowden Mountains in the background. Somewhere through the fields and small wooded glens on the island lay the *omphallos*, the sacred and spiritual center of all British druidism, but that would have to wait.

Now was the time for Jesus to take his leave of the school for a while. He had discussed the matter with Elsigar upon his arrival. His mission would take him to the other side of Ynys Môn. He would take Pirro to help him make his way to Holyhead Island, but Jesus remembered his Father's instruction. The last crossing to Ynys Lawd would be the most perilous, and he had to do it alone.

"I'll return," Jesus promised his classmates, "in time for your rite of passage."

"You must see us promoted into the ranks of the *ollamh*," Viktrica said.

"Even the chosen," Elsigar said, "have years more training in their respective specializations yet to go."

Viktrica nodded humbly.

"Until then, our classes will focus upon magic, divination, and sorcery." Elsigar eyed Jesus. "Just as well you have your own business to attend to."

Jesus understood his reluctance to share these secrets with an outlander. For his part, he now understood why his Father had sent him to learn something of the druids' philosophy and beliefs, but it would be sinful to join them in their pagan rituals and practices.

Peering into the distance, Elsigar drew Jesus aside and lowered his voice. "I have heard of the mysterious hermit who came to live on Ynys Lawd. If your god has sent you there, now is the time to go."

Chapter 13
The Chosen

Joseph

Joseph's thirst was overwhelming. His tongue was swollen, and the back of his throat hurt too much to swallow. The sail was limp, useless except to provide a little shade from the glaring sun. It was no longer a question of whether they were going to die soon, but whether it would be from exposure or drowning. The last of the fresh water was gone, and the bindings that held the raft together were unraveling. Even with no wind, they could feel the raft coming apart in the ocean swells.

As he lay on the raft alongside the others, Joseph wondered which would be the better way to die. If the raft gave out, he would drown quickly. The water would be salty, but perhaps it would feel refreshing at first, at least until he started choking on it. But if thirst was fated to be the instrument of his end, madness was not far off. Perhaps madness would mask the pain.

But then Joseph felt...something. At first it was just a slight sensation of coolness on his shoulder. He was too weak to move or try to say anything to Kendrick. The captain was in no better condition. He might even be dead already.

They were in the middle of the sea, far from land, far from any trade route that might offer some hope of rescue. A rising wind would only hasten the breakup of the raft. So, perhaps it was now more likely that death would come by drowning.

Or maybe the hint of refreshing breeze was just his imagination.

Then he felt the coolness again. The air was definitely moving, wicking the moisture from the sweat that drenched his body. Joseph willed movement to his torso and his limbs, not that it would do any good. Curious to see if this was just a localized zephyr, he raised his head. Was that a sail in the distance? God almighty be praised! He looked once more, but hope was dashed again. He wasn't hallucinating; it was indeed a sail, but it was carrying the ship away from him. It was too far off to hail.

Joseph woke with a start. He gathered his thoughts. He looked around him and began to make sense of what had happened after the despair from that memory of the vanishing sail. He was now in the hold of a ship.

The Armorican vessel had spotted the raft adrift in the sea. It had only seemed to be sailing away until it came about in the wind. Joseph tested the tightness of his throat. He, Kendrick, and Kendrick's sons had been up and about for several days now, but it still felt good to swallow without daggers of pain in his throat.

He smiled as he ventured up to the deck. The ship moved along in a perfect breeze. The dawn was breaking. The lookout gave a shout. Joseph saw telltale clouds in the distance. They had spotted the shore of Armorica.

By late afternoon the ship had docked. Joseph was now impatient to get ashore. His first order of business would be to get a portion of the coin that he had deposited with his agents. He would not withdraw the payment for a new ship today. That would wait until he found a vessel and had it under contract. But their rescuers had been most kind, and Joseph was intent on offering them a considerable reward. The rescuers were stopping at Nantes only to drop off him and his party, so Joseph was in a hurry to get the money.

The port master seemed unusually officious, demanding to identify everyone aboard before he would allow anyone to disembark. A cohort of Roman soldiers marched to the dockside. The port master waved them onto the ship and pointed to Joseph.

"Are you Joseph bar Jacob of Arimathea?"

Joseph nodded.

"I arrest you in the name of the emperor, for complicity in the false enslavement of Pirro of Delphi, a citizen under the protection of Rome!"

Jesus

At least, for a change, Pirro was not complaining.

Jesus looked at him once the two of them had settled beside the campfire for the night. The druids at the school must have worked Pirro some, but had treated him well. He didn't bear any sign of a beating, and he had gained weight. They had walked together for two days, saying little, and Pirro was actually making himself useful. Not only was he willingly carrying his share of the load, but he also displayed a little skill when they constructed a rope bridge over the strait between Ynys Môn and Holyhead.

"I am going to have to find a farmer to take you for a while," Jesus said. I will tell him you are not to be worked overly hard "God told me to make the final crossing to Ynys Lawd by myself. Otherwise, I would take you with me. I cannot leave you alone because the Celts will put you to death, if you have no one to vouch for you."

Pirro shrugged in response, sullen but accepting.

"You did well today, particularly with building the rope bridge at the crossing. It would have taken far longer to do it by myself."

Pirro just looked back at him blankly.

The next morning, at a settlement on the north side of Holyhead, Jesus arranged to leave Pirro with a farmer. He would have to pay toward food and lodging if Pirro was not to be worked as hard as the farmer wanted.

"What do you know of the hermit on Ynys Lawd?" Jesus asked.

"Scarcely anything," the farmer replied. "We never cross over there. We've a block and tackle arrangement to send bucketfuls of supplies over to him. He always has a bit of money to pay for food, and that's good enough for us."

"Has he always been alone?"

The farmer shook his head. "There were three who came to live on the island, more than fifteen years ago. Two of them died. And we haven't seen this last one in more than a week. He didn't appear for his provisions last time. Perhaps he's dead, too."

The next morning, Jesus surveyed the scene from the seaside cliff. He stood about forty feet above the water. Now the name of the island made sense. Ynys Lawd meant island of sows in heat in the Celtic tongue. The churning currents below indeed sounded just like a group of frenzied pigs, as the waves broke this way and that against the cliffs on either side, crashing first against the small island and then on the Holyhead side. The island had a small Celtic hut, but no smoke rose through the opening in the thatched roof. Jesus stood at the upper end of the bucket-lift the farmer had described. Jesus tried shouting—if the hermit heard him he could pass the end of a stronger rope that would support his weight—but there was no response. The distance to the island was not far, maybe fifty feet, but without someone on the island to secure the other end of a thicker rope, the bucket-lift was useless to him.

He waited the rest of the day. Perhaps the current would go slack at some point, the way it did at the Afon Menai. But no. He watched the tide rise and fall, mentally marking the water level against the cliffside, but the current driving the churning waves did not wane.

Shouting remained unsuccessful. If someone was alive, why was there no fire in the hut? Still, the Father had sent him all this way for a reason.

Late in the afternoon, the narrow passage seemed just as impossible. He tossed chunks of wood into the churning waves. Time after time, a wave took the stick and shattered it against the rock. No doubt the force of the wave would do the same to his bones, if he was so foolhardy as to jump in.

Then the waves pulled one piece of wood away from the cliff to a smooth patch of water. If he could make it to that patch, he might make it the rest of the way across to a small beach. From there he might climb the opposite cliffside. He cut more sticks and experimented some more. It took time to see the pattern. Every seventh wave, usually the biggest one in the set, would take the stick out to the smooth patch of water if he tossed the stick in just after the wave crashed against the cliffside.

Jesus returned to the farmhouse to spend the night. He made arrangements for the farmer to pass provisions and a large rope to him once he made it to Ynys Lawd. The Father had said he must reach the island on his own but had said nothing about how he was to make it back.

The next morning Jesus loaded the bucket with some cooked lamb, barley, and fresh water, and he lowered it to the island. He didn't know how to swim, but he had fashioned a floating vest from pieces of wood. He cinched it up, hoping it would keep him afloat. He tested the wave pattern one more time with some sticks. He was going to have one chance, and there was no room for error if he was to avoid being crushed in the seething cauldron below. He prayed for help from his Father, and then he leaped from the cliff.

The water twirled him around and sucked him down. Jesus tried to hold his breath, but the force of the water was too strong. Water entered his lungs, but just as he thought he was finished, the crude vest pulled him to the surface. He coughed out the water and gulped fresh air before the cycle repeated itself. And again. And yet again. But then the current smashed into him sideways and hurled him away from the cliff. It dragged him down and, far below the surface, while he was tumbling head over heels, the force of the water slammed against him and squeezed the last gasp of air out of his lungs. He kicked and struggled, but the current was vastly stronger than he was. But suddenly it released him, and Jesus found his head in the sunshine, the buoyant vest keeping him from sinking. He choked on the bitter seawater, caught his breath, and looked around. He was in the middle of the patch of calm water that he had seen from the cliff. He realized the current was pulling him out to sea. Inch by exhausting inch, Jesus kicked and paddled. Though he was no swimmer, the motions of his legs and arms felt like the right way to propel himself forward. He finally gained the beachhead and crawled over the rocks out of the water.

Jesus lay on the beach exhausted and coughing. At last he could stand. There was a cliff to climb from the beach, and the way up was slippery and treacherous. He slid back several times, but finally made it to the top by grabbing exposed tree roots.

He walked toward the hut. It was ominously quiet at first, but as he crossed the threshold he made out a wheezing sound. The hearth was cold, and the hermit, barely alive, shivering, lay on the hut's only bed. His face and body were gaunt from hunger and thirst. The hermit did not wake up, but his lips and tongue responded when Jesus moistened them with water. Little by little, Jesus managed to get some water into the man. Then he retrieved flints and kindling from the supplies he had passed down earlier in the bucket and got a fire going. Finally, the scent of hot lamb stew replaced the stink of dampness and cold.

It took days for Jesus to nurse the hermit back, if not quite to health, then at least to the point where he could make himself understood. In the beginning, the hermit only held down broth. When he was able to eat solid food, he continued mumbling under his breath. Slowly some color began to come back to his cheeks.

One morning Jesus got up to tend the fire and saw the hermit looking at him. "I am Jesus bar Joseph of Nazareth," he began.

"I know who you are. I have been waiting for you."

"How did you know? I was told to come here to study with a hermit who lived here. Is that you?"

"Well, do you see any other hermits about?" He coughed. "No, only me. As for how I know who you are…this is not the first time we've met, although I must say you have grown quite a bit."

Jesus moved a tripod stool to the bedside. "How could you know me? The farmer said you have been living on this island for more than fifteen years. He said you came with two others, but he thought they had died."

"I met you only once, shortly after your birth. My name is Melchior. My companions were Gaspar and Balthazar, but they died years ago. I am the last of the magi who brought you gifts the night of your birth."

"I was told you came from the east. What are you doing among the Celts and druids?"

"We followed the star to Bethlehem, expecting to meet the king of the Jews. After we left you, we were warned in a dream to avoid Herod, so we returned home. Later, the same spirit told us to journey westward and that one day you would come to us. The waiting was hard—harder still after Gaspar and Balthazar passed away. It wasn't so much the loneliness. It was knowing that they had waited until the end of their lives for you in vain. I could not help but wonder if the same fate would befall me."

"The farmer who sent you food told me you have not appeared to get your supplies for more than a week. He thought you had died."

"Sensible man. I grew so weary. I was ready for the end. I stopped caring whether I lived or died." He gave a hint of a smile. "But now you are here."

"My parents told me of your visit. They said the three of you were mysterious magi. There are still Jews living among the Persians. Are your people Jewish?"

"No, we are followers of Zoroaster. Our people came to know the Jews when they were exiled to Babylon. Some say the Zoroastrians influenced Emperor Cyrus to allow the Jews to return to Israel. We are the oldest religion that holds to a single god." He gasped for breath. "I grow weary, and I would rest now." Once again, Jesus left the old hermit to rest.

The next morning the magus was more animated. He had to hear everything Jesus could tell him about his life. He explained that he would have to know as much as possible so he could understand what it was that God wanted him to teach Jesus.

Jesus began that morning to tell the old man everything he could remember, starting with his own vague first memories and the things that Mary and Joseph had told him about those days. He spoke of his studies in the synagogue and of the time he taught in the temple in Jerusalem. He answered the man's questions about his friends and what he liked to do for play. Jesus described his adventures in Britain, good and bad, including Pirro's betrayal and punishment.

"My great dream, though, is to be a worthy Messiah for the Jewish people and lead them to freedom from the yoke of Rome."

The hermit peppered him with more questions, not finishing until late in the evening. The hermit said he was again tired and needed to rest for the night.

The next morning, Melchior said he needed to commune with the Holy Spirit through meditation. Only then would he be able to instruct Jesus. Jesus was growing impatient, but how could he argue? He busied himself with cleaning and cooking, as the hermit sat in a trance for the day. When night came, Melchior slept.

The next morning he spoke. "God, your Father, has revealed something to me, and has blessed me by once again making me the instrument of his will. He wants me to tell you that he is well pleased with you. He wishes to make you a gift of your choosing. It must be something he can grant to you in this time and space in Britain, so you cannot ask for something like a future victory against the Romans or for your mother to live forever. You can have wealth or power or the pleasure of a woman, anything, but not more than one specific thing. Whatever you choose will be granted to you, so you must think carefully what to ask for. You must think about this for the rest of the day. I will ask if you are ready to respond when the sun sets. Until then, I say no more." With that the magus went back into his meditative trance.

The sun finally dipped below the western horizon. Melchior came out of his trance and ate the supper Jesus had prepared. Then he looked at Jesus. "Are you ready?" he asked.

Jesus nodded. He drew his breath. "My mother and I are rich already in the love of God," he said. "We have everything we need. I have only one wish."

"And what is that?"

"It is about the slave Pirro. I want my Father to remove the tattoo the Britons marked on his forehead."

"There are other ways to rid yourself of him. You could sell him off or leave him so the natives will kill him as a runaway. This man has given you every reason to despise him. But you give up the chance for all the treasure one can imagine to give this criminal his freedom. Are you sure?"

Jesus nodded.

Melchior meditated for a short time before he continued. "It is done. You know you cannot expect him to be grateful."

"I know."

"Now, I am ready for my final rest."

"What about my instruction?"

"I have nothing to teach you. You have been taught by a far greater teacher."

"Who? Uncle Joseph? God, my Father?"

"I wasn't thinking of them. Your greatest teacher has been Pirro, for he has taught you compassion. Now, I must rest."

The next morning, Jesus awoke and approached the bed. The magus was no longer breathing. Jesus prayed for him. He did not know whether the Zoroastrians preferred burial or cremation. Then he remembered something the magus had said about feeding the vultures, so Jesus left the body out for them to feed upon. That would be the Zoroastrian way.

Pirro

The farmer made use of Pirro, but not in a cruel way. The work started in the early morning. There were pigs to slop, cows to milk, and stables to clean. Beyond that, the farmer had no real use for him. He did not trust Pirro to sow seed properly, and it was too early in the season for shearing the sheep. The farmer's wife used him to help tan the leather, not a pleasant job by any means, but not particularly hard on his body. Sundown marked the end of the workday. Pirro had only one more task assigned to him, to fetch a bucket of fresh water from the pond.

Jesus had said he would pay the farmer in exchange for not working Pirro too hard. The farmer had kept his word. *But Jesus will not know that.* Pirro's complaining had never worked with Jesus, so he had refrained from that over the few days they had been traveling together. *Being quiet and sullen seems to gain me some sympathy, but I cannot keep that up indefinitely. Perhaps once Jesus comes back and we leave the farmstead, I can say how cruelly the farmer used me. He will not have any way to know otherwise, unless he journeys back to the farm to ask.*

Pirro crouched at the water's edge to fill the bucket. He caught a glimpse of his reflection, and he could not believe his eyes. He stared for a long time, astonished at his own reflection. Some kind of miracle. The tattoo was gone. He could go anywhere and find a way to make a denarius, and no one would be any the wiser. They would take him for a free man—a Roman at that. He looked at his reflection again to make sure. It was gone indeed.

Pirro brought the bucket of water back to the farmhouse. *It is best that they not see me.* He called out to the family that he was leaving the water outside and that he felt too ill to eat with them. He went to the barn, but he did not stay to sleep on the straw. He grabbed a pouch of bread the wife had left and one of the sheep. *If only I could carry more. Perhaps I should set the place afire. No, that would serve them right, but it would only attract pursuit.*

Pirro looked around the barn. *Are there any other valuables? I guess not.* Pirro laughed to himself. *I never even had to tell the boy I was sorry for betraying them all at Rumps.* Then he vanished into the night.

Jesus

By the end of his third week in Bangor with Elsigar, Jesus's studies had taken a most unexpected turn. Elsigar had moved on from druidic theology; he had also finished teaching whatever conjuring, divination, and potion skills these novices had to master. *I am glad the druids covered all that while I was with Melchior. I am still a Jew, and I doubt the Father would have sent me here to learn pagan sorcery.* Elsigar had once said the advanced students must learn to think like druids. For so-called barbarians, the druids had a surprising foundation for their way of thinking—the Greek philosophers.

Jesus felt intellectually outdone, as his classmates debated the finer points of the teachings of Pythagoras and Plato. *The rabbis in Nazareth frown upon Greek ideas. Most still resent the legacy of Alexander's conquests. The Zealots, the Pharisees, the Essenes, the Sadducees—all are quick to brand Jews who take up Greek ways, or even Greek thought, as Hellenist collaborators. As a Roman, I should know these things. It is the stuff on which civilization has been built, but these so-called barbarians know more about Greek philosophy than I do.*

Jesus had trouble focusing on the subject without having anything written down. *Why do I struggle so? The Father tells me I share his divine substance. Why do I not know this the same way I know a new language? Why did Father give me a gift for the Scripture of my people and the gifts of speaking and understanding any tongue, but not philosophy? Perhaps the real learning is in this struggle—a power of ideas that is only obtained in the grappling. Or perhaps Father is testing me by making me struggle as all men do, rather than by sailing along on the power of divine gifts.*

Elsigar described how the Celts of the Danube region were neighbors of the Greeks for centuries. They had even launched a raid on the famous Greek temple at Delphi. Celtic tribes had migrated as far as Asia Minor in the classical age. *It makes sense that they would have picked up quite a bit from the Greeks.* Elsigar related a legend that said the British Celts were descended from the survivors of the destruction of Troy. *That part seems unrealistic.*

It was clear that the aesthetic life espoused by Pythagoras excited the druids. *Could this be a pathway for mortal men to touch the divine? Can they escape the troubles of the world by abandoning comfort and embracing community, humility, and simplicity?*

The discussions grew heated. Elsigar raised his wand to regain the attention of the class.

Other elder druids entered and stood solemnly in the front. "The time has arrived for us to draw this year's school to a close. Tomorrow we journey once more across the Afon Menai to Ynys Môn, where we will walk the Path of Destiny. The chosen among you will be divided from those who are not chosen. May the gods be with you all."

※

Late the next day, Jesus sat with the elder druids who lined both sides of a pathway through a patch of woods at the summit of a small hill on Ynys Môn. The main path came up the hillside and then branched into two, one branch leading down the other side of the hill to the left and the other to the right. Elsigar sat on a stone between the branches holding a wand.

One by one the novices were led up the path in blindfolds. Elsigar sat impassively as each novice stood before him in turn. Jesus noticed the elders making silent signals to each other. Occasionally, Elsigar made a signal of his own. The signals made no sense to Jesus, except at the end of each novice's evaluation. Without a sound, Elsigar pointed his wand to one side or the other, designating the pathway for the novice.

No one but the druids knew which pathway was for the chosen and which was for those not chosen, but after a few of his classmates passed by, Jesus detected a pattern. *All the best students are being led to the right.* He smiled as Genofi was brought forward and led that way. The boy was the youngest of the novices, a few years younger than Jesus, but clearly among the most gifted. Victrikta was led up a few minutes later. *Yes, she always contributes to class, and Elsigar is sending her to the right as well.*

As the last of the novices was being led down the path to the left, Elsigar turned to Jesus. "We are about to start the rite in which the chosen are graduated. They all have several years of study ahead of them in their individual specialties, but tonight we ordain them to join the ranks of the druids in spirit. You are welcome to watch."

"I would like very much to share this night with my new friends among the chosen, if you are kind enough to have me. I am sad for those who are not chosen, but they can come back to try again next year, I suppose."

"Many of them do. But before you come to the rite, we must bind your wrists and blindfold you. This is the rule when we invite outlanders. I am sure it is not necessary with you, but it would offend our gods if we took no precautions against interference."

"As you know, I come to druid rites because the spirit of my God moved me to learn and observe. This sounds as though I might be participating in some way, and that is something I cannot do and remain faithful to my God."

"You will join us only as our honored guest. You have my word that this is just a precaution to satisfy our gods that you will not interfere. It has been this way when outlanders attend since the times of the *Tuatha Dé Danann*. You are not expected to do anything except watch."

"I trust that you will not require me to do anything more." *Binding my hands seems outrageous, but these druids have so many strange rules.*

Jesus was blindfolded and led down the path to the right, where he expected to join his friends among the chosen. It felt odd. Whenever he tried to say anything, his guide told him abruptly to remain silent. He was led down a long slope. He finally sensed that he was entering a large clearing, as the air seemed to move more freely than on the confined pathway through the dense forest.

The guide stopped and pushed Jesus back against a post. "I must leave you here for a few minutes," he whispered. "I will return soon, but I need to tie you for now."

"Elsigar said nothing about—"

"Don't make me gag you," said the guide. "You must stay silent."

Jesus could hear the murmuring of an assembled crowd. Something dramatic was happening. *Elsigar should have told me I was to be bound to a post. Is this some treachery? Elsigar would never do anything to harm me—would he?*

A large forearm reached around his head and ripped away the blindfold. An apparition loomed in front of him, jogging an almost-forgotten memory of a passage he had once read in a scroll at the house of Uncle Joseph's friend in Arelate.

The wicker man stood before him, just as Julius Caesar had described in his memoir of the Gallic War. The frame was twenty-five feet tall, with outstretched arms rising even higher. A small rise of land in front obscured the view of its feet and lower legs. The figure was covered by a basketlike weaving of branches and reeds, similar to the wattle framing Celts used in the construction of their huts, but not so tightly woven. In the falling light of dusk, Jesus could see the sacrificial victims climbing through the inside. *Did they not know they were going to be trapped? Did they not know the horrible doom they faced in the flames?* Incredibly, there was no sign of panic among them. At least not yet.

A hush fell over the crowd. Elsigar and the other senior druids advanced slowly on the wicker man, chanting in syllables meaningless to Jesus. They all bore lit torches. The druids coming from the right passed in front, while the ones from the left passed behind, forming a circle around the figure. They turned to face the apparition.

As the druids advanced, the hollow at the foot of the structure appeared to swallow them—only their heads and their arms holding up the torches could be seen. In the glimmering torchlight, the faces and features of the victims could be made out. Jesus gasped. These were not strangers; nor were they the rejected candidates who had been led down the pathway to the left. There were young Genofi and Victrikta, climbing toward the top among the best and brightest, the candidates Jesus had thought surely had been chosen. *What kind of school is this? Why do they study so hard for years and try to be the best they can be, only to be offered up as human sacrifices?*

Jesus was overcome with a sense of horror. "Stop this!" he cried out. "Murder!"

Jesus's cries seemed to be the cue for everyone else. The victims inside the insidious apparition appeared to finally realize their awful fate. They cried out in fear. Then the crowd behind Jesus began shrieking for the flame.

Jesus screamed as the druids raised their torches. Elsigar applied his first, putting the flame to some kindling strategically placed in the wicker man's loins. The other druids followed suit, and a ball of flame soon enveloped the midsection of the giant figure. Jesus strained against his bonds. *Maybe I can get loose and save at least some of these victims.* Jesus wailed in anguish. One by one, the victims began to drop into the flame. Jesus prayed for them. *How they must be suffering!* Genofi was the first to drop. Victrikta soon followed. Some clawed their way higher into the arms and head, but they didn't last long there. One by one, Jesus watched his classmates fall into the flames as the crowd cheered behind him.

Suddenly an ax struck the back of the post to which Jesus was tied, and his bindings fell away. "Go!" It was the voice of his captor. "Go save your friends from death, if you can!"

As Jesus dashed forward, the crowd cheered; they were cheering for him. *What kind of people are these? First they want to see these victims slaughtered, and now they want me to save them?* But Jesus did not look back. He clenched his fists as he ran up the rise, preparing to tear the wicker man apart with his bare hands. As he reached the top, he gasped at the sight before him. The last of the victims were being helped to safety as they lowered themselves from a net stretched several feet off the ground, between the wicker man's feet. Looking up, Jesus saw that the wicker man's loins had been consumed first in the flame, leaving a path for the victims to escape below the ball of flames that continued to envelope its midsection.

The druids formed two lines, forming a pathway from the hollow up the rise towards the assembled crowd. Elsigar walked slowly between them to the top of the rise, where he faced the crowd. As he raised his arms, the structure behind him collapsed in flames. "Behold!" he cried out to the crowd. "Behold those who are chosen. Behold those who are born again!"

The druids on either side held their wands to form an archway behind Elsigar. One by one, the newly-commissioned *ollamh* emerged to the cheers of the crowd. They still had years of study ahead, but in spirit they were now druids.

The *ollamh* formed themselves into a single line, and Elsigar addressed the crowd once more. "You have seen them born again. But to be reborn in the spirit they must first die to the flesh. Thus, it has been since Bran's cauldron. Thus, it will always be."

Kegs of mead soon appeared among the crowd, and revelries began in earnest.

Genofi was the first to approach Jesus. "That was awe inspiring, don't you think?"

"It seemed so real. I was scared. I hope my screams didn't ruin it for everyone."

"Are you joking? It's great when we have an outlander watching who has read that nonsense Caesar wrote about the wicker man. Your screaming made it so real. It was the best ordination—ever!"

Elsigar joined them. "Remember what I said. To be born again in the spirit, we must first die *to* the flesh. I did not say we must die *in* the flesh."

"So the death you speak of is symbolic?"

"It's more than just symbolic," said Elsigar. "When we are born again in the spirit, we turn away from our old lives in the flesh, and in that sense we die to the flesh, but we do not destroy the flesh. We are not barbaric savages, though that is what Julius Caesar would have you believe. It's not the worst of the lies he wrote of us. Remember that druids are practiced in the art of fire building; do not try this on your own."

Joseph

"I will take an oath, but I swear only by my own Lord, the God of Abraham, Isaac, and Jacob," Joseph said as he faced his inquisitor. "I am a peaceful trader from Arimathea, a citizen of Rome, and even *noblis decurio*."

"We are not used to Jews in this province." The legate examined his scroll. "Very well, it says here that Jews need not swear by the gods of the emperor. Since you are a citizen, are you demanding trial before the emperor in Rome?"

Joseph looked at his inquisitor, who seemed green and ill-prepared. *They have detained me far too long already, and there is no telling how long it will take if they send me to Rome. They say the emperor is ill.* "I will stand trial right now." Before anyone had a chance to speak, he stated his oath his own way, promising to answer truthfully any proper questions put to him.

The inquisitor held up a letter. "This was written by Gaius Germanicus, a trader of unquestioned integrity," he said.

"An old commercial rival of mine," said Joseph. "He trades with the Cantiaci on the eastern coast of Britain."

The inquisitor handed the letter to Joseph, and Joseph read it quickly. According to Gaius Germanicus, word of Jesus's exploits at Rumps, including the way Jesus had dealt with Pirro's treachery, had spread as far as eastern Britain.

"This is not proper evidence," said Joseph. "Gaius Germanicus says nothing in this letter about what he has seen with his own eyes or heard with his own ears. He is repeating rumors picked up from the natives of Britain. Those natives would not be competent to testify against a Roman citizen in a Roman court. There is no one here competent to testify against me."

"The objection is well taken," ruled the legate.

The inquisitor questioned Joseph, but he was inexperienced at his craft. After some argument about the phrasing of the questions, he seemed confused. "What do you know directly about the outcome of the battle?"

"I was not there."

By this time the legate had lost interest, and quickly dismissed the case. "You're free to go, but you should keep an eye on that nephew of yours. From what I've heard, he seems like a troublemaker."

<hr />

Joseph and Kendrick soon had another vessel outfitted to take them to Britain. They set the course for Ynys Witrin. Between the wrecks and Joseph's imprisonment, they had been away for months. *Jesus has been off on his own on some fool's errand to the north. It will be a miracle if Daniel has held everything together with that witch of a druidess plotting against us.*

Jesus

Jesus looked across the water to the entrance of the Brue, glimmering in the morning light. A Celtic trading vessel was taking him back to Ynys Witrin, along with Arvigarus and Elsigar. He would be back in time to take supper with his mother.

Arvigarus joined him on deck.

"This has been quite an adventure for me, studying with the druids," Jesus remarked.

"I don't think I am cut out to be a druid," said Arvigarus. "My head is swimming with everything I need to remember, and this is just my first year. I don't know how my father will take it when I tell him."

"I cannot believe I fell for that performance with the wicker man. When you saw it, did you know it was just symbolic, or did you think they would truly burn the victims?"

"Everyone knows that no one actually dies in the flames."

"I feel so foolish. Everyone must be laughing at me—the way I carried on."

"You should not feel that way," said Elsigar, stepping up behind them. "Without an outlander screaming murder, the wicker man is nothing more than a ritual. Your screams helped make real the concept of dying to the flesh so we may be born again in the spirit. Do not be troubled if any laughed at your screams, for it is they who are impious."

"I think I ended up participating in this ritual more than I expected. I told you I would only watch."

"I promised that I would not require you to do anything. You chose to scream and try to save your friends. From what you could see, there were murders about to happen. Surely trying to stop murder does not offend your God?"

"My God knows my heart. I put all my faith and trust in him."

"I want to show you something. Do you remember how you described your concept of one god in three persons to me just before the battle at Rumps?

"I remember."

"You said that you were different from the druids because the god in three persons was united in purpose. You also said that most of your people accept only one single creator as god."

Jesus nodded. "Yes."

"I have been carrying this coin ever since I was a boy. It was struck in Gaul before the time of Julius Caesar." The druid held it out for Jesus to inspect. The coin depicted a bundle of snakes coiled together in a single mass. "It is called the snake egg. It depicts an ancient prophecy from the Fisher King. There will come a time when all our gods will be made one, united in purpose, perhaps just as you have described the unity of purpose of your Father, your Son, and your Spirit."

Jesus gazed at the coin. "I see we are closer than I imagined. Once people understand that a god united in purpose can live through multiple persons, the number may not matter so much. It might be easier for your people than for my people to accept the idea of a single god who lives in three persons."

Part IV
A Painful Destiny

Interlude

Pencaire Parish, Cornwall, England, 1070 A.D., during the reign of King William I of England (the Conqueror)

As Talfryn, the stonemason, explained his plan for the new guidepost to mark the path to the village church, Father Wigstan thoughtfully nodded his head. *I suppose I had better hear him out. They said this stonecutter from Looe is the mayor of that village.*

"It will carry on the tradition of this parish and remind all comers of the time our Lord himself spent here. I will carve it exactly like the worn old carving."

"Blasphemy!" exclaimed the priest. "We Saxons have allowed you Welsh to spout this nonsensical legend for far too long. There isn't a village in the south of England that does not claim that the Christ child was driven ashore in a storm, or visited them, or spent his teenage years there." *We have no time for this. The new Norman bishop will be here anon to inspect the parish. If he hears rumors that I am even discussing this drivel with this Cornish Welshman, it will be the end of me as priest in this parish.*

The stonemason turned red in the face. "It is not legend. It is absolute fact. He walked this ground."

Father Wigstan stood stunned. He was not accustomed to people opposing him, particularly laypeople on religious matters.

The sculptor puffed out his ruddy cheeks and calmed himself. "Our Lord was brought to these shores by his great-uncle Joseph of Arimathea. Scripture mentions Joseph as a rich man who later buried Jesus in his own tomb. He came here to trade with my people, and Jesus came with him as a boy and grew to manhood. Jesus visited many places, because he was working with his uncle in the tin trade. And yes, he came also to Looe, because it is on the way to the Tamar Valley where more tin was to be found."

Wigstan was about to reply, when the neigh of a horse caused him to turn.

"What are you two shouting about?" The rider was dressed in clerical robes. It was the new bishop. Engaged in the argument, Wigstan had not noticed him approach. "I heard the two of you all the way from the road."

The priest thought fast as the bishop dismounted and turned over the reins to his attendant. He waved off the stonemason. "It is a foolish business. Nothing that need concern my Lord Bishop." Wigstan led the bishop toward the church.

"No, tell me. I love to hear about legends, even silly ones."

Wigstan resigned himself to explaining the matter, but he resolved to put it in the best possible light. "These ignorant Cornish Welshmen hold to the old Celtic Church. We Saxons have tried our best to suppress it ever since the Council of Whitby, more than four hundred years ago. It's a breeding ground of Pelagian heresy."

"The only influence I have seen of the Celtic Church in this diocese is their curious crosses and patterns. They look rather attractive to me, actually. Tell me about the legend."

"These ignorant people believe that Saint Joseph of Arimathea brought Our Lord Jesus to these shores. That stonemason wants to carve a new guidepost for the church in the same form as the old timeworn one. It is one of these infernal tunic crosses. He wants to show Jesus as a boy with his arms outstretched in a gesture of greeting—which is surely not the proper way of showing him suffering on the cross to redeem the sins of the world. These crosses used to be all over the southwest of England, even beyond Glastonbury, until we Saxons came along and suppressed them, but these Cornish Welshmen are treacherous. They even had their own king until Edward the Confessor extended Saxon rule over them. That is why you still see these infernal crosses all over the diocese. I will not have that stonemason carve a fresh one in my parish."

"What is the harm in allowing these people to hold to their legend?"

"It is heretical. It is outside of Scripture."

"Scripture says nothing about the life of our Lord, from the age of twelve until he began his ministry. These Welsh people seem to use the legend as a way to be closer to Our Lord. If it helps them do that, I do not see the harm in it." He stopped and turned to face Wigstan. His tone turned cold. "You Saxons have no respect for these Welsh people, do you?"

"The Welsh are ignorant. The word itself means slaves."

"I have heard enough," said the bishop. "The king does not hold to your view. Perhaps you have heard of Cadoc?"

"No, my Lord. The name means nothing to me."

"Let me give you the news from court, then. Cadoc is the survivor of the line of Cornish kings. Our king has just created him Earl of Cornwall. If that is not reason enough for you to respect these people, you would do well to remember that you are responsible for their spiritual welfare. You will allow the stonemason to carry on with the carving of the new guidepost."

"Of course, as my Lord Bishop commands."

The bishop stomped off several paces in evident disdain. Then he turned back. "Rest assured I shall look into this matter again after the stonemason completes his work, and I had better find that tunic cross on display. Oh, and one thing more—the name of this parish—Pencaire, isn't it? Where does that come from?"

"It's the name of an old ruined Celtic hill fort atop Tregonning Hill," Father Wigstan replied. "The only real landmark within the parish. We keep it in sight when we beat the bounds." He referred to the ancient custom of taking boys around the parish boundaries and beating them, so they would remember the limits of the parish.

"This place needs a proper name, something after a good saint. I am thinking of Saint Hilary of Poitiers. I studied his works when I turned to the cloth. He wrote about how the Word was spread to the islands at the time of the apostles, well before any Saxons arrived. These Cornish Welsh people might take a liking to him."

❧ ✦ ☙

Wigstan never explained to Talfryn why he allowed him to proceed with his new tunic cross.

The sculptor suspected the bishop had overruled the priest, but he could not know for sure. Talfryn trusted neither the Saxon priest nor the new Norman overlords.

He was a descendent of the native Celtic race, survivors of so many waves of invaders. The Romans had left his people to their fate as their empire began to crumble. Then came the Saxon barbarians, but just as those bloodthirsty invaders had begun to settle down, Danes arrived, the most bloodthirsty of all. For the last four years, the Normans had been the new rulers. It was too soon to judge them.

Talfryn would carve the wording at the base in Ogham. To a Saxon or a Norman, it would look like random hash marks, but it was an ancient alphabet brought over from Ireland. Talfryn could translate it—"Look for the Secret of the Lord where the lamb turns to the beginning of his life"—though he had no idea what the words meant. All he knew was that the inscription was carved into every tunic cross.

Talfryn took one more look at his creation, before setting aside his hammer and chisel.

What mystery from the ancient past was hidden in those words?

He studied the expression on the childish face he had carved. It seemed to convey more than just a joyous greeting. There was a yearning in it, he thought. *The statue yearns to share its secret. Perhaps it will do so when the world is ready.*

Chapter 14
The Path to Calvary

Ynys Witrin, Year A.D. 14, during the reign of Augustus, first Emperor of Rome

Daniel

By Celtic custom, the return of family members from a long journey was cause for community celebration. The obligation fell upon the family to organize the feast and invite the neighbors.

Watching the Lake Villagers in the field next to Mary's house, Daniel took satisfaction in knowing that the preparations for the occasion did not disappoint. The mead flowed freely as the guests feasted, boasted, reveled, and sang.

But he felt oddly pensive, too out-of-place to join in the carousing this time. as had become his wont in the past few years, particularly in the company of his younger cousin.

Daniel smiled, watching a sight he thought he would never live to see. His father, in the center of it all, gyrating this way and that in a wild Jewish dance, to the amusement of the half-drunken Celts.

Father was back, along with a tall tale of how he had survived a shipwreck and then faced a Roman inquisition. Normally, his father would not go near any pagan festival, but this time Mary had overseen the proper preparation of the food and drink, Joseph had reluctantly agreed to attend, and within minutes he was throwing himself into the celebration.

Jesus was there, too, laughing, drinking with the Celts, and joining in Joseph's dance. *I suppose I should be glad Jesus made it back safely, and I believe I am. But, everything will center on him now. No one cares that I was the one who held everything together. No one cares what he put me through, leaving me alone to manage everything, even to look after his sick mother, while he ran off to the north.*

Grengan's suggestion to fast against Horshak had worked better than Daniel had dared hope. As he starved himself, Horshak's workmen developed a sense of shame and gradually abandoned Horshak's employ. Some of them had worked for Daniel before, but several never had. With his Roman coinage, Daniel was able to hire as many men as he needed to reverse Horshak's manpower advantage, and he quickly secured the claim to the newly discovered lode.

Elsigar was near the center of the festivities, too. He had brought Jesus and Arvigarus back with him on the boat from Bangor. The druid was staying at Ynys Witrin to sort out the search for Esmeralda's successor. The druidess was now in disgrace, her treachery and deceit exposed. Horshak had turned on her as soon as Daniel secured the claim.

But for the moment Elsigar had put these concerns aside. He was not dancing, but he smiled—a rare sight—as he watched Papa and Jesus perform a dance from their homeland.

Daniel did not know what to make of Arvigarus. He knew the Silurian prince by reputation. He could tell Jesus had struck up a friendship with him.

Daniel would not admit, even to himself, that he was jealous.

Mary's voice startled him. "I thought you liked to join these celebrations with the pagans. And yet here you are, just watching."

"I am in a strange mood," said Daniel. "I am glad that Jesus and my father are both safely back. I really am, Auntie. I know everything looks fine now. Father got the smelter going again today. He said the ore from the new lode is different, so everything about the process has changed. I would never have figured that out on my own. And with Jesus back, we'll be able to find new lodes of silver once this one runs out." Daniel breathed a sigh, and then he shook his head. "It's just…"

"You must be wondering what will come at you next," said Mary.

Daniel nodded. "How did you know?"

"It's all over your face, and I don't blame you. For months, everything has rested on your shoulders. First, your father leaves because he is angry at Jesus for taking up weapons to pursue those robbers."

Daniel looked at her. *Does she know about the prophecy of the awful death her son is facing? I know I did not tell her, and I cannot imagine that Father did, either. Maybe she figured it out. But no. She just looks confused. I guess Father's anger and the way he left so suddenly just never made sense to her.*

"Then Jesus leaves you alone to run things on your own, because he says that God is sending him on a mission to the north."

"Do you think anything will come of that mission?"

"He has grown. He is a man now. Did he tell you about freeing Pirro?"

"He told me."

"A mother sees these things. He is learning compassion. Do you know what he did yesterday? He went back to Pilton Hollow to teach the people that it was not enough for them to send the lepers away, as he told them to do before he left. To find favor with God, he told me, they had to show compassion for the afflicted. They had to provide the afflicted with food and clothing, even if the law requires the afflicted to remain apart."

"I would think a mother would worry, when her son goes off like Jesus did and does not send word for months."

"Oh, Daniel! Of course I worried, but I was comforted to know that he was in the hands of God, the Father."

She has no idea what awaits her son—that one day God will abandon and forsake Jesus on that awful cross.

"Anyway, I know it was hard to be left on your own, but we are a family. Your father and I are as brother and sister, and I know Jesus thinks of you as his brother. We will see the future through as a family, whether it holds well or ill. Just remember that you are never alone, Daniel."

He looked after his aunt as she made her way back to her house. *I guess she is not one to join the party either.* Daniel thought back to the way his cousin had described the foreshadowing of his crucifixion on that day in Lugdunum. *He said she will be there at the foot of the cross, weeping for him. How will she ever bear the pain of such a sight?*

Jesus

Jesus was beginning to feel the effects of the mead, and he needed some air and solitude. He hiked the steep path to the Tor. The raucous noise of the festivities fell away behind him. *I have not climbed the Tor in many months.*

The sky along the path will be clear now, all the way to the top, and when I get there, I can breathe in the clear night air and gaze down on the party.

There was not a cloud to obscure the stars. *I wonder if there is anything more than pagan superstition about this place.. I feel some sort of energy whenever I come here.*

The path broke clear of the trees, and Jesus stood alone at the summit. Spreading his arms, he ran this way and that, imagining himself taking flight. He remembered that morning with Brian. It seemed like a very long time ago.

Jesus settled himself on a rock, watched the revelry far below him, and listened to the faint music, shouts, and laughter. The thought of Uncle Joseph leading the merriment amused him. Then he looked out over the Levels. The patches of water below glittered faintly in the light of the moon and stars. Jesus closed his eyes and imagined all the creatures sheltered in the marsh.

It is so perfect up here, I don't want anything to change. I am so grateful for this time among the Britons, but I will be ready to return to lead Israel to freedom. I will be another David for my people. The pagans of Rome will know the wrath of the one true God, just as that same God visited his wrath upon the Egyptians when they refused to let the people go.

Opening his eyes, Jesus saw leaves swirling around him, slowly at first, then faster and faster. The gentle breeze became a gale. Then it died away.

"My entrance no longer impresses you." The voice came from no direction and from all directions.

"You are the God of the Universe, Father. A burning bush or a whirlwind, it matters not. I am your son, Your presence is all that matters."

"You have grown, my son, in body, mind, and spirit. When we first talked, I had to stop you from scurrying around to remove your slippers as Moses did in my presence. Now you are confident to sit or stand with me, and that is good. You become more connected to your divine substance every day."

"You know my heart, Father, you know my love for you, and I feel your love even when you do not reveal yourself to me."

"The time has come to speak."

"I have prepared myself for this moment, even as I have dreaded it."

"In your pride, you imagine you know my plan. That comes from your human nature, my son. But like all men, you must learn that not even you know your destiny. As I move across space and time, I see the arrogance of man. Men never understand how their fate truly rests with me, and neither do you."

"I know about the crucifixion, Father. In my visions, I have seen my mother weep at the foot of the cross. I have seen soldiers gaming over my vestures, just as the psalms prophesy."

"You do not truly understand that prophecy."

"I know I can put all my faith and trust in you. I know that, in your love for me, you will never forsake me. I will suffer, so the people see how you free me from that cross. Seeing your power, the Romans will tremble. The people will unite, and I will lead them to freedom." Moments passed. Jesus began to feel a niggling doubt. *Why does he not say anything?*

"Time and again I have entered into a covenant with my chosen people, but those covenants were never fulfilled."

"You made a covenant with David that his seed would rule your kingdom forever. Am I not his seed, Father?"

"Indeed you are, but you do not understand your kingdom. It is not of the world that you see around you."

Jesus shivered. *What is my Father saying? Surely, he does not mean to deny me the throne of Israel.*

"I covenanted with Abraham that I would make a great nation of his people, but because Abraham was an imperfect man, that covenant was imperfect. I commanded him to slay his own son as a sacrifice."

"But then, once he had bound Isaac on the sacrificial alter, you sent an angel to stay his hand," said Jesus. "You meant it as a test of Abraham's faith, and he proved he would sacrifice anything for you."

"I did not need any test to know Abraham's heart. I already know the measure of any man. I promised Abraham that his descendants would be reckoned through Isaac, and then I asked him to sacrifice his son. He trusted me. He believed I would raise Isaac from the dead, so he was willing to obey. I had no need to test Abraham, since I already knew his heart."

"Then why ask for the sacrifice, Father?"

"So Abraham could stand as an example of faith to those who followed. I provided a ram for the sacrifice so my people would know I will always provide what they need to keep covenant with me. But the covenant was nevertheless imperfect."

"Because Abraham sacrificed a ram instead of his son?"

"Even if Abraham had slain his son, the covenant would have been imperfect. Because Isaac, as a mortal man, was an imperfect being. How can the covenant be perfect if it is sealed by the blood of an imperfect creature?"

Suddenly, Jesus understood. He felt faint and weak. He slumped down on the ground, trembling.

"The time is coming," the Father said, "for a new age in which Creation is made new. It calls for a new and perfect covenant. No man can offer a perfect son in sacrifice. A son without blemish, without sin."

"No man has a such a son," said Jesus. "But you?..."

"Only I am able to bring forth such a son. Only I possess the strength to bear the pain of such a full and complete sacrifice."

"And I?"

"You must be the perfect sacrificial lamb of the new covenant, and I must bear the pain of seeing you die on the cross."

Daniel

An anguished cry pierced the night.

Daniel had been watching his father dancing and making merry among the Britons, but the cry brought the festivities to an abrupt stop. It was more than any human cry. It came from the summit of the Tor, yet it could be heard across the Levels hundreds of feet below and miles into the distance, filling the night like rumbling thunder. It was no word in any human language, not Aramaic or Celtic or Latin or Greek, but Daniel recognized the voice of his younger cousin.

"No!"

The syllable hung in the air, reverberating across the Levels.

And then Jesus, high up on the Tor, shouted: "What kind of father are you? What kind of father would condemn his own son to such a horrible death? What kind of father would sentence his own son to crucifixion, a son who has always loved him?"

Daniel and Father exchanged glances. There was no need for words. The time foretold by Joseph had come, the time for Jesus to learn of his terrible destiny.

Daniel's next thought was for Aunt Mary. She emerged from her house as if she expected to find the voice coming from nearby. She appeared confused. *She has no idea what future awaits Jesus. How can anyone tell her?*

"How many covenants have you made before, Father? Covenants that failed?" Jesus sounded as if he was sobbing. "One with Noah…Abraham…Jacob…Moses…David. You still haven't gotten it right, so you want to have another go at it? That means I have to die—shamefully, painfully, by crucifixion—for all the world to watch! I won't do it! I can't!"

Lightning flashed through the sky above the Tor.

"How could you not tell us the kingdom you promised to the house of David would have nothing to do with this world?"

Then the thunder slammed into the stunned festival-goers.

Lightning? Thunder? The night was clear and cloudless. *How can there be lightning and thunder?* Daniel looked to the Britons. The guests from the Lake Village were just beginning to appreciate how unnatural the sound and fury all about them really was.

"The gods are fighting," Elsigar shouted. "Take shelter! No mortal can face the gods when they are so angry!" But despite sounding the alarm, he stood transfixed, gazing up the Tor.

More lightning filled the sky, each bolt brighter than the last, and thunder crashed, louder, following ever closer on the lightning.

Then came a tirade of wild laughter. Daniel recognized it was his cousin's, but it sounded like a madman's laughter.

"Is that supposed to shock me into submission, Father? Is a bolt of lightning more frightening than death on that cross?"

As if in answer, another bolt of lightning cracked through the sky.

The following clap of thunder rocked Daniel to his core.

"Smite me, Father!" came Jesus's cry. "Let me die here, now, rather than suffer that awful death. Send the next bolt of lightning right through me. Let's end it now."

It seemed to Daniel that the next bolt of lightning actually struck farther away. The pause before the thunder was longer, and the peal was more of a rumble than a sharp clap.

Jesus laughed hysterically. "If you smite me now, what happens to your precious new covenant? No, you are going to keep me alive, just to abandon me later. What kind of father would do that?" Jesus shrieked, laughed, and sobbed. "What kind of father condemns his own son to die as part of a deal? That's what a covenant is, isn't it? A contract you make with your people, but I'm the one who will have to pay the price. That awful, shameful, terrible price!"

How could a voice so raspy and weak be so resonantly loud?

"What a heartless Father you are. You don't love me. You never have."

Daniel saw others coming toward him, Mary in the lead, with Elsigar, Papa, and Arvigarus close behind. In his distraction, he had not been aware how far he had stumbled from the festivities.

"Thanks be to God," Papa exclaimed. "At least you are safe."

"Where is he?" asked Mary.

Daniel pointed up the Tor. "He said he needed to get some air."

"Oh no, he cannot be up there!" Mary gazed up at the summit.

"Did you not hear him?" asked Daniel.

Mary, Elsigar, and Arvigarus all looked at Daniel in disbelief. "All I heard was some wild laughing and shouting and thunder from the top of the Tor," said Mary. "I didn't understand a word of it. I could not recognize whose voice it was."

Daniel looked at his father. The nod was all it took for Daniel to understand that Joseph, too, had heard and understood, even though the others had not.

"We must go for Jesus," Arvigarus exclaimed.

Daniel saw the confusion on Mary's face. *She looks torn. She wants to put her trust in God, but she wants Jesus back safely, too. She is not saying anything to stop us.* "Yes, let's go."

Father wanted to join them, but he was too infirm to climb. Not that Daniel could say that. "Father, you must stay behind to look after Aunt Mary."

"I forbid this," said Elsigar. "You are a prince of the Silures, Arvigarus. Your death could precipitate a war. And you are an outlander, Daniel. I cannot allow you to interfere with our gods on the Tor. I will call the men to hold you both down if I must."

Before Daniel could even frame his argument, the earth shook violently beneath their feet, an earthquake such as none of them had ever felt before. For a few seconds they looked at each other in confusion.

Lightning again flashed across the skies, and thunder made their ears pop. The earth continued to roll under their feet.

"Trying to rescue Jesus is pointless," said Elsigar. "No mortal could survive the fury of the gods. If Jesus is up there, he is already dead."

Mary gasped and then collapsed, sobbing, into Daniel's arms.

Lucifer

The Fallen One was living fat and large, feasting upon all the unredeemed souls that made their way to the depths of hell, when he felt a powerful, breaking spiritual wave. What had so jolted him out of his pleasures?

Sensing the presence of the Word among men, he was stricken with terror. He knew from the prophecies that the Son would one day live among men and offer the pathway to salvation. Ultimately, that would be Satan's destruction. *What hope is there for me once the Son becomes the light for all nations and offers the pathway to salvation for all? Who would not turn from sin if they knew that anyone had the hope to follow this Christ on the pathway to salvation?*

With a great effort, Satan calmed himself and dampened his fear. He knew there must be more at work than the presence of the Word incarnate in the world. He probed across all space and time to see what was happening. He sensed that the great spiritual wave, something like a tsunami, instead of merely spreading across an ocean, was spreading across all of Creation.

In the middle of the ocean, the force of a tsunami would pass through vast ocean depths, virtually undetectable to men in ships on the surface; but as the wave approached land, its force would be concentrated and would raise waves of monstrous destructive power. So it was with this spiritual wave. Unlimited by mortal perception, Satan grasped its unimaginable power. He sensed the immense force of the wave as it passed through hell.

Creation had seen something like this once before. When Adam ate from the Tree of Knowledge of Good and Evil, he introduced evil and sin into Creation. Though the Father had foreseen this, it was not what he had wished for or intended. Nonetheless, God so loved the world that he saved it from its own destruction. While Adam's choice meant that man could no longer inhabit the Garden of Eden and would suffer death and toil through the end of time, God nonetheless clothed men and provided for their needs, carefully keeping a balance between the good and evil he allowed in the world.

Satan traced the wave back to its source on the Tor of Ynys Witrin. Yes, both the Father and the Son had been there when it started.

Could there be some disarray among the persons of the Trinity? It was almost too much to hope for.

Satan probed Creation to discover more. Throughout the ages, the Word had lived with the Father in heaven, sharing in both his substance and divine purposes. Satan had long expected the time when the Son would put aside his divine dignity and live incarnate on Earth, but God had kept the incarnation hidden from him until now. He only now discerned that as the boy Jesus grew into manhood his divine nature had lain dormant and mostly hidden, but it had remained connected to the Godhead through the boy's love for his Father. Satan now understood what had happened: From the depths of that boy's despair, the shock of the sudden separation of the Word had set in motion a spiritual wave that the Father had anticipated but not desired.

Satan watched as the spiritual wave approached the Imperial City. The hills of Rome would be like a shallow continental shelf to an approaching tsunami, but it was not a matter of their geography. The combination of circumstance, ambition, and human vanity that lay concentrated in the capital of the Empire would provide a fertile field for the wave to wreak its havoc.

Augustus

The emperor stood on the balcony of his palace atop the Palatine Hill, gazing at the city below. He frequently boasted how he had found the city made of brick and would leave it marble. *I have done well for Rome, but much remains undone. There is too much selfishness and villainy in this city. I must lead a return to Roman virtues. The games are becoming more barbaric every day. Gladiators kill for sport, and too many people lust to see blood flowing for their own entertainment. Politicians are eager to appease that lust in exchange for votes. Romans who once were ready to fight and die for the Republic now expect barbarian mercenaries to do their fighting for them. I must replace those who lust for personal power with those filled with love for Rome. I will lead my people to a higher path, one that will make this city worthy to stand before the gods for all time.*

The sound of an opening door interrupted his reverie. His wife, Lydia, joined him on the balcony. "The city is so beautiful in the sunset," she remarked. "The colors are so vibrant, and the gathering gloom hides all the filth." She waited for him to acknowledge her. Then she continued. "We need to talk about Tiberius."

"Spare me, please. I have had enough of that confounded son of yours." *I wonder if she knows.* The emperor had signed the warrant for the arrest of Lydia's son by a previous marriage. The man was truly lecherous. August had given the order: Tiberius would be arrested and disgraced before all Rome the next day.

"You know Tiberius loves you."

"Humph! Germanicus is old enough now, and he is my blood. The people love him, and he is virtuous. When my time comes, he must succeed me. I am changing my will to assure that Rome has a worthy emperor."

Lydia chewed her lip, silently considering. Then she stepped away, leaving Augustus alone.

She knows. I should have agreed with her, to allay her fears for Tiberius. She will plot to gain the throne for her son if I give her the chance. The door opened and Lydia returned, bearing a cup of fruit.

"I am sorry that I troubled you, my dear. Have some fruit."

She must be truly desperate now to take this chance. When she poisoned Gaius and Lucius, my adopted sons, she had slaves do her dirty work. But now she comes bearing the poison herself. Augustus sighed. *I have no choice. She means to murder me by poison, and the evidence is right there in her hands. I must summon the guards.*

But at that moment, Augustus felt overcome by something he could not identify. A sense of weariness overwhelmed him. Suddenly gone was his ambition to return virtue to the public life of Rome. He was so tired, and the fruit in the bowl was so tempting. He could not help himself. He reached for a ripe pear and bit into it. He died looking into Lydia's eyes.

Lucifer

The Father would have foreseen this, but Satan knew it was not what God wanted. Augustus should have ruled Rome for many years, to be succeeded by the virtuous Germanicus. Instead, the lecherous madman Tiberius would take the throne.

Beyond this, Satan saw untold miseries laid out for Rome. The noble Germanicus would be slain in faraway Antioch through the handiwork of Lydia, who would see him as a threat to her son's rule. The son of Germanicus, Caligula, would succeed Tiberius but be driven to madness by the constant threat of death in Tiberius's court.

The short reign of Caligula would set a new low for lechery and madness, and eventually his own guards would slay him. The rule of Claudius would bring a brief respite of sanity, but his speech impediment would leave him insecure about his standing with both plebian and patrician, so he could be manipulated into launching the invasion of Britain to make his own mark. Satan chortled. What a nice touch that Jesus himself had unloosed this havoc upon the race of Britons, whom he seemed to favor. Claudius would make way for another madman, Nero. Satan would have fun with the line of Julian emperors until it petered out a hundred years after Augustus's ascension. By then, the corruption of the empire would have sown the seeds of its own destruction.

All of this havoc and more lay clear to Satan, wreaked by the spiritual wave launched that night from the summit of the Tor.

Lucifer's vision for the future overcame his earlier terror. What might have happened in the Godhead to cause such a great disturbance? *Could the Word really turn from the Father?* Lucifer had to find out, so he made his way to heaven to confront the Creator.

"I see the time has come for the fulfillment of the prophecies," began Lucifer. "The Word has become incarnate among men."

"You know that perfectly well, so why are you here?" the Father asked.

"You have not changed. Just as with Job, you build a fence around Jesus that no impure thought can penetrate, and then you say, 'Look how righteous my servant is.' With Jesus you even kept him hidden from me until now."

"Jesus is not ready to be tempted by you."

"Oh, the precious Word of God cannot be tempted by mean old Lucifer? Are you that afraid of me?"

"I have no fear of you. I only need to protect the Son from you until he is ready. Once he comes fully into his divine nature, there will be no contest."

"When will that be? When may I tempt him?"

"You will have your chance before he begins his ministry. I will allow you forty days and forty nights in the wilderness. When that time comes, you can make him suffer any deprivation you choose. You may offer him any temptation to turn away from me. But you will fail. I am his Father, and you do not know the Son as I do. You will never turn him from me. Until then, you must leave Jesus alone. That is what I command you."

"He has turned against you already. He knows you will forsake him, and he despises you for it, as well he should. I heard what he had to say. And he's right. You are a heartless Father. He knows that and I know that, and I am sure that you—omniscient you—know that, too."

The Father drew back his arm as if to strike Lucifer down.

Lucifer recoiled in terror.

"Go from here, Satan. You will have your chance to tempt Jesus. Until then, I forbid you to molest him."

"Hah! It shall be as you command, but I am not the one you need to fear. Your own Son turns against you, and that is not my doing. You think you can establish control forever, but you will fail, as you did with Job even though you do not admit it. Do not worry. You command me to leave Jesus unmolested until you say he is ready, and I shall obey. I know your tricks. You are the source of all the evil in Creation, just as you are the source of good. Why else would a truly benevolent, omnipotent, and omniscient god allow evil to run rampant throughout the world?"

"I do not answer to you. Go away."

"You speak as if a fallen angel could weary the mighty omnipotent one. Very well, I shall go."

So, Lucifer made his way from heaven down to Earth. He went among men and saw Jesus for the first time. Though he had to obey the Father, there was work to be done. Lucifer cast his eyes about. The Father had forbidden him to molest Jesus, but he had said nothing about Jesus's friends and family. Mary was too pure to be corrupted. The Arimathean was a possibility, but Jesus was too independent of him; besides, the old man kept so righteously to the Law, tempting him in any meaningful way would be difficult.

But Daniel? Satan sensed the young man's weakness. He had been Jesus's faithful companion for years, often taken for granted; surely his jealousy could drive a craving for wealth or power to prove his own mettle. Of course there was also the old standby for such a ladies' man—simple old-fashioned lust. It would take some investigating to find the best way to possess, corrupt, and destroy the young man, but the Deceiver was sure he had lit upon a fertile field for his handiwork.

Chapter 15
The Unblemished

Daniel

Throughout the night, lightning flashed, thunder rolled, and earthquakes continued to shake the ground. At first driven indoors, the people emerged and huddled in small groups in the fields around the Tor. Daniel looked up into the sky. *It is most unnatural. The stars still shine brightly, there is not a cloud in the sky, but the lightning and thunder are yet all around.*

As the violence of the night finally waned, fog rolled in from the sea, blocking the stars from view. Elsigar assured the people it was safe for them to return to their homes, but looking pointedly at Daniel, he sternly warned everyone to stay off the Tor until he could see what the gods had wrought there. "The spirits of the underworld are surely awakened. Anyone who climbs the Tor now might reopen gateways for them to get out and wreak untold havoc among the living."

Mary revived as the fog rolled in, so Daniel joined his father and his aunt as they made their way back to her house. Arvigarus joined them. It was the closest building to the Tor, where the earthquakes seemed centered, yet it appeared undamaged.

"We still could find a way to look on the Tor for Jesus," Daniel whispered to Arvigarus once they were inside. "The night is quite dark, and the fog would conceal us. We could sneak past any sentinels Elsigar might post."

"I cannot defy the archdruid!" Arvigarus was too shocked by Daniel's suggestion to keep his voice low.

Both Mary and Joseph looked up, and Mary raised her hand. "If you are thinking of going up the Tor for Jesus, there is no need. God has protected this house from the violence of this night, and surely, he did not do it just for me. If God can protect this house, then he will find a way to protect his son, too."

Daniel looked into Father's face, which was illuminated by the flickering light from the fire pit. He could see they shared the same thought. *She does not know that the violence of the night reflects the wrath her son must have stirred in God.*

Arvigarus looked to Mary. "Are you saying Jesus is the son of your god?" Getting no response, he looked to an equally nonplussed Daniel. Then he turned to Joseph.

"Jesus is very special, but your question is a deep one. It has many ramifications," Papa answered.

Mary wept softly.

"If you believe he is the son of your god, then he would likely be godly himself, at least in some ways," said Arvigarus.

"Perhaps," Joseph answered. "But this is still a trying night for all of us. We worry for his safety, and his mother is so distressed."

Arvigarus smiled, but it seemed feigned. "Soon I should be able to ask this of Jesus himself."

Daniel looked to Mary and Joseph. *Why are we all so afraid to talk about who Jesus really is?* The possible divinity of Jesus was a subject none of them had yet broached among the Britons. *Perhaps Father worries how they will react if word gets out, particularly if something has happened to Jesus.*

The prince looked to each of them in turn.

Arvigarus will want his answer before long.

A diffused light awoke Daniel after a few hours. Mary and Joseph stirred as well, but Arvigarus remained fast asleep. The light of dawn, filtered through fog that yet overhung the Levels, cast no shadows. Daniel smiled. This was the first sign for him that the natural order of his world had returned.

He rose from his bed and shook the prince. *He is used to a harsher light of dawn, where the fog does not come stealing in every morning.* "Come on, Arvigarus. The light of day will show us what the night has wrought."

Father was on his way out the door, and Mary looked as if she had not slept at all. Tightening the apron string around her waist, she followed Father. *She is in too much hurry this morning, even to start the bread.*

After they emerged onto the field, they immediately noticed the small clusters of Britons gathered around the house. A quick inspection showed Daniel and Joseph no damage. *For all the night's violence, particularly the earthquakes, it is strange that the house, so close to the Tor, stands unblemished. These people have good reason to be amazed.*

Like a slowly rising stage curtain, the fog gradually lifted. It revealed more and more of the surrounding country, but there was nothing unusual to see, at least in the beginning. Looking to the woods surrounding the field, there did not even appear to be any fallen branches. A man came up and reported to Elsigar, who was standing in one of the groups, and the astonishing word spread: nothing in the Lake Village was amiss.

The sunlight grew stronger and the day grew warmer. People suddenly pointed back to the Tor as a hush of amazement fell over the crowd. Daniel turned to see.

The Tor's perfect conical shape, rounded only at the top, had distinguished it from all other hills. Now, the lifting fog revealed a distinct ridge that marred its form.

The bank of fog lifted faster as all eyes fixed on the Tor. A second ridgeline and then a third emerged from the lifting shroud. The ridges wound around and around the Tor. From the fields around Mary's house, the Tor's conical shape appeared to be altered not only by the new ridge, but also from the side, where the entire shape was now elongated.

As the fog finally dissipated, a lone figure emerged over the second ridgeline. *It is Jesus!* As Mary dropped to her knees in a prayer of thanksgiving, Daniel watched his cousin stumble toward them. The crowd parted to make way. Jesus lurched across the field to his mother and collapsed into her arms.

"Thanks be to God for keeping you safe," Mary said. "I knew he would protect his son!"

Arvigarus raised an eyebrow.

"How did you survive the night?" Daniel asked. "The earthquakes were so powerful, they reshaped the Tor. The earth about you must have tossed like a sea in a tempest."

Jesus moaned in weariness. His words were hardly coherent. "The Father lifted me into the sky to watch as he reshaped the Tor."

"I knew he would keep you safe. You are his only son," said Mary.

"He doesn't want me." Jesus was barely audible. "He transformed the Tor into a monument to the grief I caused him. The shape of a teardrop to mark his sadness. Ridgelines like a whirlwind to remind me of his fury. I now know what it is to be blemished by sin. You should give yourself to be the Lord's handmaiden once again, Mother. Give yourself to the Father once again so he can beget the son he really wants, for you are still untainted."

Joseph spoke up. "Whatever you have said or done, Jesus, God is infinitely merciful. He will forgive you and wash it away. You only need to turn back to him."

"It's what he wants of me, Uncle, but I cannot do it. I do not even want to. I am so weary."

Jesus collapsed into a stupor, and Aunt Mary, in her element, directed Daniel and Arvigarus to carry him inside.

As he helped Jesus, Daniel noticed Elsigar watching intensely. *What must he be thinking? What will he do to Jesus and the rest of us when he realizes Jesus had some hand in reshaping this place, which is so holy for the druids? If he was afraid before that we might open the gateways to his Underworld just by climbing the Tor, what superstitions and fears must be racing through his mind now?*

Bridget

The Dobunni set a splendid table, even if their mead was weak. A couple of their warriors staged a sparring match as part of the entertainment, battering one another with blunt-edged swords. Princess Bridget picked at her food, wishing she could join them.

From an early age, she had shown a propensity for boyish sports and combat. Her mother had died years ago, leaving no sons. Bridget was her father's only hope of a successor, other than a distant cousin whom he despised. Papa hoped for her to wed a strong husband. She did not lack for suitors, but she would not be ruled.

She peered down the table toward her father. His head drooped over his trencher. *Behold, King Aghamore of the Belgae, asleep over his meal. Do our hosts not see how dull the entertainments have become?* For her part, Bridget did her best to feign interest, but Father, it seemed, could not be bothered. And who could blame him? After two nights of pointless revelries, he must be eager to get down to business. *He should just give them the ultimatum, demanding they yield the territory we need, out to the Sabrina, so we can trade with our kinsmen in Eire. These people are divided and ill prepared to fight, but Papa will not abide a war if he can avoid it. He will be the proper guest. He will wait until this stupid feasting is done and the gifts are exchanged before getting down to any business, lest he give unnecessary offense.*

Bridget caught a glance from one of the host princes. She raised her tankard for another quaff, and then she held it to her lips to conceal her amusement. *Is he flirting with me? He must not know my reputation.* The princess lowered the tankard and gave the fellow a polite smile. *Papa wants peace with these people, but he will never allow a marriage with them. I wonder what he will do if that fellow makes a bolder move.*

A bard stepped to the center of the hall, and Bridget turned her attention to him. He began singing of the outlander called Jesus. *I have heard of that fellow. They say he comes all the way from the other end of the Roman territory. He fought bravely and well at Rumps. They called him the great hero who saved the Dumnonii, but that was two years ago.*

The bard continued, accompanying himself on the harp as he set the news to verse. This time, the bard reported, Jesus had defied the gods themselves. Their fury had reshaped the great Tor of Ynys Witrin. Jesus had remained atop the summit, while everyone else quaked with fear through an unnatural, tempestuous night. They thought that Jesus must be dead, for what mortal could withstand the force of such upheavals and live to tell the tale, but Jesus did! The outlander had not made it through without adverse effect though, as the night had weakened him and confined him to bed with a fever. He yet remained at Ynys Witrin.

Bridget listened as the bard filled in more details about the mysterious outlander. Jesus was only a year, perhaps two, older than she was. *He would not be like the matches that Papa would have me make. Those men are old and lecherous.* She looked at the Dobunnian prince and grimaced. *And this Jesus fellow certainly would be no bumpkin like that one.* She looked across the table. Her father remained asleep. *How can he sleep through such a tale?*

While the bard moved on to another story, Bridget conjured in her mind a map of the precinct around Ynys Witrin. It lay near the Sabrina, not far from where she sat. She could go there as her father's emissary. An unusual journey for a girl to take, but a Celtic noblewoman could rise to a more public role. In the absence of brothers, she might even reign in her own right someday. That would be more likely if she could prove her competence now.

How do I convince him to let me go? She pondered the question as the night wore on, and then, as everyone rose to retire for the night, the idea came to her. "You don't need those men to help you back to that hut, Papa. I know you are very tired, but I can help you."

"Humph. They will say King Aghamore is feeble and drunk if he needs a woman to carry him back from a night of feasting."

"I did not say I would carry you, Papa." The two of them laughed. "Actually, there is something I wanted to talk to you about—alone."

The king dismissed his men.

"I was thinking, the whole purpose of this mission is to find a way for us to gain access to the Sabrina, so we can trade across the water with our kinsmen in Eire, but the Dobunni will be cut off to the west if we extend our lands across theirs."

"Unless the Dobunni yield that land, we cannot control our trade to the sea."

"I have thought of a way. Ynys Witrin and the area around it is a sacred precinct—neutral territory."

"That neutrality is protected under the strictest edict of the druids," he agreed.

"If the druids consent, our merchants could gain access to the Sabrina across that precinct without interfering with the Dobunni. If the Dobunni support our request, the others will go along. We avoid the war and still get what we need."

He frowned, thinking this over.

"I can go to Ynys Witrin and talk to the druids, Papa. You stay here and get the Dobunni to help."

"Let us send enough men so you will be noticed. The people must recognize your hand in securing the peace. They must gain faith in your wisdom, so they will trust you when I am no longer their king."

"Oh, Papa, you have many years ahead of you."

"I will not live forever. Go at dawn. Send me word as soon as you know what the druids have to say."

Joseph

It fell to Mary to watch over Jesus. She had only one proper bed in her house, but for two weeks she had given it up for Jesus, who lay on it, beset by an awful fever. She was still at his side when Joseph walked in. The days were growing shorter, and dusk was falling.

"I brought some wood for the fire. We may need it if the night brings a chill. How is Jesus?"

Mary sighed and replaced the cold compress on her son's forehead. "Thank you, Uncle. I have to cool his fever during the day, but we cannot let the room get too cold, either. Jesus lies still for hours, but when he thrashes about, he seems to be having a nightmare. I cannot make any sense of it. Sometimes he calls to me, and sometimes to you. Today he mumbled something about how no one would break his legs; then I could not understand anything else. He often cries out that he is forsaken." Mary wept softly. "I have never seen him like this. Even as a baby, he was never ill. I've never seen him with a weeks-long fever. Do you think we might lose him?"

"I saw him like this only once, when we crossed Gaul on our way to Britain. The fever lasted only one night. I am convinced that the fever I saw then and what we are seeing now is not entirely of this world. I think God has a great purpose for Jesus. I cannot imagine that he has looked after Jesus and seen him this far, only to lose him to a fever. God will still look after him."

"Oh, Joseph, you speak of the grand purpose that God has for Jesus and the reason he wants to keep him alive. I gave myself as the handmaiden of the Lord, and I am fully aware that God has a mighty purpose for his son. But right now all I care about is that Jesus recovers. I am simply a mother who wants her son to be well."

Joseph watched Mary sob softly. *Jesus will recover, and his ranting will begin to make more sense. She should not have to hear it that way. Perhaps it is better for me to tell her now, straight out. There is nothing more to keep from Jesus, anyway.* Joseph closed his eyes. *Please, God, help me find the way to tell her. Give me strength and wisdom.* Finally, he broke the silence. "The more I have been with Jesus since I took him from Galilee, the more I am convinced that there is something truly divine within him. There is something within him that is unlike any other man."

Mary looked up from Jesus and nodded.

"There is a mystery about him, hidden from you and me," Joseph continued. "And I think it is, for the present, somewhat hidden still from Jesus himself, although he grows into that divine nature more and more as he also grows into manhood. I was not there as much as I should have been when Jesus fell ill, but Daniel stayed with him and told me what happened."

"I saw in Nazareth how Daniel loves Jesus," said Mary. "I am thankful that Daniel was there if you could not be, Uncle."

"As we were crossing Gaul, I made Jesus watch the Romans carry out a crucifixion; I thought it was for his own good. I think that it awoke in Jesus something of the divine spark that he was not ready to handle. It caused him to be at war with his own spirit. He needed to find an answer before he could be at peace with himself. Daniel helped him find an answer, and the fever went away. Daniel told me about it, and I knew that the answer Jesus had was wrong. But I also knew Jesus was not ready for the truth, so I swore Daniel to secrecy. We have kept that secret from Jesus all these years, putting our faith in God to reveal it to Jesus when the time was right. Until now we have kept it from you, too."

"What is this strange thing that was too terrible for us to know?"

"This is hard, Mary. I must tell it to you in my own way. I think it happened that night when God reshaped the Tor. God must have shown Jesus the truth, and it made Jesus despair. I know you think that what Jesus said about God's anger came from the delirium of his fever, but what Jesus said to us right before he collapsed makes perfect sense to me. I believe Jesus is now at the crossroads of his life. He has started down a pathway that will lead him to death and pain, but it is not too late for him to turn back—not too late for him to turn back to life and happiness."

"Why would Jesus be angry with his Father for leading him back to life?"

"Jesus believes that he is the Messiah. He thinks that he can defy the Romans and lead our people to freedom. I have seen him try to prepare himself for that destiny. It is everything to him. You must know this yourself."

"I know is he skilled with the blade. Everyone tells me of his exploits at Rumps. They see him as a hero. He is, is he not?"

"He certainly is, but he thought he was indestructible. He thought that his Father would always protect him, no matter what. He thought that if the Romans tried to crucify him, everyone would see God literally lifting him off the cross. This would unite the Jewish people behind him and strike fear into the hearts of the Romans. That is what he saw through his fever back in Gaul."

"But nothing is impossible for God, Joseph. That is what the archangel told me when he said I was to give birth as a virgin, and he was right. If God wants Jesus to be the Messiah for our people, he will protect him, even on the cross."

"No, Mary, that is not what is prophesied. I have studied the Scripture all my life, and I tell you this. If the Romans put Jesus on the cross of crucifixion, he will die there."

Mary turned deathly pale.

Joseph clutched her hand to reassure her before she started breaking down. "Hold on, Mary. There is another way. Jesus can be a different type of Messiah. He can teach our people the pathway of peace. Surely, the Romans will have no quarrel with that."

"Why do you think the fever besets him now?"

"I believe his Father revealed to Jesus his error. It is not easy for him to accept that his destiny will lead him to crucifixion and death. He is angry because when he turns from the path of a freedom fighter, he gives up everything he has lived for. He will not rest until he finds an answer that satisfies both his divine spark and his human nature. The fever has returned because the answer he thought he had is false, and it will not leave him until he has a better one. Until then he will not get better—but neither do I expect he will die, for God still has a great purpose for him, and it is neither to die here in Britain on a sickbed nor to die on a cross."

Mary turned to Jesus and sighed. "What can we do for him?"

"What you have done. Try to make him comfortable while the fever remains. We must be ready to help Jesus make the right choice when the time comes. We must help him listen to his Father and accept his will."

Daniel

Distraught as everyone was over Jesus's condition, someone needed to attend to the mine, so Daniel returned to the Mendips. He hired Caden, a bright, pleasant young man perhaps two or three years older than himself. At the end of Caden's first day, Daniel noticed that his ore pile was significantly higher than those of the others. *Funny, he didn't seem to be working that hard. I am glad I didn't chastise him for goofing off, as I was about to do. Maybe the work just comes easy to him because he is so strong.* Caden was indeed very muscular. There was something odd about him, though. While everyone else was soaked with sweat and covered in grime, Caden finished the day dry and clean.

The next day, Daniel puzzled over this new worker. Not that there was anything to complain about, for Caden took the same daily wage as the others and again produced the biggest pile of ore. Every time he had crawled over to Caden through the shafts, Daniel had seen him swinging his axe; but he still felt suspicious that somehow Caden was only managing not to get caught in idleness. *I wonder what he does as soon as I turn my back?*

At the end of the day, Daniel looked at the exhaustion on the faces of the men. He wiped the grimy sweat from his own brow. Once again Caden, clean and lively, offered the biggest pile of ore.

Daniel took a sample from Caden's pile. The rock was richly veined with gray, the telltale sign of silver. "Your ore is not just plentiful, but it is the richest of anyone's. I don't know how you do it and stay so clean, but that is good work."

Caden smiled.

"Are you going home to your family tonight?"

"I am just traveling through. My family is far away on the other side of Britain. I am staying with distant cousins of mine at the mouth of the Axe."

"That's a long walk. Why don't you stay here? I could use some company for dinner. Usually my younger cousin is with me, but he is sick back on Ynys Witrin. So I've eaten alone for several weeks. Hardly anyone lives around here; Priddy is scarcely a village."

"That's very gracious of you, sir."

"You don't have to call me that. Work is done for the day."

Daniel enjoyed his evening in Caden's company. Caden was an eager listener, and Daniel delighted in telling him of his adventures in Britain, particularly all about Rumps. Caden listened as if he had never heard any of it.

As he went to sleep, it occurred to Daniel that Caden had not mentioned much about himself. No matter. Perhaps he should offer Caden a higher wage to make sure he stayed on. The quantity and quality of his production certainly justified it.

THE MAKING OF THE LAMB

Joseph

The poor horse slogged its way across the wetland, carrying Joseph back to Ynys Witrin from the mine near Priddy. Another week had passed, with Jesus still feverish in Mary's bed. The operation of the mining venture had returned to normal—nothing seemed amiss. In the long term, Jesus's help was critical if they were to continue to replenish the ore loads with new finds, but the current lode near Priddy was continuing to yield silver, and there was no sign of imminent depletion. Daniel could manage the daily mining activity well enough on his own.

Nonetheless, Joseph felt a sense of foreboding.

Kendrick would soon bring his new ship to Ynys Witrin to take the season's production to market in Armorica. After so many years, Joseph trusted the sea captain's business acumen as well as his integrity. If Jesus had not recovered by then, Joseph would stay and have Kendrick handle the transport and sale. It would not be the first time.

A gentle rain began to fall. Though Ynys Witrin was only a few miles ahead, Joseph would be soaked by the time he got there, and that would expose him even more to the nighttime chill. Hopefully, the muck around the horse's hooves would not get much wetter before he reached the house; otherwise, he would have to dismount and lead the beast.

Elsigar was not an immediate problem, but he could soon become one. The archdruid was not happy about the reshaping of the Tor. It was one of the most sacred places for the druids—the gateway to their otherworld—and it was not to be trifled with. Elsigar was still demanding to speak to Jesus. He would want to know whether the young man had practiced magic on that fateful night. If he thought it to be so, there was no telling what retribution he would demand.

Joseph had gained some time by pointing out from the writings of Isaiah that divine power, not magic, could reshape the physical world, raising up the valleys and laying low the mountains. Surprisingly, the pagan listened, at least to the point of staying his hand for a time. Joseph knew that the druids told of their gods' involvement in the reshaping of hills and valleys.

"I have learned to respect the power of your god," the archdruid had told Joseph. "But I must be sure that this is the working of a god and not some conjurer's trick. I worry that Jesus seems to be growing in whatever powers he has. That could soon surpass the power of any druid to control him. He seems to live under the protection of your god, and that could be dangerous."

The ground solidified as they emerged from wetland onto pasture, making the way easier for the horse. Through the gathering dusk, Joseph made out the smoke from Mary's hearth rising through the thatch. The warmth of the fire would soon comfort his bones, but it would not still the anxiety in his heart. The progression of Jesus's fever had been maddening to watch. *Jesus is at the crossroads of his life, he is at war with his divine spirit, and everything is uncertain. That is what brings on this fever, just as it did in Gaul. He can live a long, happy, prosperous life, but not if he continues on the path that leads to pain and death on a cross.*

Mary looked up from her son as her uncle entered. "He is much better today. The fever seems to have broken. He rests comfortably for the first time in many weeks."

"We can give thanks to God for that, but let us not raise our hopes yet. He has improved before, only to relapse."

The rain stopped, and Mary stepped outside to refresh herself in the cool night air.

A few moments later, Jesus stirred. "Is that you, Uncle? I feel so weak."

"I am here, Jesus. Your mother is taking a walk. She has been looking after you for many weeks. You have had a raging fever." Joseph felt Jesus's forehead. "You still have the fever, but you are no longer burning up. Do you remember anything that happened?"

"I remember the night on the Tor. Oh! Father and I, we were so angry. I remember what he said and what he showed me. The last thing I remember is coming down from the Tor and collapsing into mother's arms, but my head is filled with so many visions—from Jerusalem, of my future—of my own death."

"Your fever was bad. You have had nightmares—"

"They were prophetic visions, Uncle. They were real. I know they were."

"Did your Father tell you what he wants from you?"

"You were right. He does not want me to be a heroic king like David. I am not to be the instrument to free our people. It will not come in my lifetime, Uncle, but our people will rebel against Rome, and the Romans will destroy the temple."

"What? Impossible." *The boy is surely mad.* Yet Joseph remembered Jesus's destruction of his model temple as Daniel had described the day he brought Mary to Ynys Witrin.

"I've seen it, Uncle. When the Jews rebel again, the Romans will drive them from Jerusalem, just as in the days of King Zedekiah. Rebellion against Rome will not save our people."

Joseph sighed. Yes, the temple had been destroyed once, so it could happen again. "So God wants you to give up the sword and turn your life to peace."

"That is what he wants. You were right about that. I just cannot do it."

"Jesus, I know you expected to lead our people in the fight for their freedom, to be a king like your ancestor David. You expected to become the greatest king our people have ever known. But if you renounce the sword and turn toward peace, the Romans will have no quarrel with you. They will have no reason to crucify you. You can have a long and prosperous life. Perhaps you can lead our people on the same path and avoid this disastrous rebellion you speak of."

Jesus erupted in peals of wild laughter.

What is wrong with him? It must be the fever.

"Oh, Uncle Joseph, you have been right all these years, but also so very wrong. You were right about what my Father wants from me. He does want me to put away the sword, just as you have said."

"Your Father loves you. He is protecting you. He knows what the Romans will do to you if you turn against them."

"Protecting me? Really?"

"Don't you see it now, how your path will lead to pain and death on the cross?"

"That's where you are wrong, Uncle. The path of obedience is the one that will lead me there. He begat me not to be a fighter king like David. I am to be the sacrificial lamb of his new covenant."

Joseph gasped. *This makes no sense.* "Why should the Romans crucify you if they have no reason to fear you?"

"Oh, you are going to love this part, Uncle! The Romans will know of my innocence, but our own people will cry out for my crucifixion. When I teach the truth, our religious leaders will turn against me, incite the people, and convict me. They will call it blasphemy, and the ruler from Rome will put me to the cross to appease them, to avoid riot and rebellion."

Joseph collapsed as if struck down by a mighty blow. *Could this be the fever talking? Was Jesus raving?*

Once again, Jesus erupted in laughter. "Think how Daniel has always believed I am blessed to be the son of God. Would not anyone think that? I must be blessed, all right—blessed with a father who wishes me to die by crucifixion."

Joseph looked at Jesus in horror. *He must be mad. It must be the fever.* Indeed, Joseph touched Jesus's forehead and felt the burn of the fever. Jesus collapsed back on Mary's bed. By the time she returned, Jesus was ranting unintelligibly, tossing and turning. Joseph shook his head to show Mary that her son had taken a turn for the worse. *What can I say to her now?*

Excusing himself, Joseph started walking up the Tor, turning his thoughts back to what Jesus had revealed. *Maybe it was a lucid interval. Maybe it does make sense. Isaiah prophesied about a suffering servant; I must read his Scripture passage again. How could I be so wrong?*

Joseph arrived at the summit. It was his turn now to cry his anguish into the night. He spent himself until his voice failed. No one heard him, except for the Father.

Daniel

The next morning, Daniel told Caden that he had decided to raise his wage.

Caden expressed his gratitude, but it seemed to Daniel that the extra money did not make much difference.

Later that morning Daniel crawled through the shafts. Each miner worked in an individual chamber. Sometimes there was room only for one man to swing an axe. He passed a shaft that led to Caden's chamber. It was silent.

Daniel crawled in.

There was Caden, sitting on his rump. In the flickering light of the oil lamp, Daniel detected a hint of a smirk.

"I offered you more money because you produced so much ore. You're a good friend, Caden, but I cannot pay you to sit idle."

"Keep your money. I have plenty of my own."

"Then why are you working? Are you leaving?"

"Not unless you tell me to. I will have as much ore for you again tonight. I could bring up even more, but that would make the others jealous."

"How?"

"It's not difficult. Here, hand me some of that waste over there."

Daniel gathered a handful of splintered rock from the waste pile. Caden held open his hands and nodded to him. Daniel poured it in.

"Watch this," said Caden. He folded his hands together over the material. Daniel bent forward to look closer in the flickering light. Caden opened his hands. Inside was a sizeable nugget of solid gold.

Daniel gasped. "What did you just do?"

"I am richer than you can possibly imagine, Daniel. I buy anything I want. I have palaces, slaves, and women—not only in Britain, but in every land."

"How do you?—"

"When I was your age, a man gave me something. He said all I had to do was keep it with me." Caden reached into his pocket bag and brought out a talisman. The head was carved from wood, and the body was sewn together over some fiber filling.

"Do you worship that?"

"The man said nothing about worshipping it. But he said to never let it go, if I wanted to live. There was one other thing, though."

"What was that?"

"He said that I would find another talisman in my pocket bag one day, and he said that I would have to pass the second one on with the same instructions. I found this last night after you went to sleep. I thought about how you befriended me, and genuinely, not for my wealth like so many others. So I decided it should be yours."

"Are you giving this to me?"

"Yes, it's yours. Just keep it and become richer than you can possibly imagine."

Daniel rubbed his thumb over the little figure's head. He could imagine quite a bit. Riches enough to build a home to rival Castle An Dinas. Fine clothes. Fine food. Fine women. Perhaps even riches enough that Papa would have as much respect for Daniel as he did for Jesus.

A voice like that of his father resonated in his head, saying, *You shall have no other gods in my presence.* His hands trembled.

Daniel lay the second idol on the floor before him. He looked to Caden. Then he looked at the idol. "So this is now mine?"

"I give it to you."

Daniel hesitated, though he knew what must be done. "It is forbidden not only to worship false idols, but even to have them." He reached into his own pocket bag and clasped the hilt of the knife. "I worship only the one true God, and my soul is not for sale." Before Caden could stop him, he pulled out the knife and plunged it through the midsection of the talisman.

"No!" Caden cried.

Then there was silence.

He and his talismans had vanished into the air.

Daniel shivered. Only the demons of hell could work such sorcery.

Bridget

The caravan came to a stop in the field upon Ynys Witrin. An archdruid came out to greet Bridget, and the villagers gathered around to see. She could tell she was an object of curiosity.

The archdruid introduced himself as Elsigar and gestured toward one of the huts near the Tor. "Please, come in and have some food and drink."

Scarcely had she and her retinue sat at the little table, when he asked her to state her purpose.

She raised an eyebrow. This was not the usual Celtic way. A visiting emissary normally had to endure several nights of feasting before anyone got down to business.

Elsigar smiled. "I did not mean to be rude or unkind. You must be new to such ways." He spoke with a hint of condescension. "Feasting and frivolity are indeed the norm among kings and warriors, but druids prefer to be more direct."

"No offense taken, sir. Much as I enjoy the feasting that greets our diplomatic missions, getting down to business is much better."

"I am surprised your father did not send a druid to speak to me on his behalf."

"There was no time. My father is now treating with the Dobunni, and it would take weeks to summon the assistance of the druids from our home. We seek to avoid a war with them by resolving something quickly." Bridget explained the Belgae's need for a trade route to the Sabrina. She did not expect him to respond immediately.

Elsigar raised no objection. "I will need to summon Grengan. Keeping the peace is a matter for the druids, but issues of commerce fall to the king. We must consult with each other, since your proposal touches on both matters."

She stood. "Then let us be direct, and visit him now."

He waved her back into her chair. "Unfortunately, Grengan is away. We must wait until tomorrow."

"Very well. In the meantime..." Bridget toyed with a bit of bread. "There is one thing I would like to do. I have heard of a young outlander called Jesus who is staying here at Ynys Witrin, and I would very much like to see him."

"He is ridden with fever...incoherent. He cannot see anyone."

"I just want to look in on him."

"We think he may be dangerous. The Tor was a perfect cone two weeks ago. We suspect Jesus of using magic to reshape it, but he has been too ill for us to question him."

Bridget straightened her spine and looked at Elsigar directly. "I am a princess of the Belgae. Have you confined Jesus as your prisoner? Are you barring me from seeing him?"

"Of course not. I was just warning you of the danger. He is in yonder house; he built it for his mother. You should find her there, too. You can find me here with Grengan tomorrow." With that, without even offering hospitality for the night, the druid showed her to the door.

Bridget directed her retainers to find a camp site. By then her entourage had drawn a small crowd. She smiled at them, but otherwise ignored them. She whispered to the captain of her guard that he was not to come looking for her if she did not return.

Bridget walked to the house and announced her presence to the woman hovering over the figure on the bed. Aside from the absence of carved figures and talismans, it looked like a typical Celtic home. The fire on the central hearth crackled merrily, and the smell of baking bread and chicken broth filled the air.

The woman looked up at her. "I am Mary, and this is my son, Jesus. Please come in out of the chill."

"Thank you. I am Bridget. I have heard of Jesus, and I came to see him. May I?"

Mary nodded, and Bridget rounded the curtain. The lack of modesty as the young man lay atop the bed was shocking, but the sight of Jesus lying naked except for a small loincloth did not offend her. His body was not muscle-bound, as she expected in such a renowned hero. He certainly looked strong and well-defined, but lithe rather than brawny. He was slightly taller than her average countryman. His mother hadn't shaved him during his illness, and a thin beard covered his face. The olive tone of his skin marked him as an outlander and added a sense of mystery.

Bridget was so engaged by the sight of him that she didn't notice Mary speaking to her. She flushed with embarrassment at the thought that the mother must see her as a besotted fool, but she gathered that Mary must have been asking about her and where she was from. Bridget said that she was a princess of the Belgae, and she explained her father's purpose in sending her. *If the mother noticed anything, she is not letting on.*

Just then Jesus awoke, thrashing about and ranting in a language unknown to Bridget. Even through the rants, his voice sounded melodic.

Mary approached the bedside with a small bowl of soup. As soon as she touched Jesus's forehead, he calmed down and opened his eyes to look at his mother, and then he allowed her to feed him.

There is such love and compassion in his eyes. Gone now was the fear of being ruled by a brute of a husband if she ever allowed herself to be taken in marriage. *This Jesus respects women, and I do not fear to share my life and everything I am with him. He is all I could possibly want in a man. He is bedridden now, but he will not stay that way forever. What would it be like to share his bed and wake up to him showing that love and compassion for me? I will love him and bear his children, and I will do anything to make him mine.*

Daniel

Light snow dusted the pathway across the Levels towards the Tor, as Daniel made his way to Mary's house. The hard work for the season was now done. There would be chores to do, saddles to mend, and ore to refine over the winter, but at least he was done with mining until the spring. He tried to rest in the saddle, but through his weary bones, he felt each step the horse took.

Daniel had spent most of the season in the cramped tunnels, wielding his hammer and bringing up the ore to the surface. The ore in the main part of the lode had petered out shortly after Jesus had come down from the Tor and become ill, so they had to go back to another vein and dig where the going was harder. The hours were longer, and Daniel had not been able to get away for the rest of the season. *Jesus had better recover soon and find another lode, or we will need to give up.*

Daniel's spirits rose as he approached Ynys Witrin. It would be good to be back with the family. He wanted to see Jesus, in particular. According to Father, his cousin was still racked with fever, but his lucid intervals were becoming more frequent. Daniel had many questions for Jesus. Maybe he could tell his cousin about his close encounter with the demon who tempted him. He wasn't ready to tell Papa about it yet. If ever.

When Daniel arrived, his father and Mary greeted him warmly, but he was too tired to say much. It was all he could do to crawl into a corner behind a curtain, where he fell into a deep sleep. He slept much later than usual the following morning.

By that time, a willowy girl with a long braid of golden hair, had already arrived to help Mary tend to Jesus. She said her name was Bridget, and she spoke with an unfamiliar accent.

Daniel would have preferred to stay and rest—and talk with her—but Father dragged him out to help with the refining. It wasn't until late that evening, when everyone was preparing to go to sleep, that he realized that Bridget was staying in Mary's house. He wanted to ask Mary about it, but he couldn't when the girl would overhear.

The next morning, when Bridget went out to fetch water, Daniel approached Mary, who was kneading dough.

"So, Aunt Mary…who is Bridget, and why is she staying here? Doesn't she have a family of her own?"

"Bridget has been a great blessing to me for several weeks now," said Mary. "She helps me look after Jesus. She helps me cook and clean. I do not know how I would manage without her."

"Did you hire her as a servant?"

"Oh, my dear Daniel, no! You should have seen her the day she came, sparkling in her jewels. She is a princess of the Belgae. She is wearing simple clothes now because she is helping with the work. She traveled here on some diplomatic mission on behalf of her father, the king of that tribe. Once it was over, she asked to stay here until Jesus is better."

"Isn't that strange, for a princess to put aside her dignity and take up the work of a servant?"

"Is my son taking an interest in a *goy*?" Father asked. Daniel hadn't seen him get up. Joseph approached the fire to warm himself. "Perhaps it is time to bring you home to Judea to find a proper Jewish wife. No son of mine will marry a heathen."

"You have nothing to worry about, Father, but maybe Mary does. It is Jesus this woman dotes on."

"Do you think Jesus could fall in love with a Briton? Don't be ridiculous, Daniel," said Mary.

Joseph looked at Mary. "Daniel may have a point."

"Jesus has hardly said a word since he was taken ill, and what he says is in Hebrew and Aramaic. She cannot possibly understand him," Mary replied. "Besides, he is still far too young."

"He has seen eighteen summers, Mary. Take another look at that son of yours, lying almost naked atop your bed," said Father. "He looks like a man to me, and the Britons wed their children when they are much younger than that."

Over the next several days, Daniel tried to talk to Bridget whenever he could get her attention, which was hard because it was always focused on Jesus. Then the Sabbath came, and they all stayed home for their prayers. When Mary insisted that Bridget should take some time off and go outside, Daniel followed her.

They walked through the apple trees. Then, with a wry smirk, she said, "Race you," and took off running.

He sprinted after her, but it was no use. She was clearly practiced, while his legs had done nothing but heavy lifting of late. She reached the water's edge, laughing, and waited for him to catch up.

As they walked back, she spoke of life at her father's court. To Daniel's surprise, she had opinions about everything. She held her own when they argued about druids and Jewish monotheism. Even in that she found ways to make him laugh.

"You're very good around the house, for a princess," he said.

She laughed, a sound like water bubbling over cobbles. "Thank you, sir. Even highborn Belgae women must relegate themselves to domestic affairs."

"Oh, domestic affairs? Like the sprint?"

"Hah! Yes." She shook her head, and her smile drained away. "No. A queen of a strong tribe like ours may go about adorned in jewels and ornaments, but a daughter must stay in the background, properly demure, until her father forces her into marrying some horrible old man."

"Has your father pledged you in marriage?"

"No, thanks be to all that's holy, however many gods there may be." She sighed. "But I fear he will."

Daniel nodded, unable to think of a witty reply.

Daniel awoke in the middle of the night. He stretched out on the lambskins and smiled, thinking about the funny way Bridget had pouted at him with that upturned nose of hers. He thought about her body, too; like all Celtic women, she dressed modestly, but that did not conceal the curvature of her bosom or the hair escaping in golden ringlets from her braid. Though he was wide awake, he remembered dreaming about her. *The Sabbath is over. Besides, it is not a sin to dream.*

Daniel felt a tightness in his groin, and he moved his hand there. He then realized that this had been no ordinary dream. Not only was he fully erect, but his loincloth was wet. He had made himself ritually unclean, and he would need to find a natural spring to serve as the *mikvah* of living water to purify himself as soon as the day broke. There was one within a stone's throw of the door, but he did not want Mary or his father seeing him and asking questions.

His thoughts turned to the long term. His father had already spoken his mind about the inappropriateness of him marrying a gentile. However, the prospect of a journey back to Judea to find a bride held no appeal. Papa would have to arrange the marriage. Perhaps Bridget could solve the problem if she converted to Judaism. *What am I thinking? She is besotted with Jesus, not me. She can't realize that Jesus will never give her what she desires. He is truly god as well as man, and he will never love a woman as other men do. He told me that himself. I will bide my time. She will turn to me once she comes to know this.*

Daniel moved his hand back to his groin. He slowly began to rub his member. Erotic images of Bridget filled his mind. Her smooth body would be muscularly firm. He could practically feel her nipples on his tongue. *I am already unclean, so I might as well take my time and enjoy this.*

Lucifer

The Fallen One could not contain his gloating. Once again he made his way from hell up to heaven.

"So tell me, Omniscient One, how does it feel to know you have already lost?"

"What would make you think that?"

"You have gambled the hope for all of your creation on the shoulders of your begotten son. You would make him the sacrificial lamb for your new covenant, but we know, do we not, that a lamb offered in sacrifice must be unblemished. That is what you, yourself, decreed unto Moses."

"Are you saying that Jesus is now blemished by sin?"

"He said it himself to his mother. He saw the wrath he had provoked in you, and he recognized the blemish in himself." Satan's laugh crackled like a fire. "I loved it when he told his mother to offer herself up as your handmaiden once again to help you beget the son you really want."

"He did not know what he was saying."

"It does not matter. He cursed you and called you heartless. If that does not separate him from you, I do not know what would. He is now blemished, and nothing you can do will restore him to perfection."

"He was angry with me, but sometimes anger even against God can be righteous."

"I see you are up to your old tricks," Lucifer sneered. "Just as with Job. You let him off the hook even when he turned against you."

"You are a fine one to lecture me about sin separating man from God. You misunderstand the lesson of Job. I may be demanding and jealous, but I am also fair and just. Yes, Job was angry with me, but his anger was righteous. I allowed you to make his life miserable. I allowed you to take away everything he had and to afflict him with lesions and all the pain of hell. In the end, he decided not to press his righteous claim against me because of his love for me and his trust in me. I did not forgive him for a transgression; instead, I made full recompense under the law. I rendered justice, not mercy, to Job."

"But Jesus said he does not want to obey you."

"What kind of man would want to obey me in this? I have ripped away his hopes and dreams. I am sending him to a miserable, shameful, painful death."

"A truly sinless man would care only about obeying and serving his god."

"I sent Jesus to be incarnate in the world to be the pathway for a broken humanity to gain salvation. I sent him not to condemn the world, but to save it from sin. Do you think I offer salvation only to those who never fear or doubt? Do you think I offer salvation only to those who are never moved to anger at the trials I allow them to suffer in the world? Jesus is broken right now, just as his body will be broken on the cross, but he is still perfect in my eyes. He is the perfect example for a broken humanity to follow and be made perfect through my power to save and be made fit to stand before me.

"Like Adam, Jesus will make his choice," the Father continued. "He will make his choice in the wretchedness of a broken humanity, and I—not you, or even he—will be the one to judge whether he has blemished himself through sin."

"He will never choose the path of shame and death on the cross for you," Lucifer retorted.

"Then you will agree, will you not, that if he makes that choice of his own free will, that I might righteously judge him to be unblemished by sin?"

"I will concede the point, if you agree that he must make that choice on his own. Just as you have commanded me to leave him unmolested until the time comes for his temptation, so too must you agree that he is not to be offered any reward until he commits to his choice."

"Done," said the Father. "Now, leave my presence."

Chapter 16
Dark Satanic Mills

Daniel

Daniel woke early, wondering whether he should ask Jesus about Caden. Was he human or demon?

Whatever Caden was, he had vanished without a trace. None of the other miners would admit to remembering anything about him. And why would a demon offer Daniel untold wealth? What did he have that a demon would want? Was it nothing more than his imagination? Or had he lost his mind?

Mary still seemed anxious about Jesus, haunted by something. *How much has Father shared with her? Father, Aunt Mary, and Jesus have so much to worry about; I shouldn't add to their troubles. The demon is gone; that should be good enough.*

The smell of flour and oil filled the air. Mary was making the bread.

Daniel glanced over at Jesus, who was still asleep. He seemed to be resting more comfortably.

Daniel needed fresh air. He got up and smiled to Mary as he walked outside. She still seemed preoccupied, hardly noticing him. How unkind it would be to burden her more.

Winters at Ynys Witrin were mild, as winters go. The air was wet with a chill that gave it a crisp bite. As he walked among the apple trees, Daniel felt invigorated. The fog thickened around him.

"So, we meet again." The voice was unmistakable: Esmeralda! She must have been walking beside him for some time.

"I thought Elsigar banished you." Once her participation in the robbery had been exposed, the people had demanded it. He quickened his pace.

She easily matched him. "He is not here, and a druid's power cannot be undone—not even by another druid," she answered. "A druid is one with nature. Can you banish an eagle from the sky? That would be easier than banishing a druid."

"What do you want with me?"

"I want peace between us. I want peace, prosperity, and justice for my people."

"Those are noble words, but they do not match your actions."

"I am not evil, Daniel. You think I am, but everything I did was for my people. You and your family come as outlanders, take the fruits of our land, and bring a strange and powerful god with you. Jesus says he works no magic, but we know he does. It will be the destruction of the people."

"I still cannot imagine what you want with me."

"I need your strength."

He halted and turned to face her. "What?"

"Even when I plotted and schemed against you, I had to admire you. There you were, left to hold everything together after Jesus ran off and left you, with no coin to hire workers, with your Aunt Mary sick. Yet you beat me." Esmeralda hung her head. The hood of her cloak shadowed her face.

At least someone had noticed his hard work and appreciated his abilities.

"You soldiered on and held everything together," she said. "But now Jesus is back, and everyone's thoughts are on him again, aren't they?"

"I suppose so. I don't think I will ever forget how hard it was."

"That's the strength I am talking of." The druidess gripped his upper arm with a firm hand. "You do everything to hold things together, yet everyone cares only about Jesus."

"But what do you want from me?"

"The Britons need a leader. The Romans will come one day, and they will find us weak, divided, and undisciplined. I can make you king of the Britons."

He stared into her eerie, unblinking green eyes. Could she be serious? Would pagans allow a Jew to rule? Daniel certainly had the administrative skill, though he was no warrior like Tristan. He envisioned himself on a great carved throne like the one Fergus inherited from his father Uryen. Perhaps he could even convert the heathen…

Esmeralda shook him from his reverie. "All will bow down before you, if you decide to worship—"

He flung off her hand. "Away from me, witch! I worship the one true God and no other."

In an instant, Esmeralda vanished.

He was left talking into the mist.

Was it another demon, or did I imagine that? If those demons are real, they do not seem very powerful. They seem powerless if I refuse what they offer.

Bridget

A chilly, damp wind blew against Mary's house, but inside, the cheer of the fire and the fragrance of baking bread warmed the soul.

Bridget thought only briefly about attending the Imbolc festival, but the sound of the wind reminded her how dismal she would feel if she went. Besides, Mary would need her, or so she told herself. In truth, she could count on Mary to be understanding, and it would not be the first time she would have braved the elements. The real reason to miss the festival was that she did not want to leave Jesus's side.

At first, it had been difficult for Bridget to gain any sense of what he was saying. His rants always began in Aramaic, but when she spoke to him in the Celtic tongue, he would switch to that language. It was not much of a conversation—he was still ranting, and none of what he said made sense—but at least she could understand his words. He talked a lot about his father. Jesus seemed to love him dearly, but she also caught on that Jesus felt forsaken, and one day, Jesus said something that suggested that this father was sending him to his death. Yet she knew Mary's husband was dead. *What is this talk about his father? It must be madness brought on by the fever.*

As the weeks wore on, Bridget tried to solve the puzzle of his ravings. Sometimes she could ask a question and get an answer, though not always rational. Other times her questions merely inspired him to go onto something else entirely.

A week had passed since he had mentioned this seemingly cruel father figure. He talked about crucifixion, a horrible method of execution used by the Romans. Like most Britons, she had heard of this by rumor, but it had never occurred to her how monstrously cruel it was.

One day he described his "father" as the one true god, which made no sense. How could his father be a god? And how could there be just a single god in the entire universe? She asked Mary about it, and Mary explained the Jewish belief.

"But why does he call this god his father?"

Mary looked away.

Bridget's heart pounded. If Lugh could be both god and giant, could Jesus?...

She gazed again at Jesus, beautiful even in his infirmity. If anyone could be both god and man, it would be him. She turned back to Mary, her voice trembling. "If Jesus were really the son of your all-powerful god...would he not be a god himself?"

Mary sighed, dicing an onion into her soup pot. "He will be called the Son of the Most High, he will inherit the throne of his ancestor David, and he will reign over the house of Jacob forever. Or so I'm told."

That answer was almost as mad as her son's ravings.

In the hopes of gleaning sensible answers from among the crazy ones, Bridget continued posing questions to Jesus.

She could understand his despair over the cruel destiny that he believed awaited him and perhaps over the Father's bidding that he turn away from the heroic life for which he had prepared. She began to grasp his supposed dual nature as both god and man. But then he began ranting about three persons in the godhead, and she was lost again.

One day, as the first signs of spring were emerging, Mary left Bridget alone with Jesus, who was rambling in his delirium. She called to him, and he mumbled a response.

She leaned closer. "If you are divine, can you not choose your own path? Surely you are not bound to choose between fighting the Romans or letting them crucify you?"

Jesus became quiet.

Bridget paused. *He must be listening to me.* "You say the Romans will return to vanquish and subjugate the Britons. If you are truly divine, can't you stop this from happening?"

Jesus grunted something that may have been "What?"

"If your Father adopted the Israelites as his chosen people in the time of Abraham, could you not adopt the Britons as yours? You said you share his divine substance, so if he can adopt the Jews, why cannot you adopt the Britons? Unite us. Lead us to victory when the Romans invade."

Jesus sat up, wide awake, looking at her. "Who are you?"

"I am Bridget, princess of the Belgae. I have been helping your mother take care of you."

"You are right. I do have the power to create my own path in this life. Everything is my choice as much as my Father's."

Bridget nodded, smiling.

He rubbed his face. "I am weary. I must sleep. Please stay with me." Jesus drank the water she gave him. Then he settled back in his bed, no longer ranting or thrashing about. For the first time, he seemed to rest in a deep, dreamless sleep. She touched his forehead—all trace of fever was gone.

Joseph

Whatever the Father's plan for Jesus, Joseph had been certain it was not for him to die of fever in Britain. Still, he hadn't expected the illness to last so long, and it was a relief to see Jesus up and about as winter gave way to spring. He ought to talk to Jesus about what he had said, but Joseph did not want to hear Jesus confirm that God had already condemned him to die on the cross, even if Jesus were to lead a peaceful life.

Right after the sundown following the Sabbath day, after spending the day cooped up inside for prayers, Jesus, Daniel, and Bridget went out walking and left Joseph with Mary.

Joseph could tell Mary had something on her mind; all day she had seemed distracted.

"I do not know what to do for Jesus now," she said.

"So, he has talked to you."

"He told me that he talked to you, also."

Joseph sighed. "I have been trying to put it out of my mind. He said something a few weeks ago; I tried to tell myself that it was nothing more than wild talk brought on by his fever. What did he say to you?"

"I tried to tell him he should consider a different path, the path of peace, and be a different type of Messiah," said Mary. "I told him that he could live a long and happy life if he gave up his plan to wage war on Rome. Do you remember?"

Joseph nodded.

"He told me that God, his Father, already had laid that out for him." Through her sobs, Mary struggled to make herself understood. "He said our own people will turn against him and ask the Romans to crucify him. Did he say that to you, too?"

"Mary, it might be that I should have come to you about this sooner. I was hoping it was just his fever talking. When did he say this to you?"

"It was Friday, just before the beginning of the Sabbath. He was quite collected. I think he was upset only because he saw it was making me sad." She gripped Joseph's hand. "Don't blame yourself. I should have known something like this would happen. My husband and I presented Jesus at the temple shortly after he was born. A man named Simeon blessed us, saying the spirit of God had revealed to him that he would not see death before he had seen the Christ. At first we were glad, because he said that he could depart this world in peace knowing that Jesus was its salvation. But then he said that a sword would pierce my soul. I had no idea what he meant. I thought he must be a madman, but I never in all these years truly dismissed what he said from my mind. I see now he must have been a true prophet. What should we do now?"

"I curse myself for being so blind all these years," answered Joseph. "The prophecy of the suffering servant is right there in the book of Isaiah, but I was too blind to see that Jesus would suffer even more if he turned his path to peace. But that is indeed the will of God."

"Part of me wants to spit on the will of God!" Mary paced the little room. "I do not care about this new covenant that God wants to make. I am just a mother who wants her son to live and be happy." Mary started sobbing again. "What can we do, Joseph? Maybe Jesus can lead a happy and quiet life here in Britain."

"He told me the Father wants him to go back to Israel. Are you suggesting that Jesus should disobey God?"

"I cannot help it. He is my son, and no mother should have to rest a son in the grave."

"Did he tell you what he plans to do?"

"He is angry, but he loves his Father in heaven. He says he does not know what to do. He says Bridget gave him the idea, and it brought him out of the fever."

"What idea?"

"That he adopt the Britons as his people and fight to protect their freedom."

"That would mean disobeying God."

"He realizes that. That is why I thought it would be safer for him to lead a quiet life if he stays here."

Joseph stood and put his hands on her shoulders. "It is out of our hands, Mary. He will make his own decision when the time comes." Sighing, he lowered his hands. "I must pray on this."

Joseph left the house, crossed the field that led to the Tor, and climbed directly to the top, over the three ridges. As he made his way, he thought about what Jesus had said, how God had reshaped the Tor into a monument of anger and sadness. *Was it really Jesus to blame? What did the Father expect? Did he really expect his Son to react with joy at the prospect of giving up everything for which he had lived, only to die this painful and shameful death?*

At the summit, Joseph began to pray. It was not like the prayers of most people, even the most devout. He did not ask God for anything, and he did not even offer a thanksgiving. *God already knows my desires. This is the time for me to listen. I must open myself to hear what God has to say.* And so Joseph sat still for hour after hour, well into the night.

The Holy Spirit turned Joseph's thoughts to obedience and disobedience. Joseph recalled Adam's disobedience. *It was the smallest of things, really, just a bite of fruit, but it was enough to separate man in creation from God in heaven. It released all the evil in the world, all the death and sin. Adam made his choice, but what will happen if Jesus chooses differently? As the firstborn mortal man, Adam condemned the world through his sin of disobedience, but what will happen if Jesus, as both God and man, chooses obedience? Could that undo all the death and sin that Adam's act of disobedience wreaked upon the world?* Joseph remembered that is what Jesus had told him the Father had said, but neither of them understood how that would work. *Where Adam chose to disobey God just to get a bite of fruit, Jesus could choose the supreme act of obedience, even unto death. It would be the ultimate act of obedience at the greatest possible cost.* The more Joseph thought about it, the more he marveled that Jesus and Adam could be so alike, and yet so different—opposites, and yet the same, like mirror images of each other. *Perhaps Jesus can be the Adam of creation for a new age.*

But even as the Spirit led Joseph to focus on the significance Jesus's sacrifice might bring, Joseph's heart filled with despair. *He is my blood; I love him like a son. How can I ask him to carry this burden? It would be asking him to choose his own misery and death.*

As Joseph concluded his prayer, he realized that the choice before Jesus was not his to make. *Please God, give Jesus wisdom and strength. I do not know what else to pray for.*

Daniel

Daniel walked home after a long, cold day at the mine, longing for a fire to lift the chill from his bones. He flinched at every sound in the woods, anticipating another visit from Esmeralda—or whatever beast of hell had impersonated her.

He leaped across the stream that marked the halfway point between the mine and his hut. Jesus remained at his mother's house, so when Daniel was in Priddy, he had the place to himself. *Perhaps I should bring Bridget to see it. Then she'd realize I'm not just Jesus's cousin, but a man with a home and livelihood of my own.* She didn't have to know that Jesus had put as much work into that home as he had.

"Good morning, Daniel."

He turned, half expecting to find Esmeralda. But it was a Celtic lass, shorter and thinner than Bridget, with a sweet face surrounded by a cloud of auburn ringlets. He smiled. "Do I know you?"

"Probably not." On one arm, she carried a basket of pears and apples. "But I know you. Everyone knows you. Daniel bar Joseph, the famous miner of silver."

He snorted. *She must be the only one who doesn't think of me as Jesus's cousin.*

"You must be very wealthy and powerful," she said.

"Huh. Neither. We make a good living, but most of the profit goes right back into operations."

She laughed. "I'm sure you know best how to run your business."

Father does far more of the running than I. "What is your name?"

"Eurielle."

"Thank you, Eurielle. You're very sweet."

"Don't flatter me, you outlander. I know who has your heart."

"Do you?"

"It's common knowledge that you are besotted with Bridget of the Belgae."

"And is it common knowledge that she ignores me?"

She giggled, but didn't answer the question.

"How is it that I have lived in this region all this time and not met you before?" Daniel asked.

Eurielle shrugged. "Your eyes must have been elsewhere. Why should you spare your gaze on a plain girl like me?"

He laughed. "There is nothing plain about you."

"Now you are mocking my red-headedness, sir." Her voice sounded petulant, but her eyes showed mirth.

"How could I mock such beauty?"

"Hah! You are a flatterer. It will avail you not. I must go, sir." She turned aside, but after a few steps, she turned back. "Yet…let me leave you with something." She took a pear from her basket and pressed it into his hand. "Perhaps we'll meet again."

"I hope so, Eurielle."

Mary

Alone in her house, making her own prayer, Mary was not at all conflicted in her purpose.

Please God, Jesus is everything to me. I care nothing about how great he could be. I am a mother who wants her son to live and be happy. He is kind and good. He does not deserve this torment. Give him the life he deserves. If someone must suffer this horrible death, let it be me. I gladly give myself in his place.

Daniel

Daniel awoke early, alone in his hut, as hungry for Aunt Mary's bread as he was for Bridget's company. He quieted the grumbling in his stomach with a bit of old bread soaked in honey, and he set out for the mine. The morning was cold and damp, and a thick mist lay across the landscape.

Once again, as he crossed the landmark stream, Eurielle appeared. "Good morning, Daniel."

"Good morning, Eurielle." Today her basket was empty. Perhaps she had yet to do her harvesting. "You're a very industrious girl, aren't you? Out doing your gathering at the break of dawn—one of our wise men said a woman who rises before dark to provide for her family is worthy of praise."

"Sir, you are flattering again."

"I speak only the truth."

"You may be handsome and successful, but why should I allow myself to be toyed with? I would only lose you to Bridget of the Belgae in the end. Why should I suffer such heartbreak?"

"You do not know Bridget well. Her eyes are on Jesus only. She spares no interest for anyone else."

"But he will refuse her, won't he? And when he does, she'll turn to you for solace, and poor Eurielle will be out in the cold, alone."

"I daresay a pretty girl like you will never be alone for long."

"I could say the same for a handsome fellow like you. Just wait. When Jesus throws her over, Bridget will come running."

"How do you know he will do that?"

Her laugh was like water in a brook. "Everyone knows that you are the one interested in the ladies, and that your cousin will have none."

How could everyone know that? It is a thing we've discussed only between the two of us. Perhaps people noticed Jesus's behavior toward the girls at festivals, and surmised the rest.

"I tell you, Bridget has great fondness for you," Eurielle said.

"Bridget pays no attention to me."

She sighed. "You men are oblivious. She is toying with you, Daniel. Every girl knows that paying a man too much attention gives him an inflated opinion of himself. And most fellows have far too inflated opinions to begin with. She only pretends to ignore you because she wants you to pursue her."

Daniel halted. "You are mad."

She smiled coyly over her shoulder. "Perhaps in spite of all your flirtations, you do not understand women as well as you think." She continued ahead.

He followed. *I don't understand women at all. Who can?* "This makes no sense. If she wants me to pursue her, how am I to know that if she gives me no sign?"

"She will give you a sign when she is ready. And when she does, you had best be prepared to give her all a man is able to. If you can't win her at that point, you'll lose her forever."

"That's insane."

"I am giving you all the secrets of womanhood." She turned and faced him, one hand on her hip. "Do you want to know the way to understand a woman, or don't you?"

"Of course I do."

"Then listen to me. When she gives the barest sign of her true feelings for you—the touch of a hand, a kiss on the cheek—then you must return her affection with all the passion a man can muster. She will say no, no, to test your persistence. Because a man who gives up is weak. So you must press on. Otherwise you're no man at all." She spun about and walked away.

"Wait. Eurielle…" He chased after her, calling her, but lost her in the heavy mist.

Jesus

Joseph told Jesus that he should expect Elsigar to come calling now that he was out of bed, and sure enough the archdruid summoned Jesus to walk with him up the Tor.

Elsigar pointed out the mysterious ridges, but Jesus already knew what they looked like. He also knew the Tor had been reformed at its base into the shape of a teardrop.

"The reshaping of the Tor has all the signs of magic," said Elsigar, "and you were the only one at the summit that night. You understand how significant the Tor is to us. It is the gateway to the Underworld, and now it will never be the same."

"I was not the only one at the summit. God the Father was here, too." Jesus told Elsigar what God had commanded, that he give himself over to death on a cross. He told Elsigar how he had defied the Father. "It was he, not I, who reshaped the Tor. He made it into a monument to his sadness and anger."

"This Father you speak of would be the god of your people—the one true god whom you imagine to be the creator of the universe. Is that right?"

"Yes, he is."

Elsigar shook his head. "And yet you would have me believe that you defy him."

"I am not sure what I will do when the time comes, but I suppose that would be one way of putting it—that I defy him."

"I cannot allow any outlander practicing magic to stay in Britain."

"That is what you said when we first met."

"I wonder if the damage to the Tor is the price we must pay for my decision to allow you to stay. What you have told me is the most ridiculous story I have ever heard. Too ridiculous to make up, so I suppose you must believe it…and that relieves you of the accusation of practicing magic. I cannot blame you for what any god does, even if you provoked his anger. That is not the same as practicing magic."

"That is good to hear. I feel I would be starting down the pathway to crucifixion if I return to Galilee right now."

"As I have watched you over these years, I have never understood how you could worship only one god. You say he commands you to submit to a horrible and shameful death. It must be hard, having your god command you like that, if you have no other god you can turn to instead. You should think about becoming a druid; we have plenty of gods who are not nearly as demanding."

"I have not decided what I am going to do."

"Consider it. You have not studied for twenty years like our novices, but you have much of what a druid needs to know already. It will not take you that long, and it would open up a pathway in your life that will keep you off that cross."

Bridget

While Jesus was away with Elsigar, Bridget took a large basket into the wild orchard to fetch some apples. She had half-filled the container when a girl popped her head of tousled red hair from behind a tree.

"Hello, Princess Bridget. I thought I was the only one gathering fruit at this hour."

"I could say the same," Bridget answered. The girl was thin, but not thin enough to hide behind an apple tree. Where had she come from? "Do I know you?"

"Oh, no, ma'am. I'm just a common girl. I'm Eurielle. But everyone knows you. Princess of the Belgae."

Bridget stood on her toes to reach a branch, and drew it down so the shorter girl could reach. "Please help yourself, Eurielle."

"Oh, thank you, ma'am. You're very kind." The girl plucked apples from the branch and dropped them in her basket. "Everyone says so. Everyone admires your dedication in staying so long to help Jesus. Even if it is rather foolish."

Bridget loosed the branch. It snapped away, sending a couple of apples flying. "I beg your pardon?"

"I meant no disrespect, your Highness, but it's common knowledge that Jesus is devoted to his family."

"As am I."

Eurielle laughed. "No, you are devoted only to him. But when you shun his cousin…" She shook her head. "Oh, ma'am. Jesus doesn't care for people who are rude to Daniel."

"I have never been rude to Daniel."

"You scarcely speak to him. And yet he's so very handsome, and successful, and wise. His silver mines make him one of the richest men in the region."

"I don't care about riches."

"Of course you don't. You care about power. About protecting your people. But doesn't the one achieve the other? The Britons can't be protected from the Romans without funding a great army." Eurielle turned to face Bridget. "Daniel was at Rumps, too, you know. He knows what war requires."

"And what do you know of war?"

Eurielle's sweet voice turned heavy. "I've seen more than you can imagine, ma'am." She smiled. "You'll never get in Jesus's good favor if you treat his cousin poorly. They are like brothers." The girl stepped closer. "Win over one, and you may win over the other."

Bridget folded her arms. "You're saying I should use Daniel to get to Jesus."

"Daniel is already enamored of you."

"How do you know that?"

She giggled. "Everyone knows that. If you show kindness to Daniel—just sisterly kindness, nothing more—the touch of a hand, a kiss on the cheek—he may yet commend you to Jesus. And if that still doesn't work… well, you'll have Daniel. And having him would surely be the next best thing to having Jesus."

"There is no substitute. If I can't have Jesus, I'll die a spinster."

Eurielle's light laugh turned to a cackle. "That would be rather pointless, don't you think, Your Highness?" She looked at her basket. "Ah, it seems my work is done. Good day, Your Highness." She walked away, soon disappearing into the wood.

Good day, you strange little girl. But as Bridget returned to the house, she kept turning over in her mind the idea that Daniel might commend her to Jesus. Yes, he might.

Lucifer

The Fallen One chose his time carefully. He could not molest Jesus directly; God had forbidden that for now. Nor would it do for Lucifer to allow Jesus to sense his presence, so he stayed away from Ynys Witrin until one day in the spring when Jesus went on his own to look for another lode of silver ore in the Mendip Hills.

Luck was with Daniel that day, or so he thought. He was helping his father with some repairs to the refinery furnace, when Bridget came strolling by.

Lucifer and Eurielle watched from a distance. "You sowed your seeds well, little one," he told her. "I will use Daniel's lust for the girl and lead him to ruin."

"But master, that will hurt only Daniel. What about Jesus? How do we reach him?"

"Now Jesus will see Daniel's dark side. He will turn from his beloved cousin in disgust. All the other sinners now in creation and those yet to be born are strangers to Jesus. I will lay the wickedness in Daniel bare for Jesus to see, and he will understand that all men share the same wicked nature. He will never give up his life to save them from the wickedness they bring on themselves." *So much for God's plan for salvation He will yield the throne of heaven to me!*

Eurielle giggled.

"You take care of Bridget," said Lucifer. "Use her compassion. She only needs to believe for a moment that kindness to Daniel will get her what she wants."

Eurielle vanished.

Lucifer would take care of Daniel himself.

Bridget was a strong-willed woman, but Eurielle didn't need to exert complete control over her. When Bridget saw Daniel look upon her, she understood his desire for her, and she was moved to pity even without Eurielle's help. She walked with Daniel through the wood. It took the barest nudge from Eurielle to extend Bridget's hand to hold Daniel's.

Lucifer followed them closely, seeking his moment.

"I thought you cared nothing for me," Daniel said.

"You are Jesus's cousin. How can I not care for you?"

He stopped, gripped her hand tightly, and pulled her closer. "Do you?"

Bridget hesitated, trembling, as if battling with Eurielle over their next move. "Uh…of course. Like a brother." She kissed his cheek.

"Like a brother? You mock me."

"No, it's just that…Jesus is the only one I can love."

"Jesus? He cannot love you. Did he not tell you that he is only partly a man? He is also fully divine. He cannot return your love. It is against his nature. You need to share your life with a man, not a god. You need a man who's fully a man." Daniel wrapped his arm around her waist and held her close. "A man like me." He covered her mouth with his.

Eurielle held Bridget in place so she would taste that sweet, hard kiss, though Bridget pushed back with her right hand while Eurielle clung to her left.

It was enough. The strength of Daniel's will, the piety of all those years of the Arimathean's tutelage, were crushed by the raw force of his lust. It was a scant beachhead, but Satan took it.

He tore off her cloak.

Bridget pulled away. "Daniel, stop!" Eurielle fled.

He reached for the laces of her bodice and pulled them halfway open.

Again, she cried out for Daniel to stop, and part of Daniel's soul cried out likewise. But he was no longer in control. He kicked her legs out from under her. His hands tore at her garments. Lucifer had him now.

The Devil sensed her horror. She would be feeling his hardness against her body. She must know he would try to enter her. She scratched at his face and screamed.

Lucifer continued to use Daniel, who remained helpless in the face of temptation. "You wanted her," Satan whispered to him. "This is the way to get her." Daniel's sense of decency crumbled beneath the hooves of his lust.

Her cries and her struggle, her fear and hatred fueled Satan's fire.

"We can do this," Satan whispered to Daniel's soul. "She led us on. She deserves anything she gets now. Besides, surely she'll learn to love you once she partakes of the pleasure of your body."

The hope embedded in that lie destroyed what remained of Daniel's will.

But a pair of bumpkins were to foil Lucifer's plan to destroy Daniel's soul and Bridget's in a single stroke. Two young men passing through the orchard heard her screams.

They grabbed Daniel's arms and dragged him off her. He stumbled, his ankles hobbled by his own garments.

Bridget jumped to her feet. Her skirt fell into place, covering her nakedness. She battered Daniel with her fist and spat on him. "You're an animal. You tried to rape me, a princess of the Belgae! My father will see you dead!" She threw a left jab to his gut.

"You wanted me." He groaned. "You kissed me before I even touched you."

It did not matter to the two young men whether Bridget had kissed Daniel or not. The scratches on his face and her desperate screams said it all. The Celts could be crude and boisterous in their revelries, but the word "no" coming from a woman meant exactly that.

Lucifer laughed silently. *Daniel is nothing but my toy now. I cannot wait to feast upon his soul when he joins me in hell!*

Jesus

Returning from Priddy the next morning, Jesus thought he could cheer everyone with his news. He had found another rich silver lode at the foot of the Mendip Hills, easy to reach from the cavern where the River Axe emerged on the surface. He had seen the ore itself after scraping away a layer of soft rock on the cave wall. He already had the samples he would need to prove his claim to Grengan.

Arriving at his mother's house, he found everyone in despair. Bridget was crying into Mother's arms behind the women's curtain. When Jesus tried to approach them, his mother decisively waved him away.

With his head in his hands, Uncle Joseph sat in the main area near the entrance. "I cannot believe what they say about my son," he moaned to Jesus. "They say he tried to rape Bridget. The young men who rescued her say he claimed she wanted him, but they heard her scream and saw the scratches she made on his face."

Jesus wrestled with this surreal news. *Daniel? Rape? Impossible!* "Will Elsigar charge him with a crime?"

"No. He said the druids do not punish any attempted crime, but that is not end of it. Bridget's father is powerful, the king of all the Belgae.

He will come after Daniel and kill him for the insult to the honor of his family. No one will lift a hand to stop him. Elsigar has declared Daniel an anathema. No one will talk to him, even if he does show himself."

"Daniel must have some explanation. Where is he?"

"Who knows? What explanation can there be? Even if she wanted him, as he claims, it is still a great sin for him to try to do what he attempted—fornication at the least. What could he have been thinking? He has thrown away his life—on a *goy!*"

"*Goy* or not, she's a child of God, too. From what you say, he tried to have carnal knowledge of her against her will. We Jews call that rape, even if the druids do not punish the attempt. A sin like that will corrupt his soul. But he is still my cousin and your son. He needs our help."

"He is no longer my son."

Jesus took a step back. "I curse his sin, Uncle, but I still love him. He has stood by me ever since the two of you came to Nazareth, when I was in peril there." He ran his fingers through his long, unkempt hair. "What could have gotten into him? The cousin I know would never do anything like this." He shook his head. Uncle Joseph remained silent, head in his hands. "He cannot stay in Ynys Witrin; he needs to get away before the Belgae come for him. Come with me, Uncle. Your son's very life is at stake."

Joseph groaned. "I meant what I said; he is no longer my son. Go look for him if you must."

Jesus walked to Wearyall, the ridge on the finger of land jutting out into the Brue. Daniel loved to sit in a clearing atop the ridge and look out to the Lake Village or across the marshlands. That is where he found him, pacing back and forth across the clearing.

"Daniel, what happened?" Jesus asked. "What got into you?"

"Did my father send you? What did he say?"

"He didn't send me. He says you are no longer his son. He told me that you tried to rape Bridget. I want to hear your side of it."

"Rape! That is a laugh. She wanted it."

"I hear the men who rescued Bridget said she was screaming for you to stop."

"They are lying."

"Those scratches on your face do not lie. I only saw her for a moment, but Bridget was distraught."

"Did they tell you she kissed me before I even touched her?"

"Even if she did, that does not mean she wanted you to know her carnally."

"It's not my fault the bitch changed her mind. That is how women are. They lead you on. They say no when they mean yes. But you would not know about that, would you, Divine One? Before you left to study with the druids, you said you could never love a woman as men do. You don't know what it is like to want one."

"I had nothing to do with this."

"You are the one she loves. If you had not led her on, she would know she could never have you. Then she would want me."

Daniel is blaming everyone but himself. "Look, Daniel, you need to pray and get yourself right with God."

"Don't tell me what to do."

"Even if what you say is true, you are still sinning against him. From the looks of you, you must have tried to force yourself on her. She may have wanted romance, but you gave her violence instead."

"Why did you come here, if I am such a sinner? You hate me." Daniel continued to pace across the clearing.

"Daniel, I could never hate you. We are like brothers. Stop pacing and sit down."

Daniel sat down on the log next to Jesus.

"We need to get you out of Britain before Bridget's father seeks you out."

"Where will we go?"

"We must make for Armorica. You will be under the protection of the Romans there." Jesus thought out the situation. *We cannot risk waiting for Kendrick to return. Bridget's father may be only days away to the east. Crossing the Sabrina to the land of the Silures is too risky; Arvigarus is my friend, but King Cymbeline will never risk war with the Belgae to protect Daniel. No, we must head west to Carn Roz, across the lands of the Dumnonii. That is unfamiliar territory to the Belgae, and that will slow them if they try to track us. Bannoch and Tilda will remember Daniel, and the people of the village still profit from the tin trade we started. They will help conceal us until we can secure passage to Armorica.*

Jesus looked up. Daniel was shaking his head. "I am not going to Armorica. We must stay in Britain."

"Bridget's father will come for you. He will hunt you down and kill you."

"Not if Bridget realizes that I am the one she really wants."

He must be deluded. "Daniel, look what she did to your face. I left her crying in my mother's arms because you distressed her so. What more must she do to convince you she does not want you?"

Daniel turned to Jesus with a smug expression. "She's feisty, all right. All that just makes me want her more."

Now it was Jesus's turn to get up and pace. He crossed the clearing, back and forth. "Daniel, they will kill you if you stay," Jesus shouted.

"You are going to die, too. You have finally heard about the real meaning of that prophecy. How you truly will die on the cross if the Romans crucify you."

How does he know this?

"We belong here in Britain now, you and I. There is nothing for us back in Israel, nor anywhere else in the Roman empire. If we go to Armorica, we will soon be on our way back to Judea or Galilee. You know where that path leads you—to crucifixion and death."

"I can come back here on my own once you are safe."

"That's beside the point." Daniel jumped up and came close. "Make Bridget love me. I know you can. I have never asked anything from you, but I know you are fully divine, just as you said, and you can do it. Think about it: with Bridget's family joined to ours, you can adopt the Britons as your own people."

"What are you talking about?"

"I know what is to become of the Britons. The Romans will come to stay, and when their empire finally crumbles, wave upon wave of barbarian invaders will torment and enslave these people."

How can he know this? Bridget swore she would not breathe a word of this to anyone.

"You can put a stop to that," said Daniel. "Adopt these people as your own, just as your Father in heaven adopted the Jews. With Bridget's hand joined to mine, we can restore the house of David here, in Britain, where the people will love us and not betray us, and where you will become known to these people as their god. We will stop the Romans on the beaches and secure the freedom of these people for ages to come. In time, we might even lead the Britons to smash the evil empire of the Romans. The emperors themselves will cringe in terror at your feet, Jesus."

"Daniel, how do you know this, about the Romans coming to these shores? Who told you?"

"No one. I…had a vision."

Father in heaven would never send a vision like that to anyone but me. Jesus looked his cousin over. *Someone must have told him, but if not Bridget or my Father, who?* Jesus looked deep into his cousin's eyes.

The answer that came to him was horrible, but it explained everything. "Satan has taken you." Jesus said, speaking deliberately and cautiously. "You have fallen into his traps of sin and death! If you do not turn from the Devil, then I cannot help you."

Daniel laughed insanely.

"Let the Devil take you," said Jesus, "and let the Belgae king come for you and kill you. I will not form a league with the Fallen One. I cannot help you if you do not turn to God. If you change your mind, you know where to find me. You do not have much time."

Lucifer

Down in hell, the Fallen One paused from his feasting on the souls of the unredeemed to dance a triumphant jig. *The keys of heaven are practically mine! I never imagined Jesus would abandon his cousin so quickly. He sees the corruption that lies in Daniel's heart. Surely he will realize soon the futility of trying to save these mortals.*

Bridget

By the time Jesus returned to Mary's house, Bridget had regained her composure. She was eating soup Mary had prepared.

Bridget saw Mary looking at her questioningly. Then she realized what concerned her. "It's all right," said Bridget. "Jesus is not like Daniel. He will not harm me. You can leave me with him."

Mary took the hint and left, saying she had something to do outside in the herb garden.

Jesus filled his own bowl at the hearth. "May I sit at the table with you?"

"Certainly." Bridget listlessly stirred the soup. "It's strange you feel the need to ask."

"I cannot imagine how violated you must feel. I would not blame you for wanting to be alone right now…or at least away from any man. I am sorry about Daniel. He has never done anything like this before."

"I know that you, your mother, and your uncle would have stopped it if you had known." *He actually cares about my feelings! For my father, this will be about the insult to the family pride. I am the one who was almost raped, but my father will feel that he is the one who was victimized because of the insult to his honor. But Jesus is not like any Celt; he understands how a woman feels.* "You are good people," she continued. "You have all been so kind to me."

"You are the one who has been good to me," said Jesus. "You fed me and took care of me when I was sick. My mother says she could barely have managed without you."

"It was nothing. I was here on a diplomatic mission for my father, anyway."

"Elsigar tells me that mission has been over for many months. With thanks in good measure to you, I am well and walking about. I have not needed nursing for weeks. And yet you remain."

"I do not want to leave. As I said, you are all good people—"

"Bridget, do you know what it means to really love someone?"

Is he going to declare his love for me? Please, I beg the gods, please let it be so! Outwardly, Bridget just sighed and looked confused. "What does it mean to you?"

"I think it means that you care for someone more than you care for yourself. Like the love between a mother and child."

Bridget looked into Jesus's eyes. *He is so gentle and caring. No one has ever talked to me like this.*

"I care for you deeply, Bridget. I owe you so much. But Bridget, I know what you want from me, and I cannot give you what you seek."

Bridget looked at him in shock, and then she had an idea. "Are you worried about marrying a gentile? I asked Mary whether someone could become Jewish, and she said it was rare, but it could be done. Later, I asked her about where one could find a rabbi, and she said that there were rabbis in Gaul. That's what I would need to do, find a rabbi to study with, right?"

"It would take you a year at least—"

"I will do it, whatever it takes."

"No, Bridget, you dear sweet woman. Marrying you as a gentile is the least of the problems—"

"Why, Jesus, why? You just said you cared about me deeply. I see that you do, more than any man I have known."

"I care deeply about you, but you know I am not like other men. A man and woman who join themselves in marriage become one flesh, but I share the nature of my divine father. I cannot join my flesh to the flesh of any mortal woman and make it one; it would be unnatural for me. I will always be grateful to you, but I cannot give you the romantic love you deserve."

"What are you going to do about the destiny your father has carved out for you? Are you going to submit to crucifixion? What about adopting the Britons as your people?"

Jesus shook his head. "I do not know. I think of Daniel, and it all feels so hopeless. I see this man, my cousin, whom I have loved as a brother. I see how weak and wicked he has become, and I do not know him anymore. It makes me think that giving myself up to the cross will be for nothing, that no one will remember me a few days after I am gone.

"Then I think about the good life I could have," Jesus continued. "I am skilled with the sword, and I want to use it for justice. I want people to be free, regardless of whether they are Britons or Jews. I could go back to Israel and be the Messiah for my people, just as I always imagined…as the new King David, fighting to free my people from Roman oppression. Or I could stay here and adopt the Britons as my own people, and I could fight to preserve their freedom, just as you said. The path *is* mine to choose."

"Why not do that? Fight for the Jews or fight for the Britons. You will win and become the hero of the people, either here or in Judea and Galilee. Give us freedom."

"I think about that all the time now, but my Father said something else that night on the Tor. He said that by giving myself up to the cross, I would bring the hope of salvation to the world. He did not say how, and it sounds crazy to me, but it makes me wonder about the easier path, about fulfilling my birthright as the son of David. I think I can free people from Roman oppression, but then I ask myself who will free the people—the Jews or the Celts—from the wages of death and sin. I do not know right now what I must do."

The two of them sat in an awkward silence for a few minutes.

"Bridget, I think I was just too blind to see this, but there is nothing for you here now. I cannot offer what you seek from me. The time has come for you to go. You must return to your own people."

Bridget looked into Jesus's eyes. "I suppose you are right, but let me ask you for something. It will make my heart easier when I think about the future of the Britons."

"What is it?" Jesus asked.

"If you decide to obey your father, will you send to Britain word of how we can find salvation from death and sin through your sacrifice? Will you promise me this?"

"Oh, Bridget, of course I promise. I will never forget the kindness of the Britons. I make this solemn pledge: if I am unable to come myself, I will send a messenger to you."

Lucifer

Satan gnashed his teeth. He had not expected Jesus to concern himself so much with Bridget. *She will leave him, at least for now, but what if she returns? What if Jesus sees hope for these miserable mortal creatures through her?* The Devil knew he had to do something more than he had with Daniel. There must be another mortal who could be turned to death and sin—someone who could expose all the wickedness of the human spirit to Jesus and make him realize the hopelessness of trying to save them from themselves.

The Fallen One looked over the Levels and beyond, and he saw another mortal who would serve perfectly. He almost danced another jig of celebration. A runaway slave who had taken up brigandry. Even better, the slave-turned-brigand already bore hatred for Jesus. Satan had set his gaze on Pirro.

Chapter 17
Arrows of Desire

Pirro

"I did not come all this way to Ynys Witrin to raid a few farm houses," shouted Pirro, stomping his foot. "I seek a bigger prize." He looked over his motley band of a dozen brigands. "We must wait and watch for our chance. My old master and his family have silver, enough to make us all rich, but they will guard it even more closely if they suspect robbers are about. I do not care if this house is unguarded. The people are poor, and we must leave it be—for now."

Reinventing myself has been easier than I ever thought possible. Yes, they snarl at me when I tell them to leave the farmhouses alone, but they will follow me anywhere. That is not too bad for a man who's been a trader in Celtic junk and then a slave, eh?

The hunchback with five missing teeth shook his head. "It would be better to sack the farmhouses. We could spend weeks waiting for something better, and all that time we run the risk of capture." He scratched his shaggy gray hair. "Besides, if Jesus bar whatsit and his lot have all that silver, then surely they'll conceal and protect it."

"Jesus and his family do not care," said Pirro. "I saw Jesus work his magic digging for tin, and it is easy for him to find the lodes of ore. They do not think to guard their hoards because they are so easy to replace." *The hunchback makes a good point, but it does not matter. I would have made myself rich during the battle at Rumps, but Jesus foiled me. He dared to pass judgment on me and condemn me to suffer. I will have my revenge. These men need not know that I care nothing about the silver—or about them, for that matter.*

"I tell you," he said, "Jesus has more silver stashed away than you can possibly imagine. Score this one robbery with me, and you will have more than enough to live at ease for the rest of your lives."

Pirro's words failed to silence the hunchback, and a few of his cohorts started to look as if he was beginning to persuade them. *The man is tiresome, and he is not much use in a fight anyway.* Pirro drew his sword, and with one swift stroke he cleaved the hunchback's head from his broken torso. He looked over his followers. "Does anyone else have a question about what we're doing?"

Daniel

The druids gathered once again for the festival of Beltane, to call Mother Earth back to life. At first, Daniel stayed at the edge of the crowd, covering his head with his cloak so no one would recognize him. Only two days had passed since his failed attempt to make Bridget his. If he were recognized, all would shun him, or worse.

He searched the crowd for Bridget. Surely she would be at this important festival, but she was not among her people. Then he spotted her, sitting with Jesus, the two of them off by themselves. Daniel concealed himself behind a bush to eavesdrop.

"Have you decided what you will do?" Bridget asked.

"Elsigar tried to convince me to become a druid," Jesus said with a rueful smile. "When I told him what my Father in heaven wants of me, he said our one god was far too demanding. Maybe Elsigar has a point."

Bridget laughed softly. "That's the first time I have ever seen you smile."

"It is another path open to me, I suppose, though I do not think I am ready to give myself over to paganism."

"If you really believe your Father is the creator of the universe, then maybe you should trust him and go back to your homeland. This sacrifice he asks of you: doesn't he say it will be the key to the hope of salvation for the whole world?"

"Is that what you believe now, Bridget?"

"If I did not believe it, and if I did not believe that you share his divine substance, I would never leave you. I do not know why I believe it, but I do."

"Maybe the Holy Spirit is doing a good work in you, but if you believe, then you must obey the commandments. You cannot worship pagan gods."

"Mary taught me what the law of Moses says about that. It will be hard on my father." She hung her head and sighed. "I do not think my people will ever accept me as their queen if I abandon the druidic gods. If this sacrifice of yours can be the hope of salvation for all nations, not just the Jews, then we must put that ahead of our own hopes for happiness."

"I do not know if I can, Bridget. Ever since I was a small child, I have thought I would follow the path of my ancestor King David to secure my people's freedom. I thought that was my role as the Messiah. That is what made me love it here in Britain, to see your people so free. I love the idea that people should live free. My Father wants me to give that up, not only for myself, but also to know the death and destruction that awaits my people and yours. If I follow my Father's bidding, I head to the most painful and shameful death imaginable. If I die that way, I die not knowing if anyone but my mother and my great uncle will care anything about me even a week after. I will die doubting my own sanity."

"Let's not think about that now." She gripped his arm. "Do not forget the promise you made to me. I have almost finished packing, and my retinue will be here tomorrow to take me home."

He covered her hand with his. "I will never forget, Bridget. I say that not just for your sake, but out of love for all the Britons. If I go back and give myself over to death, I will see to it that word gets back to the people here: how they can claim that sacrifice to free themselves from death and sin."

Daniel gnashed his teeth as he watched Jesus hold Bridget's hand. *If she will not worship the druidic gods, it is death for her to go back to her people—but Jesus does not care! He wants her for himself. Just look at how he clings to her. I must save her from this madness. Then she will understand that her future lies with me.*

Pirro

Pirro's brigands, sent to spy on the Beltane festivities, returned late that night with a cloaked man bound and gagged. They shoved him to the ground at Pirro's feet. "The dark-bearded outlander," the tall one growled. "We saw him leave by himself once the festival ended."

A smoldering fire provided some warmth in the cool air, but Pirro made sure that his men kept the fire small so as not to draw attention.

Pirro approached, wielding his sword. He lightly scratched Daniel's face, drawing a thin trickle of blood. "You are not so high and mighty as you were back at Rumps, are you?" Pirro had his men remove the gag, but Daniel maintained a stoic silence. "What should I do with you now? It would be fun to just run this sword right through you, and then there would be one less Jew—"

"He will be worth something to his family," a youngish Celt named Waylin interjected. "If he is related to that Jesus fellow, they will pay us a nice ransom."

"His family disowned him," said the tall one. "I heard people talk about it at the festival. They say he tried to rape the daughter of the Belgae king."

"That's too bad," said Pirro. "I was thinking of selling him as a slave, just the way his cousin did to me. But if the Belgae king is on his way to seek revenge, I do not suppose anyone will buy him at the slave market. Has anyone heard whether the Belgae are offering a reward for this man's skin?" None of the band members responded. "I do not suppose they will pay much. Their king will probably figure that he is pretty much dead anyway once he hears that we have him. Maybe I should just start by cutting off his balls."

"I bet he knows where his family keeps the silver. If he wants to live he can take us there," said the tall one.

Pirro turned to Daniel and drew another trickle of blood from his cheek. "What have you to say to that? Show us where your father and Jesus keep the silver, and maybe I will let you live." *Or maybe I will kill him anyway, once I have the silver.*

"I do not care what you do with me," muttered Daniel. "Kill me if you want. That will not give you revenge on Jesus, and it will not get you the silver."

"That's easy to arrange." Pirro raised his sword.

"Hear me out. There is a way to get what you want, both revenge and the silver."

What deception is he up to? He still thinks I am a fool. It would be better to dispatch him now and be done with him. Pirro raised his sword higher, but the shouts of his men stayed his hand. They wanted to hear how they could get their hands on the silver.

"Jesus pretends he is sending this princess away tomorrow, but he wants her for himself. If you want revenge, then waylay this woman on the road tomorrow and turn her over to me. Give me the woman he holds most dear."

"That's an interesting notion," said Pirro. "Giving Jesus's woman to the man she accused of trying to rape her."

"Who cares which bastard she wants," said a stout red-headed fellow. "She is only a woman, and I do not care about taking revenge on this Jesus fellow. How will taking her and turning her over to this fool get us any closer to the silver?"

"Once I have the princess," said Daniel, "I will take you to the silver. But without her, I lead you nowhere, even if you do your worst. She is all that I live for."

The arguments went on through the night. Despite describing in gruesome detail the horrible death that lay in store for Daniel, Pirro and his thugs were unable to intimidate him into showing them the location of the silver without first capturing Bridget for him. Reluctantly, they finally agreed to do as he wished.

Daniel

Daniel watched the road like an animal stalking its prey. He and Pirro's men had concealed themselves in dense woodland near a turn. Pirro had provided him with a sword and shield. The princess and her retainers would have to come this way towards Pilton Hollow and then on to the east to the lands of the Belgae; this was the only road in that direction. Daniel and Pirro's men would have the advantage of surprise. Bridget's retainers had no reason to expect an attack in the sacred precinct of the Tor. The worst part of the wait was listening to the tawdry jokes the brigands made at Daniel's expense, about his love for Bridget.

Finally, the royal wagon emerged, accompanied by three riders. The wagon itself was little more than a four-wheel cart drawn by a team of horses, with a driver seated in front. A thick cloth canopy surrounded the space where Bridget would be sitting, protecting her from the sun and the curiosity of onlookers.

This seemed almost too easy. Bridget's riders appeared relaxed in the saddle, joking among themselves, oblivious to the men hiding in the vegetation.

Daniel felt a rush of excitement as the wagon reached the turn in the road. He imagined Bridget's body against his own, as he thought about making her his. Shutting his eyes, he ravished her in his mind.

Pirro's shout, his command to attack, startled Daniel from his reverie. The brigands struck first with arrows that whistled through the air all around him. Bridget's wagon driver had no chance to react. An arrow pierced his throat. One rider fell from his horse, wounded by an arrow through his thigh. Pirro and his men engaged the other two riders with swords. The wagon lurched as the horses began to panic. Daniel charged forward, jumped up next to the fallen wagon-driver, and grabbed the reins to control the horses.

Pirro and his men drove the two remaining riders away from the wagon. Seizing the opportunity to grab Bridget, Daniel jumped off the driver's seat and drew back the canopy, eagerly anticipating her boundless joy at his rescuing her.

An anguished cry pierced the woods. After a moment, Daniel realized it came from his own throat.

Bridget lay silent, slumped on her cushions. A single arrow, one of the volley loosed by Pirro's men but given flight through Daniels desire, had pierced Bridget's breast.

Daniel climbed into the wagon next to her, holding her in his lap as she breathed her last. His tormented wailing shredded his throat.

Pirro and the other brigands abandoned the fight and ran. Of course they ran. A royal princess was dead, murdered in the sacred precinct of the Tor. The clamor would be raised against them swiftly and surely. If caught, they would be shown no mercy.

Lucifer

From the depths of hell, the Fallen One chortled in delight. This was no longer a case of assault or attempted rape. Jesus's cousin had committed murder. Though Daniel was not the bowman, those arrows had been launched by his own lust and fury. It scarcely mattered that Satan had used that lust to subdue Daniel's better nature, or that Pirro would not have sought out Jesus without Satan's prompting. Lucifer had only drawn on the already-existing flaws in their souls.

Surely, now Jesus will see the depths of his own cousin's depravity. If this man so beloved by Jesus could be so depraved, what hope will Jesus ever find for the rest of creation, peopled by souls who are strangers to him?

Just one more little piece of work remained. Only madness shielded Daniel from realizing the import of his actions. Rather than leave him in that blissfully ignorant state, the Devil abandoned Daniel. Regaining his sanity brought the torment and self-loathing that Lucifer expected would last through the end of his days. *His life will not last long now, and his soul—when it makes its way down to hell for me to feast upon—will be the tastier for all its guilt and suffering.*

Grengan

Like all vital matters that crossed the divide between the secular and spiritual, the fate of the outlander required a discussion between the king and the archdruid. Elsigar had come to Grengan's home in the Lake Village. "Have you talked to him?" Elsigar asked.

"We've talked, but I still do not understand what happened," Grengan said. "Nor does Daniel himself understand why he did these things. He seems as horrified as we are. For all the time they have been with us, I never suspected he had it in him to commit rape and murder, and you have known him even longer from your days among the Dumnonii."

Elsigar sighed. "He was only fifteen summers old when he came to Britain, and though he was foolhardy like any youth of that age, I never saw a trace of deceit or meanness in his character. I have seen him grow into the most sober of men."

"What does the family say?"

"His father has disowned him," Elsigar replied. "I stopped at the family house on the way here, but I did not have the heart to intrude upon their grief. I did call Jesus away; he will be here anon."

"They can still remain in Britain, can they not?"

"They are outlanders, and there has been much spiritual disorder around them of late. Let us not forget the changes wrought in the Tor while Jesus was alone at the summit. I am convinced he did not practice any dark magic, but he told me that he provoked the wrath of his god. And now a princess is dead."

"This family brought prosperity to the people, and we should not forget how Daniel and Jesus both fought for the freedom of the Dumnonii," said Grengan.

"I am not sure how long they will want to stay among us, anyway. Jesus told me his god wants him to return to his homeland, although he seems loath to do so."

They fell silent at the sound of footsteps on the deck. Jesus came into the room. Grengan stood to greet him. "We are talking about what to do with Daniel. We seem to have no good options. He must be put to death for the murder of the princess."

"Did he shoot the arrow that killed her?" Jesus asked.

"Daniel was not one of the archers," said Grengan.

"He joined in the plot, so it does not matter. Under the law they are all guilty, no matter which one loosed the arrow," said Elsigar.

"Did any of them intend to slay the princess?" Jesus asked. "He wanted her to be his woman, and in his madness he thought she loved him, too. They had no reason to kill her."

"That too does not matter," said Elsigar. "They attacked her wagon, slew her driver, and wounded her guards. It is hard to believe all of that was an accident." Elsigar shook his head. "In any case, Daniel is an outlander. For him to take up arms in the sacred precinct of the Tor merits the punishment of death."

"This is not just a local matter. A princess of the Belgae is dead," said Grengan. "If we are not careful, we might provoke them. Wars have started for less. We must summon the kings and chief druids of the Silures and the Dumnonii to determine what to do, since we maintain our neutrality under their protection."

"I can speak for the druids, unless others decide to come," said Elsigar.

"May I speak with Daniel now, please?" asked Jesus.

Grengan looked to Elsigar, and the archdruid raised no objection. "However, I would not hold out much hope that you can do anything for him. He has committed murder and brigandry. I think he is sorry for what he did, but that does not change the nature of his crimes. I will tell the guards to let you see him whenever you like. You will have a few days at most before his punishment is imposed."

Jesus

Jesus rode on horseback to the place where Grengan's men held Daniel. It was halfway to Priddy, near a place called Wookey Hole where the River Axe emerged on the surface from subterranean caverns. Jesus heard the guards as he approached. At first, it sounded like the typical Celtic revelry fueled by an excess of mead, but as he drew nearer it became clear that they were taunting the prisoner. Jesus closed his eyes. *It sounds so much like the jeers of the Roman soldiers that I hear when I envision my crucifixion.*

The jeers stopped once the guards saw Jesus.

They had Daniel, bound and gagged, at the bottom of a twenty-foot sinkhole. Archers watched from the rim, ready to shoot him dead if he made any move to escape.

"Can you remove his gag?" Jesus asked. "Grengan said I could speak with him."

"You can remove it yourself when you get down to him," the captain answered. "Just don't loosen anything else. These archers have orders to shoot quickly if there is any move to escape. You can use the ladder, but we will pull it up behind you."

A guard lowered a ladder into the pit.

"May I bring him some water? He looks in need of it."

The guard pointed to a nearby bucket and cup. Jesus climbed down the ladder to Daniel, and the guards then pulled it up. Ropes held Daniel tightly in a sitting position. Jesus told him what he was about to do, and then he removed the gag. It took a few moments for Daniel to clear his throat and stop coughing.

Jesus sat next to his cousin. "Let me know when you need more water. How long have they kept you like this?"

"Since they captured me. You are the only one who has come to see me besides Grengan. He said they would have to put me to death for murder, but he seemed sad about it."

"Elsigar is very sad, too."

"What about my father? I do not suppose he feels any kinder toward me, now that I have committed murder. Does he still disown me?"

"I am sure he is heartbroken." Jesus hesitated. "But he does not talk of you."

"I am dead to him already. I cannot say I blame him. I do not know even myself, Jesus." Daniel began to cry. "I desired her from the moment

I laid eyes on her, but I do not understand what made me attack her. I am not like that!"

"I knew you would never do such a thing, even when you grabbed her the first time."

"I remember doing all those things, but I do not understand the madness that drove me. It was more than lust. I could not think straight. I even thought you wanted Bridget for yourself. Everything seems so crazy."

"This is not the first time a young woman has turned your head."

"But I have never lost control that way. I wish I had never touched Bridget, but I know I did, and she died because of my actions, and now I will pay the price. I cannot even beg for mercy. The deeds I have done deserve death. I am so wretched. Not just for incurring the punishment I face, but also because what I did was so sinful and wrong. I would give anything to make things right."

Jesus brought another cup of water to Daniel's lips. "Satan drove you to this madness. When I searched you out the other night at Wearyall, I saw how he possessed your mind. He led you to this evil, and now he has abandoned you to face the consequences on your own."

"It is so horrible, Jesus. I cannot drive away the awful memories. It was I who did those acts, but it was like watching someone else. I never wanted to do such evil."

"Let us pray together for God's compassion."

"What can God do for me now? If he is just, he will know that what I have done requires punishment."

"He sees beyond that. He sees your desires and all that you truly are. This sinkhole reminds me of how the prophet Daniel was thrown into the lions' den. Nothing is impossible for God, and he is a God of infinite compassion and mercy."

"That is not how you felt about him when you came down from the Tor."

"I will deal with God's destiny for me in good time. Right now, let us pray for God's mercy for you." Jesus prayed with Daniel for several hours, stopping only to bring him more water every so often.

Maybe Daniel is right about my feelings toward my Father. Come to think of it, this is the first time that I have prayed since I came down from the Tor. Actually, it is the first time I have even tried. I want to bare my soul to God and ask his mercy for Daniel, but for the first time in my life, I feel he is not listening. I feel so lonely, abandoned, and forsaken.

Jesus continued until he was unable to bear the pain any longer. He embraced Daniel. "I must go now, but I will be back. Your fate rests with Father in Heaven. I cannot promise you much, but I promise you one thing, Daniel. You have been my dearest friend through everything. I love you and I will stay with you until the end. No matter what happens, you will not die alone. You will have me there praying for you."

Jesus stepped back. Daniel's face was wet with tears, and Jesus felt dampness on his own. When he summoned the guards to lower the ladder, one of them came down to secure the gag and to make sure the bonds were tight.

Jesus climbed the ladder and sought out the captain. "Can you remove the bonds and the gag from my cousin? I know you must prevent his escape, but there is no way for him to get out of that sinkhole without the ladder. Your men guard him constantly from the rim, ready to shoot if he makes a move."

"He's a murderer, and our own lives are forfeit if he escapes."

"He is not the same man as when he did those things. The Devil possessed him to make him commit those crimes, and has now abandoned Daniel to wallow in his guilt and misery. My cousin is truly sorry. Even if he deserves death for his actions, there is still good in him. You would not be so cruel to an animal in binding him that way, and my cousin is so much more. He will not run, even if he gets the chance, and I pledge my own life to you that he will not even try."

"Very well. Let this be on your head as well." With that, the captain sent the same guard down into the pit to remove the ropes and gag. He also sent down the leftovers from the guards' midday meal.

Jesus watched to see Daniel loosed from his gag and bonds, and then he rode his horse down the valley of the River Axe. The Tor came into view across the marshlands of the Levels. It was late afternoon, and there was abundant light for Jesus to make out the new elongated shape of the base and the distinct ridges with which God the Father had transformed the Tor into a monument to remind Jesus of his sadness and anger. Jesus dismounted, allowed his horse to graze, and began to walk slowly across the wetland, wading through the standing water.

Stopping after a few moments, he raised his arms. "How dare you, Father?" he cried out. "It was not enough that you condemn me to crucifixion! You allowed Satan to corrupt and possess Daniel, and now he is condemned, too! You know there is good in him, and yet you forsake him to the Devil. Is it not enough for you to condemn me to death and pain and shame? Must you also hurt those I love?"

Jesus lowered his arms and dropped to his knees. His tears flowed freely. *I am even angrier now than when I faced my Father at the summit of the Tor.*

Chapter 18
Stonehenge

Jesus

Jesus visited Daniel again the next day, and as he climbed out of Daniel's prison sinkhole, Arvigarus was waiting for him.

He explained to Jesus that Cymbeline had sent him to represent the Silures because the king was too ill for the journey, and Guiderius was away on a diplomatic mission to the Ordovices tribe in northern Cymru.

"Did you come to speak to my cousin?" Jesus asked him.

"Elsigar said it would be better to wait for the Dumnonii to arrive before we question Daniel," said Arvigarus. "I thought it would be good to see you, and they said I would find you here."

"It is good to see you, but of course you understand that this is a difficult time for us."

"I am sorry about Pirro. If I had not pushed you into taking him, he would have just died instead of creating all this trouble. I doubt Daniel would have attacked the princess's wagon on his own."

"You had no way of knowing what would happen," said Jesus. "I freed Pirro on the way to Ynys Lawd. I could have chosen to let him die then, too, and none of this would have happened." *I do not want to go over everything that happened with Melchior on Ynys Lawd.* "My people believe that there is a fallen angel, the Devil, who creates evil in the world. Daniel's sin was the cunning work of that Devil. I think the Devil took Daniel first, and when he found Pirro, used him, too. We cannot keep wondering about what might have happened because of Pirro. If he had not been around, the Devil would have found someone else to use."

"Will you be able to manage without Daniel? Everyone thinks well of you and hopes your family will stay in Ynys Witrin."

"God wants me to return to Galilee, but I do not think I can."

"How can you defy your god?"

When Jesus did not respond, Arvigarus asked, "This started that night when the Tor was reshaped, did it not? I remember something your mother said: that your god would surely look after his son." Arvigarus paused, but Jesus kept his silence. "I think you would have to be his son to defy him that way. There are things only a son would get away with. Fathers have a way of forgiving their sons. My father forgave Guiderius for slaying Clotten, the man he had picked to marry my sister. And a few weeks ago I told my father that I was giving up my druidic studies; he was very angry with me at first, but then he forgave me."

"It is not the same," Jesus answered. "I would have done anything, even given my life, in any fight to free my people, but my Father in heaven wants me to die in pain and shame. He will have my own people turn on me and then will cause their destruction after I am dead."

Arvigarus thought before responding. "If that is what he has been planning for you from the start, it is hard to see how he can do any worse to you."

Jesus smiled. "I had not thought of it that way."

"Stay in Britain, then. Think of all the great adventures we can have."

Jesus became serious again. "That stage of my life is over. For all my life, I have always felt connected to my Father in heaven, knowing he shares in all my joys. Now he wants to send me to a place I do not wish to go, and I feel adrift. The joys and pleasures of this world mean nothing to me now."

"I think I must be troubling you. I will go."

"Thank you, Arvigarus. It was good to talk with you. I need to pray for my cousin now."

The next day, Fergus arrived from Castle An Dinas to speak for the Dumnonii. Fergus, Arvigarus, and Elsigar, forming the tribunal, sat in three chairs that had been set side-by-side on a wooden platform built especially for Daniel's trial. A crowd of local people gathered before the tribunal. Faces were terribly serious, reflecting the gravity of the situation. Daniel sat inside a wattle cage. *Apparently it is not their procedure to let him speak in his own defense.* Uncle Joseph stood at the rear of the crowd, listening silently with storm clouds in his eyes.

Patiently, the tribunal heard everyone who had anything to say—everyone but Daniel. The riders from Bridget's procession described in detail what had happened that day. When it was Jesus's turn to speak, he argued fervently that everyone knew Daniel would never have committed these crimes of his own volition; they must have been the handiwork of the Devil. He testified how Daniel, as a prisoner, genuinely bewailed the crimes. "He is back to his former self," Jesus claimed.

The tribunal retired to a nearby house to consider its decision.

Jesus could tell that for most in the crowd it was a simple case. They believed that Daniel was clearly guilty of murder, which called for the imposition of a slow, painful death. They grew impatient as minutes and then hours dragged by.

Mary was the only one to stay near Daniel, who waited, closely guarded, in his cage. *Mother is so kind. Look how courageous she is. If I allow the Romans to crucify me, it will be so much worse for her. How can I permit that to happen to her?*

Jesus walked up to Daniel frequently, trying to offer encouragement and hope. *The situation is hopeless, but maybe I can distract Daniel from thinking about it. Maybe he will pray with me. This is so hard, but I promised I would be with him to the end.*

Uncle Joseph never approached Daniel, keeping his head down and talking to no one as he awaited the judgment.

He keeps saying Daniel is no longer his son, but I know more than his pride is hurting. He looks as if he wants to be alone for now.

It was early evening when the three members of the tribunal emerged from the house where they had been deliberating. They took their places on the platform, and Elsigar spoke for all the members: "We know that in the eyes of Jews we are barbaric pagans, but there is not one of us who does not wish to show mercy and compassion to this outlander accused of the dreadful crimes of murder and brigandry. Grengan and I have seen him grow into manhood, and we know the truth in what Jesus said on his behalf. The prisoner has helped to bring prosperity to the people, and he risked his own life to help defend the freedom of the Dumnonii. Outlander that he is, and guilty as he is of horrible crimes, he has done much to prove himself a friend and a good person.

"On the other hand, the law is clear, particularly in this sacred precinct of the Tor. The punishment for murder and brigandry is a slow and painful death. Only by enforcing these laws can we maintain the neutrality of this sacred precinct, which is so vital to the welfare of the people and to the proper worship of our gods at Samhain. In this case, the victim is a princess and ambassador of the king of the Belgae. If we show mercy to the prisoner, that king will rightly feel insulted and will certainly set about waging war against the Silures and the Dumnonii. If we impose our judgment today, we have to follow the law and impose the punishment of painful death. That execution is not as barbaric as those used by the so-called civilized Romans, but it is nonetheless a dreadful death by flame.

"In our deliberations we decided to afford the prisoner a thread of hope. It is a thread so thin that we debated for several hours whether it would not be kinder just to end the matter here and now with that death sentence. The mercy we would show is not ours rightly to give. However, this matter is not only a crime against the Dumnonii and the Silures; it is also, of course, a crime against the king of the Belgae. We have decided to submit this case to him rather than decide it ourselves. Although he is unlikely to do so, he is the only one who can grant mercy. We leave at dawn tomorrow to bring the prisoner before King Aghamore. The prisoner's family will come with us."

Joseph

The journey was three days, a long horseback ride but not physically challenging. Grengan and Elsigar tried to spare the family any indignities as they passed the hill forts and villages. Elsigar made a point to send word to every settlement along the way that there was to be no jeering at the prisoner. Nonetheless, it was hard for Joseph to see the curious onlookers without a sense of shame for what his son had done. *He is no longer any son of mine; he is dead to me. I already sat Shiva to mourn when he tried to rape the woman, but these people will not understand that. They will think all Jewish people are cutthroats and murderers. He has shamed all the Jewish people, and through them God Almighty.*

Halfway there, a runner arrived with word that King Aghamore would meet them at Stonehenge rather than his seat at the Sarum hill fort.

Joseph spurred his horse alongside Elsigar's. "Stonehenge is a pagan monument," Joseph said. "I will not participate in a pagan ritual, even on pain of death."

"You have no reason for concern," said Elsigar. "We are not monument builders, as you well know. We conduct our rituals in forest glens. We believe the *Fir Bolg* built the site before the *Tuatha Dé Danann* arrived in the Celtic lands. It is useful for tracking the seasons, and we preserve it out of respect for the earlier people. But it is no longer a place of worship."

"Then why meet there?"

Elsigar shrugged. "Perhaps King Aghamore does not want your people in his home. Or perhaps he chose it because it's easy to find."

The procession from Ynys Witrin found King Aghamore's court arrayed across the field before Stonehenge. Several tents were set up on the near side of the field for the visitors, and everyone else busied themselves claiming their spots. Elsigar rode alone to the Belgae as the ambassador of the Dumnonii and the Silures.

Joseph found a tent for Mary, Jesus, and himself. He moved his belongings in from the carts and then stayed inside, still feeling shame. Mary came and went frequently. Joseph did not ask where she had been; he assumed that she and Jesus were still attending to Daniel, and he did not want to hear that name spoken.

The time for the evening meal approached. "Uncle, you should get something to eat," Mary said. "You have not eaten for two days."

"I'll eat whatever you bring," he said, but she tugged his arm and dragged him outside.

"I will not have you behave like an ungrateful guest," she hissed. "Come see what they have done."

It was a strange affair. The Belgae had laid out food for the visitors, but were not joining in themselves. Joseph surmised that while the imminence of the execution dampened the customary Celtic enthusiasm for revelry, the occasion still called for the Belgae to extend their hospitality. Joseph passed by the meats and contented himself with a selection of savory cakes, vegetables, and cheese. While he ate, it occurred to him that he had not seen Jesus since their arrival.

Grengan and Fergus joined Joseph at his table. Joseph nodded his greeting to them, and they kept to their silence, seeming to respect his desire to keep to himself. Joseph finished his meal and excused himself. He had not seen Jesus at the dining tables.

Joseph walked toward the wattle cage where the guards still watched over Daniel. He wanted to check if Jesus was there, but he did not want to approach too near. He drew close enough to make out the figures of Mary and the guards, but not Jesus. Joseph returned to the tent.

Sometime later—he knew not how long, for he was adrift in meditation—Mary poked her head in. "Are you hiding in here again?" She shook her head. "It is not like you to keep to yourself."

He sighed. "Have you seen Jesus?"

"Not since he asked me to bring his things to the tent." Mary studied him. "Will you come?"

"How can I be sociable now?"

She lowered her eyes, nodded, and left him alone.

As night fell, Joseph heard Elsigar return. Mary came in a short time later. "They say the Belgae king is still at his seat at Sarum."

"That's ten miles away," Joseph said.

"Elsigar had to ride there and back, but the arrangements have all been made. Aghamore will arrive early in the afternoon."

Then Grengan and Fergus will hand over Daniel for Aghamore's judgment, and the king will hear from anyone who has anything to say. Which should include Jesus. But where is he?

Just before dawn, Joseph was startled out of his restless sleep by Jesus entering the tent.

"Where have you been? Your mother and I have been worried."

"Let us go outside so we do not awaken Mother." Jesus led Joseph to a lonely campfire. The flames had died away, but the embers still glowed. Jesus placed another log on the fire. "I went to see King Aghamore. He received me after Elsigar left, but Elsigar does not know this."

"Why would you do that? The trial is not until tomorrow."

"I hoped to redeem Daniel's life."

"What do you mean by that?"

"As a child learning from the rabbi at Nazareth, I heard something about the laws under King Solomon. If a man is to be enslaved for debt, someone can redeem him from slavery by paying his debt. At Ynys Môn, I found the Celts have a broader provision under their laws. Anyone can go to the family of the victim of a crime and offer them a fine. If the fine is accepted, the prisoner must be freed."

"What happened between you and King Aghamore?"

"He received me kindly, even when I told him my purpose in coming to see him. It gave me hope that I might persuade him. I told him of the goodness that I had always seen in Daniel, and then I offered him everything you put aside for Daniel and me all these years as the fine for the slaying of his daughter."

"Did he accept it?"

"He said he died the day he heard of Bridget's death. He said there is not enough money in the world to deny his daughter the justice she deserves."

"Was there anything else?"

Jesus nodded as tears welled in his eyes. "I tried to tell him that all of us would give anything to bring his daughter back to him, but that executing Daniel would never restore her. He answered me so kindly, I knew my cause was hopeless. He said he was sorry for the loss of my cousin. I knew then that he was not acting because of any insult to his family honor but out of love for his daughter, just as I wanted to save Daniel because of my love for him."

"You should not have done this. Daniel is no longer a member of this family. You had no right to interfere. Daniel's fate is for the Britons to decide under their law."

"You have the right to say that Daniel is no longer your son, but he is still my cousin. He has been my best friend and constant companion ever since the day we left Galilee. Daniel succumbed to the Devil in a moment of weakness. The same weakness to desires affects all mortal men."

"Like all men, my son was free to choose between good and evil. He chose the path of evil, and he must now pay the consequences."

"On the night I was alone with my Father on the Tor, he said that through my death on the cross of crucifixion, I could redeem the whole world from sin. Did you hear that, Uncle? He said that my death would be the hope for redemption for everyone, not just the few, not just the strongest or the worthiest, but everyone. Daniel has always been a good and righteous man, until he fell into sin for one short period, for which he most sincerely repents. I have now done everything I can to redeem him." Jesus gritted his teeth and clenched his hair in his hands. "If I cannot redeem just one righteous man, how can I possibly redeem the whole world?"

"No one can know how God works his will. You are called to a great trial, Jesus, as much as any prophet of old. Did Jonah imagine that God would find a way to release him from the belly of that whale? I am sure Jonah thought his situation was as hopeless as you feel yours is right now, and yet God heard his voice and found the way to save him. I have lived all my life in obedience to God. You must decide for yourself if you will do the same."

Lucifer

Once again, the Fallen One made his way to heaven to confront God the Father on his throne. "I see you still think you can trick me. You know that Jesus will never surrender himself to death for the love of you, and so you use his love for his cousin. You just used the Arimathean to extend him hope that his death might still redeem that cousin of his."

God considered what the Devil had said. "I might concede the point. After all, what credit would it be to Jesus to give of himself for someone he loves and who has always loved him? So, let us say that I take away any hope Jesus might have for Daniel. Instead, Jesus must make his choice to surrender himself to death for the sake of someone he despises."

"That will never happen," said Satan.

"If Jesus does that, will you in turn concede that he is unblemished, and that his sacrifice on the cross of crucifixion is worthy to seal a new covenant with my people?"

The Devil considered his choice. *It seems fair, but if I concede the righteousness of the sacrifice I will end up consumed in my own fires at the end of all things. It matters not. The boy does not have the strength to sacrifice himself if God removes any hope for Daniel.* "Fine, it is done," Satan answered.

Jesus

In the morning, the Belgae laid out another splendid meal for the travelers, but Jesus was not hungry. *Our hosts do not partake because they know this is no occasion for revelry.*

Going to the cage, Jesus put his hand through an opening in the wattle, and the two cousins clasped hands for some time without speaking. Jesus took back his hand and dipped his finger in a small vessel of oil he had brought with him. He spread the oil upon Daniel's forehead, and then led Daniel in a prayer, asking God in Heaven for forgiveness. *Daniel seems comforted, but I am not. I call to my Father, but I hear nothing.*

"Daniel, I need to pray by myself for a while. King Aghamore will arrive, and your trial will begin anon. I will be in the crowd praying for you. I will be there through the end, and you will not be alone." Jesus put his hand through the opening, and the cousins clasped hands again. Turning away, Jesus saw his mother approach to take his place. She had food with her and a moist cloth to wipe Daniel's face. *Mother always knows what to do for those who suffer.*

Jesus walked away at a brisk pace, into the woods, and then he began to run. He ran far enough that no one would hear him shout. He dropped to his knees and closed his eyes, picturing in his mind the image of the Tor, reshaped into the monument to God's anger and sadness. "Father, you say that the time is nigh for me to return to my homeland, to return to my kinfolk who will turn against me and offer me up for crucifixion. If I go, I bring no hope for freedom in this world for the Jews. If I go, I will never return to these shores and to the Britons I have come to love, and I abandon them to conquest. I know the path you would have me walk through this world is still a long one. It will be many years until the end, but I know now where it leads, so now is the time, here and now, for me to make my choice—obedience unto shame and death, or the fullness of life that comes with the awful price of separation from you.

"You say this sacrifice will bring redemption and the hope of salvation to a broken world racked by sin, but at the same time, it seems that I cannot even redeem just one man." Jesus continued to shout. "Father, Daniel is a good man, but the Devil bewitched him in a moment of weakness. You know his repentance is true. If I cannot redeem a man such as this, how can I possibly redeem anyone else? Let me redeem Daniel, and I will do it.

Show me how I can redeem this dear man, and I will give myself to death on the cross for you. It is all I ask."

Hearing nothing, Jesus wept and pounded his fists into the ground.

Arvigarus

The Belgae cheered as King Aghamore made his way through the pillars and under the lintels of Stonehenge. A full council of druids followed closely behind. The king passed by a pyre in the center of the monument, already constructed by his people so he could consign the prisoner to the flame without delay. The king seemed to pay it no mind. The Belgae druids who were to judge the case took their seats in front of the monument, facing the visitors across a small open space. King Aghamore and his retainers took seats on either side.

Arvigarus cast his eyes about nervously. Joseph, Fergus, and Grengan were in their places, and guards held Daniel by a halter. Even Mary was there, although she was not essential to the proceedings. *Where is Jesus? He said he wanted to be here so his cousin would not be alone at the end.* Arvigarus sensed some movement behind him and was relieved to see Jesus make his way to his place in the front of the visitors.

The guards from Ynys Witrin led Daniel before King Aghamore and handed the halter to the king's retainers.

Arvigarus and Fergus stated that the Silures and Dumnonii had decided, because the crime had been committed against a princess of the Belgae, to yield jurisdiction to the Belgae.

King Aghamore rose to speak, first addressing Arvigarus and Fergus. "As representatives of the Silures and Dumnonii, you have honorably fulfilled your obligations by delivering the prisoner for justice." Turning his attention to Daniel, the king pointed his finger and howled with rage, addressing the druids sitting in judgment. "This man attempted to rape my daughter and then killed her. I died the day I heard she was dead, but it was not just a crime against me. I have no sons, and now I have no heir of my body to rule my kingdom after me. It was a crime against all my people, a crime against my house, and a crime against my daughter. I demand justice."

Arvigarus recognized the chief druid of the Belgae, who was to preside over the trial—Aelhaern. At the druidic school in Bangor, he had been a hard taskmaster who focused upon rote memorization of druidic teachings. Aelhaern opened the trial for anyone to speak.

Joseph rose first and offered his apology to King Aghamore and all the Belgae. He explained the Jewish custom of sitting *shiva* for the dead. "I did this when I first heard of the attempted rape, because I considered Daniel dead to me."

King Aghamore nodded courteously. "I understand your sorrow at the loss of a son. I bear no ill will against you and your family."

Joseph sat down without looking at Daniel, who hung his head in pain, muttering that he deserved to die. One by one, the witnesses rose to speak. Each of the surviving riders who had attended Bridget that day said they had seen Daniel attack her driver with a sword.

Fergus spoke eloquently of how Daniel risked his life at Rumps to preserve the freedom of the Dumnonii.

"While Daniel's heroism at Rumps was commendable," Aelhaern said, "it is not relevant to this crime."

Grengan stood. "It is unlikely that anyone intended to kill the princess. Her death was the consequence of a stray arrow." He pointed a finger at the druids. "An arrow. If Daniel attacked the wagon with a sword, he could not have been the one who loosed the fatal shot."

A murmur ran through the crowd.

One of the druids said, "King Grengan's arguments matter not, because as an outlander Daniel has earned the punishment of death simply by taking up arms in the sacred precinct of the Tor."

Jesus stood to object. "Any violation of the neutrality of the sacred precinct is not properly part of the case, because that would not be a crime against the Belgae, only against the Dumnonii and the Silures."

That gave rise to a heated discussion among the druids, but then Aelhaern ruled that Jesus was correct. "Does anyone else wish to speak?" Aelhaern asked.

Mary wept but said nothing. Daniel hung his head and remained silent.

The Belgae druids retired to a nearby grove to consider their decision.

Within a few minutes the druids filed back. With great solemnity they took their seats, except for Aelhaern. None of them looked at Daniel.

Aelhaern raised his voice, as if to make his pronouncement heard all the way to Ynys Môn. "The only possible decision is that Daniel be put to the flame." Mary cried out in horror, but Aelhaern ignored her and continued. "It matters not whether anyone intended to kill the princess, or whether Daniel himself shot the fatal arrow. The evidence is clear that the prisoner was in league with brigands and that they intended to attack Princess Bridget's wagon. In these circumstances, Daniel is responsible for the consequences of the attack, regardless of intent and regardless of whether he loosed the fatal shot."

On Aghamore's signal, the Belgae druids and the people behind them stepped back to clear a path for the guards to bring Daniel to the stake.

As they led Daniel through, Jesus stood and cried out, "Stop! I will redeem the prisoner!" All eyes turned to him.

"I will not deny my daughter justice for any price," the king replied sadly.

"You seek justice, and that is what I offer—not just silver. I am the son of the one true God in heaven, and I offer up my own life in place of Daniel's. If you execute Daniel, the recompense she receives in mortal blood will fade from memory, but execute me in his stead, and your bards will sing for ages of the recompense she receives from the divine."

Aelhaern looked stunned, and then he laughed. "You not only come as an outlander and expect us to accept your god, but you say that you are divine yourself! I have never heard of anyone so bold. You have taken leave of your senses!" Aelhaern looked over to Elsigar. "Do you see now why I said it was foolish of you to bring an outlander to Bangor?"

Joseph and Daniel were shocked into silence at first, and then both shouted out to Jesus at the same time. They looked at each other, and Joseph went ahead. "You are innocent of any crime," he said to Jesus. "Daniel must be the one to pay the penalty."

"My Father in heaven told me I must surrender my life to redeem the whole world from sin that is not my own. I would sooner die here and now, knowing my sacrifice redeems the life of at least one worthy man."

The crowd buzzed like a nest of angry wasps.

Aghamore held up his hand for silence. "I am moved by the gallantry of your offer, Jesus, senseless though it is. I know what the so-called civilized people of the world think of druids and Celts. They say we are barbarians. The Romans say we are ignorant and cruel, while they gorge themselves with the sight of blood in their arenas and watch their victims slowly suffer death on their crosses. Even the Jews—yes, I know something of your ways, ignorant barbarian that I am—even the Jews call us pagans.

"Let no one say that Britons are without mercy and compassion," the king continued. "I commute the sentence! We shall not consign the prisoner to the flame. Let his death be merciful and quick, and let it stand as a testament to the goodness and mercy of my daughter." The king turned to the captain guarding Daniel. "Let it be done at once."

Before anyone realized what was happening, the captain wound a cord tightly around Daniel's throat. He placed a stick in the garrote and turned it, lifting Daniel from behind. Daniel choked and clawed the air.

Jesus cried out and ran to Daniel. His cousin expired just as Jesus grasped out to hold him. Mary shrieked in anguish as Jesus and the guard released the body, which fell limp onto the ground.

Arvigarus joined Jesus and his mother as they wept over the body.

Joseph turned away.

Jesus rocked the body of his cousin like a child. "No. Daniel, no." Jesus's breathing grew rapid and shallow. He looked at his mother. "How can this be? Why does God hate me so?"

"He doesn't—"

"He must! He wants to destroy me to save the world, but he won't let me save the one person I most desire to save."

Grengan sent men to fetch a wagon to carry off the body.

Jesus clung more tightly.

Mary put her hand on his arm. "You must let him go, Jesus."

Jesus winced and bowed his head. He lay the body on the ground, and stood over it. "I don't understand." His voice was hoarse. "I was willing to sacrifice myself, just as my Father wants. Why did I fail?"

Arvigarus tried to recall all that Jesus had said about the extraordinary prophecy of his sacrifice. "I gather...your god...your Father, you call him...wants this sacrifice to be your choice."

"I was willing to die for Daniel, but my Father doesn't care."

"I don't understand all about your...father...your god...but..." Arvigarus looked over his shoulder but could not find Joseph, who was no doubt better suited for this strange conversation. Mary was bent over the body, murmuring prayers in her native language. "Could it be that it's not enough to make the sacrifice out of love for the one being redeemed? Maybe you have to make the sacrifice out of obedience to your god. Or love for him."

Jesus closed his eyes and sighed. "Oh. Yes. Of course." His eyes flew open. "Both."

The chief druid came forward and sneered at Jesus. "You say you are the son of the one true god, and yet he has commanded you to surrender your own life to redeem the world. We have seen that you cannot redeem even one man. You will die, as all men do, but your death will mean nothing. Elsigar told me how your god will have you die on the cross. It will be for naught. No one will remember you."

"My Father in heaven says that all who claim me shall have redemption."

"And you will give your life for this. Is that so?"

"That is my choice. I make it here and now."

"Let us say that only one hundred righteous men remember you and claim you, as your father says. Would you die for one hundred? I think that would be quite a generous estimate, to be honest."

"I would die to save one hundred souls."

"Let us say you lack ten to make one hundred—"

"I will die to save ninety."

"Let us say it is only ten—perhaps a mighty king, a couple of worthy men, a few women, and some slaves. Let us say that they are the ones who remember you and claim you. Would you die for them as well?"

"I would die to save just ten."

"Let us say that all of them were slaves. Would you die for ten slaves?"

"Yes, I would suffer the cross for slaves."

Aelhaern held up his hands and walked around, mocking Jesus. "This son of a mighty god would yield up his very life, for what?—just a few slaves. Some all-powerful and almighty god that must be!" The Belgae laughed along with the druid. Even some of the Dumnonii and Silures joined in.

"Well, Jesus, suppose it were just one slave. Suppose it were not just any slave—no. Let us suppose it is this slave." With that, Aelhaern turned and pointed to a figure crouching on the ground, held tightly by the neck with a collar and chain.

"Save me, Jesus!" the figure cried.

It was Pirro.

"I see that you know each other," the druid continued. "Elsigar told me about you and him. We caught him the other day trying to escape across our territory." The druid poked at Pirro with his staff, drawing yelps from him and guffaws from the crowd. "He deserves to die just as much as your cousin, but he is such a pathetic creature, and his death would hardly restore honor to the Belgae. He is not worth our trouble. He is yours to redeem—that is, if you want him. What will it be, Jesus? Will you give your life for him?"

Jesus looked at Pirro, and slowly closed his eyes.

"Think about it." Aelhaern continued to circle. "We all know the story. Think of how this slave tried to betray you to your enemies at Rumps. Think of how that caused the death of Fedwig. Think of how you ransomed his freedom once already and how he squandered that gift. Now tell us, Jesus. Will you die for one pathetic creature such as this?"

Jesus opened his eyes, glanced at Pirro, then turned to Aelhaern. Jesus looked the druid directly in the eye. "I will die for him. I will suffer all the pain and humiliation of crucifixion for him. If his were the only soul written in the Book of Life, I would die for him still."

"Excellent!" exclaimed Aelhaern. "What shall it be? I suppose we could arrange a crucifixion if you like, but that is not something druids do, and we would hate to frighten the children. We could burn you at the stake—the pyre is still there. I also offer you the choice of garroting—you can go the same way your cousin went—it is quick and painless."

"My Father will have me return to my homeland," said Jesus, "and fulfill my ministry first."

"So is that the catch?" Aelhaern shook his head, as the crowd laughed again. "I love the way these outlanders do business," he said, turning to the crowd. "Yes, I will give my life in torment to redeem this poor soul. But no, I can't do it *now*." The crowd roared. "I must go home and do my ministry first, but don't worry, just spare me the life of this murderer, and somewhere and sometime, maybe a year from now, maybe ten or maybe twenty, sometime when it is a little more—how do I put this?—sometime when it is a little more *convenient*, I will go through with all that torture and death." Aelhaern shook his head. "Jesus, you may call us barbarians, but we are not fools." He turned to the guard holding Pirro and pointed to his prisoner. "Burn him at the stake."

As the crowd laughed, a stroke of lightning flashed from the sky and struck one of the lintels of Stonehenge.

Arvigarus looked up. A dark cloud appeared overhead. The earth shook. One by one, some of the lintels and pillars of the monument crashed to the ground. A massive voice filled the sky, coming from nowhere and everywhere.

"Do not doubt the promise of my begotten son!" The lightning, thunder, and earthquake suddenly stopped, and stillness fell.

Suddenly Jesus was standing next to Arvigarus. "What happened?" he asked Jesus. "You were over there and now you are here."

"God my Father took Elsigar and me away across time and space, and then brought us back. I'm sorry to startle you. I forgot where I was standing before."

Joseph pointed at Elsigar and said, "Look how his face glows, just like Moses."

"Who is Moses?" Arvigarus asked.

"He was a great prophet," said Jesus. "One of the very few to see God…until now."

"What happened to Elsigar's face?"

"He too has seen God."

Elsigar raised his hand and a hush fell over the crowd. "When the earth and sky were formed there was a creator," he began. "The Fisher King taught the *Tuatha Dé Danann* of this in the ages before all human knowledge. The Jews know him by many names. Yahweh, among others. To the Fisher King he was simply the Creator. The Creator has shown me that Jesus is indeed his begotten son, and he has taken me to the time and place where Jesus will die on a dreadful Roman cross. I have seen his suffering, torment, and death. The Creator has shown me that for the divine there is no present, no past, no future. Jesus has chosen the path of obedience, and his suffering and death are real in the here and now."

Elsigar began chanting in a tongue Arvigarus did not understand.

"What's that?" Arvigarus asked.

"He's calling the spirits of the earth," said Jesus, "in the language of the *Fir Bolg*."

"In whose language?"

"That of the *Fir Bolg*," Jesus said.

Arvigarus gave him a blank look.

"The druids believe the *Fir Bolg* are the giants who ruled the earth before the coming of the *Tuatha Dé Danann*," Jesus explained. "They were the ones who lost the Battle of *Mag Turied*."

Elsigar raised his arms to the sky as he completed his chant. Suddenly, a burning cauldron, solid gold, brightly reflecting the sunlight, appeared in the sky above them. The druid turned to Jesus. "I am sure you remember the Mabinogion, the story of the Cauldron of Bran that I told you at Samhain. It brought back to life the slain warriors. According to the teachings of the *Tautha de Danaann*, it was destroyed by Efnisien, the British hero. But there are certain ordinances, burned deep in the fabric of the earth, that transcend the *Tautha de Danaann,* and that each archdruid has passed in secret to the next generation from the days of the Fisher King. Among these, it was written that when the heroic son lays down his life for the despised slave, Bran's cauldron will be restored unto him."

The cauldron hovered over Jesus's head, dissolved into a stream of golden particles that enveloped him, then vanished into the air.

"Redeem your cousin, Jesus," Elsigar cried. "Then go and redeem the world."

Jesus turned to the body of his cousin and pointed at him. "Daniel, rise up!"

Someone laughed. But then Daniel began to move. A hush of amazement fell over the crowd. The bruising and gashes from the garrote faded and disappeared. Daniel rubbed his eyes as if waking from a sleep. He rose to his knees, then stood and looked around at the people as if unsure of where he was.

Elsigar lowered his arms, and the glow faded from his face. He addressed the crowd. "I am diminished. The time of the druids and the *Tuatha Dé Danann* has passed. A new age is here, and the people will know the true godhead. I leave for Eire, and from thence I will sail to the west."

The archdruid turned and walked away, never to be seen again.

Epilogue

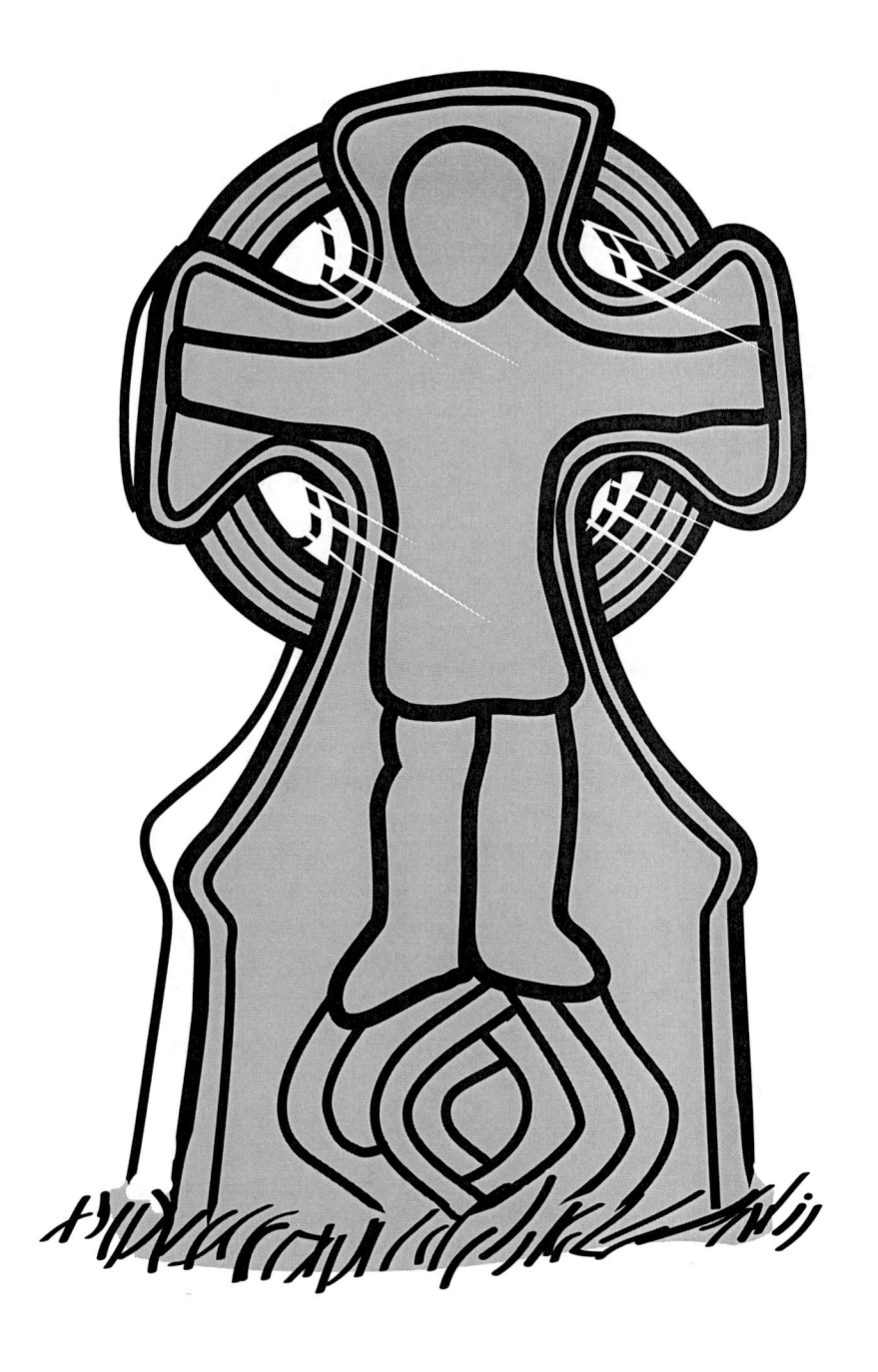

Judea, the River Jordan, A.D. 29, during the reign of Tiberius, second emperor of Rome

John

John knew people thought of him as a wild man, but he cared not. His raiment was made of camel hair, and a leather girdle wrapped his loins. He fed upon locusts and wild honey. He cried out to the people to repent, for the kingdom of heaven was at hand. His was the voice crying in the wilderness to prepare the way of the Lord and to straighten his paths.

People came to him to be baptized, and he did so. "I baptize you with the waters of the river," he told them. "But one is to come, one mightier than I, whose shoes I am not worthy to bear. He will baptize with the Holy Spirit and with fire."

A figure emerged from the crowd and waded into the river to be baptized. It was Jesus.

John held up his hand, bidding Jesus to stop. "I am the one who has the need of you to baptize me," John said to Jesus. *Why am I to baptize you, since you are already without sin?*

"Suffer it to be so now," Jesus answered. "It becomes us to fulfill all righteousness."

John lowered Jesus into that cool, clear water. Jesus rose up, water running from his long brown hair. The heavens opened, and the Spirit descended like a dove and lighted upon him.

A voice from heaven said, "This is my beloved Son, in whom I am well pleased."

John shuddered, staring at Jesus.

Jesus smiled gently and embraced him. "I must go. Farewell." Gathering his belongings, he walked away.

John looked about the crowd. To one side, he spotted a well-dressed gentleman to whom he was distantly related. *The Arimathean is getting on in years. Will he recognize me? It has been so long.*

Seeing no others waiting, John walked out of the river toward Joseph, who greeted him with an outstretched hand.

"This is a fine day," said Joseph. "You will be remembered for this."

"I am humbled," John answered. "Yet I am perplexed. Jesus did not answer my question."

"I know."

"Jesus is the unblemished one, the one without sin. Was he not already reconciled fully to God?"

"Look at him, now, as he makes his way to the wilderness," said Joseph.

John looked into the distance, where the tiny figure of Jesus walked slowly across the rocky terrain.

"He is being led by the Spirit," said Joseph. "The path before him remains a long one, but it is still the path of the lamb who is led to the slaughter. Yet, he walks the path of obedience, to suffering and death, without complaint. It was not always so for him."

"Are you saying that he rebelled against the Father in Heaven? The Lamb of God must be unblemished!"

"I did not say he rebelled or was blemished. Only that he complained. Who are we to judge whether Jesus or anyone else is blemished? God alone is the judge. Nevertheless, Jesus is now baptized: that means he is perfectly reconciled to God, and he will remain so. That is the true path of salvation that Jesus lays open for all, including those who come broken. I believe this baptism signifies the reconciliation of Jesus to his human nature. Many years ago, God called him to the painful task that lies before him. He had choices open to him, and there was much sound and fury, but in the end he chose to obey the Father.

"I was there to see it. All the sound and fury of Jesus's anger signified something, for the depth of that fury was overcome by a far greater abiding love between Father and Son."

I think it was for Jesus as it was with Job, who remained a righteous man in the eyes of God, even though his tribulations stirred him to great anger. It was his friends who were called to account by God for telling Job to make an insincere repentance. Because God is just, he made recompense to Job, and thus they were reconciled. A righteous man can be stirred to righteous anger with God. He can be without sin and yet call for reconciliation.

Ynys Witrin, Britannia Province, 73 A.D., during the reign of Vespasian, ninth emperor of Rome

"There you are, young man." Brother Kenan said. "Walk with me."

Ponticus turned and followed the older man, though Kenan was going in the opposite direction. A dusting of snow lay on the ground. He pulled his cloak tighter against the chill breeze. The basket of food he carried weighed on his hand. He shifted it to the other side.

"Settling in all right?"

"Yes, sir. Thank you."

A smile crinkled around Kenan's eyes. "What brought you to our little brotherhood?"

"My bishop in Lugdunum sent me here to study."

"All the way from Gaul. Very good. And are your studies going well?"

"Yes, very. Only…"

"What?"

"Why do you call yourselves *Culdees*, sir? It means *refugees*, does it not?"

"Indeed it does. Our founders fled Jerusalem with the master, soon after the Lord's death and resurrection."

"I see."

Kenan led him along the base of Wearyall. "You're tending our master these days, are you not?"

"I am, sir. A great privilege for one so new." The master was the same Joseph of Arimathea who had buried Jesus in his own tomb. "To even see him, let alone to care for him, is an unutterable joy."

"Indeed. Now look here." They approached a thorn, unaccountably in bloom.

"How…how is it possible?" Ponticus asked.

Kenan put down his toolbox and threw back the hood of his cloak, revealing a head bald but for a thin ring of silver hair. "Upon arriving at Wearyall—the boats put in right there"—Kenan turned and gestured to the water—"Joseph declared he had no further need of an old man's walking stick. He planted his staff in the ground to claim the country for Christ. In the ground right here." He walked around the tree, gazing up at its budding branches. "The staff sprouted into this mysterious thorn, the only one of its kind that blooms twice a year—once in rhythm to the native thorns of Britain, and again in rhythm to the thorns of Galilee."

"That's…that's impossible," Ponticus said.

Kenan glared at him. "That's miraculous, young man."

Ponticus nodded.

Kenan took a hatchet from a loop on his belt and pointed to a flowering branch. "Hold that."

Ponticus held the branch while Kenan hacked at it. "Do the Culdees own the whole island, sir?"

"Arvigarus, king of the Silures, granted the community twelve hides of land, including the Tor and the island. We've been working this land and spreading the good news to the Britons for more than forty years now."

"The Romans don't try to stop you?"

"I do wish you'd say *us* instead of *you*, lad."

"Sorry, sir."

"The Romans have been Britain's rulers, ostensibly, for these last thirty-some years. Fortunately, they see this as a backwater of a backwater, so we have escaped the persecutions our brethren faced under Emperor Nero." With a final blow, the branch came loose in Ponticus's hand. "Take that back to our master."

Ponticus put the branch in the basket alongside the cheeses and bread, and he turned toward the Tor.

Kenan walked silently beside him.

"Is it true what the brothers say about the church?" asked Ponticus. "That it was not constructed through the art of any man?"

Kenan nodded. "Our Lord Jesus himself built it as a home for his mother Mary, when Master Joseph brought him to Britain as a young man. The local folk refer to it as 'Secret of the Lord.' Some say that the Virgin Mary returned with Master Joseph and was buried here, but they keep that a big secret. There are many wonderful tales of Jesus's doings in Britain. Ask Master Joseph. He'll surely answer you. Good day." Kenan turned away, and Ponticus continued toward the Tor.

The wattle-and-daub church, the largest of twelve buildings arrayed in a circle, sat near the foot of the Tor. Ponticus walked to the house directly opposite the church. He paused at the master's threshold. Joseph was now aged, bedridden and infirm. The master might be a frail whisper of a man, but he was a giant figure among Christians, the great-uncle of Lord Jesus Christ himself.

"Who are you?" the old man grumbled from his bed.

"I am Ponticus, sir. I will tend to your needs today, as I did yesterday and the day before." He walked in and put the basket on the little table.

"Bah. You're not one of the brothers. Send for Lazarus. He knows how to take care of me."

"I am sorry, Master, but Lazarus is working in the orchard with all the brothers. They are harvesting the apples and pears, and they left me to tend to you."

"So, you will have to do."

Ponticus smiled. They'd had the same conversation over the last two days.

"Brother Kenan sent this." He handed Master Joseph the thorn tree branch, a sprig the length of his forearm. It was covered in tiny white flowers. "Ah, it blossoms still." He gave a hacking laugh and placed the sprig on the little table near his bed.

Ponticus offered Joseph porridge and apple juice for his breakfast. Lazarus had left some rabbit hides to be made into a blanket, so Ponticus got out needle and sinew, and started piecing them together. As he worked, he took Kenan's advice to ask questions of Joseph. "The brothers told me that you brought Jesus to Britain, but the accounts written by Mark, Luke, and Matthew say nothing about the Lord's time here. They only mention you as the man who buried the Lord after the crucifixion. I hear that John of Ephesus is writing an account. Do you think he will be telling more about your part than Matthew, Mark, and Luke did?"

The old man sat up in bed and glared at Ponticus. "He'd better not! Luke was the physician to Paul of Tarsus, and he wrote to me after Paul was martyred. He asked me to send him something to include in his account of the life of Jesus from the time he taught in the temple until he began his ministry. I wrote back and told him he should only say that after the time he taught in the temple at the age of twelve, Jesus grew in his wisdom and in the favor of God and man. I did not want any of them to include the part about how I buried Jesus, but they said that was important because it fulfilled the prophecy that a rich man buried him, as if I were rich..."

Ponticus became concerned by the old man's coughing and choking, until he realized it was only laughter. "Why did you want to exclude the wonderful story of Jesus in Britain?"

"It makes the message too confusing. We are trying to bring the good news to the Romans and to the world beyond. The Romans have always despised the druids. I didn't much care for them myself. But Jesus learned much from them, and he taught them, too. I believe they had an important role in bringing out his divine nature so he could understand it from a human perspective. I believe the Romans will come to accept the good news one day—but not if they confuse it with druidism, which it is not."

"What influence did the druids and the Britons have upon Jesus?"

"I think everyone Jesus encountered in his life nurtured him in some way, within the context of God's plan. The most important thing was coming to accept his destiny to suffer death on the cross, because that was the purpose of his incarnation to live among us. It need not have happened in Britain. It could have happened elsewhere."

"But you were there that day at Stonehenge. You saw all that business with Bran's Cauldron, did you not?"

"There is only one true God, who lives through the Father, the Son, and the Holy Spirit. Scripture talks of all sorts of supernatural creatures; it mentions seraphim, angels, archangels, and demons, to name a few. I never understood who the Tuatha Dé Danann really were, but I am sure they were just different creatures of our almighty God. Whatever happened that day at Stonehenge was ultimately the work of the true God. The Lord works in mysterious ways, and it does not matter if he uses Tuatha Dé Danann, whatever manner of creature they be, to accomplish his purposes."

"Why would God use the druids, of all people?"

"Jesus told me later that the whole point of his sacrifice was that it had to be his own exercise of free will, not only of his divine nature, but something embraced by his human nature as well. For Jesus's sacrifice to become the pathway of salvation for a broken world, he had to suffer all the doubts and pain of a broken humanity. He had to make his choice as a true sacrifice, not from the expectation of resurrection and glory. Bran's Cauldron appeared only after Jesus made his choice to suffer death upon the cross. He told me later that he never saw it coming when he, in his human nature, made the choice to obey the Father even unto death."

"What happened to Jesus and Daniel after that day at Stonehenge?"

"God, whether in the person of the Father, the Son, or the Holy Spirit, works across all time and space. I believe that Jesus truly connected with his divine nature when he made the choice to suffer death on the cross, and after that he lived every day of his life in the pain of his crucifixion. He told me that his days in Britain gave him strength to bear the pain, because he could also live in the happier times he had here before he understood the path of suffering and pain he was destined to follow. He said that he came to call those years his days of 'awe and joy.'"

"Awe and joy," Ponticus repeated. "It makes me happy to know Our Lord experienced that, and that it helped him to bear the pain of his sacrifice."

"I brought Jesus and Mary back to Galilee," the master continued. "He traveled the known world, learning everything he could before the time came for his ministry. Daniel stayed in Britain and married a Celtic woman. He preserved Mary's house until I returned after the Lord's Passion. These days, Daniel preaches throughout Britain."

"I've seen no druids since I've come to this country. What happened to them?"

The Master sighed. "By the time the Romans came, druidism was already weakened. Some of them followed Elsigar across the seas and were never heard from again. Some of them embraced the good news I brought back to Britain. The Romans brutally suppressed any that still clung to their old ways. The final straw occurred when the druids harbored fugitives from Rome on Ynys Môn. The druids thought their own gods and the fast flowing waters of the Afon Menai would protect them. General Gaius Suetonius Paulinus proved them wrong. He crossed the waters with his army at slack tide and slaughtered those he found on the island. The only druids who now remain anywhere in the world are those in Eire and Caledonia."

Ponticus prepared to ask another question, but Master Joseph waved him off.

"I am tired now, Ponticus. You must let me rest. You ask good questions. I will answer more when I am able."

The Arimathean dozed off, but he never made good on his promise. Within hours he had a high fever. From time to time he awoke, but he kept coughing up fluid and could not speak coherently.

All the brother hermits gathered around Joseph's bedside that evening, knowing their Master's time was nigh. Once again, the Arimathean awoke from his fever-ridden sleep. He propped himself up on one elbow, and his eye fell upon a carving against the far wall. "Jesus!" he cried, reaching out his hand. He tried to get out of bed, but his knees buckled, and he collapsed on the floor. He continued to hold out his hand and call to the statue.

The brothers rushed to help him. "It is only a carving, Master," said Lazarus, gripping the old man's shoulders.

Ponticus had been aware of the carving, but he had never looked at it carefully. Now, he studied it for the first time. The carving depicted a boy before a Celtic cross, with his arms held wide in greeting.

"It is a carving we made to portray the Lord when he first arrived in Britain with you," Lazarus said. "It is not Jesus himself."

Joseph coughed up more fluid and lowered his hand. Lazarus and Ponticus lifted him back into his bed.

Master Joseph's voice ran thin. "That carving brought back the memory of those days of awe and joy. It matters not. I will be with Jesus soon." He looked from one face to another. "I can see it in your faces. My time is short." He looked back to the carving and pointed to it. "You must make more of those when I am gone. They will remind the Britons of the Lord's visit here."

"It shall be done, Master," said Lazarus.

"Where is that novice who was taking care of me?"

Ponticus stepped forward, wringing his hands.

"You have a sharp and discerning mind," Joseph told him. "You ask intelligent questions. The brothers will tell you the stories of the time Jesus was in Britain. Write them down, but keep them well hidden. God will cause them to be found when the world is ready to hear them."

The Arimathean settled back and looked around the room. Once again his eye settled upon the tunic cross statue on the far wall. "Put some clue of where to find the stories, in those statues you will be sending out. Make it something hard to figure out, so the secret is revealed only with the inspiration of God."

"We will," said Lazarus.

"My work is done," Joseph closed his eyes. "I commend my soul to Jesus." The brothers kept a vigil over the Arimathean as he rested comfortably.

Dawn brought a diffused light filtered through the thick mist. It cast no shadows, and it revealed that this giant among the followers of the Way breathed no more.

Saint Hilary's Parish, Cornwall, A.D. 1997, during the reign of Queen Elizabeth II of England

The day after he met Father Walters, Ned returned with his parents for the Sunday service at the quaint parish church. It was quite a change from the simple "ordered" services the family was used to. His father whispered that it was hard to believe this was Church of England. When the thurifer swung the censor to bless the people, Ned's father complained the incense upset his allergies. His parents started straight for the door at the conclusion of the service, but with no plans other than to relax at the bed-and-breakfast for the afternoon, they raised no objection when Ned said he wanted to stay behind and explore.

As the pews emptied, Ned wandered the church and looked over the icons. In the back, he discovered a picture of Jesus at the age of twelve teaching in the temple.

Suddenly, Father Walters was standing next to him.

"This is the last we hear of Jesus from the Bible," said Ned, "before he began his ministry. Is that right?"

"Some people call that period the Missing Years," said Father Walters. "It is quite a gap in the account of his life."

"Yesterday you mentioned the legend that Christ came to Britain when he was my age, but people back then didn't just take a trip like that for a holiday."

"According to the legend," Father Walters agreed, "his great uncle was Joseph of Arimathea, a trader of tin. The archeologists tell us that this area of Cornwall has been a major source of tin ever since the Bronze Age."

"My dad says there was a big monastery in Glastonbury, and the monks started the legend in the Middle Ages to attract pilgrims to raise money to replace the buildings that had burned down."

"Glastonbury was one of the biggest monasteries in Britain until King Henry VIII dissolved them all. It is true that a big fire burned the entire complex at the end of the twelfth century, but the legend is older than that. You probably know that Pope Gregory sent Augustine to take Christianity to the Anglo-Saxons about the year 600. Augustine reported that he encountered a Christian church among the native Celtic people. The bishops told him of a church built by the very hands of Christ, at what is now Glastonbury. Gildas, the first British historian, wrote about other parts of the Glastonbury legend at about the same time."

༺ ❈ ༻

The Jacobs family was booked in the bed-and-breakfast for the week. The Old Vicarage did not have a television or video games, so aside from occasional day trips with his parents, Ned found himself frequenting the church and spending time with Father Walters.

Near the end of their stay, Ned was talking to Father Walters about the tunic cross in the churchyard.

Father Walters imitated the boy's gesture holding his hands out. "It might be a greeting."

Ned looked at the stone, and then Father Walters. "I feel that boy might have a secret he wants to share."

Father Walters's arms dropped to his sides. "What do you mean, Ned?"

"It was something I thought of the first time I saw the statue. The way the boy is holding out his arms. It just reminded me of my mates at school, how we sometimes like to share secrets."

Father Walters put a heavy hand on Ned's shoulder. "Ned, please make it a point to come see me before you leave. I might have something important to share with you, but I must think about it overnight, and pray."

Ned thought Father Walters's request quite strange. The family was scheduled to leave the next day. Nonetheless, he was intrigued. "Yes, Father. I'll come."

⁂

"Ned, thank you for stopping by," said the priest, as Ned walked up the path the next morning. "Do you remember what you said yesterday about the figure on the tunic cross having a secret to share?"

"You seemed surprised."

"I may know what the secret is, but I cannot figure out what it means. The secret has been passed down in this parish across many generations. I am going to retire soon, and I doubt the rector replacing me will have any interest in preserving the legend of Christ's visit to Britain. I had no one to pass this secret to, but what you said gave me the idea of sharing it with you. I prayed about it last night. You are awfully young, but you have a discerning and inquiring mind. I believe the secret will be in good hands with you, if you will let me share it."

Ned nodded. Who would say no to such a thing?

"Shortly after I first came to this parish, I noticed that part of this tunic cross had fallen into disrepair. The cement holding Father Donoghue's plaque to the bottom had eroded. When I inspected it, the plaque fell off in my hand. I found a hollowed crevice, and inside was a very old stoppered bottle. Inside was a paper that bore the traces of some kind of rubbing. It did not seem like much to me, just some random horizontal and vertical marks, but I thought it strange that someone had taken such care to preserve the pattern, so I took everything I found to some experts at the British Museum."

"Could they read it?" asked Ned.

"The bottle itself was the easiest to track down. The museum experts said it was a medicine bottle manufactured in the 1920s and 1930s. I talked to one of the older parishioners, and she told me that according to her grandmother, Father Donoghue's plaque had been placed on the cross by Father Bernard Walke in the aftermath of the famous riot that happened here in 1932."

"This churchyard seems so peaceful. It is hard to imagine anyone starting a riot here."

"The rubbing required carbon-dating, and the people at the museum said it dated back to the early or middle part of the seventeenth century, about the time of the English Civil War."

"Wow, that's brilliant!" said Ned.

"The pattern in the rubbing turned out to be an ancient script made with hash marks against a baseline. The hash marks represent different letters depending on their length and angle. The script is called Ogham, it comes from Ireland, and it dates back to the early Dark Ages. A museum expert in Old Gaelic and Ogham translated it. This is what the rubbing said: 'Look for the Secret of the Lord where the lamb turns to the beginning of his life.'"

"Huh?" Ned frowned. "That's the big secret?"

"I have no idea what it means."

Ned repeated: "Look for the Secret of the Lord where the lamb turns to the beginning of his life. It sounds really weird. How are you supposed to know where some lamb turned round centuries ago?"

"You have your whole life ahead of you, Ned." Father Walters put his hands on Ned's shoulders. "Just remember the secret. Maybe you will discern its meaning during your lifetime. If not, just remember to pass it on before you die."

Ned smiled. "That's really cool, Father." *Discern the meaning...* "I will remember that."

"Ned!" His father bellowed from the road. "Time to go."

THE MAKING OF THE LAMB

Glastonbury, Somerset, A.D. 2010, during the reign of Queen Elizabeth II of England

The bus rumbled down the A361. Geoffrey battered a drum rhythm on his lap. "That was a great festival, wasn't it?"

"Fantastic," Ned answered his friend. "Can't believe they got so many of the latest bands—"

"In Pilton, I know, right?"

The girl in the seat in front of them turned around. "Oi! What you got against Pilton?"

"Nothing, nothing," Geoffrey said.

"If you're not from around here," she said, "what are you doing on the Glastonbury bus?"

"How can you tell we're not from around here?" Ned asked.

"You sound like a Londoner," she said. "So why aren't you headed that way?"

"Did you see that car park?" Ned pointed his thumb back the way they'd come. "Who wants to deal with that? We thought we'd have a look round Glastonbury and give the traffic time to thin out."

"Huh. Tourists." The girl turned back around.

Ned looked out of the window at the green farmland rolling by. The festival had been a welcome change of pace from his studies. Having made it through his first year at theological college, he was preparing for ordination. His call to the ministry had been quite a shock to his parents, as well as to all his mates—including his oldest school chum, Geoffrey—who remembered him as an adventurous prankster.

They got off the bus in the High Street, which was already full of tourists on their summer holiday to the West Country. In addition to ordinary tourists were many new-age types, identifiable by their long, flowing hair and clothes adorned with beads and flowers. Among them, Ned even spotted a few men and women dressed as druids.

He pulled out a map. "Glastonbury Abbey that way." He pointed ahead. "Guided tours…museum… Oh! Just up the street"—he pointed back over his shoulder—"there's an archeological museum with artifacts from an iron-age lake village."

Geoffrey looked up from his phone. "A what?"

"An old archeological site discovered a hundred years ago on the Somerset Levels."

"Whatever." Geoffrey pointed to the other end of town. "What's that, then?"

Ned turned to see. Looming over the village was an oddly shaped hill with mysterious ridges descending in a triple helix from the top. A medieval tower on the summit gave the Tor a distinctive silhouette. "Glastonbury Tor."

"Hiking up there might be cool," Geoffrey said. "Must be quite a view."

"Right, then."

"Oh, blimey!" Geoffrey stared at his phone. "No!"

"What?"

"I can't leave for five minutes."

He'd been gone three days, not that it mattered. Ned craned his neck to see the screen. "What's wrong?" he asked.

"The web server's bolloxed up again." Geoffrey looked around, then pointed. "I'll be in this Internet café awhile fixing this."

"On a phone?"

"I've got my laptop in my backpack, haven't I?"

Of course. He carries the thing everywhere.

"I'll text you when I get it sorted. Have a look about in the meantime."

Ned's father had not hesitated to inform his son what an insensible career choice he was making taking up the cloth, but the ministry couldn't possibly be worse than running Geoffrey's Internet startup.

"No worries, I'll just go check out some of the shops. See you later."

Geoffrey disappeared into the café, and Ned stopped at a little teashop across the street. They seemed to offer every herbal variety imaginable, but he only wanted his favorite English breakfast. After a night of partying, he needed the caffeine. His order somehow disturbed the matron's cosmic aura, as she flustered about preparing it instead of her typical herbal concoctions.

Stepping onto the pavement with his takeaway cup, he looked up and down the street. Spying a new-age shop, he thought it might be amusing to browse among the pagans. His first impression was that he had stepped into a shop for witches and wizards: *Diagon Alley,* remembered Ned, from the Harry Potter movies. Packets of every manner of incense were neatly arranged on one wall. Maps showing lay lines passing through the Tor in all directions hung on another. Cauldrons and wands were offered, as was a modest collection of books. That was more to his liking.

Most of the collection revolved around new-age spiritual concepts that held little interest for Ned, but among the books he spotted a thin used paperback called *The Traditions of Glastonbury: The Biblical Missing Years of Christ—Answered*. The author was an archeologist, E. Raymond Capt. The cover featured a tapestry showing young Jesus and an older man paddling up a stream at the base of the Tor. *How did this get in here? Maybe the shop owner thought it would sell from local interest.* Ned thumbed through it, recalling what Father Michael Walters had told him, thirteen years before, of the legends surrounding Christ's visit to Britain, how Joseph of Arimathea founded Glastonbury Abbey as the first house of worship in all Christendom, and even something of King Arthur. *I wonder whatever happened to Father Walters? That was such a crazy motto he had me memorize. Look for the secret of the Lord where the lamb turns to the beginning of his life.*

Turning another page, Ned spotted an image of a time-worn architectural feature on a doorway: a carving of a lamb beneath a cross. At first glance the image seemed like a typical Agnus Dei image for "the Lamb of God, which taketh away the sin of the world," but there was something odd about it that Ned could not immediately place. He continued reading, and then it hit him. *The lamb is facing the wrong way!* The typical Agnus Dei image showed the lamb and the cross facing the west, towards the end of Christ's life—his death and resurrection. But according to Capt's book, this lamb was facing the east, the direction associated with the sunrise, representing the beginning of Christ's life with his future before him. *That's it! A lamb turned to the beginning of his life!*

Ned turned the page again. The doorway feature was on a chapel in Cornwall. According to the book, the north transept of that chapel held an example of Ogham script carved into a panel on the wall. *Could this piece of script be a link in the mystery?* Ned hadn't given much thought in the last decade to Father Walters and the mystery, but now he wondered about it. *Only one way to find out...*

Ned paid for the book and hurried out to fetch Geoffrey. He found him at a high table, typing madly on his laptop. "Geoff, can you hurry? I've got...look, I'm sorry, but I've got to cancel that climb up the Tor."

"What's got into you, Ned?"

"I've got something I need to take care of. Immediately."

"One minute." Geoffrey typed a few more lines of code, and they left the café. They caught the next bus back to the festival car park. The traffic had improved, but not much. As they crept down the road, Ned beat the steering wheel.

"What's up, mate? I'm usually the impatient one," Geoffrey muttered.

"Maybe nothing," said Ned. "But maybe...just maybe...something really amazing."

Finally they got onto the A361 and then the A37 north from Shepton Mallet.

Ned packed Geoff off at the Bristol train station and took the M5 west to where it ended, an hour later, just south of Exeter.

Ned debated whether he should find a room to stay for the night, but he knew he was too excited to sleep. He continued on the two-lane into Cornwall, swinging around each of the roundabouts at full speed. He crossed Bodmin Moor at midnight. An hour later he pulled over to the side of the road just outside Truro and slept.

The light of breaking dawn awoke Ned from his light sleep. Stopping only for a coffee, he proceeded south on the A3078. He was used to driving between the hedgerows, and the road narrowed only occasionally to force two lanes of opposing traffic down to one.

He had to park the car some distance from the chapel, and he walked to it on a public path. He took a look at the photograph in the book and compared it to the chapel. Yes, it was certainly the right building. The chapel was attached to a larger estate house called Place Manor. According to the sign, the chapel was a decommissioned church, no longer consecrated ground for the Church of England, now in the custody of the C of E Conservation Trust. He approached the old oak door, darkened with age. He tried it, and it creaked open. By now the sun was up, illuminating the interior through tall lancet windows. Ned gazed around at the memorials, stretching back hundreds of years in commemoration of various members of the family that owned the house. Where was that Ogham script sample for which he had come all this way?

He found it on the wall of the north transept, just where Raymond Capt said it would be. Ned took out a pencil and some paper, and he made a rubbing.

He stared at his work as he walked back down to the car. He had the inscription. Now he needed to find someone to read it. Maybe that museum expert Father Walters knew.

I bet the man will be surprised to hear from me after all these years. Tracking down Father Walters took a number of phone calls, but eventually Ned found the priest living in a retired housing scheme operated by the Church of England Pensions Board.

Ned arrived without calling ahead. The staff showed him to Father Walter's room. Ned knocked and entered a narrow room, barely big enough for a twin bed and a recliner. The old priest sat in his recliner by the window, a shadow of the man Ned remembered from more than a decade earlier.

"Hello, Father. I don't suppose you remember me."

Father Walters looked at him blankly.

I hope he hasn't gone senile. "I'm Ned Jacobs. We met at St. Hilary's shortly before you retired." The priest still showed no sign of recognition. "You shared a secret with me, from the tunic cross."

Father Walters suddenly became animated. "Ned, after all these years! Did you figure it out? Did it lead you to the Holy Grail?" The priest laughed and clutched Ned's hand.

Ned smiled. "Not quite yet, Father, but I think I'm close to something." Ned showed Father Walters the rubbing and explained how he'd found the Ogham inscription. "Can you tell me who translated the other one for you?"

"Oh, my boy, that was so long ago…" Father Walters lowered the footrest of the recliner and pressed the arms of the chair to help him stand. "Let's see if I can find it."

A bookcase stood nearby, packed chockablock with all sorts of books. Father Walters pulled out a battered old Moleskine notebook. He snapped the elastic back and opened the book. Glancing over Father Walters's shoulder, Ned saw pages filled with penciled notes and sketches. As Father Walters flipped through it, newspaper and magazine clippings came loose and fluttered to the floor. He seemed not to notice. Ned stooped to gather them up. "Must be in here someplace," muttered Father Walters to himself. "Somewhere." Ned tucked the clippings back into the notebook as the priest continued to turn pages. "Ah, here it is."

Father Walters showed Ned the page. Ned took out his phone and tapped the name into a web browser. The search results seemed to take forever to appear, but at last they came. "Ha. He still works at the British Museum." Ned gave the Father a grin. "Want to come with me?"

Though Father Walters was eager, it took some doing to check him out of the home. "Luv, 'e's too frail to travel," the head nurse moaned.

"Would you deny an old man a bit of fresh air?" Father Walters protested. "You think I'm not in my right mind?"

After a complaint to the director, a ream of paperwork, a suitcase crammed with spare clothes and toiletries, and instructions to Ned about the old man's medication schedule, they were finally on their way.

"It describes a location," said the British Museum specialist. "Measured by paces from the altar of a place called Lammana Priory. Whatever that is."

"Never heard of it," admitted Father Walters.

Ned pulled out his laptop and looked it up. "It's on Looe Island."

"In Cornwall?" Father Walters asked.

"Where else?" Ned laughed. "The abbots of Glastonbury owned the priory at least since the Dark Ages. It's also called Saint George's Island, just off the coast."

"Well, then, young man." Father Walters stood, looking more spry than he had in the home. "Let's get going."

Within a few days of the old priest's liberation from the retirement home, he and Ned were driving down the A387 toward the twin villages of East Looe and West Looe.

"We have the distances to pace out from the altar," said Ned. "But how do we find the altar?"

"My boy, we don't have to. It's already been found."

"It has?"

"The altar was found. But not whatever is buried at the site described in the Ogham message."

"Right, right." Ned shifted his grip on the wheel. "What do you mean the altar was found?"

Father Walters opened his Moleskine notebook and searched through the magazine clippings. "I have quite a collection of articles," he said. "I seem to remember one... Ah, young man, here it is."

He handed a clipping to Ned.

"A few years back," Father Walters said, "I saw this article about an archeological dig on St. George's Island. I'm always interested in things like that. There was also a special about it on the B.B.C."

Ned looked over the clipping. Under a bold headline—*"Archeologists Uncover Christian Altar Dating from Roman Antiquity"*—he saw several color photos of khaki-clad students and professors with trowels and brushes, standing in a trench.

"It gives the location of the altar?" asked Ned.

"Precisely."

"Ha!"

Ned found a marina in East Looe and rented a small motorboat. As they set out across Looe Bay, the sun glinted on the whitecaps. Ned turned to the priest. "Good thing the manager didn't ask many questions. The island's a wildlife refuge. No telling how long it would take to get permission to dig."

Father Walters chuckled. "It's often easier to obtain forgiveness than permission."

Ned laughed, the wind ruffling his hair.

The island was not far from the harbor entrance. Ned steered the boat toward it.

The delight shining in the old man's eyes must look something like his own, Ned thought.

They had done it! Decoded the clues. Solved the mystery.

Saint Joseph's buried secrets would soon be theirs.

Author's Afterword

Before I get started, let me give a word of warning: This afterword will have some plot spoilers. Please read the book first. I will cite some of my sources, but this is not a full bibliography. For more information, I invite you to visit www.makingofthelamb.com.

How did this book come to be written and what purpose does it serve?

The Making of the Lamb was first conceived as I was preparing for my baptism in 2004. I was doing quite a bit of sailing with my good friend, Austin Mill, and he gave me a small plaque for my sailboat honoring Saint Joseph of Arimathea. Joseph is the patron saint of sailors, miners, and funeral directors. Austin also introduced me to the Jerusalem Hymn, which sets in music the legend that Jesus traveled to Britain during his "missing" teenaged years, which are left out of the Bible. In the course of my travels with Austin, one of us got the idea that the legend would be a good basis for a novel.

I started researching with *The Traditions of Glastonbury: The Biblical Missing Years of Christ: Answered* (1983, revised 1987, 2005) by E. Raymond Capt. Then I delved into primary sources closer in time to the legend, going back as far as Gildas, the first British historian. I also encountered some works that fictionalized the legend: *I, Joseph of Arimathea* by Frank C. Tribbe (2000) and *Uncle of God, The Voyages of Joseph of Arimathea* by M. E. Rosson (2010).

As I kept going, both with the book and the preparation for my baptism, I read *The DaVinci Code* (2003) by Dan Brown and some non-fiction works that flesh out Code's backstory that Jesus survived the crucifixion and went on to father a bloodline that can be traced through the Dark Age Merovingian kings. Among these is *Bloodline of the Holy Grail* by Laurence Gardner (1996). From my church's adult formation class, I recognized the elements of Arian and Gnostic heresy. Heresies are studied in Christian formation classes because, by contrast, they give rise to a greater understanding of orthodox Christian belief. As I saw these books taking off in the popular culture, I watched distinguished commentators treat them as a valid alternative to traditional Christian teachings, perhaps equally valid.

That was when this book got its name and really took form. I realized that *The Making of the Lamb* could take the legend well beyond anything already written about Christ's visit to Britain. What was needed was much more than an ancient travelogue. I realized that I had an incredible opportunity to show Jesus as a teenager in a distant land, struggling with his destiny to die such a horrible death on the cross. Such a Jesus could touch the emotions of my readers and thereby really drive home the significance of his death and resurrection.

My hope is that my readers will find this book fun, engaging, and thought provoking, regardless of whether they are Christians or not. We read how the largest growing denomination now is "unaffiliated." This book is tailor made for these questioning, doubting people, who sometimes fear walking into a church lest they be expected to drink the Kool-Aid.

One of the most surprising things I found from going to church was the level of discernment I found going on all around me. One of my favorite passages from the Episcopal Church's Book of Common Prayer is from the prayer said for the newly baptized. We don't pray for them to obediently accept and pass on canned proselytizations. Instead we pray for God to give them "an inquiring and discerning heart." People who enjoy thought-provoking books may be surprised to find out how much they can enjoy going to church.

Thought-provoking fiction can be a great tool for evangelization. It can be a way to break the ice with potential newcomers. I hope readers and others will come to www.makingofthelamb.com, and post their experiences and ideas about this on the blog.

Is this portrayal of Jesus consistent with Scripture?

Putting Jesus front and center as a main character in a work of fiction creates a dilemma for a Christian writer. Conflict is the driving force for good fiction. There's not much point to putting Jesus up against a mortal antagonist—that fight is going to be over almost before it starts. The only really worthy opponents would need to be divine, but Christian doctrine seems to belie any notion of discord among the members of the Holy Trinity. Perhaps that is why many Christian authorities frown on any fictional accounts of Jesus's life. I put the spiritual tsunami into Chapter 14 to show how any sort of discord within the Trinity might unleash untold havoc on Creation.

Another problem is that we want our fictional characters, even our heroes, to be flawed. But doctrine says that Jesus is the unblemished perfect man as well as the divine God. At first that may seem difficult to square with this novel's truculent teenager, who screams his defiance from the summit of the Tor when he discovers his true destiny.

Nonetheless, there is a strong case to be made within Scripture for my portrayal of a teenaged Jesus. We need to start with the significance of Jesus's incarnation. In his divine nature, he has been a coequal member of the Trinity since the beginning of all time. But at the time of his incarnation, he put aside his divine dignity to take our human nature upon himself. He came into our world as a helpless baby, and he had to be nurtured like any other baby through his childhood.

The last we hear about Jesus in Scripture before the onset of his ministry is at the end of the second chapter of Luke, when Jesus, at the age of twelve, tarries behind to teach in the Temple. His parents lose him for three days, much to their sorrow, and when they find him his Mother asks why he has dealt with them so (Luke 2:41-48). Rather than defend Jesus's behavior, the gospel writer puts it in the context of natural human growth: "And Jesus increased in wisdom and stature, and in the favor of God and man" (Luke 2:52). In other words, at the onset of his teenage years, Jesus in his human nature was an unfinished work with some growing to do.

Even as an adult, the Gethsemane episode on the eve of the crucifixion shows that Jesus submitted to death on the cross because he was obedient to God, the Father, not because he wanted to. When we see from the Bible how Jesus obediently suffered so much for our benefit, we can accept the concept of an adult Jesus living without sin, but do we even understand what it would mean to apply that concept to Jesus as a teenager? What would a "perfect" teenager ever do?

In the novel, Jesus suddenly discovers that everything he has lived for is being ripped out from under him. The promised throne of David is not going to be of this world. He will suffer a horrible death at an early age. He will never become the conquering heroic messiah of his people. Perhaps worse than the prospect of such personal pain and suffering is the emotional pain of knowing that he will die helpless to ward off the coming suffering for both his own Jewish people and the Britons, whom he has come to love. Despite all this, he starts traveling the path of obedience, which he knows will lead to Calvary.

Is our concept of perfection in Christ's human nature so rigid that we would really deny Jesus the emotional space he needs, even as a teenager, to deal with all of this? I believe that if we do, we make so much of Jesus's lack of sins that his human nature effectively becomes indistinguishable from the divine. Perhaps he can be Emmanuel, the God living with us, in a physical sense, but not with the same emotional connection. If Jesus had never struggled to accept his destiny, his sacrifice would seem less meaningful.

If Jesus had any human nature, then the teenaged Jesus portrayed in the novel would not have been the first righteous man to struggle with God. It's not clear from the passage in Genesis whether Jacob wrestled with God or with an angel sent by God when he was on his way to meet Esau. In the Book of Job, God holds Job to be his worthy servant throughout the sound and fury of Job's anger with God for all his tribulations. Ultimately, they are reconciled as God renders justice to Job. It is Job's friends who are called to account for telling him to make an insincere repentance. Job is sometimes considered a figure in the Old Testament who actually foreshadows Jesus. In *Putting God on Trial: The Biblical Book of Job* (2004), Robert Sutherland provides an objective guide to the subtle nuances in the Book of Job that a reader needs to understand.

The question of how Jesus came to accept his destiny to die on the Cross is a great mystery of the Bible that wants exploring. This book does not purport to be a book of theology. It's a novel, hopefully a thought-provoking one. I have had people tell me with great fervor that Jesus must have been aware of his true destiny from his childhood. Others were equally fervent that Jesus knew nothing about that until the onset of his ministry. In debating this, we cannot help but realize the significance of Christ's sacrifice. That is why I hope people will come to www.makingofthelamb.com and sound off on the blog.

Is *Making of the Lamb* Historically Accurate?

The job of the historical novelist is both to educate and to entertain. We create a story around known facts of history. Particularly when so much of the story deals with prehistoric people, it is necessary to take what is known and fill in many blanks. In this short space I discuss some of the issues I encountered, but I would also love to have people blog their questions and comments on www.makingofthelamb.com.

Some people have questioned the relatively advanced level of the late Iron Age portrayed in the book, but the archaeological evidence shows that the Britons of this period were remarkably sophisticated. The Celts at this time carried on trade over extensive networks. Julius Caesar admitted that their seafaring skills were superior to those of the Romans. They were adept with metals and all manner of crafts. The reeve system of their farms evidences a sophisticated division of labor. *Iron Age Communities in Britain, An Account of England, Scotland and Wales from the Seventh Century BC Until the Roman Conquest* (1974, 4th edition 2005) is Professor Barry Cunliffe's advanced college-level archeological textbook. Cunliffe has also written a number of other books that do not require a background in archaeology, such as *Britain Begins* (2013). Other noted works include *The Atlantic Iron Age* (2007) by Jon C. Henderson and *Exploring the World of the Celts* (1993, reprinted 2002) by Simon James. Artifacts from Iron Age Britain and related exhibits can be seen in the British Museum in London, the Iron Age Museum in Andover, and the Jewry Wall Museum in Leicester.

The methods of navigation and sail rigging that I describe are more of my own hypothesis, because there is scant archaeological evidence on this. The lateen rig was known to the Romans by the middle of the first century BC. This fore-and-aft rig greatly improved the ability of sailing vessels to progress into the wind over square-rigged vessels, but the swinging gaff high above deck and the unbalanced force of a triangular sail would have been problematic for craft venturing far into the stormy North Atlantic. The lug rig would have been a relatively simple adaptation of the square rig. By adding a single spar along one vertical side of the square rig, a leading edge can be presented to the wind when the sail is swung into a fore-and-aft position. At the same time, the force of the wind is much more balanced over the mast than with a triangular sail. An adaptation such as the lug rig would have been essential for the Celts to easily maneuver against the Roman vessels in battle without oars the way that Julius Caesar described.

Navigation certainly would have been problematic over one hundred miles of open water between the tip of Armorica and the tip of Cornwall. The compass had not yet been invented, and late-eighteenth-century mariners were still trying to find an accurate method for resolving longitude. Nonetheless, we know that ancient Phoenicians sailed vast distances across blue ocean waters. Indigenous Pacific islanders used wave patterns and ocean swells, and I hypothesize that the Celts might have supplemented their navigation this way when clouds obscured sun and stars.

Archeology tells us a great deal about how people lived, but not so much about what they believed. The druids abjured writing, particularly anything of a spiritual nature. Some of the tribes minted coins with Greek letters, and they had calendars, but we don't have anything more substantial written down by the Celts themselves. Julius Caesar wrote about the druids in his account of his war against the Gauls, but one needs to take what he said with a grain of salt because the Celts were his enemies, and his annals were a propaganda piece against people he wanted to portray as barbaric. Irish folktales were written down centuries after the time of the druids by Christian monks who brought their own biases.

As I conceived this book, I knew that Jesus would have encountered druids if he stayed in Britain for any length of time, but everything I read about them just sent me in circles. I finally came across Jean Markdale's book, *The Druids, Celtic Priests of Nature* (1999), and this became my guide to sorting out the pantheon of druidic deities and making some sense of them. Some of the concepts, such as the idea that they learned Greek philosophy, might very well be overly romanticized. On the other hand, we know that the Celtic people often crossed paths with the classical cultures of Greece and Rome and that each druid went through twenty years of training.

E. Raymond Capt and several writers before him rightly take note of the British tin trade in advancing the theory that Joseph of Arimathea might have traveled to Britain as a trader in tin, a metal essential for making bronze. There is indeed strong evidence for this from archaeology and classic writers such as Diodorus Siculus and Pytheas. Nonetheless I think it is overly simplistic to assume that this trade continued through Jesus's lifetime. Cunliffe writes of how the conquest of Gaul vastly disrupted the ancient Atlantic trading zone and shifted the trading pattern to the east where Romans could sail to Britain between Calais and Dover within sight of land, avoiding the hazards of sailing the blue waters. It is unlikely that the Arimathean would have become rich by simply following what others of his time were doing. If he traveled to Cornwall and made a fortune at it (as the Bible might suggest), he would have done so as the contrarian businessman of his day, taking risks and finding his own path for a competitive advantage, as I portray in the novel.

How much of the tunic cross story is factual?

Tunic crosses are found across Cornwall. As far as I know, E. Raymond Capt was the first writer to suggest that they might represent an ancient memory of Jesus's visit to England. I came across the tunic cross in St. Hilary's Parish churchyard during my visits in 2004 and 2005. The more modern plaque marking the burial of Father O'Donohue was attached to it. Father Bernard Walke and his wife, Annie Walke, were real, but Father Walke's involvement with the cross and its secret is fictional. The story of the riot that took place in 1932 is loosely based upon Father Walke's account in his autobiographical *Twenty Years at St Hilary* (1935, 2002). The discovery of the Roman altar on St. George's Island and the related BBC documentary are real. All of the other events and characters associated with the tunic cross are fictional.

Who helped you with The Making of the Lamb?

Let me start with friends and family members who reviewed the manuscript. Some of these people made hundreds of detailed notes on the manuscript. Others wrote up commentaries or gave me valuable suggestions in other ways. I considered every suggestion that was made, and every one of these people made an important contribution to the book. So, going in alphabetical order, I want to thank Mario Ashby, Cory Bear, William Bear, Daphne Byron, Benjamin Coleman, Lesley Cross, Peter Duncan, James Edmondson, Barney Harris, Laurita Liles, Tina Mallett, Austin Mill, Fred Nicholson, John Orens, Joyce Parker, Robert Portch, William Prather, Janet

Wamsley, Linda Wilkinson, and Charles Zagrieb. I should single out Austin Mill and Lesley Cross. Austin traveled with me to Britain in 2004 and 2005 to visit the sites where Jesus might have been, and he helped me get started with the early stages of the writing. Lesley has been working tirelessly as my proofreader-in-chief and as an additional line editor.

I have been fortunate to engage two extremely talented and hard-working professional editors. My developmental editor was Kristen Stieffel (www.kristenstieffel.com) and my line editor was Mason McCann Smith (www.madscavenger.com). Both are also authors in their own right.

Kristen has had a distinguished career in the newsroom of the Orlando Business Journal and as a freelance editor. She is under contract for her fantasy series, *The Prophet's Chronicle*. The first book, *Alara's Call*, was published in 2013. She is an ordained elder in the Presbyterian Church.

Mason is the author of several historical novels: *When the Emperor Dies* (Random House, Hamish Hamilton in the UK), *La Venganza de Beatrice* (Grijalbo Mondadori, Spain), *March on Magdala*, *Oliver in Bronze*, and *The Stained Glass Virgin*. He is a full-time writer, editor, and book designer.

My cover designer was Peri Poloni-Gabriel of Knockout Design (www.knockoutbooks.com). She sent me an incredible assortment of cover concepts to choose from and then did a wonderful job when I asked for the hardest one. She has been a cover designer and interior book designer for many years.

Guiding me through the publishing minefield was my consultant, Peter Bowerman (www.wellfedsp.com), the author of *The Well-Fed Self-Publisher*. (2007)

I also want to thank Tim Leonhart and the highly professional staff at Bookmasters (www.bookmasters.com), who are handling production and distribution.

Robert Harley Bear

Glossary of Place Names

Through the centuries, many place names have changed. The following glossary may guide the reader to the current location of events in The Making of the Lamb. Names rendered in bold type are those used in the book. Numbers in brackets indicate pages where the bolded place name may be found on a map.

Acre (Modern) – Port City in Lebanon. Ptolemais (Latin). [14]

Albion (Latin) – See "Britain".

Afon Menai (Welsh) – Menai Strait (modern). It separates the island of Ynys Môn fron the Cymru mainland. [225]

Arar (Latin) – Saone River, France (modern). A navigable tributary of the **Rhodanus** (Rhone) River that joins it at Lugdunum (Lyons) and forms a trade route leading north to the roads leading in turn to the narrowest passage across the English Channel. [15]

Arelate (Latin) – Arles, France (Modern). [15]

Armorica (Latin roots) – Brittany (Modern), a region of northwest France. The modern name comes from British Celts who fled the Anglo-Saxon invasion centuries after Jesus. [15]

Arimathea (Biblical) – Referred to in the Bible as the home of the man Joseph who buried Jesus. Supposedly, a small village about five miles north of Jerusalem.

Bangor (Modern). A town in Northwest Cymru, across the strait from Ynys Môn. It was a center of druid teaching. [225]

Belerium (Latin) – Name used by Roman geographers (*i.e.*, Diodorus) for the British southwest peninsula of modern day Cornwall, Devon and parts of Somerset and Dorset. [100]

Bembont (Fictional) – Bembridge (Modern). A seaside town on the east side of Vectis (Isle of Wight) with a little recreational harbor. The Welsh word for bridge was used because of the likely Germanic origin of the English word. [15]

Brest (Modern) – Port city in northwest France. Gesocribate (Latin). [15]

Britain (Latin roots) – British Isles. Used interchangeably with "Albion" although Albion technically would exclude Eire (Ireland). "England" is a distinctly Anglo-Saxon name that would have been unknown at the time of Jesus. [225]

Brue (Modern, Unknown origin) – River flowing to the Severn from Ynys Witrin. It was navigable prior to the draining of the Levels in the Middle Ages. [101]

Caer Leir (Celtic) – Leicester, UK (modern) [225]

Caer Wysg (Fictional name) – Caerleon, Gwent, Wales (Modern) The modern name is Welsh for "place of the legion", a reference to Roman times that is clearly subsequent to the time period of this novel. The Romans themselves referred to the place as "Isca", after "Wysg", the Welsh name for the present-day River Usk that runs through the town. The fictional name combines the Celtic word for place or fort ("Caer") with the name the people used for the river. [101]

Calais (Modern) – Gesoriacum (Latin) [15]

Castle An Dinas (Celtic) – Actual Iron-Age hill fort site near St. Columb Major, Cornwall. [100]

Carn Roz (Fictional name) – St. Just in Roseland, Cornwall (Modern). The parish history refers to a legend that Jesus and Joseph of Arimathea came there. The tidal pool is real. A prominent rock on the shoreline (removed in the 20th century) was said to be where Jesus stepped ashore. [100]

Cheddar (Modern) – The same name is used for a gorge and river that cuts through the Mendip Hills. [101]

Creta (Latin) – Crete, Greece (Modern). [14]

Cymru (Celtic) – Wales (Modern) [225]

Dvrobrivae (Latin) – Rochester, UK (Modern) [15]

Dubris (Latin) – Dover, UK (Modern) [15]

Eire (Celtic) – Ireland (Modern) [225]

Gaul (Latin) – France (modern) [15]

Holy Island (Modern) – Also known as Holyhead (Modern), a smaller island on the northwest of Ynys Môn (Anglesey). [225]

Ictis (Latin) – Bronze/Iron-Age port located somewhere in southwest England or southern Wales. Leading archeologist Barry Cunliffe cites evidence for placing the locale at Mount Batten (Plymouth) or the mouth of the Severn River. This work follows the legendary stories that place Ictis at Mount St. Michaels, near Marazion, Cornwall. [100]

Liger (Latin) – Loire River, France (modern). [15]

Looe (Modern, unknown origin) – Modern-day twin towns of lie on either side of the mouth of the River Looe in Cornwall. St. George's Island lies a short distance to the southwest of the mouth of the river. [100]

Lugdunum (Latin) – Lyons, France (modern). [15]

Lysarth (Latin) – Lizard Head, UK (modern). [100]

Mare Internum (Latin) – Mediterranean Sea (modern). [14]

Massilia (Latin) – Marseilles, France (modern). [15]

Mendip Hills (Modern) – A range of hills north of Glastonbury, a site of silver and lead mining in ancient times.[101]

Nantes (Modern, Celtic roots) – Port City at the mouth of the Loire, France. Condevincum (Latin). Modern name likely has its origins from the Namnetes tribe of Gauls. [15]

Oceanus Britannicus (Latin) – English Channel (Modern). [15]

Pencaire (Modern) – A hillfort complex on Tregonning Hill, Cornwall. It actually has three hillfort rounds. [100]

Pendennis Castle (Modern) - Fort in Falmouth constructed by Henry VIII on the site of Pen-Dinas. It was one of the last Royalist holdouts in the English Civil War. It had given sanctuary to Queen Henrietta Maria and the Prince of Wales (Charles II), before their escape to France.

Pen-Dinas (Fictional). The use of this site in Falmouth harbor as an Iron-Age hillfort is only a possibility. [100]

Pilton (Modern) – A town to the east of Glastonbury. The parish banner shows St. Joseph of Arimathea bringing Jesus to the site by boat. [101]

Pomparles Bridge (Latin) – A bridge that crosses the River Brue between Weary-Al in Glastonbury and the Town of Street, Somerset County. It is the site where Excalibur is said to have been returned. [101]

Priddy (Modern) – A town to the north of Glastonbury atop the Mendip Hills. It is sometimes said, "as sure as the Good Lord came to Priddy". The parish history refers to a legend of a visit by Jesus. [101]

Rhodanus (Latin) – Rhone River, France (modern). [15]

Rock (Modern) – A village near Padstow, Cornwall. [100]

Rumps (Modern) – Iron-Age cliffside castle near Padstow and Rock, Cornwall. [100]

Sabrina (Latin) – Severn River (Modern) [101]

Salamis (Latin) – Famagusta (Modern) Port city on Cyprus. [14]

Sequana (Latin) – Seine River (Modern) [15]

St. Hillary (Modern) – A parish near Marazion, Cornwall.

Snowden (Modern) – A mountain range in northwest Wales. [225]

Tamar (Modern, Celtic origins) – A river that joins the Plym at Plymouth and forms the eastern boundary of County Cornwall (Kernow). [100]

Tor (Celtic) – A prominent hill in Glastonbury (Ynys Witrin). The mists that surround the Tor at sunrise and the mysterious ridges are real phenomena. [101]

Tregonning Hill (Modern) - A hill near Mounts Bay, Cornwall, about four miles east of St. Hilary's parish church. [100]

Vectis (Latin) – Isle of Wight (Modern). An important trading center in Roman and pre-Roman times. [15]

Wearyall (Modern) – A ridge on the south of Ynys Witrin (Glastonbury). [101]

Yengi (Celtic) – Hengistbury Head, near Christ Church, Dorset, UK. This was a major iron-age port on the south coast of Britain at least until the time of Julius Caesar, with significant trade possibly continuing thereafter. [15]

Ynys Lawd (Celtic) – Short Stack (modern). A small island with a modern lighthouse off Holyhead Island, Wales. [225]

Ynys Môn (Celtic) – Also known as Mona (Celtic). Anglesey, North Wales (modern). Together with nearby Bangor, this was a center of druid teaching and spirituality. [225]

Ynys Witrin (Celtic) – Glastonbury, Somerset (modern). Before the draining of the Somerset Levels in the Middle Ages, this area surrounding Glastonbury and the Tor in Somerset County, England was an actual island. This is a legendary site where, according to legend, Joseph of Arimathea brought Jesus and where he later brought Christianity to Britain and founded the Glastonbury Abbey, which was among the richest and most powerful of monasteries in England until its dissolution at the hands of Henry VIII. The site is also significant to followers of Arthurian Legends, modern-day druids, New-Age Spiritualists, and fans of the annual music festival. [101]